DON'T CRY NOW

DON'T CRY NOW

Joy Fielding

HEADLINE

First published in Great Britain in 1995
by HEADLINE BOOK PUBLISHING

10 9 8 7 6 5 4 3 2 1

British Library Cataloguing in Publication Data

Fielding, Joy
Don't Cry Now
I. Title
813.54 [F]

ISBN 0-7472-1526-X

Typeset by Avon Dataset Ltd., Bidford-on-Avon, B50 4JH

Printed and bound in Great Britain by
Mackays of Chatham PLC, Chatham, Kent

HEADLINE BOOK PUBLISHING
A division of Hodder Headline PLC
338 Euston Road,
London NW1 3BH

For Owen Laster,
with respect, admiration and love

ACKNOWLEDGMENTS

I would like to thank Jane Lonergan for her help and support in driving me through Boston and suburbs during the worst snow storm in decades. Her heart, as well as her home, is always open. Special thanks as well to George Kampoures for introducing me to the world of reptiles and giving me much needed information and insight. Once again, thanks to Dr. Terence Bates for his medical expertise.

Chapter One

She was thinking of palm trees. They were tall and brown and bent by decades of high winds, their long green leaves fluttering like empty gloves towards a magically clear blue sky.

Rod had mentioned the possibility of her accompanying him to Miami next month. A few days of meetings with the network affiliates, he told her, and then the balance of the week for the two of them to make like Burt Lancaster and Deborah Kerr on the beach – how did that sound to her? It sounded great, hence the visions of palm trees that had instantly imprinted themselves on the inside of her eyelids, appearing every time she closed her eyes. It meant creating some problems of her own at work – she'd have to lie to her principal, tell him she was sick when she was always boasting that she was one of those disgustingly healthy individuals who were never felled by colds or nasty flu bugs; she'd have to have her daily lessons precisely detailed and laid out in advance so that whoever they brought in to supply for her would know exactly what to do and at what pace to proceed. Minor inconveniences when compared to the thought of a romantic week in the sun with the man she loved. Illicit even, were it not for the fact that the man in question was her husband of five years.

Bonnie took a deep breath, readjusting her focus to eradicate all traces of swaying palms. Minor inconveniences, maybe. But how would she go about disguising a decidedly unsickly-looking tan to a suspicious high-school principal? How would she be able to look the man in the face without blushing, speak to him without stammering, deal with his solicitous inquiries as to how she was feeling? She hated lying, was terrible at it, valued honesty above all else. ('You're my good one,' her mother had often said.) And she was proud of the fact that in almost nine years of teaching, she'd never missed a day. Could she really skip five days in a row just to roll around with her husband on a Florida beach?

'Besides,' she said out loud, glancing down at the soft golden doll that was her three-year-old daughter, 'how could I leave you for five whole days?' She reached over and stroked Amanda's cheek, her fingers tracing the thin scar that snaked across the child's cheekbone, the result of a recent tumble from her tricycle. How fragile children are, Bonnie thought, leaning over, inhaling her daughter's sweet smell. Immediately, Amanda's blue eyes opened wide. 'Oh, you're up, are you?' Bonnie asked, kissing her daughter's forehead. 'No more bad dreams?'

Amanda shook her head, and Bonnie smiled with relief. Amanda had wakened them at five in the morning, crying from a nightmare she couldn't quite recall. 'Don't cry, baby,' Bonnie had whispered, allowing Amanda into their bed. 'Don't cry now; everything's going to be okay. Mommy's here.'

'I love you, sweet thing,' Bonnie said now, kissing her again.

Amanda giggled. 'I love you more.'

'Impossible,' Bonnie countered. 'You couldn't possibly love me more than I love you.'

Amanda crossed her arms over her chest, assumed her most serious face. 'Okay, then we love each other exactly the same.'

'Okay, we love each other the same.'

'Except I love you more.'

Bonnie laughed, swinging her legs out of bed. 'I guess it's time to get you ready for school.'

'I can get myself ready.' In the next second, Amanda's round little body, all but hidden inside a pink and white Big Bird nightgown, was running down the hall toward her room.

Where do they get so much energy? Bonnie wondered, crawling back between the covers, letting her tired body luxuriate in the stillness of the early spring morning.

The phone rang, its shrill sound slamming against her brain with such unexpected force, Bonnie felt as if she had been rear-ended by a car. Her shoulders tensed, then jerked, contracting at the base of the neck, as if she'd been suddenly shrunk. Who would be calling now, at barely seven o'clock in the morning?

Bonnie forced her eyes open, staring toward the phone on the night table beside the king-size bed, reluctantly pushing herself onto her elbows, reaching over with an impatient hand to pluck the receiver from its carriage. 'Hello?' She was surprised to find her voice still coated with sleep, and cleared her throat, waiting for whomever was on the other end of the line to declare themselves.

'Hello,' she said again when no one did.

'It's Joan. I have to talk to you.'

Bonnie felt her heart sink, her head snapping toward her chest, as if she'd just been felled by a guillotine. Not even seven o'clock in the morning, and already her husband's ex-wife was on the phone. 'Is everything all right?' Bonnie asked, immediately fearing the worst. 'Sam and Lauren . . . ?'

'They're fine.'

Bonnie expelled a grateful breath of air from her lungs. 'Rod's in the shower,' she said, thinking it a little early even for Joan to be hitting the bottle.

'I don't want to talk to Rod. I want to talk to you.'

'Look, now isn't a great time,' Bonnie told her, as gently as she could. 'I have to get ready for work . . .'

'You don't have to work today. Sam told me it's a PE day.'

'PD,' Bonnie corrected. 'It stands for professional development.' Why was she explaining anything to this woman, to whom she owed no explanations at all?

'Can you meet me later this morning?'

'No, of course I can't meet you,' Bonnie told her, amazed at the request. 'I'm in lectures all morning. I'm being professionally developed, remember?' Like a photograph, she almost added, then didn't. Rod always complained his ex-wife had no sense of humor.

'At noon then. You must get a break for lunch.'

'Joan, I can't . . .'

'You don't understand. You have to.'

'What do you mean, I have to? What don't I understand?' What was this woman talking about? Bonnie looked helplessly toward the bathroom door. The shower was still running. Rod was tearing into a rousing chorus of 'Take Another Little Piece of my Heart'. 'Joan, I really have to go.'

'You're in danger!' The words emerged as a hiss.

'What?'

'You're in danger. You and Amanda.'

The cold hand of panic immediately and instinctively grabbed for

Bonnie's gut. 'What do you mean, we're in danger? What are you talking about?'

'It's too complicated to explain over the phone,' Joan answered, her voice suddenly eerily calm. 'You have to meet me.'

'Have you been drinking?' Bonnie demanded, angry now, despite her best intentions.

'Do I sound like I've been drinking?'

Bonnie had to admit that she didn't.

'Look, I'm doing an open house this morning at four hundred and thirty Lombard Street. That's in Newton. I have to be out by one o'clock when the owner comes home . . .'

'I told you, I'm in lectures all day.'

'And I told you you're in danger!' Joan repeated, as if there were a period between each word, as if each letter were capitalized.

Bonnie opened her mouth to protest, then decided against it. 'All right,' she agreed. 'I'll try to get there on my lunch hour.'

'Before one,' Joan instructed.

'Before one,' Bonnie agreed.

'Please don't say anything to Rod about this,' Joan added.

'Why not?'

Bonnie's answer was the sharp click of a receiver being dropped none too gently into its carriage as the line went dead in her hands.

'Always a pleasure hearing from you,' Bonnie said, hanging up the phone, staring at the white ceiling in frustration. What crazy idea had Joan gotten into that confused mind of hers this time?

Although she didn't sound confused, Bonnie acknowledged, lifting her feet out of bed and shuffling toward the bathroom. She sounded clear and focused, as if she knew exactly what she was saying. A woman with a mission, Bonnie thought, washing her face and brushing her teeth, then padding across the plush taupe carpeting toward the walk-in closet. It was probably time to change the closet around for the warmer weather, although what was that silly saying her friend, Diana, was always quoting? Don't change a thread until April is dead? Yes, that was it, Bonnie remembered, blocking her ears to other, more ominous voices, and exchanging her white nightshirt for a rose-colored sweater dress. *You're in danger,* Joan's voice insisted again. *You and Amanda.*

What was Joan talking about? What danger could she and her daughter possibly be in?

4

Please don't say anything to Rod about this.

'Why not?' Bonnie asked again, smoothing the dress across her slim hips. Why didn't Joan want her to say anything to her husband about her strange proclamation? Probably because he'd think she was crazy. Bonnie laughed. Rod already thought his ex-wife was crazy.

She decided against meeting Joan. There was nothing the woman had to tell her that she wanted to hear. Nothing that would benefit her in any way. Yet even as she was making this decision, Bonnie knew her curiosity would get the better of her, that she'd end up sneaking out of the lecture early, probably missing the best part, and driving all the way over to Lombard Street, only to discover that Joan wouldn't even remember having called her. It had happened before. Drunken calls in the middle of the night, frantic ravings at dinner time, sad laments at bed time. None of it recalled later, *What are you talking about? I never called you. Why are you trying to make trouble for me? What on earth are you talking about?*

Bonnie had indulged her. Despite everything she knew to be true about the woman, about the anguish she'd caused Rod, Bonnie couldn't help but feel some sympathy for her. ('You're a good egg,' her mother would say.) She had to keep reminding herself that Joan's problems were largely self-inflicted, that she'd made a conscious decision to start drinking, keep drinking. It was too easy to excuse her behavior on the grounds that it wasn't unnatural for a woman to turn to alcohol after the kind of tragedy she'd endured.

Still, even the tragedy had been largely her own fault. Certainly it could have been averted had Joan not been so careless, had she not left her fourteen-month-old baby alone in the bathtub, even for less than a minute, as she later frantically claimed. She had all sorts of explanations: Sam and Lauren were fighting in the other room; Lauren was screaming; it sounded as if Sam might be hurting her; she'd simply rushed out of the bathroom briefly to find out what was going on. By the time she got back, her youngest child was dead, and her marriage was over.

Please don't say anything to Rod about this.

Why upset him first thing in the morning? Bonnie asked herself, deciding against telling her husband about Joan's call, at least until after their meeting. Rod had enough to worry about at the studio – a difficult afternoon time slot, an impossible hostess, a tired format. How many tabloid talk shows did the public really need? Still, under his expert direction, the ratings had been steadily improving. There was growing talk of national syndication. The convention in Miami next month could prove pivotal.

Again, the palm trees magically appeared, dotting the surface of her lavender bedroom walls like patterns on wallpaper. Imaginary soft breezes followed her to the small vanity table and mirror that sat opposite her bed beneath a muted print of a Salvador Dali nude, a faceless woman sketched in blue, all round hips and elongated limbs, rays of something-or-other streaming from the top of her bald head.

Maybe baldness was the answer, Bonnie thought, trying vainly to fashion her chin-length brown hair around her narrow face the way her hairdresser had shown her. 'Give it up,' she told her mirror image, abandoning her unruly hair, deciding that despite the tiny lines around her deep green eyes, she didn't look that bad. She possessed the kind of clean-cut cheerleader good looks that never really went out of fashion, that made her appear younger than her almost thirty-five years. Well scrubbed was how Joan had once described her.

Multiple images of Rod's ex-wife rudely replaced the palm trees, like a painting by Andy Warhol, one of those silk screen images of Elizabeth Taylor or Marilyn Monroe. Joan, Bonnie repeated, trying to stretch the word to two syllables, to make it more soothing, easier to contend with. *Jo-oan. Jo-oan.* It didn't work. Joan remained on her lips, as she did in life, resolutely unchangeable, impossible to alter or tone down.

She was a big woman, close to six feet tall, with large brown eyes she constantly referred to as sable, flamboyant red hair she preferred to label titian, and a bosom that was spectacular in anyone's lexicon. Everything about her was an exaggeration, which was no doubt at least partly responsible for her success as a real-estate agent.

What was she up to this time? Why the melodrama? What was so complicated she couldn't discuss it over the phone? What kind of danger was she talking about?

Bonnie shrugged as Rod's shower shuddered to a halt. She'd find out soon enough, she decided.

Bonnie pulled her white Caprice into the driveway of four hundred and thirty Lombard Street at exactly twelve thirty-eight – there'd been an accident on the Massachusetts Turnpike and it had taken her over half an hour to get here – parking directly behind Joan's red Mercedes. Joan was obviously doing very well for herself, Bonnie decided. Despite the fluctuations in the real-estate market, she seemed to have survived the latest prolonged slump quite nicely. But then, Joan was a survivor. It was only those around her who perished.

This house shouldn't be too difficult to sell, Bonnie thought, squinting into the cool sun as she walked past the large sign on the front lawn that announced the open house and mounted the outside steps to the front porch. The house was two stories high and wood-framed, like most of the homes in this upscale suburb of Boston, and it had recently received a fresh coat of white paint. The front door was black and slightly ajar. Bonnie knocked timidly, then pushed the door open further. Immediately she heard voices coming from one of the back rooms. A man and a woman. Maybe Joan. Maybe not. Possibly in the middle of an argument. It was hard to tell. At any rate, she wouldn't eavesdrop. She'd wait a few minutes, cough discreetly a few times, let them deduce someone else was in the house.

Bonnie looked around, helping herself to one of the many fact sheets that Joan had left stacked on a small bench in the front foyer next to an open guest register. According to the information on the sheet, the house was three thousand square feet over two floors, with four bedrooms and a finished basement. A wide center staircase divided the house into two equal halves, the living room to one side, the dining room to the other. The kitchen and the family room were at the back. A powder room was somewhere in between.

Bonnie cleared her throat softly, then again, more loudly. The voices continued. Bonnie checked her watch, wandered into the beige-and-cream-colored living room. She'd have to leave soon. As it was, she'd be late getting back, miss the first part of the lecture on how today's schools had to adapt to today's teens. She checked her watch again, tapped her foot on the hardwood floor. This was ridiculous. While she hated to interrupt Joan while she was trying to make a sale, the fact was that the woman had insisted she be here before one o'clock, and it was almost that now. 'Joan,' she called out, returning to the hall, walking down the corridor toward the kitchen.

The voices continued as if she hadn't spoken. She heard snatches – 'Well, if this health plan is implemented . . .' 'That's a pretty lame-brained assessment' – and wondered what was going on. Why would people – Joan, of all people – be involved in such a discussion at such a time? 'I'm going to have to cut you off, caller,' the man's voice suddenly announced. 'You don't know what you're talking about and I feel like listening to some music. How about the always classic sound of Nirvana?'

It was the radio. 'Jesus Christ,' Bonnie muttered. She'd been wasting her time discreetly coughing so that a rude radio host could finish hurling invectives at some hapless caller! Who's the crazy lady here? she wondered, losing her patience, raising her voice over the sudden onslaught of sound that was Nirvana. 'Joan,' she called, stepping into the yellow and white kitchen, seeing Joan at the long pine table, her large sable eyes clouded over with booze, her mouth slightly open, about to speak.

Except that she didn't speak. And she didn't move. Not even as Bonnie approached, waving her hand in front of the woman's face, not even as she reached out to shake her shoulder. 'Joan, for God's sake . . .'

She wasn't sure at what precise moment she realized that Joan was dead. It might have been when she saw the bright patch of crimson that was splattered across the front of Joan's white silk blouse like an abstract work of art. Or perhaps it was when she saw the gaping dark hole between her breasts, and felt blood on her own hands, warm and sticky, like syrup. Maybe it was the awful combination of smells, real or imagined, that was suddenly pushing its way toward her nose that convinced her. Or maybe it was the screams shooting from her mouth like stray bullets, the ungodly sound creating a strangely appropriate harmony with Nirvana.

Or maybe it was the woman in the doorway screaming with her, the woman with her arms full of groceries who stood paralyzed against the far wall, the bags of groceries glued to her sides, as if they were all that were keeping her upright.

Bonnie walked over to her, the woman recoiling in horror as Bonnie pried the groceries from her arms. 'Don't hurt me,' the woman pleaded. 'Please don't hurt me.'

'Nobody's going to hurt you,' Bonnie assured her calmly, laying the bags on the counter and wrapping one arm around the shaking woman. The other arm reached toward the wall phone and quickly pressed in 911. In a clear voice she gave the operator the address and told her that a woman appeared to have been shot. Then she led the still-trembling owner of the house into the living room where she sat down beside her on the textured tan sofa. Then she put her head between her knees to keep from fainting and waited for the police to arrive.

Chapter Two

They burst through the front door like a violent thunderclap in the middle of a storm, expected but terrifying nonetheless. Their voices filled the front hall; their bodies swarmed into the living room, like bees to a hive. The woman beside her on the sofa jumped up to greet them. 'Thank God you're here,' she was saying, her voice a wail.

'Are you the one who called the police?'

Bonnie felt the woman's accusatory finger pointing toward her, was aware of all eyes turning in her direction as the room filled up around her. Reluctantly, she forced her eyes to theirs, although initially, all she could see was Joan, fiery titian tresses falling in frenzied ripples around her ashen face, her wide mouth slightly agape and outlined by her trademark fluorescent orange lipstick, sable eyes milky with death.

'Who's been shot?' someone asked.

Again the woman pointed, this time toward the kitchen. 'My real-estate agent. From Ellen Marx Realty.'

Several faceless young men, wearing the white coats of medical personnel, rushed toward the back of the house. Ambulance attendants, no doubt, Bonnie concluded, strangely detached from the proceedings, this sudden detachment allowing her to absorb the details of what was happening. There were at least six new people in the house: the two paramedics; two uniformed police officers; a woman whose posture identified her as a police officer but who looked barely out of her teens; a big man of about forty who was obviously in charge, with bad skin and a gut that protruded over his belt, who had followed the paramedics to the kitchen.

'She's dead,' he announced upon returning. He was wearing a black-and-white-checkered sports jacket and a plain red tie. Bonnie noticed a pair of handcuffs dangling from his belt. 'I've notified forensics. The medical examiner will be here soon.'

Forensics, Bonnie repeated in her mind, wondering where such strange-sounding words came from.

'I'm Captain Mahoney and this is Detective Kritzic.' He nodded toward the woman on his right. 'Do you want to tell us what happened here?'

'I came home . . .' Bonnie heard the owner of the house begin.

'This is your house?' Detective Kritzic asked.

'Yes. I've had it up for sale . . .'

'Name, please.'

'What? Oh, Margaret Palmay.'

Bonnie watched the woman police officer jot this information down in her notepad.

'And you are . . . ?'

It took Bonnie an instant to realize Detective Kritzic was addressing her. 'Bonnie Wheeler,' she stammered. 'I'd like to call my husband.' Why had she said that? She hadn't even realized she'd been thinking it.

'You can call your husband in a few minutes, Mrs Wheeler,' Captain Mahoney told her. 'We need to ask you a few questions first.'

Bonnie nodded, understanding it was important to maintain a sense of order. Soon, people would be arriving with strange instruments and powders for measuring and testing, carrying video cameras and green body bags and yards of yellow tape with which to cordon off the area. *Crime Scene. Do Not Cross.* She knew the routine. She'd witnessed it often enough on television.

'Go ahead, Mrs Palmay,' Detective Kritzic directed gently. 'You were saying you'd had your house up for sale . . .'

'Since the end of March. This was our first open house. She said she'd be out by one.'

'So you have no way of knowing how many people went through the house this morning,' Captain Mahoney stated more than asked.

'There's a guest book in the hall,' Bonnie offered, remembering such a book beside the stack of fact sheets in the front foyer.

The officers nodded toward each other, and Detective Kritzic, whom Bonnie now noticed had red hair almost the same shade as Joan's, disappeared for several seconds, returning with the book in hand. A silent signal passed between the officers.

'And when you came home . . . ?'

'I knew she was still here,' Margaret Palmay told them, 'because her

12

car was in the driveway, and I knew someone was with her because of the other car right behind hers. I had to park on the street. I would have waited until they left, but I had all these groceries, and some things that had to be put in the freezer before they melted.' She stopped, as if her mind had gone suddenly blank, and perhaps it had.

She was a pretty woman, Bonnie thought, a little on the short side and nicely rounded, with soft blond hair that curled toward the bottoms of her ears, and a nose that was narrow and beak-like between pale blue eyes. Her mouth was small, but her voice was clear and steady.

'What happened when you came inside the house, Mrs Palmay?'

'I walked straight to the kitchen, and that's when I saw her.' Again an accusatory finger extended itself beyond the camel-colored sleeve of her coat, pointing at Bonnie. 'She was standing over Joan. Her hands were covered with blood.'

Bonnie's eyes shot to her hands, a gasp escaping her throat when she saw the dark red blood that encrusted her fingers, like a child's fingerpaint. A flush of heat washed through her body, moving quickly from her head to her toes, like liquid through a straw, robbing her of energy. She felt dizzy, faint. 'Do you mind if I take my coat off?' she interrupted, not waiting for anyone to respond before pulling her hands through her coat sleeves, trying to keep the blood on her fingers from touching the coat's smooth silk lining.

'Who's Joan?' Captain Mahoney asked, eyebrows crinkling toward his nose.

'The victim,' Margaret Palmay answered, the word sounding out of place on her tongue.

Who did he think they were talking about? Bonnie wondered.

Captain Mahoney checked his notes. 'I thought you said her name was Ellen Marx.'

'No,' Margaret Palmay explained, 'Ellen Marx is the name of the real-estate agency she worked for. The victim's name is – *was* – Joan Wheeler.'

'Wheeler?'

Dark eyes grew darker still; all eyes turned toward Bonnie.

'Wheeler,' Captain Mahoney repeated, eyes narrowing, as if fitting Bonnie into the sights of a gun. 'A relative of yours?'

Was she? Bonnie wondered. Was there such a thing as an ex-wife-in-law? 'She was my husband's ex-wife,' she answered.

13

No one spoke. It was almost as if they'd been asked to observe a moment's silence, Bonnie thought, knowing something had changed, some current in the room had been subtly altered.

'All right, let's back up here for a moment,' Captain Mahoney said, clearing his throat, and directing his attention back to Margaret Palmay. 'You said you saw Mrs Wheeler standing over the body of the victim, and that there was blood on her hands. Did you see a weapon?'

'No.'

'Then what?'

'I started screaming. I think she was screaming too, I'm not sure. She saw me, and walked toward me. At first I was afraid, but she just took the groceries out of my arms and called the police.'

'Do you agree with Mrs Palmay's statement?' Captain Mahoney inquired, turning to Bonnie, who said nothing. 'Mrs Wheeler, do you disagree with anything that Mrs Palmay has said?'

Bonnie shook her head. Margaret Palmay's version of the facts sounded straightforward enough.

'Why don't you tell us what you were doing here?'

This would be more difficult, she thought. She wondered if this was how her brother had felt the first time he'd been questioned by the police, if he'd been this nervous, this unsettled. Although no doubt he'd gotten used to it, she decided, shaking her head free of such troubling thoughts. Her brother was the last person she needed to be thinking about now. 'Joan called me first thing this morning,' she began. 'She asked me to meet her here.'

'I take it we can assume you weren't house-hunting.'

Bonnie took another deep breath. 'Joan said there was something she had to tell me that she couldn't discuss over the phone. I know,' she continued without prompting, 'it sounds like something you'd hear in the movies.'

'Yes, it does,' he agreed flatly. 'Were you and your husband's ex-wife friends, Mrs Wheeler?'

'No,' Bonnie replied simply.

'Did you find it unusual that she called and said she had to speak to you?'

'Yes and no,' Bonnie answered, continuing only when the look on his face demanded further explanation. 'Joan had a drinking problem. She would phone the house from time to time.'

14

'I'm sure you couldn't have been too happy about that,' Captain Mahoney said, with what Bonnie supposed was an attempt at an understanding smile.

Bonnie shrugged, not sure how to respond. 'Could I call my husband now?' she asked again.

'How did your husband feel about you meeting with his ex-wife?' Captain Mahoney asked, using her question as a stepping stone for one of his own.

Bonnie paused. 'He didn't know.'

'He didn't know?'

'Joan asked me not to tell him,' Bonnie explained.

'Did she say why?'

'No.'

'Did you always do what your husband's ex-wife told you?'

'Of course not.'

'Why today?'

'I'm not sure I understand what you mean?'

'Why did you agree to meet with her today? Why didn't you tell your husband?'

Bonnie brought her fist to her open lips, quickly returned it to her lap when she tasted blood. Joan's blood, she realized, swallowing the urge to gag. 'She said something strange to me over the phone.'

'What was that?' Captain Mahoney took a few steps toward her, his pen poised to record her response.

'She said I was in danger.'

'She said *you* were in danger?'

'Me and my daughter.'

'Did she say why?' Captain Mahoney was asking.

'She said it was too complicated to discuss over the phone.'

'And you had no idea what she was talking about?'

'None.'

'So you agreed to meet with her.'

Bonnie nodded.

'When did you get here?'

'Twelve thirty-eight,' Bonnie answered.

Captain Mahoney looked surprised by the preciseness of her response.

'The clock in my car is digital,' Bonnie told him, her words suddenly striking her as hopelessly inane. She giggled, watching as shock replaced curiosity on the faces of everyone else in the room. A woman was dead, for God's sake. Murdered. And not just any woman – her husband's ex-wife. And she had been discovered standing over the body with blood on her hands. This was definitely not a funny situation. Bonnie laughed again, this time more loudly.

'Do you find something amusing here, Mrs Wheeler?' Captain Mahoney was asking.

'No,' she told him, strangling a fresh burst of laughter in her throat, so that her voice sounded gnarled, like an old piece of driftwood. 'Of course not. I guess I'm just a little nervous. I'm sorry.'

'Do you have anything to be nervous about?'

'I don't understand.'

Detective Kritzic stepped forward, sat down beside her. 'Is there anything you'd like to tell us, Mrs Wheeler?' Her voice assumed maternal overtones that conflicted with her girlish face.

'I'd like to call my husband,' Bonnie told them again.

'Let's just finish this first, can we, Mrs Wheeler?' Detective Kritzic's voice resumed its earlier timbre, all traces of the indulgent mother suddenly gone.

Bonnie shrugged. Did she have a choice?

'You arrived at twelve thirty-eight,' Captain Mahoney reiterated, waiting for her to continue.

'The door was open, so I came inside,' Bonnie explained, replaying the events in her mind. 'I heard voices from the back of the house and I didn't want to interrupt, so I waited in here a few minutes, then I went into the kitchen.'

'Did you see anyone?'

'Only Joan. There was no one else here. The voices I'd heard were on the radio.'

'And then what?'

'And then . . .' Bonnie hesitated. 'At first I thought she was just passed out. She was sitting at the table and she had this blank look in her eyes, and so I walked over to her and I think I touched her.' Bonnie stared at her bloodied fingers. 'I must have touched her.' She swallowed. It hurt her throat. 'That's when I realized she was dead. Then there was all this screaming – mine, hers.' She looked toward Margaret Palmay. 'I called the police.'

'How did you know the victim had been shot?'

'Pardon?'

'You told the dispatcher that a woman had been shot.'

'Did I?'

'It's on tape, Mrs Wheeler.'

'I don't know how I knew,' Bonnie replied honestly. 'There was a hole in the middle of her blouse. I guess I just assumed.'

'Did anyone see you arrive, Mrs Wheeler?'

'Not that I know of,' she answered. Why was he asking that?

'What do you do, Mrs Wheeler?'

'Do?'

'Your occupation?'

'I'm a teacher,' Bonnie answered, wondering how what she did for a living was relevant.

'In Newton?'

'Weston.'

'Which school is that?'

'Weston Heights Secondary School. I teach English.'

'So you left the school at what time?'

'Actually, I wasn't teaching today. It was a PD day.' PE day, Joan had called it. 'Professional development day,' Bonnie explained. 'And I was attending a symposium in Boston. I left a little before twelve.'

'And it took you over forty minutes to drive from Boston to Newton?' he asked sceptically.

'There was an accident on the Turnpike,' Bonnie told him, 'and I was held up.'

'Anyone see you leave?'

'See me leave? I don't know. I tried to be pretty quiet about it. Why?' she said suddenly. 'Why are you asking me these questions?'

'You're saying your husband's ex-wife was dead when you got here,' he stated.

'Of course I'm saying that. What else would I be saying?' Bonnie jumped to her feet. 'What's going on here? Am I a suspect?' Of course she was a suspect, she realized. What else would she be? She'd been discovered standing over her husband's ex-wife, with blood on her hands, for God's sake. Of course she was a suspect. 'You haven't answered me,' she persisted. 'Am I a suspect?'

'We're just trying to find out what happened here,' Detective Kritzic told her calmly.

17

'I'd like to call my husband now,' Bonnie said.

'Why don't you call him from the station?' Captain Mahoney closed his notepad, dropped his hands to his sides.

'Am I under arrest?' Bonnie heard herself ask, thinking the voice must be coming from someone else. Maybe the radio again.

'I just think we all might be more comfortable at the station,' came the unsatisfactory response.

'In that case,' Bonnie said, hearing her brother's voice filtering through her own, 'I think I'd better call my lawyer.'

Chapter Three

'Where have you been?' Bonnie demanded, making no effort to hide her frustration. 'I've been trying to reach you for half the afternoon.'

Diana Perrin stared at her friend in astonishment. 'I was with clients,' she answered calmly. 'How was I to know that my best friend was going to get hauled down to the police station for questioning in a murder case?'

'They think I killed Rod's ex-wife!'

'Yes, I think they might,' Diana agreed. 'What the hell did you say to them?'

'I just answered their questions.'

'You answered their questions,' Diana repeated numbly, shaking her head. Bonnie noticed that her long dark hair was neatly tied into a lawyerly bun at the back of her head. 'How many times have you heard me say that one never talks to the police without a lawyer present?'

'How could I not talk to them, for God's sake? I found Joan's body!'

'All the more reason.' Diana took a deep breath, plopped down into the chair across the table from Bonnie.

They were sitting on opposite sides of a long table, maybe light walnut, maybe dark oak, in the center of a small, brightly lit, poorly furnished room, with a scuffed linoleum floor and light, institutionally green walls that were in need of a fresh coat of paint. The ceiling lights were recessed and fluorescent; the walls were bare; the wooden chairs were straight-backed, cushionless and uncomfortable, obviously designed to make the user wish to spend as little time in them as possible. A window interrupted one interior wall, allowing a clear view of the inside of the small suburban precinct. Not much was happening. A few men and women busied themselves at their desks, occasionally glancing in Bonnie's direction. She hadn't seen either Captain Mahoney or Detective Kritzic for the better part of half an hour.

'So, what exactly did you tell them?'

Bonnie again recounted the events of the early afternoon, watching for any signs of emotion on Diana's usually expressive face. But Diana's face registered nothing, her cool blue eyes remaining fixed on Bonnie's lips as she spoke. Diana was a beautiful woman, Bonnie thought, knowing how hard Diana worked to downplay her good looks, at least during the working day, sticking to little make-up, severely tailored suits, like the mustard-colored number she was wearing today, and low-heeled, practical shoes. Still, nothing could disguise the fact that Diana Perrin, age thirty-two and already twice-divorced, was a stunner.

'What are you staring at?' Diana asked, suddenly aware of Bonnie's perusal.

'You look gorgeous.'

'Shit,' Diana muttered. 'This must be what the cops meant when they said some of your reactions were less than appropriate.'

'Are they going to arrest me?'

'I doubt it. They don't have enough evidence to charge you, and since they didn't Mirandize you, they can't use anything you said against you.'

'Mirandize me?'

'Read you your rights.'

Bonnie thought how wondrously accommodating the English language was, the ease with which it had permitted a man's proper name to become a verb. 'Did I really say anything that was so bad?'

'Well, bearing in mind that my practise is primarily corporate and commercial, and that I haven't had anything to do with criminal law since I got out of law school, let's see what I can come up with: the victim was your husband's ex-wife; you were something less than friends, but you still agreed to meet with her and not tell your husband; you snuck out of a meeting and told no one where you were going; you claimed you were stuck in your car at the time of the murder . . .'

'There was an accident on the Turnpike. They can check it out . . .'

'They are, I assure you. Just as they'll be checking your phone records, your school records, the symposium you claimed you attended this morning . . .'

'I was there, for God's sake.'

20

' . . . the mileage on your car, Margaret Palmay's neighbors, the message you gave to 911.'

'What possible motive could I have for killing Joan?'

Diana lifted her elegantly long fingers into the air, counting off the reasons one by one. 'One – she was your husband's ex-wife, which some might consider motive enough. Two – she was a nuisance. Three – she was a financial drain on your resources.'

'They think I would kill her to save on alimony payments?'

'Many have killed for far less.'

'Jesus, Diana, I didn't kill her. You have to know that.'

'Of course I know that.' Diana suddenly snapped around in her chair, as if she'd just realized she'd misplaced something important. 'Where's Rod? Does he know what's happened?'

'Not yet. I couldn't reach him until about twenty minutes ago. I can't tell you how frustrating it was. I couldn't find anyone. You were in meetings; Rod was at lunch. The only person I could get a hold of was Pam Goldenberg.'

'Who?'

'Her daughter is in day care with Amanda. We carpool together. I asked her if she'd mind keeping Amanda at her house until I get out of here.'

'Good thinking.'

'About time.'

Diana reached across the table to her friend's hand. 'Don't be too hard on yourself, Bonnie. It's not every day you stumble across the body of your husband's ex-wife.' She looked toward the ceiling. 'How do you think Rod will take it?'

Bonnie shrugged, pushed herself out of her chair. 'I guess that after the shock wears off, he'll be okay. It's Sam and Lauren I'm worried about. How are they going to cope with the fact that their mother's been murdered? What will this do to them?'

Diana's voice grew timid. 'Doe this mean they'll be moving in with you?'

Bonnie paused. 'What other choices are there?'

She closed her eyes, the images of Rod's two teenage children leaping into focus: Sam, sixteen years old and a student at Weston Secondary, very tall and very skinny, with shoulder-length hair newly dyed jet black, and a tiny gold loop earring wrapped around his left nostril; Lauren, age fourteen, a mediocre student despite attending the best private girls' school in Newton, model-thin and doe-eyed, with her mother's head of luxuriant long reddish hair and full, sensuous lips.

'They hate me,' Bonnie muttered.

'They don't hate you.'

'Yes, they do. And they barely know their half-sister.'

Diana looked toward the inside window. 'Here comes Rod.'

'Thank God.' Bonnie jumped to her feet, watching as the tall, handsome man who was her husband was directed by a young woman in a wrinkled blue uniform toward the small interior office. Bonnie stepped toward the closed office door, hand reaching for the knob, then stopped dead.

'Tell me that's not who I think it is,' Diana said, voicing Bonnie's thoughts out loud.

'I don't believe it.'

'What's she doing here?'

The door opened. Rod stepped inside, the woman behind him momentarily detained by a young man who was thrusting something at her for her to sign, a crowd already gathering around her. An excited buzz filled the air. *Isn't that Marla Brenzelle?* a voice asked. *Is that really Marla Brenzelle?*

Marla Brenzelle, my ass, Bonnie thought. I knew her in high school when she was plain old Marlene Brenzel, back in the days before plastic surgery gave her a new nose and a new set of boobs, before her teeth were capped and her tummy was tucked, before her thighs were liposuctioned and her hair was bleached the color of ripe corn. I knew her when the only people she could get to listen to her were those hapless souls she cornered in the hallway between classes, long before her daddy bought a television station and made her the star of her own television talk show. The only thing about Marlene Brenzel that hadn't changed in the intervening years was her brain, Bonnie thought. She still didn't have one.

'Oh Rod, I'm so glad you're here.'

'I got here as fast as I could. Marla insisted on driving me.' Rod surrounded Bonnie with his arms. 'What's going on?'

'They haven't told you?' Diana asked.

'Nobody's told me anything.' Rod spun around in Diana's direction, obviously startled by her presence. 'What are *you* doing here?'

22

'I called her when I couldn't reach you,' Bonnie explained.

'I don't understand.'

'Maybe you should sit down,' Diana advised.

'What is it?'

'Joan is dead,' Bonnie said softly.

'What?' Rod grabbed at the back of a chair for support.

'She was murdered.'

Rod's normally pale complexion turned paler still. Now in his early forties, his hair had started turning gray in his late twenties, and contrary to accepted wisdom, it had actually made him look younger, emphasizing the deep brown of his eyes, and giving the harder edges of his face – his long nose, his square jaw – a much-needed softness. 'Murdered! That's impossible. How . . . who . . . ?'

'It looked like she'd been shot. They don't know who did it.'

Rod took a moment to digest her words. 'What do you mean, it looked like she'd been shot? How would you know what it looked like?'

'I was there,' Bonnie answered. 'I found her.'

'What do you mean, you found her?' The confusion in Rod's voice carried out into the hall, attracting the attention of the former Marlene Brenzel, who stopped mid-autograph, her body swaying toward them.

'I don't want her in here,' Bonnie said.

Rod quickly stepped into the outer room, his hand reaching out, stopping on Marla's shoulder as he bent over to whisper something in her ear. Bonnie watched the woman's eyes fill with surprise, although her facial muscles didn't move. They probably couldn't, Bonnie thought.

'She's had so much plastic surgery, she looks like a quilt,' Diana muttered, echoing her thoughts. 'Her chin is so pointed, she's liable to stab someone with her face.'

Bonnie had to bite down on her lower lip to keep from laughing, the laugh dying instantly in her throat as Rod walked back into the room.

'Do the kids know?' he asked.

'Not yet.' Bonnie walked to his side, put her arm through his.

'What am I going to say to them?'

'Maybe I can help,' Captain Mahoney offered, emerging from the crowd around Marla Brenzelle, and entering the small room, shutting the door behind him. 'I'm Randall Mahoney, captain of the Detective Bureau. Detective Kritzic and I are the ones who escorted your wife down here.'

23

'Will you please tell me exactly what happened.'

Bonnie watched her husband's posture as he absorbed the news: his wide shoulders slumping forward with the confirmation that his ex-wife had indeed been shot and killed; his large hands dropping lifelessly to his sides with the revelation that Bonnie had agreed to meet with Joan that morning without telling him; his head shaking back and forth in denial when he learned that it was Bonnie who had called the police and then refused to cooperate further until she spoke with her lawyer.

'She's a goddamn corporate lawyer, for Christ's sake,' Rod whispered, not even trying to conceal his long-standing distaste for Diana. 'Why did you call her?'

'Because I couldn't reach you. And I didn't know who else to call.'

Rod turned back to Captain Mahoney. 'Surely you don't suspect my wife,' he stated more than asked.

'We're just trying to find out as much information as possible at this stage,' Randall Mahoney told him.

Bonnie heard something new in the policeman's voice, a subtle hint of conspiracy, as if what he were really saying to her husband was: we're both men; we know how these things work; we don't let our emotions get the better of us; now that you're here, maybe we can start making some progress.

'Do you mind if I ask you a few questions?' Captain Mahoney asked as Detective Kritzic opened the door and stepped inside.

'That's quite a crowd,' she muttered, clearly flushed by her brief encounter with celebrity.

'Mr Wheeler, this is Detective Natalie Kritzic.'

Natalie Kritzic nodded, self-consciously tucking an autographed picture of Marla Brenzelle behind her back. 'I understand you're her director,' she said. 'I'm a big fan.'

I'm in serious trouble, Bonnie thought. The world is in serious trouble.

Rod accepted the compliment graciously. 'Whatever I can do to cooperate, I'll be happy to . . .'

'You're Joan Wheeler's ex-husband?' Captain Mahoney asked.

'Yes.'

'May I ask how long you were married?'

'Nine years.'

'And you divorced when?'

'Seven years ago.'

24

'Children?'

'A boy and a girl.' He looked to Bonnie for help.

'Sam is sixteen and Lauren is fourteen,' she offered.

Rod nodded. Everyone watched while Randall Mahoney jotted down this latest information.

'Did your ex-wife have any enemies that you know of, Mr Wheeler?'

Rod shrugged. 'My ex-wife wasn't exactly Miss Congeniality, Captain. She didn't have many friends. But enemies . . . I couldn't say.'

'When was the last time you saw your ex-wife, Mr Wheeler?'

Rod gave the question a moment's thought. 'Christmas, probably, when I took over some gifts for the kids.'

'And the last time you spoke to her on the phone?'

'I can't remember the last time I spoke to her on the phone.'

'And yet, according to your wife, she often called your house.'

'My ex-wife was an alcoholic, Captain Mahoney,' Rod said, as if this somehow explained everything.

'Were you on good terms with your ex-wife, Mr Wheeler?'

'Don't answer that,' Diana advised from across the room, her voice quiet but forceful nonetheless. 'It has no relevancy here.'

'I have no problem answering the question,' Rod informed Diana curtly. 'No, of course we weren't on good terms. She was nuttier than a fruitcake.'

'Good one,' Bonnie heard Diana mutter, not quite under her breath, as she raised her hands in defeat, her eyes rolling to the top of her head.

Captain Mahoney allowed a slight smile to crease the corners of his mouth. 'According to your wife, your ex-wife called her this morning to warn her she was in some kind of danger. Do you have any idea what she might have been referring to?'

'Joan said you were in danger?' Rod asked his wife, his voice echoing the look of incredulity that had settled, like a mask, over his regular features. He brought his hand to his forehead, rubbed it until it grew pink. 'I have no idea what she was talking about.'

'Who would profit by your ex-wife's death, Mr Wheeler?'

Rod looked slowly from Captain Mahoney to his wife, then back to Captain Mahoney. 'I don't understand the question.'

'I advise you not to answer it,' Diana interrupted again.

'What are you asking?' Rod asked impatiently, although it was hard to tell whether his impatience was directed at the police or at Diana.

'Did your ex-wife carry any life insurance policies? Had she made a will?'

'I don't know whether or not she had a will,' Rod answered, each word carefully measured. 'I know she carried life insurance because I paid the premiums. It was part of our divorce settlement,' he explained.

'And who is the beneficiary of that policy?' Captain Mahoney asked.

'Her children. And myself,' Rod added.

'And how much is that policy for?'

'Two hundred and fifty thousand dollars,' Rod replied.

'And the house at thirteen Exeter Street? In whose name is it registered?'

'It's in both our names.' Rod paused, cleared his throat. 'Our divorce agreement stipulated that she could live in the house as long as the kids were still in school, then she'd have to sell, and we'd split the profits.'

'How much would you say the house is worth in today's market, Mr Wheeler?'

'I have no idea. Joan was the real-estate agent, not me.' Rod looked pained, his eyes narrowing in growing frustration. 'Now, I think it's time I took my wife home . . .'

'Where were you today, Mr Wheeler?'

'Excuse me?' Rod's cheeks flushed hot pink, like rosy circles painted onto the faces of porcelain dolls.

'I have to ask,' Captain Mahoney said, almost apologetically.

'He doesn't have to answer,' Diana reminded him.

'I was at work,' Rod said quickly. Again Diana's eyes rolled toward the ceiling.

'All day?'

'Of course.'

Bonnie felt suddenly confused. If he'd been at work all day, where was he when she called?

'Your wife tried for over an hour to reach you, Mr Wheeler,' Captain Mahoney said, as if reading Bonnie's mind.

'I took several hours off for lunch,' Rod explained.

'I'm sure you have witnesses . . .'

Rod took a deep breath, made a sound halfway between a laugh and a sigh. 'Well, no, actually, there aren't any witnesses. The fact is, I didn't eat lunch. I told the switchboard that I was going out for lunch and that I couldn't be reached, but what I really did was grab a few

26

hours' sleep in my office. We didn't get a lot of sleep last night. Our daughter had a nightmare.'

Bonnie nodded confirmation.

'Nobody saw you?'

'Not until after two o'clock, when I went into a meeting. Look,' he continued, unprompted, 'I may not have been one of my ex-wife's biggest fans, but I certainly never wished her any harm. I feel terrible that this has happened.' He hugged Bonnie tight against him. 'I'm sure we both do.'

There was a long pause during which nobody spoke. From outside the small room, Marla Brenzelle's high-pitched laugh reverberated. She's working the room, Bonnie thought, watching as the woman pranced around the station in her bright yellow Valentino suit, dragging an imaginary microphone with her, thrusting it into the faces of her adoring fans.

'I think that's all for now,' Captain Mahoney was saying. 'Of course, we'll probably want to speak to you again.'

'Anything we can do to help,' Rod offered, although he no longer sounded as sincere as he had earlier.

'We'll have to interview Sam and Lauren,' Detective Kritzic said.

Rod looked startled. 'Sam and Lauren? Why?'

'They lived with their mother,' Detective Kritzic reminded him. 'They might be able to shed some light on who killed her.'

Rod nodded. 'Can I speak to them first? I mean, I just think it would be better if I were to break the news to them.'

'Of course,' Captain Mahoney stated. 'We'd like your permission to search the house later. There may be some clues . . .'

Rod nodded. 'Any time.'

'We'll come by in a few hours. In the meantime, I'd appreciate it if you wouldn't move anything in the house. If the kids should say something, or you think of anything that might be helpful, I hope you'll call us immediately.'

'Will do.'

Rod squeezed Bonnie's shoulder, led her to the door.

'Oh, by the way,' Captain Mahoney said as they were about to exit, 'do either you or your wife own a gun?'

'A gun?' Rod shook his head. 'No,' he said, the single syllable managing to convey enough outraged indignation for several complete sentences.

27

'Thank you,' Captain Mahoney said as Marla Brenzelle extricated herself from her fans and walked toward them, arms outstretched in a theatrical display of sympathy. 'I'll see you in a few hours.'

Something to look forward to, Bonnie thought, as the former Marlene Brenzel locked her in a suffocating embrace.

Chapter Four

The suburb of Newton is only minutes from downtown Boston, its eighteen square miles housing almost eighty-three thousand inhabitants. It is composed of fourteen diverse villages, including Oak Hill to the southeast and Auburndale to the northwest. Joan Wheeler and her children resided in West Newton Hill, the site of the most exclusive homes in Newton.

The house at thirteen Exeter Street was large and mock-Tudor in style. Several years ago, Joan had painted the entire exterior of the house a kind of greenish-beige, including the wood trim, and replaced all the front windows on the main floor with panels of stained glass. The result was a structure that looked like it couldn't quite make up its mind what it wanted to be – house or cathedral. The stained-glass panels themselves were primitive and puzzling: a man in long flowing robes, a dog playing at his feet; a woman in modern dress balancing a pitcher of water on her head; a man tilling the land; two pudgy children playing by a waterfall.

Rod lowered his head into his hands as Bonnie pulled her car into the driveway.

'Are you all right?' Bonnie asked.

Rod leaned his head back against the leather headrest. 'I just can't believe she's dead. She always seemed so much larger than life.' He looked toward the front door. 'I dread like hell going in there. I don't know how I'm going to break the news, what I can say to make things easier . . .'

'You'll find the right words,' Bonnie told him. 'And you know I'll do everything I can to help them.'

Rod nodded silently, opening the car door and stepping outside. A few clouds hovered, threatening rain.

April is the cruellest month, Bonnie recited silently, recalling the poem by T. S. Eliot, and thrust her hand inside her husband's as they marched solemnly up the front walk.

At the large wooden double door, Rod stopped, fumbling in his pocket for the keys.

'You have keys?' Bonnie asked, surprised.

Rod pushed open the door. 'Hello,' he called, as they stepped into the marble foyer. 'Anybody home?'

Bonnie checked her watch. It was almost four thirty.

'Hello,' Rod called again as Bonnie took several tentative steps toward the living room on the right.

The room was lushly papered in a textured pale blue satin. An antique-looking sofa in pale pink silk and two blue-and-gold armchairs were grouped around a large brick fireplace, several obviously expensive Indian rugs scattered in seemingly random fashion across the dark hardwood floor. Several charcoal drawings hung in simple frames: a woman hugging a young girl to her side; two middle-aged women lying with loose-legged abandon in the afternoon sun; two old women sewing. 'These are very nice,' Bonnie said, eyes lingering on the sketches.

She walked through the dining room, running her hand along the top of the long, skinny oak table that occupied the center of the room, framed on either side and at each end by high-backed oak chairs with burnt-orange leather upholstery.

The kitchen was at the back, a huge room which ran the entire width of the house. The floors were bleached oak, the cabinets dark burgundy against winter-white walls, the entire back wall a window that overlooked a tastefully landscaped back yard. Like the living and dining rooms, this room was immaculate. A far cry from her own kitchen, Bonnie thought, conscious that there was nothing sticky on the floor, no wayward patterns of dried-up sauces on the walls, no fingerprints on the large glass kitchen table. Did anyone actually live in this house, let alone a woman with two teenagers? she wondered, pushing a second door on the other side of the kitchen and returning to the front hall. 'Rod?' she called, wondering where her husband had disappeared.

'In here.'

Bonnie followed his voice into the small room to the left of the front door. Rod stood behind a gilded antique desk, his right hand caressing a large crystal paperweight. Built-in bookcases lined three walls; a burgundy leather sofa stood against the fourth, an oval-shaped Dhury rug in front of it.

'This used to be my favorite room,' Rod said, his eyes a decade away.

'Everything's so neat,' Bonnie marveled. 'It's kind of spooky.'

'Since when did neat equal spooky?'

'Since we had Amanda.' Bonnie was suddenly aware of someone moving about overhead. She walked quickly back into the front hall, Rod right behind her.

'Who's there?' The voice was small, tentative. 'Mom? Is that you? Do you have someone with you?'

'Lauren?' Rod answered, approaching the staircase. 'Lauren, it's your father.'

There was silence. Bonnie waited beside Rod at the bottom of the steps. What was he going to say to the girl? How was he going to tell his fourteen-year-old daughter that her mother was dead, that she'd been murdered?

'Lauren, can you come down here a minute?' he said. 'I need to talk to you.'

A face appeared over the top railing, pale and wary, her eyes wide, her lips slightly parted, her hands tightly gripping the banister. She hung back at the top of the stairs for several seconds before allowing herself to be coaxed down, moving ever so slowly, ever so carefully down the stairs, looking only at her feet, refusing to glance up at either her father or her father's wife, like a wild animal being tempted by food in a human palm.

She was wearing the green-and-ivory uniform that distinguished the students of Bishop's Private School for Girls: green kilt and matching knee socks; ivory, long-sleeved blouse; green-and-gold-striped tie; black Oxfords. Her long auburn hair was pulled into a ponytail at the back and secured by a dark green scrunchie. The ugliest school uniform money could buy, Bonnie thought, mindful of the huge tuition fees Rod had to pay each year. Another condition of his divorce settlement.

'Hello, Lauren,' she said, noticing for the first time how much Lauren resembled Amanda, how much their father was present in both faces.

'Hello, sweetheart,' Rod echoed.

'Hi, Daddy,' Lauren said, as if Bonnie hadn't spoken, as if she weren't there. 'What are you doing here?'

'I came to see you,' Rod answered.

31

'How come?'

'Where's your brother?' he asked.

Lauren shrugged. 'Out. He had a PD day today.' She looked toward the front door. 'Mom's late,' she said. 'She's usually here by the time I get home from school.'

'Do you have any idea when Sam might be getting back?' Rod asked.

'Is something the matter?'

'Maybe we could sit down,' Bonnie began, stopped when she realized that no one was listening to her.

'What's wrong?' Lauren demanded, a curtain of fear descending across her huge hazel eyes.

'There's been an accident,' Rod began.

'What kind of accident?' Lauren was already shaking her head back and forth, as if denying the reality of what she was about to hear.

'Your mother's been hurt,' Rod said gently.

'Was she in a car accident? Is she in the hospital? What hospital did they take her to?' The questions ran together as one.

'Lauren, honey,' Rod began, then faltered, looking to Bonnie for help.

Bonnie took a deep breath. 'Sweetheart,' she said, 'we're so sorry to have to tell you this . . .'

'I'm talking to my father,' the girl said sharply, the force of her rebuke throwing Bonnie off balance, as if she had been physically pushed out of the way. Bonnie grabbed for the railing, lowering herself down until she was sitting on the stairs. 'What happened to my mother?' Lauren demanded of her father.

'She's dead,' he said simply.

For several seconds, Lauren said nothing. Bonnie wanted desperately to go to her, to take the child in her arms, tell her not to worry, that they would look after her, that she would love her as if she were her own, that everything would be all right, but Lauren's invisible hands were on her shoulders, holding her down, refusing her comfort.

'She was a lousy driver,' Lauren was whispering. 'I was always telling her to slow down, but she never would, and she was constantly yelling at everyone else on the road, calling them all sorts of names, you should have heard her. I kept telling her to calm down, that there was nothing anyone could do about the traffic, but . . .'

'It wasn't a car accident,' Rod interrupted.

'What?' The word froze on Lauren's lips. Obviously, she couldn't imagine any other possibility. 'How then?' she asked finally.

'She was shot,' Rod answered.

'Shot?' Lauren's eyes frantically searched the room, inadvertently connecting with Bonnie's before turning abruptly away. 'You mean she was murdered?'

'The police aren't exactly sure what happened,' Rod hedged.

'The police?'

'They'll be here soon,' Rod said.

'My mother was murdered?' Lauren asked again.

'It looks that way.'

Lauren walked to the front door with purposeful strides as Bonnie rose to her feet. Where was the girl going? But Lauren reversed herself when she got to the door, striding with equal purpose back into the front hall, although there was no purpose that Bonnie could determine, other than to keep moving. Maybe that was purpose enough.

'Who?' Lauren asked. 'Do they know who . . . ?'

Rod shook his head.

'Where? Where did this happen?'

'An open house your mother was having on Lombard Street.'

Tears filled Lauren's eyes. She walked briskly back to the front door, pivoted sharply on the thick heels of her black Oxfords, and returned to the middle of the hall. 'How did you find out about this?' she asked suddenly. 'I mean, why did the police contact you, and not me and Sam?'

'I'm the one who found her,' Bonnie replied after a pause.

It was as if time suddenly stopped, Bonnie thought later, as if none of what was happening was actually taking place at this moment, as if it had already occurred long ago and somewhere far away, and they were merely watching a replay of the whole horrible scene through one of Rod's television monitors, everything happening in slow motion, and just so subtly out of sync: Lauren's head spinning toward Bonnie a frame at a time, her ponytail lifting lazily into the air, then slapping against her right shoulder in a series of exaggerated jerks, tears hovering under widely expanded pupils, hands shooting into the air, scratching it like fingernails across a chalkboard, her mouth opening in a silent scream.

And then there was chaos as the scene snapped back into the present, unwinding with ferocious and unforgiving speed. Bonnie watched in horror as Lauren flew across the room toward her, her fists connecting with Bonnie's chest and face, her feet targeting her legs. The onslaught was so sudden, so terrifying, so unexpected, that Bonnie had little time to defend herself against the blows. Suddenly, everyone was screaming.

'Lauren, for God's sake,' Rod was yelling, trying to disengage his daughter, to tear her away from Bonnie.

'What do you mean, you found her?' Lauren cried. 'What do you mean, you found her?'

'Lauren, please,' Bonnie began, just as Lauren's left fist connected with her mouth. Bonnie fell back against the stairs, tasting blood for the second time that day, although this time the blood was her own.

'For God's sake, Lauren, stop it!' Rod finally managed to secure his daughter around the waist, and drag her, still kicking and screaming away from Bonnie. 'What's gotten into you?' he shouted, his breath coming in short, angry bursts. 'What are you doing?'

'She killed her!' Lauren was screaming, her hair breaking loose of its green scrunchie and whipping across her face, several strands clinging to her tear-streaked cheeks, as if secured by glue. 'She killed my mother!' Lauren made another lunge in Bonnie's direction.

'She didn't kill her, for Christ's sake!' Rod cried, restraining her.

'She just happened to find her?' Lauren demanded. 'You're trying to tell me she just happened to find her?'

Bonnie's head was spinning, her eyes closing against the possibility of further attack, afraid to open, her ears buzzing around the awful things Lauren was saying. Her jaw ached. Her lower lip stung where it had been cut. Her arms and legs were no doubt covered with bruises, or would be by the time the police arrived. And wouldn't that make an interesting addendum to their notes?

'Lauren,' Bonnie said softly, each word an ordeal, 'you have to know I had nothing to do with your mother's death.'

'What were you doing at her open house? Are you trying to tell me it was just a coincidence that you happened to be there, a coincidence that you were the one who found her?'

'Your mother called me,' Bonnie began, then burst into tears, burying her head in her hands. She couldn't tell it again. She couldn't go through the awful events of the morning one more time.

'Let's go into the living room,' Rod said softly. 'Maybe if we all sit down and discuss this thing rationally, we can figure something out.'

'I'm going up to my room,' Lauren said instead, breaking away from her father's arms.

Instinctively, Bonnie recoiled as Lauren approached, her hands moving to protect her face from further blows. In the next minute, she felt the painful vibrations of Lauren's heavy black Oxfords as they pounded up the gray-carpeted stairs. A second later, a door slammed overhead.

Rod was instantly at Bonnie's side, his hands gingerly pushing the hair from her eyes, his lips kissing away the blood at the side of her mouth. 'Oh, my poor baby, I'm so sorry. Are you all right?'

'My God,' Bonnie muttered. 'She really hates me.'

There was a noise at the front door, scuffling, laughter, the sound of a key turning in the lock. Sam, Bonnie realized, her body tensing automatically.

Brace yourself for the second round, it said.

Chapter Five

The door opened and Sam Wheeler spilled inside, like a tall glass of water. He was wrapped in a multitude of layers, an open khaki jacket over an army-style camouflage shirt, itself worn over an olive-green T-shirt, all of which hung over the top of a pair of faded and baggy brown pants. On his feet were expensive name-brand high-topped sneakers, their laces undone and twisting around his feet, like snakes. His hair was uncombed and so black, it radiated blue, blotting out the natural color of his eyes, so that they looked like two empty sockets, incongruously nestled beneath extraordinarily long lashes. A small gold loop curved around the outside of his left nostril.

Right behind Sam was another boy, not as tall, a little more muscular, a series of tattoos running up and down his bare arms. Long brown hair framed a decidedly handsome face, but there was something almost rude about the boy's good looks, a sneer in his gray eyes as well as his posture. He wore a black T-shirt over black jeans and black pointed-toed leather boots. The pungently sweet odor of marijuana surrounded him like an overpowering cologne, his trademark, Bonnie knew. Wasn't that why everyone called him Haze – because he was always in one? Her eyes moved rapidly back and forth between the two teenage boys.

'What's going on?' Sam said instead of hello, although neither his face nor his voice registered any surprise at seeing them there.

'Hey, Mrs Wheeler,' Haze said, his eyes focusing in on her torn lip, like a camera lens. 'What happened to your face?'

'My wife had a little accident,' Rod explained quickly.

Hadn't he used the same word when describing Joan's death to his daughter? Bonnie found it an interesting choice, in that it absolved anyone of blame.

'That your car in the driveway?' Sam asked Bonnie, barely acknowledging that his father had spoken.

Bonnie nodded. 'We need to talk to you, Sam,' she said.

Sam shrugged. So talk, the shrug said.

'Maybe it would be better if we could talk alone.' Rod glanced toward Haze.

'Maybe it wouldn't,' Sam told him.

Beside him, Haze chuckled.

'This is Harold Gleason,' Bonnie said, introducing her husband to his son's friend. 'He's in my first period class.' He's disruptive, he never does his assignments, he's failing, she could have added, but didn't. 'Everyone calls him Haze.'

'Looks like someone hit you, Mrs Wheeler,' Haze said, ignoring her introduction and moving a step closer, the scent of marijuana radiating provocatively from his hair and clothes, stretching toward her like a third hand. 'Yeah,' he observed. 'Looks like somebody nailed you one pretty good there, Mrs Wheeler.'

'Sam, this is important,' Rod said impatiently.

'I'm listening.'

'Something's happened to your mother,' Rod began, then stopped, looking up the stairs.

Sam's eyes followed his father's. 'What's the matter with her? Did she get drunk and fall out of bed? Did she call you to come over? Is that what you're doing here?'

'Your mother is dead, Sam,' Rod said quietly.

There was silence. Bonnie watched Sam's face for any hint of what he might be feeling, but his face was resolutely blank, betraying nothing of whatever might be going on behind those inexpressive black eyes.

'How'd it happen, man?' Haze asked.

'She was shot,' Bonnie answered simply, still monitoring Sam's face for some reaction. But there was none, not a tear, not a twitch, not even a blink. 'I was the one who found her,' she continued, automatically taking a step back, protecting her mouth with the back of her hand.

Still no response.

'She called me this morning, said there was something she had to tell me, asked me to meet her at an open house she was having on Lombard Street. When I got there, she was dead.'

Sam's eyes narrowed slightly.

'Do you have any idea why she wanted to see me, Sam?' Bonnie asked.

Sam shook his head.

'I think she was trying to warn me about something,' Bonnie elaborated. 'Maybe if we knew what . . .'

'Who shot her, man?' Haze asked, nervously rubbing the side of his nose with his fingers. Bonnie saw his arm muscle flex beneath his black T-shirt, a red tattooed heart swelling involuntarily with the motion. MOTHER, it said above the heart; FUCKER, it said below.

'We don't know yet,' Bonnie told him, grateful that someone was asking the appropriate questions.

'What happened to her car?' Sam said.

'Pardon?' Bonnie was sure she'd heard him incorrectly. Had Sam really asked about his mother's car?

'Where's her car?' Sam repeated.

'I guess it's still on Lombard Street,' Bonnie told him, the words emerging slowly.

'That's an expensive car,' Sam said. 'The police can't impound it, can they?'

Bonnie didn't know how to respond. She hadn't given a thought to Joan's car. 'I don't know what the procedure is,' she said, glancing at Rod, who looked as confused as she was.

Sam shuffled aimlessly, his eyes refusing to linger more than half a second in any one spot. 'Is Lauren home?'

'She's upstairs.'

'You told her?'

Bonnie nodded.

'So now what?' he asked.

'I'm not sure,' Bonnie admitted. 'The police will be here soon . . .'

'I should get going,' Haze announced instantly, hands reaching for the door, as if the police were already at his back, guns drawn. 'I'm real sorry about your mom, Sammy. Catch you later, man.' The front door opened and closed, a hint of cool April air grappling with the stale scent of marijuana.

'I have nothing to say to the police,' Sam said.

'I don't think you have any choice in the matter,' Rod told him.

'Look, what are you doing here, anyway?' Sam looked from his father to Bonnie and then back again to his father. 'I mean, you came, you saw, you delivered the bad news – ding dong, the witch is dead – so you don't have to stick around here anymore, do you? You can go back to your new home and your new family and forget all about us for another seven years.'

Bonnie felt the scene around her starting to unravel, like a skein from a fat ball of yarn. *Ding dong, the witch is dead?!*

'Sam?' a thin voice called from the top of the stairs.

All eyes looked toward the pale young girl who stood trembling on the upstairs landing.

'Did you hear what happened?' Lauren whimpered, eyes unfocused, as she moved slowly down the steps, as if in her sleep. 'Did you hear what happened to Mommy?'

'It'll be a few days before we get the final report back from the medical examiner,' Captain Mahoney was saying, his large body all but overpowering the delicate blue-and-gold living room chair in which he was sitting. Sam, fidgeting and looking bored, and Lauren, not moving and barely breathing, sat across from him on the pink silk sofa, while Bonnie perched at the end of a dining room chair that Rod had brought into the room. Both Rod and Detective Kritzic remained standing, Rod by the large brick fireplace, Detective Kritzic in front of the stained-glass windows.

'What do you want to ask us?' Sam said.

'When was the last time you saw your mother?' Captain Mahoney asked.

'Last night.' Sam tucked a strand of wayward hair behind his right ear. 'I went in to say goodnight to her at around two o'clock.'

'And how did she seem to you?'

'You mean, was she drunk?'

'Was she?'

Sam shrugged. 'Probably.'

'What about you, Lauren?' Detective Kritzic asked, her voice gentle and soft.

'I went in to kiss her goodbye this morning before I went to school.'

'I thought it was a PD day,' Captain Mahoney interjected, eyes on Bonnie.

'I go to a private school,' Lauren told him.

'Did your mother say anything to you about her plans for the day?'

'She said she had an open house this morning, and that she wouldn't be late.'

'Did she sound anxious or worried about anything?'

'No.'

'Did she say anything about meeting with Bonnie Wheeler this morning?'

'No.'

'Did she say anything about wanting to warn Bonnie Wheeler that she was in danger?'

Lauren shook her head. 'What kind of danger?'

'Do you have any idea who might have wanted to harm your mother?' Captain Mahoney's gaze travelled between the two teenagers.

'No,' Sam said simply.

Lauren looked over at Bonnie. She said nothing, though the inference was clear.

My new family, Bonnie acknowledged silently. A boy who doesn't seem to give a damn that his mother has been murdered, and a girl who thinks I killed her. Great. Well, at least they have each other, she thought, although looking at them now, sitting side by side, like two ceramic figurines, not touching, features etched in stone, blank eyes directed inward, it was unlikely they would be of much comfort to each other in the difficult weeks ahead. And they certainly aren't about to let me comfort them, Bonnie thought, knowing any such gesture wouldn't be tolerated, let alone appreciated. They barely know me, but they know they hate me.

Could she blame them? Hadn't she felt the same way toward the woman her father had married after her parents' divorce? Hadn't she openly rejoiced when that marriage had fallen apart? Even now, weren't her feelings something less than cordial toward wife number three? And what about the brother she hadn't spoken to since their mother's untimely death? How much comfort had he ever provided?

Bonnie closed her eyes, fighting back bitter tears. Now was hardly the time to reopen ugly wounds, to drag old skeletons from the closet. She had far more immediate concerns.

We have a lot in common, she wanted to tell Lauren. I can help you, if you'll let me. Maybe we can help each other.

She felt movement around her and opened her eyes. Captain Mahoney had risen to his feet and was motioning toward the front hall. 'I'd like to have a look around now,' he said.

Chapter Six

'My God, what happened here?' The words were out of Bonnie's mouth before she had a chance to stop them.

'I guess she didn't have a chance to clean up yet,' Lauren replied defensively.

'Watch where you step,' Captain Mahoney cautioned. 'Try not to touch anything.'

Together, they filed into Joan's upstairs bedroom: Bonnie; her husband; his children; Captain Mahoney and Detective Kritzic. They walked as if they were tiptoeing on glass, taking exaggerated steps, knees lifting high into the air, feet careful where they landed. No one spoke, their silence more shocked than respectful, although the expressions on the faces of Joan's children reflected little of anything at all.

'She just didn't have a chance to tidy up yet,' Lauren repeated, finding an empty patch of carpet beside an open closet door.

'It's always like this,' Sam said, leaning back against one pale pink wall.

'It wasn't like she was expecting company,' Lauren said.

Company? Bonnie thought, turning in small circles in the center of the room, trying to overcome her natural revulsion, to wipe her face clean of judgement. The room was a disaster area, a war zone, a dump site, barely fit for any form of human life, let alone company.

Bonnie's eyes swept across the room like a broom, as if she were trying somehow to visually transport all the assorted debris into its center, to pull together all the old newspapers that grew along the sides of the walls like weeds, to scoop up the various books and magazines that lay open and twisted on the rose-colored broadloom, to rake in the layers of discarded clothing that spilled from the closet and were strewn everywhere, like autumn leaves, to pick up the multitude of crusted-over dishes and half-empty cups of coffee, to empty the scores of ashtrays that fell across every available surface, like dominoes, their ashes spilling onto the carpet and the once-white bed sheets, the bed looking as if it hadn't been made in weeks, maybe months. Empty liquor bottles lay across the pillows, necks entwined, like lovers in repose; a white phone, its cord hopelessly twisted and looped around an open address book, sat in the middle of the bed, beside a half-eaten hamburger, relish and mustard still clinging to its paper wrapper. More empty bottles protruded from just underneath the bed. Wine bottles, Bonnie recognized, trying not to stare. How could the woman live this way?

'It's so neat downstairs,' Bonnie muttered, trying to reconcile the two areas.

'No one ever uses the downstairs,' Sam said.

'What about dinner?' Bonnie tried not to focus on the half-eaten hamburger. 'Who made dinner? Where did you eat?'

'We ate out,' Sam said. 'Or we ordered in, ate in our rooms.' He said this as if it were the most normal thing in the world for families to behave this way.

'The real-estate business isn't exactly nine to five,' Lauren continued. 'It's hard to coordinate everybody's schedules. My mother did the best she could.'

'Of course she did,' Bonnie agreed.

'A little mess isn't the end of the world.'

'No, of course it's not.'

'Who asked you?' the girl said.

Bonnie was aware of Captain Mahoney standing by the bed, watching this exchange, his large hands diligently working to extricate the address book from the phone wire. She felt faint, the odor of discarded food and stale cigarettes swirling around her head like a dense fog, summoning forth reminders of earlier odors, even more unpleasant. The smell of blood and torn flesh and human wastes. The smell of violent, unexpected death.

Bonnie felt Rod's arms wrap protectively around her, as if he knew what she was thinking, and felt her own body sway, then sink against his side.

Captain Mahoney lifted the open address book from the bed, the phone wire snapping back against the sheet like an elastic band. 'Anybody know Sally Gardiner, Lyle and Caroline Gossett, Linda

Giradelli?' he read, the address book obviously open to the letter G.

'We used to be friends with the Gossetts,' Rod remarked. 'They live across the street.'

'My mother had a lot of friends,' Lauren said.

'Drinking buddies,' Rod whispered under his breath.

'What about a Dr Walter Greenspoon?'

'The psychiatrist?' Bonnie asked.

'You know him?'

'I know *of* him. He writes a weekly column for the *Globe.*'

'And we've used him as a consultant on our show a number of times,' Rod added.

'Any chance your ex-wife might have been a patient of his?'

'I have no idea.'

Captain Mahoney looked toward Sam and Lauren. Both shrugged. The police captain flipped to another page. 'How about Donna Fisher or Wendy Findlayson?'

Rod and Bonnie shook their heads. Again Sam and Lauren shrugged.

'Josh Freeman?'

'There's a Josh Freeman who teaches at Weston Secondary,' Bonnie said, startled by the familiar name.

'He's my art teacher,' Sam concurred.

'Is that the school's phone number?' Captain Mahoney stretched the book toward Bonnie.

'No,' she said, picturing the tall, slightly rumpled-looking widower who was new to the school this year, wondering what Joan would have been doing with his home number.

Captain Mahoney handed the red leather address book to Detective Kritzic, then turned his attention to the bed, pushing the phone and the partly eaten hamburger aside, and pulling back the sheet. 'What have we here?' he asked, although the question was obviously rhetorical.

Bonnie watched him lift a large paper scrapbook into his arms, and open it, quickly flipping through the pages. 'Anybody know a Scott Dunphy?' he asked after a moment's pause.

Bonnie felt an uncomfortable twinge of recognition, although she wasn't sure why. She didn't know anyone named Scott Dunphy.

'What about Nicholas Lonergan?'

Bonnie gasped, the small twinge twisting into a large cramp, filling her stomach.

'I take it the name is familiar,' Captain Mahoney stated, eyes narrowing and lifting toward Bonnie.

'Nicholas Lonergan is my brother,' Bonnie said. Her back stiffened even as she felt her legs turn to jelly.

'Interesting,' Captain Mahoney remarked casually. 'I see he got himself into a bit of trouble a few years back.' He flipped to the next page.

'I don't understand . . .'

'What about a Steve Lonergan?'

Bonnie felt as if she had just stepped into some kind of peculiar time warp, as if the words she was hearing, the words she was speaking, were coming from somewhere and someone else. 'My father,' she acknowledged. What was going on? What were her father and brother, two men she hadn't spoken to in over three years, doing here in this room with her now? In what perverse way had Joan's murder served to reunite them?

'You might want to have a look through this,' Captain Mahoney said, dropping the open scrapbook into her arms. It felt surprisingly light, considering he had just dumped the entire weight of her past into her hands.

Bonnie glanced down at the first page, almost afraid of what she might see. A small newspaper clipping occupied the center of the otherwise blank space. *The marriage is announced of Bonnie Lonergan to Rod Wheeler on 27 June 1989. Ms Lonergan is a high school English teacher. Mr Wheeler is the news director at television station WHDH in Boston. The couple will honeymoon in the Bahamas.*

Why would Joan have saved her wedding announcement? Bonnie wondered, turning the page, conscious of Rod reading over her shoulder, his breath warm on the back of her neck. A small line of perspiration broke out along her upper lip as she read the second clipping, dated 5 November of that same year. *Warrants issued in land fraud scheme,* the article headlined. *Warrants have been issued for two men believed to have been involved in a scheme to defraud investors of hundreds of thousands of dollars. Scott Dunphy and Nicholas Lonergan, both of Boston, are believed to have spearheaded an attempt to defraud hundreds of potential investors . . .*

'My God,' Bonnie whispered, skipping the balance of the article she knew by heart, and moving quickly to the next page, seeing a large, grainy black-and-white photograph of her brother in handcuffs, his handsome face obscured by chin-length shaggy blond hair. Then on the next page – *Pair acquitted in land development scheme. Judge cites lack of evidence.*

And then another small announcement in the middle of an otherwise blank page: *The marriage is announced of Steve Lonergan to Adeline Sewell on 15 March 1990. Mr Lonergan is an employment counsellor. Ms Sewell runs a travel agency. They will honeymoon in Las Vegas.* The announcement neglected to mention it was the third marriage for each of them.

The next page was filled with news about Rod: a flattering profile, including photographs, of the hotshot director of news at station WHDH; the announcement of the creation of *Marla!* with Rod at the helm, a picture of the dynamic duo arm in arm; a chart of the program's growing success.

And then back to more unflattering shots of her brother in handcuffs, looking a little older, a lot more haggard, an oddly smiling Scott Dunphy beside him, this time under the lurid headline, *Pair Found Guilty of Conspiracy to Commit Murder.*

Bonnie quickly turned the page. She had no desire to relive those awful months wedged between her mother's death and the birth of her child, both announcements suitably enshrined on the next few pages, Bonnie noted with mounting unease.

The last page in the album was entirely taken up with a newspaper picture of her daughter, Amanda, snapped this past Christmas when they were in Toys 'R' Us. A photographer had caught the child standing wistfully in front of a giant stuffed kangaroo, one hand at her mouth, her thumb lost between her lips, the other hand in the paw of the huge stuffed marsupial. The photograph had made the front page of the Life section of the *Globe.* Bonnie had a large framed copy of it sitting on her desk at home.

'I don't understand,' Bonnie said again, her voice echoing the numbness she was feeling. She looked over at Sam and Lauren. 'Why would your mother keep a scrapbook like this?'

But Sam and Lauren said nothing, their silence underlining either ignorance or disinterest, perhaps a combination of both.

'There's a Nick Lonergan listed in here,' Detective Kritzic announced, holding Joan's address book into the air, as if it were a Bible.

Bonnie was conscious of her heart starting to race. 'That can't be,' she protested, feeling that she was sinking into quicksand, and grabbing for Rod's arm for support. 'They didn't even know each other.'

Detective Kritzic read the number aloud.

Bonnie nodded recognition. 'That's my father's number,' she said, then lapsed into silence. How many times could she say 'I don't understand'?

'Did your mother own a gun?' Captain Mahoney asked, switching the focus of his questioning to Sam and Lauren. If he had any more questions about what her brother's name might be doing in Joan's address book, he was keeping them to himself.

'Yes,' Lauren said.

'She kept it in the top drawer of her dresser,' Sam added, pointing to the tall walnut armoire that stood beside the window on the wall opposite the bedroom door, its bottom drawers open, several bright-colored blouses hanging over the sides.

Two large strides brought Captain Mahoney to the armoire. He pulled open the top drawer, sweeping his hand across Joan's more intimate belongings, several pairs of pantihose escaping his grasp to float aimlessly to the floor and land gently across the top of his black shoes. 'What kind of gun was it, do you know?'

'I don't know anything about guns,' Sam said.

'Ask my dad,' Lauren told him. 'It was his gun.'

All eyes turned to Rod, who looked as stunned as Bonnie had felt only moments ago.

'I thought you said you didn't own a gun, Mr Wheeler,' Captain Mahoney reminded him.

'I used to have a .38 revolver,' Rod stammered, after a pause. 'Frankly, I'd forgotten all about it. Joan kept it after we separated. She claimed she was afraid to be alone.'

'There's no gun here,' Captain Mahoney stated, after checking each drawer in turn. 'But we'll do a more thorough search after you leave.'

'Where are we going?' Sam asked.

'You'll come home with us,' Bonnie told him, looking to Rod for confirmation, receiving only a blank stare in reply. 'Why don't you throw a few things into a suitcase. We can come back later in the week for the rest.'

48

'What if we don't want to go with you?' Lauren asked, panic evident in her voice.

'You can go with your father or I can take you to Juvenile Hall,' Captain Mahoney intervened. 'I think you might prefer going with your father.'

Bonnie nodded gratefully. Surely the fact that he was encouraging Sam and Lauren to go home with them meant that he didn't seriously consider either one of them a suspect.

Sam and Lauren took several seconds to consider their options, then turned and walked silently from the room, Bonnie and Rod following numbly after them.

Sam's bedroom was immediately across the hall from his mother's, his bed unmade, the top of his dresser covered with books and paper and what looked like hundreds of loose pennies. There was a poster of Guns 'n' Roses' star Axl Rose in his underwear beside a picture of a topless Cindy Crawford. An acoustic guitar, its surface scratched, one string broken, lay on the brown carpet beside a discarded flannel shirt, an open pack of Camel cigarettes protruding from its pocket. A rectangular glass tank sat on the sill beneath the bedroom window. A large snake lay stretched out inside it.

'My God,' Bonnie whispered. 'What on earth is that?'

'That's L'il Abner,' Sam answered proudly, his face noticeably animated for the first time since he'd come home. 'He's only eighteen months old, but he's already over four feet long. Boa constrictors can grow to nine, maybe even twelve feet. Longer in the wild.'

Captain Mahoney walked past Bonnie to the tank. 'He's a beauty,' he said. 'What do you feed him?'

'Live rats,' Sam answered.

Bonnie grabbed her stomach, fought down the urge to throw up. Surely they weren't really standing in the room of a young boy who had just learned that his mother had been murdered, listening to him talk about feeding live rats to his baby boa constrictor. It couldn't be happening.

'Your mother didn't mind you having such an exotic animal as a pet?' Captain Mahoney asked.

'She just hated it if the rats escaped,' Sam said.

Bonnie looked from her husband to his son, straining to find a resemblance between the two. It was there, but only faintly, in the abstract

49

as opposed to the particular, manifesting itself more in their general posture than their individual features, the way each tilted his head when asked a question, the slight pursing of their lips when they smiled, the way each absently rubbed at the side of his nose when distracted.

Perhaps there'd been a mistake, Bonnie postulated. Perhaps there'd been one of those awful errors at the hospital that you sometimes heard about, and Sam and another baby had been switched at birth, and this wasn't really Rod's son at all. Rod's son was a normal young man with ordinary brown hair and no gold loops sticking through his nostrils, a boy who cried when told of his mother's death, and liked dogs and goldfish.

'I'm ready,' Lauren announced from the doorway, a large tote bag over her shoulder, a small overnight bag in her hand.

'What's going to happen to the house?' Sam asked.

'It's too early to think about that now,' Rod answered.

'I don't want to sell it,' Lauren told him.

'It's too early to think about that now,' Rod repeated.

'How am I going to get to school?' Again, panic filled Lauren's eyes.

'We won't worry about school for a few days,' Bonnie told her.

'I'll drive you when we get Mom's car,' Sam answered, turning to Captain Mahoney. 'When can I get my Mom's car?'

If Captain Mahoney was surprised by the question, he didn't let on. 'We can probably have it back to you within the week.'

Detective Kritzic entered the room carrying a small file folder that she promptly opened for the captain's perusal. Randall Mahoney took several moments to scan the contents, glancing over at Bonnie and Rod periodically. 'Why don't we go into the hall,' he suggested casually when he was through reading. Too casually, Bonnie thought, following the officers out of the bedroom.

'Did you find something?' Rod asked.

'You didn't tell me that your wife's insurance policy carried a double indemnity clause,' Captain Mahoney stated.

'Double indemnity?' Bonnie repeated, twisting the words around her tongue, not comfortable with the sound.

'In the event of either accident or murder, the death benefits double,' Captain Mahoney explained. 'That would make your ex-wife's death worth half a million dollars.'

'So it would,' Rod said evenly.

'Are there any other policies I should be aware of, Mr Wheeler?' the police captain asked.

'I have life insurance policies on my entire family,' Rod told him.

'Including your current wife and children?' Captain Mahoney pulled his notepad from his rear pocket.

Bonnie's back stiffened at the word 'current', as if her position was merely transitional and might shift at any moment.

'Everyone,' Rod answered.

'Double indemnity?' asked Randall Mahoney.

Rod nodded. 'I believe so.'

Sam appeared in the hallway, his guitar slung over one shoulder, the large snake wrapped across his neck and arms like a fur stole, its forked tongue flicking menacingly into the air. 'I'll need some help with the tank,' he said.

Chapter Seven

Bonnie stood by the side of her bed and stared at the phone for several long seconds before lifting the receiver, then hesitated again before pressing in the appropriate numbers. 'Please be there,' she whispered. 'It's after midnight. I'm so tired. Where have you been all night?'

The phone was on its sixth ring when it was finally picked up. 'Yes?' the woman's voice said clearly. Not 'hello', but 'yes'. Almost as if she'd been expecting Bonnie to call.

'Adeline . . .' Bonnie began.

'Bonnie, is that you?'

Bonnie felt a wave of panic, surprised the woman had identified her so quickly, understanding it was too late to turn back now. 'I need to speak to my father.'

'Is something wrong?'

'I just need to speak to my father.'

'I'm afraid he can't come to the phone right now. His stomach has been acting up. Do you want to tell me what this is about?'

'Actually, it's really Nick I need to talk to. Is he there?'

There was silence.

'Adeline, is my brother there? Tell me.'

'He's not here.'

Bonnie took a deep breath. 'You know I wouldn't be calling if this weren't very important.'

'I assumed as much, since this is the first time we've heard from you in over three years.'

Bonnie closed her eyes. She was too tired to go into all this now. 'Look, I just need to get a hold of Nick.'

'All I can do is give him the message you called,' Adeline said.

Bonnie pictured the woman on the other end of the phone. She was little, barely five feet tall, with soft blue eyes, short gray hair, and a will of iron. At almost seventy years old, she was still a formidable force, even over the phone. Bonnie was no match for her, never had been, she conceded, smiling sadly at Rod as he walked into the room, watching him unbutton his shirt. 'Fine. Just tell my father I called,' Bonnie said. 'Tell him it's extremely important that I speak to Nick as soon as possible.'

'I'll give him your message.'

'Thank you,' Bonnie said, although the woman had already hung up. 'Tell me this is all a bad dream,' she instructed her husband, as he came forward to wrap her in his arms.

'This is all a bad dream,' he said, obligingly, kissing her forehead, taking the phone from her hand and returning it to its carriage.

'The kids settled?'

'More or less.' He kissed the side of her cheek.

'I'll go say goodnight to them.'

'I think I'd leave them be,' Rod advised gently, his voice wrapping around her ankles like an anchor, securing her in place.

'I just want them to know that I'm here for them.'

'They know,' he told her. 'And they'll come around. Just give them a little time, a little space.'

She nodded, hoping he was right.

'Let's get to bed.'

'My father might be calling . . .'

'I didn't say we had to go to sleep.' Rod's lips moved provocatively to hers.

'You want to make love now?' Bonnie asked, her voice incredulous. She'd just spent possibly the worst day of her life. She'd discovered the murdered body of her husband's ex-wife, been dragged down to the police station for questioning, inherited two hostile stepchildren, not to mention a four-foot baby boa constrictor. She'd been beaten up and beaten down. From her stepdaughter to her stepmother. She was confused and angry and exhausted. And her husband was . . . what? Her husband was amorous. 'Careful of my lip,' she cautioned as he kissed her again, this time more forcefully, his hands moving across the front of her dress. Well, why not? she thought, responding to his caresses, despite her fatigue. Did she have any better ideas?

'Mommy!' Amanda's voice scraped against the air, like a pebble on the pavement, bouncing unsteadily toward its target. 'Mommy!'

Bonnie slowly extricated herself from her husband's embrace. 'I guess it's just too much excitement for one night.'

'Mommy!'

'Coming, sweetheart.' Bonnie hurtled down the hall, passing both the guest room that Lauren was now occupying and the small study in which Sam and his snake were ensconced. 'What's the matter, baby?' she asked, stepping inside Amanda's bedroom.

Amanda sat in the middle of her small four-poster bed, surrounded by a veritable zoo of stuffed animals: a giant pink panda bear; a small white kitten; a medium-sized brown dog; two miniature black and white teddy bears, and Kermit the frog. The large stuffed kangaroo she'd fallen in love with at Toys 'R' Us stood on the floor at the foot of her bed, its arms outstretched, as if warding off evil spirits.

'I can't sleep,' Amanda said.

'I know. It's hard.' Bonnie approached the bed, watching Amanda's round little face grow increasingly visible through the darkness, as if she were being lit from within. And perhaps she was, Bonnie thought, marvelling that she could have played a part in creating anything so beautiful, so absolutely perfect. Amanda Lindsay Wheeler, she repeated to herself, all blond curls and puffy chipmunk cheeks, huge navy-blue eyes and tiny turned-up nose. *Sugar and spice and everything nice. That's what little girls are made of.* Bonnie brought her hand to her lip, felt it sting.

And then they grow up, she thought.

Soon the chipmunk cheeks would thin out and become more sculpted; the eyes would grow less curious, more fearful; the lips would narrow from smile to pout. Already the toddler's skin had been shed to make room for the little girl. Already, the sleeping adolescent loomed, threatening to burst prematurely out of its cocoon.

'Do you think Lauren's pretty?' Amanda asked suddenly, catching Bonnie off guard.

'Yes, I do,' Bonnie answered. 'Do you?'

Amanda nodded vigorously. 'Is she going to be my big sister now?'

'Would you like that?'

Again, Amanda nodded, throwing up her arms for emphasis.

'Get some sleep now, sweet thing.' She kissed her on the forehead, tucked her back under the covers, walked to the door.

'I love you,' Amanda called after her.

'I love you too, angel.'

'I love you more.'

Bonnie stopped, smiled at what was becoming a nightly ritual. 'You couldn't possibly love me more.'

'Okay,' Amanda giggled. 'We love each other exactly the same.'

'Okay,' Bonnie agreed, walking to the door. 'We love each other exactly the same.'

'Except I love you more.'

Bonnie threw her daughter another kiss from the doorway, watching as Amanda reached up to pluck it from the air and glue it to her cheek. Then she stepped back into the hall.

The light was still on in the den, beckoning to her from under the closed door. Bonnie hesitated, then knocked gently, gingerly pushing open the door when Sam failed to answer.

Sam lay spread across the sofa, which doubled as a pull-out bed, wearing only his baggy brown pants, a lit cigarette dangling from his lips, ashes dropping onto his bare chest. He jumped up when he saw her, and the ashes spilled onto the taupe carpeting.

'I know I'm not supposed to smoke in the house,' he said quickly, looking around for a place to extinguish his cigarette, finally butting it out between his fingers.

Bonnie looked helplessly around the small den, once intended as her sanctuary, a room to which she could retreat to mark essays and exams, to prepare her lessons, to read, to relax. Now, clothes hung over the top of the large-screen TV, a guitar stood propped against one soft green wall, grey ashes mingled with the yellow and green flowers of the sofa-bed, and a large glass tank had all but overtaken the top of her stately oak desk, pushing the framed photograph of Amanda unceremoniously off to the side and relegating her computer to the floor. She froze. 'Where's the snake?' she asked, her brain suddenly registering that the tank was empty.

Sam raised one long skinny arm and pointed toward the window. 'Right there – on the windowsill. He thinks he's a cat.'

Reluctantly, Bonnie's eyes veered toward the window at the far end of the room. The mint-green curtains were partially open to reveal the coiled body of the snake behind them.

'Would you mind keeping him in the tank when we're home?' Bonnie asked, her voice small, fighting the almost overpowering urge to run screaming down the hall.

'Sure thing,' Sam said, though he didn't move.

Bonnie stood in the doorway. 'Are you all right?' she asked. 'Is there anything you'd like to talk about?'

'Like what?' the boy asked.

Bonnie didn't know what to say – How about the weather? Or the Boston Red Sox? How about the fact that your mother was murdered this morning? – so she said nothing. She waited, trying to penetrate the boy's opaque features, finding it ironic that boys so often resembled their mothers, while girls tended to look more like their dads. At least such was the case with Sam and Lauren. And such had been the case with her and Nick. 'Goodnight, Sam,' she said finally, wondering if her brother would call. 'See you in the morning.'

Bonnie stepped out of the room, closing the door behind her just as the door to the guest room opened and Lauren appeared. Instinctively, Bonnie took a small step back.

'I'm just going to the bathroom.' Lauren motioned toward the small room at the end of the hall.

'There are fresh towels and a new bar of soap,' Bonnie said as Lauren brushed past her. 'If you need anything else . . .'

Lauren entered the bathroom and closed the door behind her.

' . . . just call,' Bonnie said. 'Give her time and space,' she reminded herself, returning to her bedroom, seeing Rod already under the covers. 'I'll just be a minute,' she said, pulling her dress over her head, dropping it to the floor, sliding out of her underwear and into bed beside her husband, looking forward to the luxury of his arms. Maybe he was right. He'd always known exactly how and where to touch her. She snuggled in against him, felt the steady rise and fall of his bare chest.

He was asleep, she realized with a smile, running her hand along his warm skin, delicately kissing his slightly parted lips. He looks like a little boy, she thought, the troubled lines around his eyes and mouth now smooth with sleep.

She'd never sleep, she realized in that same moment, getting up and going to the bathroom, brushing her teeth and splashing some soap and water on her face, careful not to rub too hard around her swollen lip. Her mind was too full of disturbing sounds and images: Joan's voice on the phone that morning; Joan's body at the kitchen table in the house on Lombard Street; the gaping hole in the middle of her chest; Joan's bedroom; Joan's scrapbook; her brother's name in Joan's address book;

57

the insurance policy with its damned double indemnity clause; a life brutally extinguished; two motherless children. Why? What did any of it mean?

'I'll be awake all night,' Bonnie moaned, crawling back into bed and closing her eyes. In the next instant, she was asleep.

In Bonnie's dream, she was standing in front of her high school class, about to hand out their final exams. 'This is a difficult test,' she was telling her students, peering across their bewildered faces, 'so I hope you're prepared.'

She moved quickly among the rows of desks, dropping an exam paper in front of each student, hearing assorted groans and giggles. Looking up, she realized that someone had decorated the room for Halloween, as one would a kindergarten class: large cut-outs of witches balancing on broomsticks; silhouettes of black cats with their backs arched; orange pumpkins with horrific faces, their eyes large, empty black holes. 'You can start as soon as I finish handing these out,' she told her students, concentrating on the task at hand. There was loud laughter. 'Would somebody mind telling me what's so funny?' she asked.

Haze pushed himself away from his desk, and sauntered toward her. 'I have a message for you from your father,' he said, a hand-rolled cigarette falling from his shirt pocket to the floor.

'No smoking in this room,' Bonnie reminded him.

'He says you've been a bad girl,' Haze told her, looking toward the window, Bonnie's eyes following his gaze, seeing a large cut-out of a boa constrictor woven through the old-style, thick Venetian blinds.

'No,' Bonnie protested. 'I'm a good girl.'

The fire alarm suddenly sounded, students bolting for the door, knocking Bonnie down in their rush to escape, trampling her under their heavy boots. 'Somebody help me,' Bonnie called after them, torn and bloody, as the cut-out of the snake dropped to the floor and bounced to life, slithering toward her, its mouth opening in a chilling hundred-and-eighty-degree angle, as the fire alarm continued its shrill cry.

Bonnie bolted up in bed, arms stretched out protectively, the alarm still ringing in her ears.

It was the phone.

'Jesus,' she said, trying to calm the rapid beating of her heart with a series of deep breaths. She reached across her sleeping husband and

58

grabbed for the phone, noting the time on the clock radio. Almost two a.m. 'Hello?' Her voice was husky, hovering between panic and indignation.

'I understand you were asking about me?'

'Nick?' Bonnie leaned back against the headboard, feeling vaguely sick to her stomach, inadvertently dragging the phone wire across her husband's face. Rod stirred, and opened his eyes.

'What can I do for you, Bonnie?'

He either didn't know, or didn't care, that it was the middle of the night, Bonnie thought, picturing her younger brother as he spoke, his dirty blond hair falling across his close-set green eyes and small delicate nose, a nose that seemed altogether wrong for the rest of his tough-guy face. His voice was the same as always – a mixture of charm and impudence. She remembered how he used to make her laugh, wondered at what precise moment the laughter had ceased.

'I didn't know if you were out of jail.'

'You should call more often.'

'You're living with Dad?'

'Condition of my parole. Is there a point to this conversation?'

'Joan Wheeler was murdered today,' Bonnie said and waited for his response.

'Is that supposed to mean something to me?' her brother asked after a lengthy pause.

'You tell me, Nick. The police found your name in Joan's address book.'

The phone went dead in her hands.

'Nick? Nick?' She shook her head, handing the phone over to Rod. 'He hung up.'

Rod sat up, running a tired hand through his tousled hair, and dropped the phone back into its carriage. 'You think he could have had something to do with Joan's death?'

'Joan calls first thing in the morning to warn me that Amanda and I are in some kind of danger,' Bonnie said, thinking out loud. 'A few hours later, she turns up dead, and my brother's name turns up in her address book. I don't know what to think.'

'I think we should let the police handle it.'

'The police think *I* did it,' she reminded him.

Rod put his arm around his wife, hugged her close to his side. 'No, they don't. They think *I* did it. I'm the guy with the life insurance policies on all of you. Double indemnity, remember?'

'Thanks.'

'Any time.' They settled in against the pillows, Bonnie's backside pressed into her husband's stomach, Rod draped, spoon-like, around her.

'Of course, there's also Josh Freeman,' she said several seconds later.

'Who?'

'Josh Freeman, Sam's art teacher. He's also in Joan's address book, and he's another link between us.'

'Get some sleep, Nancy Drew.'

'I love you,' Bonnie whispered.

'I love you too.'

'I love you more,' Bonnie said, and waited. But Rod merely squeezed her arm and said nothing.

Chapter Eight

Joan's funeral took place the following week.

Bonnie sat in her front-row seat in the small chapel beside Rod and his children, amazed by the large number of mourners, trying to figure out who each one was, to determine what, if any, relationship each had with the deceased.

Rod had said Joan had no friends, only 'drinking buddies'. And yet the room was literally filled to the rafters, well over a hundred people crowded into the narrow benches and pressed against the walls, and they couldn't all be casual acquaintances with whom Joan had merely shared a few glasses of wine. Nor could they all be business associates, although the back row's coterie of immaculately dressed women whose hair never moved were unmistakably Joan's cohorts from Ellen Marx Realty. True there were probably a number of people present who hadn't known Joan at all, who were there out of morbid curiosity, intrigued by the newspaper and television coverage, aroused by the specter of sudden, violent death in the midst of their normally peaceful community.

Bonnie's gaze stretched across the room, like an elastic band, gathering all those present into her line of vision, and then slowly popping them out, one at a time. Captain Mahoney and Detective Kritzic stood near the rear door, the captain in dark blue, the detective in light gray, their eyes alert for any movement that might seem even slightly out of place. And there were undoubtedly several undercover officers, although, like the agents from Ellen Marx Realty, they seemed fairly easy to spot: the young man with the brownish-blond hair and blue-striped tie who sat near the back of the room and trailed after everyone with his watery brown eyes; the two balding men in casual dress, standing near the rear door, whispering to one another through loosely spread fingers. Who were these people, if not the police?

But what of all these others, these men and women with tears in their eyes and noticeable catches in their throats? Who were the middle-aged couple consoling one another in the third row on the other side of the center aisle? Who were these people immediately behind her, sharing hushed memories of the dear friend they had lost? Could they really be talking about Joan? Bonnie pushed back in her seat, straining to catch part of their conversation, but their voices suddenly stilled, as if aware of her interest.

Joan had no living relatives outside of her children, no sisters or brothers to mourn her. An only child. Lucky her, Bonnie thought, warily glancing over her shoulder, half prepared to see her brother waltz through the door, something he would do if only for the perverse pleasure of seeing the shock on her face. She wondered absently whether the police had contacted him, then pushed him rudely from her mind, concentrating on those present. She smiled at her friend, Diana, there to lend moral support, nodded at Marla Brenzelle, sitting in the row behind Diana, dressed in a hot pink number that made her look more like a mother of the bride than a mourner at a funeral. But Marla was staring just past her, looking dramatically solemn for the several photographers who hovered nearby. Was everything a photo opportunity to this woman? Bonnie wondered, catching her breath as Josh Freeman entered her line of vision. Why hadn't she noticed him before?

He looked exactly the way he did at school, she thought, handsome in a careless sort of way, as if his good looks were something of an inconvenience, a fact of life he'd learned to accept but never really felt comfortable with. His first appearance in the staff room at Weston Secondary had created an immediate buzz among the female staff, everyone wanting to know more about the soft-spoken widower from New York. But Josh Freeman had proved as inaccessible as he was attractive, sticking mostly to himself and rarely socializing with the other teachers, although he was unfailingly pleasant and polite whenever Bonnie had approached him. What was he doing here? she wondered now. How well had he known Joan?

'Mr Freeman's here,' she whispered across Rod to Sam, who glanced back at his art teacher and waved, as casually as if he'd just spotted a friend at a baseball game.

A woman gingerly approached, her steps halting, her eyes swollen with tears. 'Lauren,' she began, taking the girl's hands inside her own. It was hard to determine who was trembling more. 'Sam,' she acknowledged, trying to smile, but her lips began quivering uncontrollably, and she had to clamp the palm of her hand over them to still them. 'Lyle and I are so sorry about your mother,' she managed to whisper. 'We just can't believe this has happened.'

Bonnie became aware of a short, heavy-set man standing behind the tall, blond woman, a protective hand on her shoulder. 'She was such a wonderful person,' the woman continued. 'I know I wouldn't be here today if it weren't for your mother, and everything she did for me. I just can't believe she's gone. I can't believe anyone could have hurt her. She was a great lady. She really was.' A loud sob escaped the woman's lips. Her husband's grip tightened on her shoulder, creasing the delicate silk of her navy dress.

A great lady? A wonderful person? Who on earth was this woman talking about? Bonnie looked toward Rod, who was staring at the woman with bemused detachment.

Lauren stood up, drew the woman into a close embrace.

'I'm the one who should be comforting you,' the woman told her, pulling back, wiping stubborn tears from her eyes.

'I'll be all right,' Lauren assured her.

The woman's hand reached out and gently caressed Lauren's cheek. 'I know you will.' Again she tried to smile, this time with marginally more success. 'Your mother loved you so much, you know. She talked about you all the time. Lauren this and Lauren that. My Lauren, she would say, my beautiful Lauren. She was so proud of you . . . of both of you,' the woman added in Sam's direction, belatedly seeking to include him.

Sam nodded, quickly looked away.

'Anyway, if there's anything we can do . . .' The woman broke off as Lauren lowered herself back into her seat. ' . . . you know where to reach us.' The woman's eyes scanned across Bonnie, stopping at Rod.

Rod rose quickly to his feet. 'Caroline,' he said, extending his hand. 'I'm sorry we had to see each other again in such sad circumstances. Hello, Lyle.'

'Hello, Rod,' the man said, coolly.

'Rod,' the woman acknowledged without taking his hand. 'You look well.'

'You sound disappointed.'

'I guess I keep expecting justice.'

Bonnie found herself holding her breath, her eyes moving warily between the two obvious adversaries. Who were these people? Why the hostility toward her husband?

'Thank you for coming today,' Rod said, his voice very low, almost inaudible.

The woman turned her attention to Bonnie. 'You must be Bonnie. Joan spoke very highly of you.'

'She did?'

'Take care of her children,' the woman urged, before turning on her navy patent heels, and marching back up the aisle, her husband trailing after her.

Bonnie turned immediately to her husband. 'What was that all about? Who are those people?'

'The Gossetts,' Rod explained, sitting back down, folding his hands across his chest.

Bonnie quickly recalled their names from Joan's address book. Lyle and Caroline Gossett. They lived across the street from Joan. 'Former friends' was how Rod had described them. 'I take it you weren't on the best of terms.'

'Can't please everyone,' Rod said easily.

What happened? Bonnie was about to ask, but thought better of it. Now was hardly the time or place to expose and explore old wounds, she thought, deciding to ask Rod about it later.

Bonnie heard sniffling, looked past Sam to his sister, who seemed lost inside a loose-fitting long blue dress. 'Are you all right?' she asked, but Lauren said nothing, her hands twisting in her lap. 'Do you want a tissue?' Bonnie extended one to Lauren, who refused to acknowledge its presence.

Bonnie slipped her hand into Rod's. Help me, she pleaded silently. Help me to get to know your children. Tell me how to reach them.

How could he? she wondered, when he barely knew them himself.

They had refused to set foot in their father's new house, to become part of his new life. Over the years, conflicting timetables and increasingly divided loyalties had reduced Rod's once-weekly visits to his children to hit-or-miss affairs. It wasn't his fault. It wasn't their fault. It wasn't anybody's fault. It was just, sadly, the way things were.

The week had been a difficult one. Bonnie was obviously still a suspect. The police had been back several times to question her further, and to talk to Sam and Lauren. Bonnie wasn't privy to those conversations, and neither Sam nor Lauren had shown any interest in sharing the contents of these discussions with either her or their father. In fact, they said little about anything, volunteered nothing, withdrew every time Bonnie approached. They left their rooms only to eat, and then only reluctantly. After several days of this, Rod had returned to work. Bonnie had been tempted to do the same, especially since her presence at home was less than appreciated. But she felt she couldn't leave Sam and Lauren alone in a strange house. Not yet. She had to be there in case they needed her. At least until after the funeral.

'You're a good girl,' she heard her mother say, and Bonnie's eyes welled up with tears at the memory of another woman who had died much too soon. How ironic, she thought, that she was missing a week of school after all, although this wasn't exactly the romantic holiday she'd been imagining. 'You're my good one,' her mother's memory repeated, as Bonnie swivelled around in her seat, wondering if her brother might be among the mourners.

'What's up?' Rod asked, his arm encircling her shoulder, pulling her toward him.

Bonnie shook her head, her eyes returning to the flower-laden casket at the front of the room. She adjusted the collar of her gray silk blouse and smoothed out the pleats of her black skirt, though there was nothing wrong with either of them. She heard a shuffling in the aisle, looked up to see Sam's friend, Haze, pushing his way in amongst a group of women on the other side of the aisle.

'Hey there, Mrs Wheeler,' he said. 'How's it goin'?'

A tall, gray-haired man assumed the podium at the front of the chapel. 'It is with deep sadness and regret,' he began, his voice low, 'that we gather here today to mourn Joan Wheeler. And it says something of the high regard in which Joan was held that there are so many of you here today. Her kindness, her spirit, her dedication, her sense of humor,' he continued, and Bonnie wondered again exactly whom he was eulogizing, 'are qualities she never lost, despite other tragic losses.'

The man continued, proudly listing Joan's accomplishments, rhapsodizing on the love she had for her children, alluding only obliquely to the circumstances of her youngest child's death, providing suitable euphemisms for Joan's subsequent descent into alcoholism, mentioning that in the days immediately preceding her death, Joan had been filled with fresh resolve, had told him that she was determined to pull herself together, to put her house in order.

Not an easy task, Bonnie thought, remembering the state of Joan's bedroom. She found herself drifting in and out of the rest of the eulogy, unable to relate the things Rod had told her about Joan to what she was now hearing. She listened as quiet sobs filled the crowded room. Who was this woman so many were crying for? She looked over at Sam. And why were her son's eyes so dry?

And then the service was over and the pallbearers approached the casket, hoisting it onto their shoulders. Rod and his children followed after it, Bonnie hanging slightly back, keeping her eyes resolutely straight ahead, refusing to establish eye contact with anyone, almost afraid of what she might see. The doors at the rear of the small chapel opened to reveal a blindingly bright afternoon sun, although the air was cold. I should have worn a jacket, Bonnie thought, shivering as she watched the casket being loaded into the hearse.

She was suddenly aware of noise, of cars going by on busy Commonwealth Avenue, of people crowding around her. She wondered absently how many of them would be driving to the cemetery. None, she would have guessed before the service. Almost all, she would probably say now.

She spotted Josh Freeman out of the corner of her eye.

'Mr Freeman,' Bonnie called after him, wending her way through the mourners, wondering fleetingly why she was addressing her colleague by his proper name. 'Excuse me, Mr Freeman. Josh . . .'

He stopped, turned around. 'Mrs Wheeler,' he acknowledged, a slightly puzzled look settling across his face. Was he surprised to see her here? Hadn't he known that she was Sam's stepmother?

'I hadn't realized you knew Joan,' Bonnie began, not sure where, in fact, she was heading with this.

'Sam is in one of my classes.'

'Yes, I know.' Bonnie waited for him to say more, but he didn't. She felt a hand on her elbow, turned, saw Diana.

'I'll call you later,' Diana said, kissing her on the cheek, not really stopping as she continued toward the parking lot.

Bonnie returned her attention to Josh Freeman, focusing on his brown eyes, lighter and clearer than Rod's. His hair was wavy and slightly tousled, as if he'd struggled with it and lost, but it suited the sly curve of his lips and the slightly crooked line of his nose. 'Were you and Joan friends?' she asked, trying not to stare.

'Yes,' he said. Then again, nothing further.

'Do you think we could talk about her some time?' Why had she asked that? What did she want to talk about?

'I'm not sure what there is to say,' he said, his words echoing her thoughts.

'Please.'

He nodded. 'You'll be back in school soon?'

'Monday.'

'I'll see you then.'

'Wasn't that a wonderful eulogy?' Marla Brenzelle was asking loudly. Bonnie turned toward the voice as Marla, looking like a giant cone of pink candy floss, extended her arms toward Rod's children. 'You must be Lorne and Samantha.'

'Sam and Lauren,' Bonnie corrected, turning back to Josh Freeman. But he was already gone.

'I'm so sorry about your loss,' Marla continued, undaunted.

'Thank you,' Lauren said.

'I finally got a chance to meet your brother a few weeks ago,' Marla said.

It took Bonnie a moment to realize that Marla wasn't talking to Lauren, but to her. 'I'm sorry. What did you say?'

'Can my friend have your autograph?' Sam asked suddenly.

Marla's face lit up, as if someone had just shone a spotlight on her. 'Of course.'

Bonnie looked over at Haze, who stood there grinning, magic marker in hand.

'You could just sign here,' he said, handing Marla the marker and holding up one tattooed arm. MUFF, the tattoo proclaimed above a picture of a beaver. DIVER, it said below.

'Haze,' Marla repeated, after asking his name and how to spell it. 'That's an interesting name.'

What's going on here? Bonnie wondered, waiting impatiently while Marla added the *le* that transformed Brenzel to Brenzelle, with an exaggerated flourish. 'What do you mean, you met my brother?'

Marla flashed her a perfectly capped smile. 'Well, I never did get to meet him in high school. I'd already graduated by the time he got there.

But I remember hearing stories about how wild he was, how *hot*, as the kids would say today. So I've always been curious about him, especially since you've always been such a goody two-shoes.'

Bonnie ignored the slight, intended or otherwise. 'How did you meet my brother?'

'He came by the studio to talk to Rod. Didn't Rod tell you?'

Bonnie spun around, looking for her husband, but he was speaking to one of the undertakers beside the chapel door. Rod had met with her brother without telling her? Why?

'Apparently he had some crazy idea for a series,' Marla said, answering Bonnie's silent question. 'Rod told him it would never fly, but I think I may have talked him into appearing on one of our shows. I think he'd make a great guest, don't you? He's very good-looking, and so charming.'

'My brother is a crook and a con artist,' Bonnie said flatly, wanting only to get away from this woman as fast as she could.

'Exactly my point.'

'I really have to get going,' Bonnie told her, moving briskly from her side. 'Thanks for coming,' she added, tossing the words over her shoulder like a crumpled piece of paper.

'Hopefully, the next time we see each other will be under pleasanter circumstances,' Marla called after her.

Don't count on it, Bonnie thought.

'Why didn't you tell me you'd seen Nick?' Bonnie asked, watching as her husband spread numerous cartons of Chinese food across the round white kitchen table. The room was longer than it was wide, and opened into an eating area at the front of the house, overlooking the street. The cabinets were bleached oak, the tile floor and appliances almond, the walls white. A Chagall lithograph of a cow suspended upside down over a rooftop hung on one wall; Amanda's painting of a group of people with square heads hung on another.

'You talked to Marla,' Rod stated, his voice calm, his manner unruffled.

'I don't understand, Rod.'

He placed the last carton on the table, absently licked his fingers. 'It's simple, sweetheart. Your brother dropped into the studio a few weeks back, without an appointment, of course. He had some crazy idea for a series. I had to tell him it wouldn't work.'

'Fly,' Bonnie corrected.

'What?'

'Marla said you told him it wouldn't fly,' she said testily, tears of anger springing to her eyes. How could he not have told her?

Rod crossed to where Bonnie stood leaning against the warm oven door. 'Ah, come on, honey. It was no big deal. I didn't tell you because I knew how much it would upset you.'

'As opposed to the way I'm feeling now?'

He lowered his head. 'It was stupid not to tell you. I'm sorry.'

'So, you'd already seen him when the police found his name in Joan's address book,' she stated more than asked, trying to get the facts straight in her mind. 'Why didn't you say something then?'

'What was I supposed to say? "Oh, by the way, your brother came to see me last week"? It didn't seem relevant.'

'What about later, when I was trying to reach him?'

'I thought about telling you.'

'But you didn't. Not even after I spoke to him.'

'I didn't see what good it would do. The whole thing was starting to feel very complicated. I still say if he's involved in any way in Joan's death, we should let the police handle it.'

'That's not the point,' Bonnie cried.

'What is the point?' Rod asked, his eyes moving into the hall, obviously concerned that his children might overhear them.

Bonnie instantly lowered her voice. 'The point is you should have told me.'

'Agreed,' he said. 'But I didn't. I don't know why. Probably I was trying to avoid exactly the kind of scene we're having now.'

There was silence.

'The food's getting cold,' Rod ventured.

'Did you know he was staying at my father's?' Bonnie asked, as if he hadn't spoken.

'No. I didn't ask and he didn't say.'

'Did you talk about Joan?'

'Why in God's name would we talk about Joan?'

'Why would his name be in her address book?'

'I repeat,' Rod said, his square jaw clenched tight, clipping the ends off his words, like garden shears, 'let's let the police deal with this.'

'Did you know that stupid woman has asked him to be a guest on your show?' Bonnie asked, switching gears.

'Marla?' Rod laughed.

'You think it's funny?'

'He won't do it.'

'Of course he'll do it. If only to aggravate me.'

'Then don't let it.' Rod kissed the tip of her nose. 'Come on, honey. Don't let them get to you. I'm sorry I didn't tell you. Really, I am.'

Sam casually sauntered into the room, his sister trailing after him. 'You think Marla Brenzelle is stupid?' he asked, the laces of his sneakers dragging across the ceramic tiles of the floor.

Bonnie wondered how much of the conversation they had overheard. 'Let's just say the woman has a poorly defined sense of irony.'

'What's that?' Sam folded his long body inside one of the tall wicker chairs.

'Irony?'

'That.' Sam pointed toward one of the plastic containers.

'Lemon chicken,' Rod told him. 'Help yourself.'

'I think she's cool,' Lauren said, sitting down and spooning a large helping of fried rice onto her plate.

'You do?' Bonnie made no effort to contain her surprise. 'What about her do you find "cool"?'

Lauren shrugged. 'I think she helps people.'

'Helps them? How – by exploiting them in front of millions of people?'

'How is she exploiting them?' Lauren asked.

'Can you pass me the chow mein?' Sam said.

'She exploits them because she misleads them into thinking that by confessing their problems in front of millions of people, they can solve them. She offers thirty-second sound bites as solutions. And she provides a forum for every kook and exhibitionist in the country. She legitimizes their highly questionable behavior by making it sound like the norm, which it definitely is not.' Bonnie paused, her mind still reeling from her earlier confrontation with Rod, anger fueling her words. 'How many twin lesbians are out there who have seduced their mother's boyfriends, for God's sake? Or Peeping Toms who married their first cousins after spying them making love to their fathers? Do you think that's normal? Do you think that by having these people on her show Marla Brenzelle, whom I used to know as Marlene Brenzel, by the way, is interested in helping anyone other than herself and her precious ratings? I mean, whatever happened to discretion? Whatever happened to common sense?'

Her unexpected outburst brought silence to the room.

'That was some speech,' Rod said quietly.

'I'm sorry,' Bonnie quickly apologized. 'I'm not sure where that came from. I didn't mean to sound so . . .'

'Disdainful?' Rod asked, pointedly.

'I'm sorry. I really didn't mean . . .'

'I hadn't realized you had such strong feelings about what I do every day,' Rod said.

'When did you know Marla Brenzelle?' Sam asked.

'We went to school together,' Bonnie told him, eyes on Rod.

'Cool,' Sam said.

'Look,' Bonnie said to her husband. 'I wasn't trying to denigrate what you do . . .'

'Good thing you weren't trying,' he said.

'She asked me if I'd like to come on the show some day,' Lauren said, dragging a forkful of long yellow noodles into her mouth. 'She said it might help me to come to terms with what's happened if I were to talk about it.'

'It would certainly help you to talk to someone, yes,' Bonnie quickly agreed. 'But talk to your father. Talk to a therapist. Talk to me,' she offered.

'Why would I want to talk to you?' Lauren asked.

'Lauren,' Rod cautioned. 'Take it easy.'

'Well,' Bonnie began, the words emerging painfully, scratching against the sides of her throat, 'I know what it's like to lose a mother you love.'

'I didn't *lose* my mother. She was murdered. Was yours?' Lauren asked provocatively.

'No,' Bonnie said. Not exactly, she thought.

'Then you don't know anything.' Lauren pushed her chair away from the table. 'I'm not very hungry. Can I be excused?' In the next instant, she was gone.

Rod reached across the table to pat Bonnie's hand. 'Sorry, honey. You didn't deserve that.' He laid down his fork, stared out the front window at the quiet suburban street. 'It's been a horrible day for everyone.' He ran his hand through his hair, pushed his plate away. 'I'm not that hungry either.' He stood up, stretched. 'Actually, I'm kind of restless. Would you mind if I went out for a bit?'

'Now? It's after nine o'clock.'

'Just for a short drive. I won't be long.' He was already on his way out of the kitchen. Bonnie quickly followed him into the hall. 'I just need some time to clear my head,' he said at the front door.

'Rod, I'm sorry,' Bonnie began. 'You know I didn't mean to criticize you.'

'You have nothing to be sorry for.' He kissed her gently on the mouth, one hand reaching behind him to open the door. 'Want to come along?' he offered suddenly.

'How can I leave Amanda?' Bonnie pictured her daughter asleep in her bed.

'Sam and Lauren are here,' Rod reminded her.

Bonnie looked toward the staircase, thought of Sam in the kitchen and Lauren in her room. '*Don't even think of using my kids as baby-sitters. They're not here for your convenience,*' Joan had berated her one memorable evening soon after Amanda's birth.

'I better not,' Bonnie said, thinking of how Joan had done everything in her power to keep Sam and Lauren from knowing their half-sister. How spiteful and mean and cruel she had been. Certainly not the paragon of virtue Bonnie had heard eulogized this afternoon.

'Be back soon,' Rod said, shutting the door after him.

Sam was still sitting at the table, hunched over his food, the light from the overhead fixture picking up the midnight blue of his hair, when Bonnie returned to the kitchen.

'I'm glad that someone has an appetite,' she said.

Sam turned around, orange sauce coating his lips like a heavy lipstick, the same shade his mother used to wear, the same shade she'd been wearing when she died.

Bonnie took an involuntary step back, as if she'd seen a ghost. Sam smiled, something dangling from his right hand, like a pocket watch on a chain, except this wasn't a chain, Bonnie realized, clutching her stomach. It was a tail.

'Oh, God,' she said. 'Tell me that's not what I think it is.'

'It's just a little white rat,' Sam said, laughing. 'I let him nibble on some sweet and sour pork. Kind of a last meal sort of thing before I feed him to L'il Abner.' He stood up, and Bonnie tried not to notice the slight orange halo around the doomed rat's twitching nose and mouth. 'Want to watch?'

'No, thank you,' Bonnie whispered, as Sam left the room. Then she sank down into one of the kitchen chairs, across from Joan's ghost, and waited for Rod to come home.

Chapter Nine

Bonnie pulled her car into the staff parking lot at the front of the Weston Secondary at exactly seven twenty-nine the following Monday morning. 'The clock in my car is digital,' she remembered telling the police not long ago. And then she'd laughed. Not long, not loud. Just long enough to increase their curiosity, just loud enough to arouse their suspicions. They'd been back over the weekend to question her again, covering the same familiar territory, probably hoping she'd contradict herself, say something suitably incriminating, enough to justify Captain Mahoney clamping the pair of handcuffs always dangling from his belt around her wrists, and taking her away. They seemed unconcerned about whatever danger she and her daughter might be in, the danger Joan had warned her against. They probably think I made the whole thing up, Bonnie thought, frustrated by how little the police had revealed about their investigation, other than the coroner's conclusion that Joan had been killed by a bullet from a .38 caliber revolver, quite possibly the one still registered to Rod.

'Yo, Mrs Wheeler,' someone called as Bonnie reached the front door of the one- and-a-half story reddish brick building. 'Let me get that for you.'

Bonnie turned to see Haze running toward her. Well, no, not exactly running, she thought, watching him, mesmerized by the easy insolence of his gait. More like loping. A sleek, muscular white stallion, dressed all in black, and totally tuned to his own body rhythms.

'You look real nice today, Mrs Wheeler,' he said, pulling open the heavy door and standing off to one side so that Bonnie could enter first. 'Nice to see you back,' he said as they stepped into the cafeteria.

Bonnie smiled. 'And what can I do for you, Haze?'

Haze lowered his head, his voice teasingly soft, so that she had to lean forward to hear him. 'You're not still expecting that essay for today, are you?' he asked.

She almost laughed, would have if not for the sudden tension in the boy's face, the noticeable stiffening of his smile.

'I'm afraid I am,' she told him, the noise and smells of the room crowding around her. 'You've had over a month.'

Haze said nothing, a subtle smirk replacing his frozen smile, as he slowly backed into a group of students hovering nearby. Bonnie watched him disappear, the rat being swallowed by the giant snake, she thought, feeling somewhat unsettled by their encounter, although she wasn't sure why. She proceeded out of the cafeteria, nodding at several boys roughhousing in one corner, and walked briskly down the corridor. A long fluorescent light ran down the center of the high ceiling, like a single line on a highway, casting shadows on the yellow brick walls, lending an eerie glow to a large framed photograph of recent graduates, their smiling heads severed and mounted in a series of small neat ovals, hanging outside the door to the staff room. Bonnie pushed open the door, heading straight for the pot of coffee percolating on the side counter, quickly pouring herself a cup.

'Hi, there, everyone,' she said to no one in particular, walking to a chair by the long wall of windows. The view – a small inner courtyard with a single tree – was something less than spectacular.

There were perhaps half a dozen teachers scattered about the predominantly blue and beige room, several grouped in conversation around the water cooler, others seemingly absorbed in the morning paper, all a careful study of casual nonchalance. A smattering of 'hi's' reached her ears. Someone asked how she was; she said okay. 'It's nice to be back,' Bonnie volunteered, noting that Josh Freeman was nowhere around.

'It must have been horrible,' Maureen Templeton, a science teacher with frizzy yellow hair and a pronounced overbite, offered, and everyone nodded, further embellishment not required.

'Yes, it was,' Bonnie agreed.

'Do the police . . . ?'

'Nothing yet,' Bonnie said.

'Rough week?' asked Tom O'Brian, the suitably brooding dramatic arts teacher.

'The pits.'

'Well, anything we can do to help . . .' Maureen Templeton offered, while the rest nodded.

'Thank you.'

'Sam's in my third period class,' Tom O'Brian stated. 'He's a real talent, a natural-born actor. How's he doing?'

'Better than you might expect,' Bonnie answered, still not sure what to make of Sam's behavior. The police had released Joan's car, and Sam had happily volunteered to drive his sister to and from her school in Newton for the balance of the school year. 'Did you know his mother?'

'I met her at parent-teacher interviews back in November. She seemed nice enough.' Tom O'Brian shook his head. 'Awful thing. Hard to believe.'

There didn't seem anything left to say, and the room fell silent. Gradually, everyone returned to whatever each had been doing before Bonnie's entrance. Bonnie reached for a section of the *Boston Globe* that lay on the formica coffee table in front of her chair, flipping through it, relieved her name was no longer front and center on the pages. Other murders, bloodier, more sensational, had rendered her old news: a murder-suicide in Waltham; a drive-by shooting on Newbury Street; a couple stabbed while having dessert at a trendy bistro.

Bonnie quickly traded the first section for the Life section, scanning the recipes for low-fat brownies and high-fiber apple crumble, ignoring an article on sex and the elderly, and focusing on House Calls, an advice column shared by two doctors, general practitioner Dr Rita Wertman, and family therapist Dr Walter Greenspoon.

What had Dr Greenspoon's name been doing in Joan Wheeler's address book?

Dear Dr Greenspoon, the first letter began. *I'm the mother of a hyperactive seven-year-old girl who is driving my husband and me crazy. She refuses to get up in the mornings, screams when I take her to school, and won't eat her supper or go to bed. My husband and I are exhausted, and are constantly at each other's throats. I'm afraid our marriage won't survive this child, and I don't know what to do.*

Dear Frustrated Mom, began Dr Greenspoon's reply. *You and your husband need to learn how to act as a unit . . .*

'Excuse me, Mrs Wheeler,' a voice interrupted.

Bonnie looked up, the paper dropping to her lap. Josh Freeman stood before her, tall and lean, a shy smile on his lips, looking appealingly boyish, although there was something about his posture that warned her not to get too close. 'Mr Freeman,' she acknowledged, awkwardly.

'You said you'd like to talk to me.'

'Yes, if you wouldn't mind.' Bonnie nodded toward the chair beside her. Josh Freeman hesitated, then sat down. 'How are you enjoying Weston Secondary?' Bonnie asked, not sure how to begin, feeling as awkward as if this was their first date. What was she doing? Why had she asked to speak to him? What exactly did she want to speak to him about?

'I like it here very much,' Josh Freeman told her. 'Lots of talented, creative kids. I don't have to do much to motivate them. But I don't think that's what you wanted to talk to me about, is it?'

So, he wasn't one for small talk, Bonnie thought, normally a trait she admired. 'I was surprised to see you at Joan Wheeler's funeral,' she ventured.

Josh Freeman said nothing.

'I hadn't realized you were friends.'

Still nothing.

'You're not saying anything,' Bonnie said, staring at his lips, almost afraid to look into his eyes.

'You haven't asked me anything,' he told her.

She smiled, understanding she would have to be specific if she hoped to learn anything, although exactly what she was trying to learn puzzled her. 'How well did you know Joan?'

'We met in November at parent-teacher night. We talked a number of times after that.'

'She had your home phone number.'

'Yes, she did.'

Bonnie took a deep breath, forced her eyes to his, was momentarily startled by their clarity, by the intensity with which he returned her gaze. 'You're not making this very easy for me.'

'I'm not trying to be difficult,' he said. 'I'm just not sure what you're getting at.'

'Have the police contacted you?'

'I've spoken to the police, yes.'

'May I ask you what you talked about?'

'You may not,' he said evenly.

Bonnie felt her cheeks grow red. 'Did you know about my connection to Joan?' she asked.

'I know that you're married to her ex-husband.'

'Did Joan tell you that, or did the police?'

'Joan told me.'

'What exactly was your relationship with Joan?'

'I'm not sure that's any of your business,' Josh Freeman said, glancing at the large clock on the wall. 'And the bell's about to ring. I should get moving.'

'We have another five minutes.'

'What is it about my relationship with Joan that you want to know?'

'So, there *was* a relationship,' Bonnie stated.

He said nothing.

'Did she ever talk about me?' Bonnie asked. 'Or my daughter? Did she ever tell you she thought we might be in danger?'

A look of concern flickered briefly through Josh Freeman's eyes, then disappeared. 'I'm not sure what you're getting at,' he said, standing up, 'and I find I'm getting very uncomfortable with this conversation. I really should get to my class.'

Bonnie rose immediately to her feet. 'Can we talk after school?'

'I don't think so.'

'Please.'

'We'll see,' he said, clearly torn. Before she could protest further, he was gone.

Bonnie took a deep breath and pushed open the door of her classroom. Immediately, those students who were still grouped in front of the long side window raced for their seats. They were a motley group, all hair and denim and pierced body parts, an approximately equal number of young men and women from relatively affluent homes, determined to look as impoverished as possible, their blank eyes reflecting a collective cynicism beyond their years. Whatever happened to sweet sixteen? Bonnie wondered.

There was some giggling, and many nervous glances, as Bonnie scanned the faces of the twenty-four students in her first period junior year English class. From the back of the room, Haze winked and nodded his head up and down, like a ventriloquist's dummy. Bonnie approached her desk at the front of the class and edged herself into her seat, quickly checking to make sure everything was as she'd left it. The chalkboard had been wiped clean; the bulletin board on the east wall was a familiar assortment of maps, signs and playbills. LITERATURE THROUGHOUT THE AGES 1400 – 1850, one sign announced. Next to it were student-drawn posters illustrating some of the things her classes were studying: *Catcher in the Rye; I Know Why the Caged Bird Sings; Cyrano de Bergerac; Macbeth.*

'What did the supply teacher do with you last week?' she asked, lifting her copy of *Macbeth* from the top of her desk.

'Not much,' someone said, and laughed.

'Out, out, damned spot,' Haze bellowed. More laughter.

'He was pretty incompetent,' one of the girls said from the first row. 'He just had us work on our own most of the time.'

'Good. Then there shouldn't be any excuses for not having your essays handed in today,' Bonnie reminded them to a series of loud groans. 'In the meantime, let's turn to page seventy-two.'

A hand reached up, fluttered into the air.

'Yes, Katie?'

'What was it like to find a dead body?' the girl asked shyly.

There was a moment of stunned silence. Well, of course they would be curious, Bonnie realized. They'd read the papers, knew all about Joan's murder, were aware she'd found the body. 'Awful,' Bonnie told the girl. 'It was awful.'

'Did the body feel cold?' another girl asked.

'It felt cool,' Bonnie told her.

'Cool,' a chorus of voices repeated.

Cool, Bonnie thought. Had they misinterpreted the word?

'Did you do it?' The voice was male and deliberately provocative. Bonnie knew without having to look that it belonged to Haze.

'Sorry to disappoint you,' Bonnie said, struggling to keep her voice even, 'but the answer is no. Now, I think we should turn to page seventy-two.' She flipped through the small text, hands noticeably shaking. 'Macbeth's speech at the top of the page.'

She glanced toward the window, pleased with spring's progress. Despite the less-than-seasonal temperatures, the trees were all budding, some already in bloom. It looked as if someone had taken a finger through a chalk drawing, she thought, smudging the boundaries of the branches, engulfing them in a soft green mist. It was her favorite time, Bonnie realized, watching as several girls ran across the large back field, obviously late for class. One of the girls dropped a notebook and had to run back to retrieve it. Bonnie followed her with her eyes, saw the girl bend forward, her short black skirt riding up to reveal a pair of plaid boxer shorts. Bonnie smiled, about to return her attention to the text, when something else caught her eye: a man standing at the far end of the field, not quite hidden by the trees. Was he watching the girls? Bonnie wondered. Or something else?

She walked to the window, leaned forward, pressed her nose almost to the glass. As if he knew he was being watched, the man stepped away from the trees and out of the shadows, affording her a clearer view. He was wearing a tan windbreaker over a pair of blue jeans, large sunglasses covering his eyes. Mirrored sunglasses, Bonnie knew, gasping, taking a step back, bumping against one of the student's desks.

'Mrs Wheeler, are you all right?' someone asked.

'Tracey, take over until I get back,' Bonnie said, already on her way to the door. 'Work on your essays,' she instructed.

'What's going on?' someone whispered.

'Who is that guy?' someone asked.

Bonnie walked briskly down the corridor, mindful of the sign that cautioned against running in the hall, to the exterior door. She pushed it open, running through the back field toward the trees where she'd seen the man.

Except he wasn't there.

Bonnie stopped, turned in a full circle, then turned again. Goddamn him, she thought, angry tears springing to her eyes. She wasn't going to let him do this. She wasn't going to allow him to start playing games with her head. 'Nick!' she called out, the wind carrying her voice across the field, like a football tucked beneath a quarterback's arm. 'Nick, where are you? I know you're here. I saw you.'

There was a shuffling noise. Bonnie turned, squinting into the sun, as a man walked lazily toward her. Bonnie cupped her hands over her eyes, strained to make out the man's face.

'Something wrong?' the man asked.

Even before she saw his face, she knew it wasn't Nick. The voice was all wrong. It was kind and solicitous, two adjectives she could never apply to her brother.

Bonnie approached the dark-haired, middle-aged man, who was

wearing the gray uniform of the school custodian. 'Did you see a man lurking around here?' She motioned vaguely toward the trees. 'Tall, blondish, mirrored sunglasses,' she continued, positive about the sunglasses even though she really couldn't be sure. Nick had always favored mirrored sunglasses. That way, no one could see his eyes. The mirror of the soul, she thought. Except that he didn't have one.

The custodian shook his head. 'Sorry, no. Didn't see anyone. But I can't say I like the sound of someone lurking about. I'll keep my eyes open. That's for sure.'

Bonnie took a last look around, then reluctantly headed back toward the school, aware of her students watching her from the classroom windows. Maybe she'd been mistaken. It might not have been Nick. What would he be doing out here anyway? No, it was probably her imagination. A shadow she'd shaped into a man, like a piece of clay. No one really there. Except that others in her class had seen him too. 'Who is that guy?' she distinctly remembered someone asking.

'He left as soon as you ran out of here,' Haze greeted her upon her return to the classroom.

'Did you see where he went?' Bonnie asked.

'Toward the parking lot,' someone answered.

'Who was it?' several voices asked in unison.

Bonnie lifted her hands into the air. 'Someone I thought I knew. Anyway, enough of that. Please turn to page seventy-two, and let's get started on this speech.'

At the end of the period, Haze ambled toward her, one hand in the side pocket of his black jeans, the other round a clipboard, from which a few loose pieces of blank paper protruded. He stopped only inches from her face, the omnipresent scent of marijuana covering him like a second skin. 'Uh, Mrs Wheeler,' he began, 'I haven't had a chance to do that essay yet, and I need a little more time.'

'You've had more than enough time,' Bonnie reminded him.

'Well, the last week was kinda busy, what with the murder and everything,' he said.

Bonnie opened her mouth to speak, immediately closed it again. Was he really using the murder of his friend's mother as an excuse for not having his English assignment completed on time? And was she really surprised? 'I'm not sure I follow.'

82

'I need more time.'

'You know the rules, Haze. You lose marks for every day your assignment is late.'

'Look, I really need to pass this course.'

'Then you really need to start doing some work.'

'Don't be such a tight-ass,' Haze mumbled out of the side of his mouth.

'Excuse me?'

'Sam's mother was a tight-ass,' Haze continued, eyes locking onto hers. 'Look what happened to her.'

For a moment, Bonnie was too stunned to speak. 'What are you trying to say?'

'I really need to pass this course,' he repeated, and walked out of the room.

Bonnie sat in the staff room at the end of the long day, drinking her third cup of coffee, and trying to relax. She wasn't cut out for all this intrigue. She liked things simple and straightforward. No beating around the bush, no second-guessing. It was one of the reasons she'd always had trouble with poetry. 'Why don't they just say what they mean?' she often found herself asking, the same question she was asking herself now. She thought of Josh Freeman and his refusal to confide in her, of her brother, skulking in the bushes like some would-be child molester, of Haze, with his guarded threats.

She should probably call the police, report his strange remarks, although she doubted that would accomplish anything. The police had made it obvious she was still their prime suspect. 'What about the danger Joan talked about?' she repeatedly asked them. 'The danger to myself and my child?' To that, they said nothing. Was there no one who could provide her with any satisfactory answers?

She checked her watch. It was after three. Where was Josh Freeman? Hadn't he agreed to speak to her again after school?

Well, no, she had to admit. He hadn't agreed to any such thing. In fact, he'd been most reluctant to speak to her again, offering only a tepid 'we'll see' when pressed.

Bonnie looked around the room, the sun throwing an afternoon spotlight on the aggressively ugly blue-and-beige curtains bunched at either end of the long window. Anthony Higuera, a teacher of Spanish, sat marking papers in the far corner; Robert Chaplin, a teacher of chemistry, was reading the morning paper and shaking his head. Josh Freeman was nowhere to be seen.

He was an interesting man, Bonnie decided, an enigma, pleasant but aloof, although something in his eyes told her that he hadn't always been that way. He'd kept mostly to himself since coming to Weston Secondary, as if he was afraid to let anyone get too close. She remembered hearing that his wife had died in some kind of horrible accident, but as far as she knew, he'd never discussed this, or any other aspect of his personal life, with anyone. How much of his personal life, she wondered, had he shared with Joan?

Maybe he was waiting for her in his classroom, Bonnie realized, jumping up from her chair so abruptly she almost knocked it over. It was certainly worth a shot, she decided, departing the staff room and heading down the corridor toward the staircase at the back of the school. Even if he wasn't waiting for her, maybe she'd be able to head him off . . .

'Oh, Mrs Wheeler,' a voice called, and Bonnie turned to see one of the secretaries, a plump young woman dressed all in red, running after her. A tomato with legs, Bonnie thought, as the woman approached, hand over her heart to still her breathing. 'I'm glad I caught you.'

'Is something wrong?'

'There was a phone call from your daughter's day care. They want you to call back as soon as possible. They . . .'

Bonnie didn't give the startled young woman a chance to finish her sentence. She bolted for the office and the first available phone.

'Problem?' Ron Mosher asked, stepping out of his office and into the general waiting area.

'Claire Appleby, please,' Bonnie said into the receiver, acknowledging her principal's concern with a slight lifting of her shoulders. 'It's Bonnie Wheeler calling.'

'Mrs Wheeler,' Claire Appleby's voice repeated a second later. 'Thank you for calling back so quickly.'

'What's wrong? Is Amanda all right?'

'She's fine now. I don't want you to be alarmed.'

'What do you mean, she's fine *now*?'

'There was an incident.'

'An incident?'

'I want to stress that your daughter is unharmed . . .'

If the woman said anything further, Bonnie didn't hear her. She'd already dropped the receiver and was racing down the corridor toward her car.

Chapter Ten

The school which housed Amanda's day-care center was a two-story red-brick building with lots of windows, located on School Street, normally a two-minute drive from Weston Heights Secondary. Bonnie got there in under sixty seconds.

She pulled her car into the long driveway, slamming it into a parking space at the side of the school, then ran along the small walkway, nicknamed Alphabet Lane, to the day-care center, located at the back of the school, next to the playground.

Bonnie immediately spotted her daughter through the window and pushed open the glass door with considerably more force than necessary, almost falling into the large room. Amanda looked up from her miniature table, where she sat playing with a stack of colorful building blocks. 'Mommy!' the child shouted, the word reverberating with pleasure.

Amanda was wearing an unfamiliar pair of blue overalls and a red jersey, her blond hair pulled away from her round face and secured by a pair of red barrettes. Hadn't she dressed Amanda in a green cotton jumpsuit this morning? Whose clothes was her daughter wearing?

One of the childcare workers, a young woman with curly dark hair and a canary-yellow dress, was sitting on a small chair beside Amanda. Bonnie fought with her memory for the woman's name, remembered it just as Amanda came leaping toward her. 'What happened, Sue?' Bonnie asked the woman, scooping Amanda into her arms, her eyes quickly scanning the child's face and body for any signs of bruises, her hands fingering the strange apparel.

'Bad person threw something at me,' Amanda said.

'What do you mean? Who threw something at you? What did they throw?'

'Let me get Mrs Appleby,' the childcare worker offered. 'She said to notify her as soon as you got here.'

'Are you all right?' Bonnie asked her daughter, her trembling hand tracing the delicate lines of her child's face, her heart pounding wildly against her chest. She had to calm down, she told herself. She had to stay calm, at least until she found out exactly what happened.

Somebody had thrown something at her daughter. Someone had tried to harm her innocent little baby. No, that was impossible. It had to have been some kind of an accident. Why would anyone want to hurt a three-year-old child?

You're in danger, Joan had warned. *You and Amanda.*

'No,' she whispered, stiffening. It couldn't be.

'What, Mommy?'

'Mrs Wheeler,' said Claire Appleby, startling Bonnie, who hadn't seen or heard her come in. 'I'm so sorry this has happened.' Claire Appleby was a tall, middle-aged woman with a flat chest and wide hips. She wore a simple powder-blue shirtwaist dress that unfortunately emphasized both.

'What exactly is it that's happened?' Bonnie caught sight of something sticky coating a few of the hairs behind her daughter's left ear.

'Perhaps Sue could take Amanda outside,' Claire Appleby suggested gently.

Amanda tightened her grip around Bonnie's neck, threatening to cut off her supply of air. Like a boa constrictor, Bonnie thought uneasily, gently loosening the child's arms. 'It's okay, sweetie,' she told her daughter, lowering her to the floor. 'I'll only be a few minutes. Then we'll get an ice cream.'

'Strawberry?'

'If that's what you want.'

'A bad person threw blood all over me.'

'What?!'

'Sue,' Claire Appleby said, her hand lifting nervously to her blond hair, 'please take Amanda into the playground.'

'I want to go to the swings,' Amanda directed.

'I'll race you,' Sue said.

The playground was equipped with an enormous jungle gym, three slides of assorted shapes and sizes, a giant sand box, and several sets of swings. Bonnie watched Sue as she harnessed her daughter inside one of the smaller swings, aware that she was holding her breath, feeling it painful and tight against her chest. She wanted to demand answers to the hundreds of questions that were pummeling against the sides of her brain, but she was unable to find her voice. Tears were already falling the length of her face, disappearing down her neck and under the collar of her white blouse. Don't cry now, she admonished herself silently. Now is not the time for tears.

'It's not as bad as it sounds,' Claire Appleby was quick to reassure her.

'What exactly happened here?' Bonnie whispered, each word like a knife chipping at her throat.

'You know that we keep a very watchful eye on the children . . .'

'I know that. That's why I don't understand . . .'

'I'm so sorry, Mrs Wheeler. I can see how upset you are. I know this has been a terrible time for you. I've been following the papers . . .'

'Please tell me exactly what happened,' Bonnie urged.

'The children were outside in the playground,' Claire Appleby began immediately. 'Sue and Darlene were with them. Apparently, Amanda wandered over to the laneway. She told Sue later that someone called her name.'

'Someone called her?'

'That's what she said.'

'Did she say who it was?'

'She didn't know. Apparently, whoever it was was wearing a hood or something, and as soon as Amanda got close enough, they just emptied this pail over her head.'

'A pail filled with . . . blood?' Bonnie asked, her voice incredulous.

'We *think* it was blood,' Claire Appleby said quietly. 'We're not sure. It was dark and red and at first we thought it might be paint, but . . .' Her voice drifted off.

'But . . . ?'

'It wasn't paint. Sue said she almost fainted when she saw Amanda because she assumed she'd fallen and cracked open her head. We didn't realize she hadn't actually hurt herself until we'd washed most of it off. It was all over her face and clothes. We have her clothes for you in a plastic bag,' Claire Appleby added.

'Wait a minute,' Bonnie instructed, needing to get the facts straight in her mind. 'You're telling me that there was a strange person in the laneway wearing a hood and carrying a pail of blood, and nobody noticed him?'

'I'm afraid that's right,' Claire Appleby admitted.

Bonnie felt her legs go weak, thought they might go out from under her, reached for something to grab onto. There was nothing. She stumbled, fell toward one of the tiny tables.

'Why don't you sit down?' Claire Appleby helped her into one of the tiny chairs, attempting to sit down beside her, her ample backside refusing to wedge itself into the small seat. 'Amanda's all right,' the woman said, as she had said earlier. 'She was just frightened.'

Bonnie looked helplessly around the room, casually absorbing the many imaginative mobiles that hung from the ceiling, the large paper letters of the alphabet that ran along the walls, the bright posters of wild animals, the boxes of toys, the series of bold fingerpaint sketches tacked to the far wall. 'How long ago did this happen?'

Claire Appleby checked her watch. 'Not long ago. Twenty minutes, maybe. Half an hour, tops. We cleaned her off and called you.'

'Did you call the police?'

Claire Appleby hesitated. 'We decided to contact you first. Naturally, we'll be filing a report.'

'I think we should call the police,' Bonnie stated, staring out the window at her daughter, who was laughing and shrieking with glee as she sailed high into the air, the ugly incident earthbound and forgotten.

'Do you have any idea who might have done this?' Captain Mahoney was asking. Behind him stood his friend, Detective Haver of the Weston police force. Since this latest incident had happened in Weston, and not Newton, Captain Mahoney had explained, it was technically out of his jurisdiction.

Bonnie shook her head. Why was he asking her that? How would she possibly have any idea who could have done such a horrible thing? 'Should we take her to the hospital?' Bonnie asked. 'Should she have an AIDS test?'

'Why don't we wait and have the blood analyzed first?' Captain Mahoney suggested, his voice kind. 'The odds are it's not human blood.'

'What do you mean?'

'There are a lot of farms in the area, Mrs Wheeler,' Detective Haver reminded her. He was a stout man of medium height, his skin the color of dark chocolate. 'There are some farms over in Easton where they even slaughter their own cattle.'

'Easton?' Bonnie repeated, numbly.

'Your father lives in Easton, doesn't he?' Captain Mahoney remarked casually.

Too casually, Bonnie thought, starting to tremble, recalling the sight of her brother lurking in the trees behind the school earlier in the day. 'Have you spoken to him?' Bonnie asked.

'Briefly.'

'And to my brother?'

'We spoke to him as well.'

'And? Did he have anything interesting to say?'

'Why don't you ask your brother?'

Bonnie swallowed, looked at her daughter, who was now dangling upside down from one of the high bars of the jungle gym, the childcare worker hovering anxiously nearby, her arms a safety net. 'My brother and I aren't exactly on the best of terms, Captain,' Bonnie told him.

'May I ask why not?'

'You saw Joan's scrapbook,' Bonnie reminded him. 'I would think the answer is self-evident.'

'Do you think he had something to do with Joan Wheeler's death?'

'Do you?'

'Your brother has an alibi for the time Mrs Wheeler was murdered,' the captain told her.

'He does?'

'You sound surprised.'

'Nothing about my brother surprises me.'

'Now you sound disappointed.'

'I guess I'd better keep my mouth shut,' Bonnie said, watching Captain Mahoney smile. He wants to like me, Bonnie thought. He wants to believe I had nothing to do with Joan's death.

'Any reason to think he might have been involved in what happened here this afternoon?'

'Why would Nick want to hurt my daughter? He's never even met her,' Bonnie said, more to herself than to the officers. And yet, he'd been here this morning, only a few blocks away. Was he the danger Joan had been trying to warn her against?

What was keeping her from giving this information to the police? Could she still be trying to protect her younger brother?

You're a good girl, she heard her mother whisper. Bonnie shook the voice aside with a toss of her head.

'Do you think that what happened to Amanda could be just some silly teenage prank?' Bonnie asked hopefully, pushing logic roughly aside.

Captain Mahoney loosened his red-and-black-striped tie, pulled the collar of his white shirt away from his prominent Adam's apple. 'I suppose someone might have read about you in the paper, and decided to have a little sick fun,' he said, obviously thinking out loud. 'There's a lot of wackos around, even in a supposedly safe haven like Weston.'

Bonnie nodded. There was no denying the truth of his words. Nowhere was really safe anymore, even a 'safe haven' like Weston, where they'd moved when she became pregnant. Boston probably wasn't the best place to raise a family, she and Rod had decided reluctantly, selecting Weston because, despite its proximity to the city, it felt more like the country. Each house rested on one and a half acres of land, and there was an abundance of trees and ponds and good clean air. The ideal place to raise a family. Just fifteen minutes away from downtown. Around the corner from their friends Diana and Greg. Far enough away from Newton and Joan. Even farther away from Easton and what was left of her family.

Except that Diana and Greg had divorced soon after Amanda was born, and Diana now spent most of her time in the city. And it appeared that nothing could be too far away from either her relatives or Rod's ex-wife. The past is always closer than you think, Bonnie reflected.

'I'm sorry, did you ask me something?' Bonnie realized she hadn't been paying attention.

'I asked whether you're a popular teacher,' Captain Mahoney repeated. 'Popular?'

'Do you think your students like you, Mrs Wheeler?'

'I think so,' she stammered. 'I *like* to think so,' she immediately qualified, thinking of Haze, picturing him as he advanced toward her, stopping only inches from her face. Could he have been responsible for the attack on her daughter? Could he have had something to do with Joan's death? Could he be the danger Joan had been referring to? 'There's one boy,' she said. 'Harold Gleason. Haze, everyone calls him. He's in my junior year English class. He's been giving me a bit of trouble, and he knew Joan. He's a friend of Sam, my stepson,' she added, the word feeling clumsy on her tongue. She told the captain exactly what Haze had said to her this morning, watching as he took note of this latest information, his face frustratingly void of all expression.

'Do you know where Harold Gleason lives?' he asked.

Bonnie closed her eyes, trying to picture the address written on the boy's student index card. 'Eighteen Marsh Lane,' she said finally, her breath catching in her lungs. 'Easton.'

Chapter Eleven

Bonnie had been driving for the better part of an hour through the wide, twisting streets of Easton. Many of the streets had the same names as streets in Weston: Glen Road; Beach Road; Country Lane; Concord Street, among others. She knew them all. They hadn't changed in the more than three years since she'd been up this way, had barely changed, in fact, since she was a child. What was she doing here? It would be getting dark soon. She should probably go home. What was she hoping to accomplish by coming out here?

The police had told her they would handle Haze, that she should take care of her daughter, get her that ice cream cone she'd promised her. She'd done that, then promptly taken her to see their family physician, who'd examined her thoroughly, and pronounced her in perfect health, advising Bonnie to wait until after she got the results from the police lab before subjecting Amanda to any blood tests. The child had seen enough blood for one day, the doctor advised.

So she'd taken her daughter home, feeling like an unwelcome intruder as she pushed open her front door, hostile rap music blasting at her from the upstairs bedrooms. She'd tried to call Rod, was told he was busy filming a promo and couldn't be disturbed, and so she'd busied Amanda at the kitchen table with some paper and a box of crayons, and tried to think what Sam and Lauren might like for dinner, deciding on home-made macaroni and cheese. All kids loved macaroni and cheese, she thought, wondering if the way to a child's heart was as straightforward as that to a man's.

Rod called just as they were sitting down to eat, saying he'd be late, that he'd just grab a sandwich at the studio, would she be all right alone with the kids? She heard Amanda giggle, looked over to see Sam making a face out of his macaroni, Lauren smiling indulgently. In the next instant, all three were making faces in their macaroni, something which would have horrified Bonnie's mother, but which filled Bonnie with something approaching pride – her dinner was a success. Yes, she told Rod, they'd be all right.

After dinner, Bonnie got Amanda into bed, then called Mira Gerstein, an elderly woman who lived down the street, and asked her to baby-sit. She wouldn't be long, she told her, wondering where she was going, what she was planning to do. Stay out of it, she felt Rod admonish as she climbed into her car and backed out of the driveway onto Winter Street. But how could she just sit home and do nothing when her child was at risk? How could she hope to rebuild her family until Joan's ghost was laid to rest, until her killer was caught? Only then could they move forward; only then would they be safe.

'So just what is it you think you're doing?' Bonnie asked out loud, once again turning her car onto Marsh Lane, driving slowly past the old wood-framed houses that irregularly interrupted the landscape, eyes peeled for number eighteen.

It was the oldest house on the small street, or at least, it looked that way, neglect covering it like a second coat of paint. Haze lived in this house with his maternal grandparents, his mother having abandoned him after she, herself, had been abandoned by his father. Bonnie slowed her car down further, so that she was almost crawling, trying to peer inside the curtainless windows of the single-story home. But the interior of the house was in darkness; it didn't look as if anybody was there, although there was an ancient blue Buick in the driveway. What kind of car did Haze drive? she wondered, stopping, debating whether to get out of her car, knock on the door, demand to speak to Haze's grandparents, neither of whom she remembered ever meeting.

And what good would that do? she asked herself, returning her foot to the gas pedal. Just what was she planning to ask? Where was their grandson immediately after school? Had they noticed anything strange about his behavior lately? Did they believe he could be guilty of murder?

Sure, great. Terrific detective work. Let the police deal with it, Rod had told her, and he was right. She'd done her part, told them everything she knew.

Except that she hadn't told them everything she knew.

She turned onto Spruce Street, then again at Elm Street, and again at Cherry. She hadn't told them about seeing her brother. She turned again at Meadow Road, stopped the car at the end of the long street.

Two long blocks to the right and another to the left, and she'd be there – the old brick house she'd grown up in, the house her mother had willed to her brother. Nick had immediately turned around and sold the house to his father.

Just one right turn, and then another, then one more to the left, and she'd be there. She wouldn't go there now, Bonnie decided, knowing that she was already on her way, that it had been to this house, this haunted house, so full of skeletons and ghosts, that she'd been headed all along.

She drove as if on automatic pilot, her fingers barely touching the steering wheel. She hadn't been back to the house since her mother's death, refusing to even think about it on a conscious level, although sometimes, when she closed her eyes in sleep, the dark walls of her childhood reappeared, closing in on her like a coffin. It was then she saw the heavy floral wallpaper that she'd always held responsible for the slightly sickly odor that permeated every room.

'What am I doing here?' Bonnie wondered, stopping her car in front of the house at four hundred and twenty-two Maple Road, not sure for a moment if she had make a mistake, turned at the wrong street. 'What have they done?' she asked, stepping outside, her legs wobbling as her feet touched the pavement.

The red-brick exterior had been painted gray, and there were white shutters around each window. Brightly colored pansies sat in two large clay pots on either side of the white door and in a long window box suspended outside the kitchen window. The scent of freshly mowed grass wafted toward her nose as Bonnie inched her way slowly up the front walk. 'What am I doing here?' she asked again, thinking that there was still time to turn back, that no one had seen her, that she could crawl back into her car and leave with no one being the wiser.

The front door suddenly opened, a woman appearing on the outside landing, watching Bonnie, as if she had been aware of her presence all along. 'My goodness,' the woman said. 'It *is* you.'

'Hello, Adeline,' Bonnie said, surprised to hear her voice so strong. She stopped, her feet immediately taking root.

'I thought it was you when I saw your car pull up. I said to Steve, "I think we have a visitor. I think it's Bonnie." '

'And what did he say?' Bonnie asked.

The woman shrugged. 'You know your father. He doesn't say much.'

97

Bonnie nodded, not sure whether to stay where she was or to continue up the pathway. Not that her feet gave any indication they would cooperate, she realized.

'I kind of thought we might get a visit after your phone call,' Adeline continued. 'I said to Steve, "I bet Bonnie pays us a visit." '

'Here I am,' Bonnie acknowledged.

'So I see.'

'This isn't easy for me,' Bonnie said.

'It doesn't have to be so difficult.'

'Is my brother here?'

'Not at the moment.'

Bonnie felt her shoulders sink, although she wasn't sure whether it was with disappointment or relief.

'Why don't you come inside and spend a few minutes with your father?' the woman continued. 'Seeing as you've come all this way.'

Was she being sarcastic? Bonnie wondered, fighting the urge to turn around and flee. The truth was, she didn't know this woman her father had married very well at all. She'd seen her only seldom since their wedding, talked to her only when she had no other alternative. Exactly the same way Rod's children had treated her. What goes around comes around, Bonnie thought.

'We won't bite,' Adeline Lonergan added, her wide smile revealing both rows of teeth.

Bonnie was about to say no, but her feet, rather than backing their way down the front path, suddenly propelled her forward. 'I see you've made some changes,' Bonnie said, nearing the front door.

'About time, wouldn't you say?' Adeline's blue eyes almost twinkled under the soft gray fringe of hair.

Bonnie was too busy staring at the interior of the small house to reply. The heavy flowered paper that had once covered all the walls had been literally whitewashed. White walls were everywhere – the halls, the kitchen, the living and dining areas. Pale green sheers had replaced the dark velvet drapes of the main rooms, light maple substituted for heavy mahogany. Whites, yellows and greens stood in for burgundy and black.

'Like it?' Adeline asked, inviting Bonnie into the living room, and motioning her to sit down on the pale yellow sofa.

'It's certainly different,' Bonnie allowed, the only concession she was willing to make. In fact, her heart was racing. She felt giddy and light-headed, as if she were Dorothy newly awakened in the technicolor world of Oz.

'Those dark colors were so oppressive. And depressing,' Adeline added, lowering herself into a mint-green chair. 'How have you been?'

Bonnie took a second to calm herself. 'All right,' she said, then wondered what the question had been.

'Everyone is well, I hope?'

'We're all fine, thank you.' Bonnie fidgeted in her seat. She noticed a Bible sitting on the coffee table beside the latest edition of *Vanity Fair*. 'My father . . . ?' Bonnie looked toward the hall, head spinning, her brain unable to digest the changes her eyes were perceiving. She felt her body reel, grabbed the arm of the sofa to steady herself.

'He knows you're here. He'll be down in a minute, I expect. Old bladders are just one of the joys of ageing.'

Bonnie nodded, already regretting her decision to come inside. 'You're looking well.'

'I watch what I eat and try to stay in shape. I have a Debbie Reynolds tape that I exercise with a few times a week, and your father and I go for long walks every day.'

Bonnie stood up, walked to the window, stared outside, trying to picture her father walking by with her mother, but the image refused to come. Her father had always been too busy to go walking with her mother. 'What about your travel business?'

'Oh, my daughters took that over several years ago. Your brother is working there now.'

Bonnie's head swiveled toward her father's third wife. 'Really? And how is that working out?'

'Very well, from what my daughters tell me. Nick has changed a lot in the past eighteen months.'

'I hope you're right.' Bonnie checked her watch. It was almost seven-thirty. 'Look, I have to go. Will you tell my father . . .'

'Tell me what?' a voice asked from the doorway.

Bonnie's head snapped toward the sound.

'Hello, Bonnie.'

'Dad,' Bonnie acknowledged, the word heavy on her tongue, like a wad of cotton.

Steve Lonergan folded his hands against his chest and drew his shoulders back, a gesture Bonnie remembered from her youth, one that had always filled her with anxiety. Even now, she felt her pulse quicken, although the almost delicate old man who stood before her, his white hair receding into nothingness, his skin oddly translucent, was hardly a figure of fear. Age was shrinking him, Bonnie realized, common sense telling her he'd never been as tall as he stood in her memory, but surprised anyway by his obvious mortality. His face still bore a thin veneer of toughness, but there was a softness in his light hazel eyes that Bonnie couldn't remember having seen before.

'What brings you out this way?' Her father walked into the living room, easing himself into a green-and-yellow-striped wing chair and beckoning her back to the sofa.

'A student of mine lives in the area, and I needed to drop something off for him,' Bonnie heard herself reply, feeling the soft cushions of the sofa collapse under her.

Her father chuckled. 'You were always a terrible liar.'

Bonnie's face flushed a deep red. Was she a bad liar because she hated lying, or did she hate lying because she was so bad at it? 'A student of mine lives in the area,' she repeated, 'and I was hoping to talk to Nick,' she admitted after a brief pause.

'Nick's not here,' her father said.

'I know.'

'Adeline gave him your message. Didn't he get in touch?'

'Yes, he did.'

'You're looking a little tired,' her father said suddenly, and Bonnie felt her eyes well up with tears. 'Working hard these days?'

'Well, it's been a busy time.'

'So the police tell me,' her father said. 'I guess now I have *three* grandchildren I've never seen.'

For an instant Bonnie was speechless.

'How *is* my granddaughter?' her father asked.

'She's fine,' Bonnie whispered, her words wobbling into the air, dropping to the ground. Someone emptied a pail of blood over her today, she almost shouted, but didn't. She wanted to jump from her seat and run from the room, from this house where she'd known only unhappiness, from the oppressive dark flowers that were threatening to burst through the whiteness of the walls, but she couldn't move. Imaginary vines had wrapped themselves around her ankles and wrists, tying her to the sofa, securing her to her past, refusing to let her break free.

'She's how old now? Three? Four?'

'You know how old she is,' Bonnie reminded him.

Steve Lonergan nodded. 'Well, let's see. She was born two months after your mother died . . .'

'I don't want to talk about my mother.'

'Really? I thought that's why you might be here.'

'I'm here to see Nick.'

'Nick's not here.'

Bonnie closed her eyes. This was stupid. Why had she come? Again, she tried to push herself out of her seat, but her body refused to cooperate. 'Did Nick ever say anything to you about his relationship with my husband's ex-wife?' she ventured.

'He has an alibi for the time of her death, if that's what you're getting at.'

'You?' Bonnie scoffed.

'It was his day off work,' Adeline interrupted, 'and he was helping us around the house.'

'You're his alibi?' Bonnie repeated incredulously.

'Why would we lie?' Adeline asked.

'And what about today?' Bonnie demanded, ignoring the question. 'Another day off?'

'I believe it was, yes. It varies from week to week, from what I understand. But I don't know where Nick went today. He'd already left by the time we woke up.'

'That's all right,' Bonnie told them, using her hands to push her body away from the sofa, rising unsteadily to her feet. 'I know where he was today.' She walked to the front door, refusing to glance up the stairs, to acknowledge the ghosts waiting just behind the bedroom door. 'Just tell him to stay away from my daughter,' Bonnie said, throwing open the front door and racing up the pathway to her car before anyone could say another word.

What was the matter with her? Bonnie glared at her reflection in the car's rearview mirror. Her eyes stared back reproachfully, tears still hovering, lids already showing signs of swelling. 'Don't you cry,' she warned. 'Don't you dare cry.' What had possessed her to go back to that house? What had she hoped to accomplish by confronting her father and his wife? Had she expected her father to throw himself at her feet and beg her forgiveness? I'm sorry I was such a lousy father; I'm sorry for the pain I caused your mother; I can't live any longer with the guilt of her death. Is that what she'd been hoping to hear?

What was her father doing living in that house? Hadn't he been all too eager to leave? Wasn't he the one who'd walked out, the one who left her mother alone with two children? What right did he have to be back there? To be happy there? How would her mother feel if she knew?

'I should never have gone there. I'm stupid. Stupid.' Bonnie hit the side of her head with her hand. 'I need my head examined, is what I need. How could I have gone back there?'

What was it her father had said? That he assumed she'd come to talk about her mother? Why had he assumed that? What could he possibly think she'd have to say to him? What could he possibly think she'd want to hear from him?

'Just as long as you give Nick my message,' she said out loud, sighing with relief when she saw the sign announcing she was back in Weston.

Of course, it was possible Nick hadn't had anything to do with what happened to Amanda. What possible motive could he have for wanting to hurt her child, after all? What could he possibly hope to gain?

The only person who had anything to gain from something happening to either Amanda or herself was Rod, Bonnie realized with a gasp, her foot inadvertently pressing down on the brake, jolting the car to a sudden stop. The car stalled. 'Now you're really being stupid,' she said, restarting the engine, grateful there'd been no one behind her. 'I won't have to wait for someone to shoot me,' she said. 'I'll get myself killed.'

What was she thinking about? Rod was the kindest, sweetest man in the world, despite what a few of Joan's friends and neighbors might think. What exactly had Caroline Gossett meant at Joan's funeral anyway? 'I guess I keep expecting justice,' she'd said. What did that mean?

So what if Rod had insurance policies on her and his children? Lots of men carried life insurance policies on their families.

On their children? a little voice asked. Double indemnity?

Rod didn't have an alibi for the time of Joan's death, the unwanted voice continued. He'd met her brother without telling her.

He'd been sleeping in his office at the time of his ex-wife's death, Bonnie silently countered. Her brother had come to see him about some wild idea for a series. Rod hadn't told her because he hadn't wanted to upset her.

Or maybe there was another reason for Nick's visit to the studio. Maybe the two men had other things to discuss.

Like what?

Like murder, the little voice said.

Again Bonnie's foot slammed on the brake. This time, loud honking erupted around her. Bonnie glanced in her rearview mirror to see the man in the car directly behind her giving her the finger, his angry lips contorting around the words, 'Women drivers!' 'Great,' Bonnie said. 'Thank you very much.'

Don't forget about Haze, the little voice continued as soon as Bonnie's foot reached for the gas.

'Haze had no motive for killing Joan,' Bonnie said. 'She may have been a tight-ass, but I hardly think that's motive enough for murder. He may not think much of me as a teacher, but killing me isn't going to get him a passing grade.'

Unless he, too, stood to gain financially from Joan's death. Unless someone had offered him a share of future spoils. Possibly a friend who cared more about his mother's Mercedes than he did about the bullet through her heart. *Ding dong, the witch is dead!?*

'Jesus Christ,' Bonnie said. Could she really be thinking these things? Could she really suspect her husband and her stepson of murder?

Bonnie turned the car onto Winter Street, her house appearing, like a mirage, at the second twist of the road. Rod's car was in the driveway, and Bonnie pulled hers in beside it and shut off the engine.

Home sweet home, she thought.

Chapter Twelve

The next day she went to see Caroline Gossett.

The modern bungalow was painted yellow, with gray shingles and black awnings. It stretched across the land like a lazy yawn, open and twisting in odd and unexpected directions. Rather like my life, Bonnie thought, as she proceeded slowly up the winding stone walkway to the black front door, careful to avoid looking over her shoulder at Joan's house across the street. 'What am I doing here?' she asked out loud, a question she seemed to be asking with alarming frequency of late. 'I must be nuts.'

Bonnie pressed the doorbell twice in rapid succession, heard it respond with the first bar of 'London Bridge is falling down'. There was a long, narrow panel of glass on either side of the front door, and Bonnie tried to peek inside, but her view was hampered by the gathered sheer curtains that fell across the windows like a heavy film. What she could see of the interior of the house looked elegant and upscale – dark wood floors, a baby grand piano in what was likely to be the living room at the back, a tall brass sculpture of what appeared to be a nude woman.

She should have phoned first, she decided now. She should have phoned and asked whether she would be welcome, what would be the most convenient time to drop by. That would have been the reasonable thing to do, the polite thing. As it was, she'd simply obeyed a sudden, unfortunate impulse and driven here directly after school was finished. She didn't even know if Caroline Gossett would be home. It was barely past three in the afternoon. The woman was probably still at work. If she worked. Bonnie had no idea what Caroline Gossett did with her time, whether she was a busy executive or a stay-at-home mom, if she did volunteer work or if she worked out eight hours a day at the local gym. She knew nothing about Caroline Gossett at all, other than that the woman lived across the street from her husband's ex-wife, and that she'd obviously thought the world of Joan.

Every time Bonnie had tried to broach the subject of Caroline Gossett with Rod, he'd waved her questions aside with an impatient hand and a frown. He had no interest in discussing the past, he'd told her. Caroline Gossett was a frivolous and superficial woman with misplaced loyalties. He'd had no use for her when he was married to Joan; he certainly had no use for her now.

So what am I doing here? Bonnie wondered again, by-passing the bell to knock loudly on the door. *Joan spoke very highly of you,* she remembered Caroline saying at the funeral. Why had Joan spoken of her at all?

'Hold your horses,' a voice called from inside, footsteps approaching. A woman's face appeared behind the soft fabric of the side-panel curtains, pulling them sharply aside, her blue eyes obviously taken aback by what they saw. 'You're Rod's wife,' Caroline Gossett said, opening the door and staring at Bonnie with undisguised curiosity.

Caroline Gossett was as tall as Bonnie remembered, but thinner, less imposing now that she was out of her navy silk dress and into a pair of jeans. Her blond hair was pulled into a short ponytail, and her pink cotton shirt hung loose over her hips. She wore no make-up. Even so, she retained a certain elegance.

'I was wondering if we could talk,' Bonnie heard herself say.

'Sure,' the woman said easily, backing into the front foyer. 'Come on in.'

Bonnie stepped inside. 'Thank you. I know I should have called . . .'

'No, it was probably better that you didn't. The element of surprise and everything.' Caroline Gossett closed the front door and motioned toward the kitchen. 'Would you like some lemonade? I just made a fresh pitcher.'

No, I shouldn't, Bonnie thought. 'Actually, yes,' she said. 'I'd love some.'

'This way.'

Bonnie followed Caroline Gossett into her large square kitchen. The room was white and yellow, with earth-toned Mexican tiles on the floor, and a series of framed charcoal drawings of women and children on the walls, obviously by the same artist as the pictures in Joan's living room. Either the women had very similar tastes or there'd been a sale at a local gallery. 'These are lovely,' Bonnie remarked, her eyes moving from a picture of a mother holding her newborn baby in her arms to one of a middle-aged woman cradling an old woman, probably her mother.

'Thank you.'

'I'm sorry if I'm disturbing you,' Bonnie ventured, thinking she should probably say this, even if she didn't mean it.

'Actually, I'm glad for the break. I was getting a little cross-eyed.' Caroline Gossett opened the refrigerator, took out a large pitcher of pink lemonade and poured them each a glass.

'Cross-eyed?'

'I'm working on a sketch for a new painting.'

'A sketch? Then you did these?' Bonnie's eyes swept across the walls with fresh appreciation. The person who had done these remarkable drawings was obviously a skilled artist and a very sensitive woman. She could hardly be described as frivolous and superficial.

'Rod didn't tell you I'm an artist,' Caroline said.

'No, actually. He didn't tell me anything.'

'So he doesn't know you're here,' Caroline said, in that disconcerting way she had of stating all her questions.

'I didn't know myself that I was coming.'

'That's interesting.' Caroline handed Bonnie the tall glass of lemonade.

Bonnie took a long sip of her drink, felt her lips contort into an involuntary pout.

'Too sour?'

'It's fine.' Bonnie returned the glass to her lips, didn't drink.

Caroline smiled. 'Anybody ever tell you you're a lousy liar?'

'Everybody.'

Caroline's smile widened. She was very pretty when she smiled, Bonnie thought. Almost girlish.

'Joan always used to complain that my lemonade needed more sugar. She had a real sweet tooth. Just like you.'

'I don't have a sweet tooth,' Bonnie said, uncomfortable at being in any way compared to Rod's ex-wife.

'That's what she used to say.' She smiled. 'How are the kids?'

Bonnie took a deep breath. 'I'm not sure. They haven't exactly confided their feelings in me.'

'Give it time. It's a hell of an adjustment to have to make.'

'Were they very close to their mother?'

Caroline gave the question a moment's thought. 'Not as close as Joan would have liked,' she said finally. 'Sam was something of an odd duck, he kept to himself most of the time, and Lauren was always more of a daddy's girl. Joan tried, but . . . what can you do?'

Bonnie followed Caroline Gossett out of the kitchen and into the art-filled living room. Aside from the large bronze nude, there were several other pieces of sculpture – a woman's torso, a child's head, a small figurine of a ballerina. Paintings – some oil, some pastel, some pen and ink – were everywhere.

'Did you do these?'

'Most of them.'

'They're beautiful,' Bonnie said. 'I especially like this one.' Bonnie pointed to an oil painting of a woman staring into a mirror, her older reflection leaping out at her in shades of blue and violet.

'Yes, I knew you would. It was Joan's favorite as well.'

Bonnie instantly backed away from the painting, felt the grand piano at her back. 'Do you play?'

'Not very well,' Caroline plopped down in the middle of the white sofa. 'Why don't you sit down and tell me what I can do for you.'

Bonnie perched on the end of a white tub chair. 'I was curious about a few things you said at the funeral.'

'You'll have to refresh my memory.'

'You were talking to Rod and you commented that he looked very well. He said you sounded disappointed.'

'Oh, yes. I remember thinking that there must be a very ugly painting of your husband hidden at the back of somebody's closet,' Caroline said, the index finger of her right hand tapping her bottom lip.

'My husband is hardly Dorian Gray,' Bonnie said. Was the woman implying that Rod had made some sort of pact with the devil? 'You said, "I guess I keep expecting justice." What did you mean by that?'

Caroline raised her glass to her lips, drank half the lemonade in one long sip. 'What is it you don't understand?'

'Why you don't like my husband,' Bonnie replied truthfully.

Caroline shook her head, her hair coming loose of its ribbon and scattering around her face. 'Why does it matter what I think of Rod?'

'It doesn't,' Bonnie said quickly, lowering her gaze to the floor to hide her lie, instantly raising it again. 'I'm not sure why it matters,' she corrected. 'But it's been bothering me ever since the funeral. I couldn't help but wonder what had happened between the two of you for you to dislike him so intensely.'

'You didn't ask him,' Caroline stated.

Bonnie said nothing.

'Let me guess.' Caroline pushed the stray hairs behind her ears, looked toward the ceiling. 'He said that I was a silly busybody who was part of an unfortunate past he no longer wanted to think about.' She looked directly at Bonnie. 'Close?'

'Close enough.'

Caroline laughed. 'I like you. But then that's not too surprising. Rod always had great taste in women.'

'What happened between you and Rod?' Bonnie repeated.

'Between the two of us? Nothing.'

'Then why the ill will?'

Caroline finished the rest of her lemonade, put the glass down on the red-and-black hand-painted coffee table beside the sofa. 'You're sure you want to hear this?'

'No,' Bonnie conceded. 'But tell me anyway.'

Caroline took a deep breath. 'How can I phrase this gently?' She paused, obviously searching for just the right words. 'Your husband is a philandering, insensitive prick. How's that?'

Bonnie winced, thought of leaving, didn't move. 'Can you be more specific?' She almost laughed. The woman sitting across from her had just called her husband a philandering, insensitive prick, and Bonnie's response was to ask her to be more specific. Good one, as Diane would say.

'You want examples,' Caroline said.

'I'd appreciate it.'

'I'm not sure you will.'

'Tell me anyway.'

'No, you tell me. What's the story he's given you all these years? That he was the long-suffering husband of an irrational drunk?'

Bonnie tried to keep her face blank, failed.

'I thought so. It's the story he tells most people. Maybe he even believes it. Who knows? Who cares?' She stood up, walked to the piano, stopped. 'Did he happen to mention that one of the reasons Joan drank was because he was never home? That he was an irresponsible husband and a disinterested father? That he was too busy playing around with other women to be much of either? No, I can see by your face that he neglected to mention that.'

'Joan told you these things,' Bonnie said, adopting the other woman's habit of asking questions in statement form.

'If you're suggesting that I simply believed everything Joan told me, you're wrong. I saw Superman myself one night when he was supposed to be working. Lyle and I were having dinner at the Copley Square Hotel, and there he was just two tables away, nibbling on the ear of a stunning brunette.'

'It was probably business, for God's sake. My husband is a television director. It's not like he doesn't come into contact with gorgeous women every day.'

'And night,' Caroline added, with infuriating calm. 'Trust me, this wasn't business.'

'Be that as it may,' Bonnie said, 'my husband didn't leave Joan for another woman.'

'And why did he tell you he left?'

Bonnie took another sip of lemonade, felt it bitter on her tongue. 'He said that after the baby died . . .'

'Go on.'

'He just couldn't bear to be around her anymore.'

'Yes, he was a big help after Kelly died,' Caroline said.

'You're being very judgemental.'

'I thought that's what you wanted.'

'How can you know what my husband was feeling, what he was going through?'

'I know what I saw.'

'And what was that?'

'A man who cheated on his wife at every opportunity, a man who was never there when she needed him, a man who walked out on her when she needed him the most.'

'He couldn't stay,' Bonnie tried to explain. 'Every time he looked at Joan, he saw his dead little girl.'

'Then that was more than he saw of her when she was alive,' Caroline snapped, leaving both women temporarily speechless. 'I'm sorry,' Caroline said quietly, after a long pause. 'That was pretty crass, even for me. Your husband obviously brings out the best in me.'

Bonnie felt herself dangerously close to tears, held them tightly in check. 'You don't know my husband very well.'

'Maybe you're the one who doesn't know him,' Caroline responded.

'My husband is not the one who let a fourteen-month-old baby drown in a bathtub,' Bonnie reminded her.

'Now who's being judgemental,' Caroline observed.

'Facts are facts.'

'And accidents happen. And people make mistakes. And if they're lucky, they get a little help and understanding from those around them. Two people died the afternoon Kelly drowned,' Caroline said quietly. 'Joan's funeral was just a little late.' Tears threatened the corners of her eyes.

'You said something else at the funeral,' Bonnie ventured.

Caroline shrugged, waited for Bonnie to continue.

'You said that you wouldn't be here today if it weren't for Joan. What did you mean?'

'I went through a rather difficult time myself a few years ago,' Caroline began, speaking on a lower register than before. 'Sparing you the gory details, I learned I could never have children.'

'I'm sorry,' Bonnie said, genuinely.

'Joan was there for me every day. She made sure I ate, that I got out, that I had someone to talk to. She didn't tell me everything was going to work out just fine. She didn't tell me that I'd get over it, that I could adopt, that it was God's will, that it was for the best. She knew how unhelpful, and downright hurtful, those handy little clichés really are. She'd heard them all herself. She knew that what I needed was someone to talk to, someone who would hold me and listen while I cried and moaned and bitched and railed against my fate. And it didn't matter that I said the same things day after day. She was there to listen, to agree that it was unfair and a goddamn shame. She didn't try to minimize my feelings or ignore my anger. Even after months, when my sisters and everyone else were telling me it was time to get on with my life, Joan didn't abandon me. She told me I'd get on with my life when I was good and ready.'

'She was a real friend,' Bonnie agreed.

'Yes, she was. I couldn't have gotten through those months without her.' Caroline took a deep breath, forced a smile. 'There's more,' she said.

'More?'

'Just when I was starting to get back on my feet, my mother fell and broke her hip, had to be hospitalized. My father is dead; my sisters both live out of town. It was up to me to make all the arrangements. My mother had to go into a convalescent hospital, and then a nursing home, because she couldn't really take care of herself anymore. Joan just took charge. She talked to the doctors, made all the arrangements, made sure my mother got the best care. She was amazing. I guess again, because of what she'd been through with her own mother after Kelly died.'

Bonnie felt a sudden chill. 'What do you mean?'

'You don't know about Joan's mother.' Another question disguised as a statement of fact.

'Just that she's dead.'

'Dead?' Caroline looked astonished. 'Who said Joan's mother is dead?'

'She isn't?'

'Not as far as I know.'

Bonnie realized she was holding her breath. She tried to release it, but nothing came. It was as if she wasn't breathing at all. 'What happened after Kelly died?'

'Her mother began behaving very irrationally. She'd forget things and go outside in her underwear, stuff like that, and she was talking pretty crazy. She'd had a problem with alcohol for years. It just got worse. Joan finally had to have her committed. More guilt for her to deal with. Naturally, her handsome hubby was nowhere to be seen.'

'Do you know where she is now?'

'Melrose Mental Health Center in Sudbury. It's a private facility, relatively nice as far as mental hospitals go.'

'Who paid for it?'

'Joan's inheritance,' Caroline replied, sardonically. 'At least that's what Rod used to say.'

'Do you think her mother knows that Joan is dead?'

'I don't think she knows much of anything anymore. From everything Joan told me, she'd pretty much retreated into her own little world.'

'Do you know her name?' Bonnie surprised herself by asking.

'Elsa,' Caroline said. 'Elsa Langer. Why?'

'I'm not sure,' Bonnie said honestly. The truth was that she wasn't sure of anything. 'Can I ask you one more thing?'

112

'Shoot.' Both women looked aghast. 'Sorry. Unfortunate choice of words.'

'You said at the funeral that Joan spoke highly of me.'

'That's right.'

'What sort of things did she say?'

Caroline raised her eyes to the ceiling. 'Let me see . . . that you were a nice person, that you were a good mother, that she admired you.'

'Did she seem obsessed?'

'Obsessed?'

Bonnie told Caroline about the scrapbook the police had found in Joan's bedroom.

'Really? I've never known her to be that organized.'

'Anything else you remember that she might have said?'

'I do remember one thing,' Caroline told her after a pause.

'Yes?' Bonnie asked, waiting, curiosity building.

'She said she felt sorry for you.'

Tears immediately sprung to Bonnie's eyes. Don't cry, she admonished herself silently. Not here. Not now. 'I really should get going.'

'It's been an interesting afternoon for you,' Caroline observed, leading the way to the foyer.

'Thank you for your time,' Bonnie said, opening the front door, grateful for a strong gust of wind that blew some much-needed air into her face. She opened her mouth, gulped at it like water.

'Who's that?' Caroline asked, stepping outside, directing Bonnie's attention across the street.

Reluctantly, Bonnie's eyes traveled toward Joan's house, watching as a dark green car pulled into the driveway and stopped. The door opened and a pair of well-shaped legs swung slowly out of the car, hands adjusting the hem of the narrow beige linen skirt before stepping onto the pavement. The woman had beige hair to match her beige skirt, jacket and shoes. She looked around, aware that she was being watched, and smiled pleasantly in Bonnie's direction, before starting up the driveway to the house.

'Nobody's there,' Caroline called after her.

'That's all right,' the woman called back, not bothering to turn around. 'I have a key.' She waved it in the air.

Immediately, Bonnie was across the road, Caroline at her side. 'Excuse me,' Bonnie persisted, 'but you can't go in there.'

The woman turned around. Her make-up was the same color as the rest of her. Put her up against a beige background, Bonnie thought, and she would likely disappear. 'I'm sorry. Is there a problem?' the beige woman asked.

'The woman who lived here died,' Bonnie told her, not sure what else to say. There was something vaguely familiar about the woman. Bonnie had seen her somewhere before.

'Yes, I know. I'll be careful not to disturb anything.'

'Who are you?' Bonnie asked. Instinctively, she knew she wasn't with the police.

'Gail Ruddick.' The woman extended her hand, displaying a small white card.

Bonnie extricated the calling card from the woman's manicured beige nails, aware that Caroline was reading it over her shoulder. 'Ellen Marx Realty,' Bonnie read. From behind her, Caroline made a slight whistling sound. 'I saw you at Joan's funeral,' Bonnie remarked, suddenly aware why the woman looked familiar. The back row with the hair, she thought.

'That's right.' Gail Ruddick looked distinctly uncomfortable. 'Awful thing that happened. Just awful.' She swiveled toward the house, then back, as if she were on a rotating stand. 'We've been asked to have a look around, determine what the house is worth.'

'The police asked you to do that?'

'No,' Gail Ruddick answered. 'Not the police.' Clearly she was reluctant to volunteer any further information.

'Who, then?' Bonnie demanded.

'I'm sorry,' the woman said. 'I really don't think I should be discussing this with strangers.'

'I'm hardly a stranger,' Bonnie qualified. 'This house belongs to my stepchildren. And my husband,' she added, unease tickling at her throat, causing her words to tremble upon contact with the air.

Gail Ruddick broke into a large, expansive smile, the white of her teeth something of a shock next to all that beige. 'Well then, there's no problem. Your husband's the one who asked me to have a look-see. In fact, he's the one who gave me the key. If you'll wait just a second, I'll open the door and give it right back to you. It'll save me having to return it later.' She proceeded to the front door, opened it, then returned with the key. Bonnie added it to her key chain, trying to keep her hands from shaking. 'Tell your husband I'll get back to him with an estimate as soon as I can.'

Bonnie nodded as the woman continued up the walk to the front door. 'Tell me,' Bonnie said over her shoulder to Caroline, her eyes never leaving the woman from Ellen Marx Realty, 'did Joan ever tell you she thought my daughter and I were in any danger?'

'No,' Caroline answered. 'Do you think you are?'

Bonnie said nothing.

'Take care,' Caroline said. 'Remember I'm here if you ever need to talk.'

Bonnie watched as Gail Ruddick disappeared inside Joan's house. Behind her, she heard Caroline's footsteps retreating, turned to see her closing the front door after her. Bonnie stood alone on the sidewalk, a little girl lost, waiting for someone to take her hand and show her the way safely home.

Chapter Thirteen

The Melrose Mental Health Center was located on over one hundred acres of land in the adjoining suburb of Sudbury, close to the Sudbury River, and only a short drive along Route 20 from Weston Heights Secondary School. Bonnie drove there directly from work the next afternoon.

'What are you doing?' she asked herself out loud, a slight variation on the ever-popular 'What am I doing here?'

'I'm trying to find out what's going on. I'm trying to get some answers,' she told the frightened-looking woman reflected in her rearview mirror. Why hadn't anybody told her that Elsa Langer was still alive?

Bonnie turned her car up the long driveway toward the magnificent white building that looked like something out of the old South, with its large pillars and air of decayed gentility. It was a beautiful day, a slight wind tickling the leaves on the trees, the temperature warm. People strolled the grounds of the facility in groups of twos and threes. Patients, probably, Bonnie realized, acknowledging a friendly wave with a nod of her head. Someone she knew? she wondered, dismissing the possibility. More likely one poor lost soul recognizing a kindred spirit.

She pulled her car into the large visitors' parking lot. When had she started thinking of herself as a poor lost soul?

She pushed open her car door, and swung her legs around, instantly recalling Gail Ruddick's similar gesture of the previous afternoon.

'Well then, there's no problem. Your husband's the one who asked me to have a look-see. In fact, he's the one who gave me the key.'

Bonnie thought back to yesterday. She'd waited all afternoon to talk to Rod, but he'd called at dinner time to say he'd be late, that they were laboring mightily to get everything ready for the convention in Miami, and that he'd grab a sandwich at the studio, she shouldn't wait up.

She'd waited up anyway, but she could see from his expression the minute he walked through the front door that this wasn't the best time to confront him. Not that she wanted to confront him exactly. Just ask him a few questions. Why had he sent a real-estate agent to Joan's house that afternoon? Why hadn't he told her Joan's mother was still alive? Was it true what Caroline had said about his many extramarital affairs?

She'd been rehearsing the questions all afternoon, trying to make them sound as innocent, as non-threatening, as possible. She didn't want Rod to think she was accusing him of anything. She wasn't, after all, accusing him of anything. She was just curious. Her life had been turned upside down, and far from starting to right itself with time, it seemed perilously close to securing itself in this position forever, leaving her balancing on her head and spinning like a ball on the nose of a seal, and if this was the way it was going to be, well then, she had a few questions. Was that too much to ask?

'Can I talk to you?' she'd ventured as Rod was climbing into bed, pulling the blankets around himself.

'Can it wait till tomorrow? I've had a really rotten day.'

'I guess so.'

He'd promptly turned around, planted a delicate kiss on her right shoulder. 'Sorry, sweetie. That's not fair. My kids giving you a hard time?'

'It's not the kids.'

'What then? Tough day at school?'

Bonnie shook her head. 'I went to see Caroline Gossett today.'

Rod propped himself up on his elbows, the blankets falling from his bare chest. 'Why, for God's sake?'

'I'm not sure. I guess I was confused about the things she said to you at the funeral.'

Rod took a deep breath, closed his eyes. 'And now, let me guess – you're more confused than ever.'

Bonnie smiled. 'How'd you know?'

'Caroline has that effect on people.'

'She seems like a very nice woman.'

'Things aren't always what they seem.' Rod laid his head back against his pillow, brought his left arm across his forehead, his hand falling across his handsome face. 'So what did she tell you? That I drove my ex-wife to drink because I was never there, that I was too busy running around with other women to pay her the kind of attention she needed, that I deserted her in her hour of need?'

'Sounds like you've heard it before.'

'She's been singing that song for years.'

'*Were* you playing around?' Bonnie asked, tentatively.

Rod lifted his hand from his face, looked Bonnie straight in the eye. 'No,' he said. 'Although God knows I had ample opportunity. God knows I thought about it often enough. Does that make me guilty?'

Bonnie leaned over and kissed Rod gently on the lips in response.

'Can I go to sleep now?' he asked, about to turn over.

'Did you know that Joan's mother is still alive?'

'Elsa's still alive? No, I didn't realize that.'

'She's in a mental health facility in Sudbury.'

Rod said nothing, drawing Bonnie's arm around his waist as he flipped back onto his side. 'Wherever she is is no longer any concern of mine,' he mumbled.

'Have the kids ever said anything about her?'

'Not to me. Can we talk about this tomorrow?'

Bonnie lapsed into silence. 'I love you,' she whispered, after a slight pause.

'I love you too, sweetheart. I'm sorry. I'll have more energy in the morning.'

'Can I ask you one more thing?'

'Sure.' His voice was muffled, balancing on the brink of sleep.

'You didn't tell me you were having a real-estate agent look at Joan's house.'

Rod said nothing. Beneath her arm, Bonnie felt his body stiffen.

'The real-estate agent came by as I was leaving Caroline's house,' she explained.

'What's your question?' Rod's voice was as taut as the muscles beneath Bonnie's fingers.

'I was just wondering why you were having someone look at the house . . .'

'Why shouldn't I have someone look at it?'

'It just seems a little . . . premature,' Bonnie ventured.

Rod sat up, impatiently pushed the covers off him, got out of bed. 'Premature? The house is mine, for God's sake. I've been paying the mortgage on it for over ten years. It belongs to me and my children. It's their future we're talking about, and I want what's best for them. Is there something wrong with that? Don't you think I should have some idea what the house is worth and what my options are?'

'I was just worried what the police might think . . .'

'I don't give a damn what the police think. It's what *you're* thinking that's concerning me.'

'I just wondered why you hadn't said anything to me about it, that's all.'

'Probably because I've been working my tail off trying to get ready for this damn conference in Miami, and I haven't had two minutes to think, let alone fill you in on every little insignificant detail that's been going on in my life.' He threw his hands up in the air, paced back and forth in front of the bed, naked except for a pair of light blue boxer shorts. 'You want details? Okay, here's details. I'm up to my eyeballs at work, Marla's got her back up about something, and I get a phone call from some real-estate agent who says I should be thinking about selling the house now while the market is back on its feet, because who knows how long that's going to last. Is this detailed enough for you?'

'Rod . . .'

'So I said I thought it was probably too early to be thinking about selling at this point, and she said, what harm would it do to go in and have a look around, give me some idea of what we could get for the place? I said that sounded reasonable, but then, what do I know? I'm just some philandering s.o.b. who deserted his ex-wife and kids.' He stopped pacing, facing Bonnie directly. 'Maybe I even arranged to have the woman killed.' He paused. 'Is that what you're thinking, Bonnie? Is that what these questions are really all about?'

Bonnie said nothing. Was he right? Could that really have been what she'd been thinking?

Rod's features suddenly softened, saddened. His voice trailed after him, like a small child searching for an adult's hand. 'Bonnie, answer me. Do you honestly think I could have had anything to do with Joan's death? Because if you do . . . I mean, what are we doing here? How can you bear to be in the same room with me, let alone in the same bed?'

He was right, Bonnie thought, her head spinning. What was the matter with her? Had she not realized the way her questions would be interpreted? What other way *could* they be interpreted, for God's sake? 'Rod, I'm so sorry,' Bonnie said, wanting to touch him, but afraid she'd be rebuffed. 'I don't know what to say. I know you had nothing to do with Joan's death. I never meant to imply . . .'

Rod shook his head slowly from side to side. 'Okay, okay. It's okay. It'll be okay,' he repeated, as if it were a mantra, as if the very repetition of the word would make it so. 'Let's just get some sleep.' He climbed back into bed. 'I'm tired. I'm not thinking straight. I'm probably overreacting. I'm sorry if I jumped down your throat. It'll be okay. I'll be all right in the morning. All I need is a good's night's sleep. We'll talk in the morning.'

But by the time Bonnie came out of the shower, he'd already left for work. The note on the kitchen table said he'd be late again, she shouldn't wait up.

'So, what is it I hope to accomplish?' Bonnie asked, walking toward the sprawling premises of the Melrose Mental Health Center. 'Am I trying to clear my name, to put this family together? Just what do I hope to find out from some poor old drunk who lives in her own little world?' So now she was talking to herself, she thought, cutting across the front lawn. 'I'll fit right in.'

An elderly woman sitting on a nearby bench waved her over. 'I know you,' the woman declared, as Bonnie approached, trying to place the woman's wrinkle-lined face. 'You're that famous actress. The one who died.'

Wonderful, Bonnie thought, quickly spinning around on her heels, feeling them sink into the grass, as she made her way to the front entrance.

Inside, the place assumed the air of forced joviality common to most such institutions. Wide hallways, peach-colored walls, Picasso lithographs of flowers and harlequins, an attractive middle-aged woman behind a large ivory-colored desk in the spacious, well-lit reception area. Bonnie approached the desk cautiously.

'Yes,' the woman said, her wide smile revealing her entire upper gum. 'Can I help you?'

You can tell me to turn around and go home, Bonnie thought, fixing on the woman's violet eyes, wondering if they were real or contacts. You never knew these days. Things weren't always what they seemed. Wasn't that what Rod had said? 'Where would I find Elsa Langer?' she heard herself ask.

The receptionist referred to her computer. 'Langer, you said?'

'Yes, Elsa Langer.'

121

'Elsa Langer. Yes, here she is. Room three hundred and twelve in the south wing. The elevators are over there.' She pointed to her right.

'Thank you.' Bonnie didn't move.

'You can go right up.'

Bonnie nodded, willing her legs to move. They didn't.

'Is something wrong?'

'It's just that I haven't seen Mrs Langer in a long time,' she lied, wondering if the receptionist could read her as easily as Caroline Gossett had, 'and I'm not sure what to expect.' That part, at least, was the truth.

Bonnie stepped off the elevator at the third floor, and took a slow look around. The walls were blue; Matisse had replaced Picasso as the artist of choice. A visitors' lounge was located several steps to the right, situated across from a nursing station. Several large arrangements of flowers sat on the counter waiting to be delivered. Maybe she should have brought Elsa Langer some flowers, Bonnie thought, tucking two newly purchased magazines under her arm, *Vogue* and *Bazaar*. The latest in spring fashions. Just what the woman needed.

Several nurses were busy chatting as Bonnie approached the station. They looked up, noted her presence, returned to their conversation. Clearly, customer service wasn't a high priority. Bonnie waited, glancing toward the visitors' lounge, noting a young woman seated silently between a middle-aged man and woman, probably her parents, the mother in tears, the father staring absently into space, as if he couldn't quite believe this was happening to him. Another woman sat with her arm around a young man who was ferociously picking invisible lint off his clothing. 'There, there,' the woman kept muttering. 'There, there.'

Bonnie turned to the nurses. 'Excuse me, but could you direct me to room three hundred and twelve?'

'That way,' one of the nurses pointed, without bothering to look up.

'Thank you.'

In the next instant, Bonnie was standing in front of the closed door to room three hundred and twelve. What was she supposed to do now? Knock? Barge right in? How about turning around and going home?

'Come in,' a voice called out before she could choose.

Bonnie took a deep breath and pushed open the door.

A woman sat in a wheelchair by the window. Her hair was dyed dark brown, although at least an inch of gray roots was showing, and her skin was dotted with the assorted moles and liver spots of the elderly. Shapeless legs, like two large blocks of wood, protruded from underneath a quilted pink housecoat. Even sitting down, she was an imposing figure. Like mother, like daughter, Bonnie thought uncomfortably, although there was little other resemblance to Joan that Bonnie could see.

'How did you know I was there?' Bonnie stepped into the room, feeling the whoosh of the door as it closed behind her. Had the woman been able to sense her presence? Had she somehow known she was coming?

'I heard footsteps,' the woman said. 'They stopped in front of the door.'

Bonnie laughed. So it was as simple as that. How quick we are, she thought, to overlook the obvious. 'Are you Elsa Langer?'

'Maybe.' The woman smoothed her housecoat across her wide knees. 'Who's asking?'

'Bonnie . . . Bonnie Wheeler.'

The woman's thin eyebrows furrowed, moved closer together across the top of her wide nose.

'I have something for you.' Bonnie took several tentative steps toward the woman, laid the magazines across her lap.

The woman glanced down, looked back up at Bonnie. 'Thank you. What did you say your name was again?'

'Bonnie. Bonnie Wheeler,' Bonnie said, emphasizing her last name, hoping it might jog the woman's memory, continuing when it elicited no response. 'I knew Joan.'

'Did you?'

'Yes.' Bonnie wondered what to say next. Did the woman know her daughter was dead? Had anyone told her?

'I knew a Joan once too.'

Bonnie nodded.

The woman began making strange motions with her mouth, as if struggling with an errant piece of food, twisting her lips back and forth, in and out, ultimately popping a top set of dentures out of her mouth, balancing them on the tip of her tongue, then snapping them back in place with a sharp click.

'Has anyone spoken to you about Joan?' Bonnie ventured, trying to avoid looking at the woman, who was once again trying to push her dentures into the open air.

'Joan is dead,' the woman said, her words slurring together as she struggled with her dentures.

'Yes,' Bonnie said, her eyes casually absorbing the blue walls, the small dresser, the twin hospital beds. One of the beds had been neatly made, the other left untended, its covers bunched at the end and piled high in the center, as if there were someone still in it. 'My God, there's someone there,' Bonnie said, drawing closer to the bed, the shapeless lump in the center of it slowly assuming human form. Bonnie held her breath, trying to remember her mother in the days before her death, afraid to look too closely at the still figure in the center of the bed.

The woman's skin and hair were both ash gray, her cheeks sunken, her brown eyes open and blank, unseeing, as if she were blind. For a minute, Bonnie thought the woman might be dead, but she suddenly emitted a strange little sound, a rippled cry that disappeared upon contact with the air. 'This is Mrs Langer, isn't it?' Bonnie asked the woman in the wheelchair.'

'Maybe,' the woman said. 'Who's asking?'

'Bonnie,' Bonnie repeated. 'Bonnie Wheeler. Do you know the name, Mrs Langer?' she asked the woman lying in bed.

'She won't talk to you,' the woman in the wheelchair said. 'She won't talk to anyone since they told her Joan is dead.'

'I'm so sorry about your daughter,' Bonnie continued, gently touching Elsa Langer's shoulder.

'She used to visit every month. Now, no one comes to visit.'

'Mrs Langer, can you hear me?'

'She won't talk to you.' Again, Bonnie heard the sound of dentures clicking back and forth.

Bonnie knelt down beside the bed until her eyes were level with Elsa Langer's. 'I'm Bonnie Wheeler,' she told her. 'Rod's wife.' The woman's eyes blinked rapidly several times. Bonnie inched her body closer. 'Did Joan ever mention me?'

'Joan's dead,' the woman in the wheelchair pronounced.

'Joan was worried about me,' Bonnie continued. 'She said she had something to tell me, but she died before we had a chance to talk. I was wondering if maybe she'd ever said anything to you . . .' Bonnie broke off. What was she doing? The woman was a breath away from death, for God's sake. She probably couldn't even see her, let alone hear her, let alone understand what she was talking about. 'I just want you to know that Sam and Lauren are okay. They're living with Rod and me now, and we'll take good care of them. Maybe I can even bring them one afternoon to visit you, if you'd like. I'm sure they'd like to see their grandmother.' Why had she said that? They'd never so much as mentioned her.

Elsa Langer said nothing.

Bonnie rose unsteadily to her feet. 'I guess I should get going.'

'I told you she wouldn't talk to you,' the woman in the wheelchair said, a note of triumph in her voice.

'Did she ever talk to you?' Bonnie asked, glancing at the woman, whose dentures continued flicking in and out of her mouth, like the tongue of a snake.

'Maybe. Who's asking?'

Bonnie closed her eyes in defeat. 'Bonnie,' she said. 'Bonnie Wheeler.'

'The name is familiar,' the woman told her. She brushed her hand across her lap, knocking the magazines to the floor.

'Is it?'

'Maybe. Who's asking?'

Bonnie retrieved the magazines from the floor, and deposited them on Elsa Langer's bed, glancing furtively at the woman buried inside the crisp white sheets. A lone tear was running the length of Elsa Langer's cheek. It curved toward her lip, dribbled down her chin, like drool, then disappeared into the pillow. 'Mrs Langer? Mrs Langer, can you hear me? Did you hear what I said before? Can you understand me? Can you talk to me, Mrs Langer? Is there something you want to tell me?'

'She won't talk to you,' the woman in the wheelchair said.

'But she's crying.'

'She's always crying.'

'Is she?'

'Maybe. Who's asking?'

Bonnie exhaled a deep breath of air. 'Don't cry, Mrs Langer,' she told Joan's mother. 'Please, I didn't mean to upset you. I'm going to go now, but I'll leave my phone number with the nurses in case you ever want to reach me.' She leaned forward, touched the woman's soft gray hair. 'Goodbye.'

'It's been nice meeting you,' the woman in the wheelchair said.

'It's been nice meeting you too,' Bonnie told her.

125

'Liar, liar, pants on fire,' the woman sang out as Bonnie fled the room.

Chapter Fourteen

As soon as Bonnie got home, she called the office of Walter Greenspoon.

'Dr Greenspoon's office.' The secretary's voice was husky and smoke-filled, as if Bonnie had caught her in mid-puff.

'I'd like to make an appointment to see Dr Greenspoon as soon as possible,' Bonnie told her, trying to understand what she was doing. She hadn't intended to make this call. She'd spent the better part of the drive home from Sudbury convincing herself to let the police deal with Joan's murder, to stay out of it. Except how could she stay out of it when she was right in the middle of it, when she and her daughter might be in mortal danger?

'Are you a patient of Dr Greenspoon's?'

'What? Oh, no, no, I'm not.'

'I see. Well then, the first appointment we have available for new patients is on July the tenth.'

'July the tenth?! That's two months from now.'

'The doctor is very busy.'

'I'm sure he is, but I can't wait that long. I have to see him right away.'

'I'm afraid that's not possible.'

'Wait a minute, don't hang up,' Bonnie said, sensing the woman was about to. 'I have an idea.' She did? 'When is Joan Wheeler's next appointment?'

'I beg your pardon?'

'I'm Joan's sister,' Bonnie said, hearing her voice crack under the weight of the lie.

The secretary's voice also changed, becoming softer, even deeper. 'We were all very shocked and saddened by what happened,' she said.

'Thank you,' Bonnie told her, amazed by the things coming out of her mouth. 'I know that Joan thought very highly of Dr Greenspoon, and I'm having a pretty hard time right now dealing with everything, and I just thought maybe I could use Joan's next appointment . . .' She stopped, the lie too heavy on her tongue to carry further.

'I'm afraid we've already filled that time,' the secretary apologized.

Bonnie nodded, about to hang up. You see, her conscience whispered, lying gets you nowhere.

'But we have a cancellation for this Friday,' the secretary continued quickly. 'I guess I could give you that, although I'm really not supposed to. Can you come for two o'clock?'

'Absolutely,' Bonnie agreed quickly.

'Fine. May I have your name please?'

'Bonnie Lonergan,' Bonnie said quickly, temporarily resuming her maiden name, finding it an uncomfortable fit, like a too-small shoe. Why had she picked Lonergan, for God's sake? Hadn't she been all too eager to leave that part of her life behind? She hung up the phone before the secretary could change her mind. Two o'clock, Friday. She'd have to miss her final class. That was all right. She'd tell the principal she had an appointment with a therapist about Sam and Lauren. Which was the truth. Or at least not a complete lie. She did have an appointment with a therapist. At some point during the session, she would no doubt mention the puzzle that was Sam and Lauren. In fact, she might speak at length about them. So she wasn't really lying at all.

Bonnie suddenly became aware of music vibrating through the kitchen ceiling from Sam's bedroom. Well, not music exactly, she thought, taking some vegetables from the fridge, preparing to cut them into a salad. Rhythmic noise was a more accurate description – loud, insistent, relentless.

Bonnie pictured Sam lying on his bed, shirt unbuttoned and falling open, staring at the ceiling, thinking . . . what? Bonnie had no idea. Despite her repeated efforts, Sam had never confided his thoughts to her. Or anyone. Not to Bonnie, not to Rod, not to the principal or the vice-principal, not to the guidance department or the social worker or the school psychologist, all of whom had tried in the last week to get him to open up. It was useless. Sam came to school, did his work, hung out with his friends, played his guitar, fed his snake, smoked his cigarettes, and said nothing.

Lauren was much the same, refusing to accept professional counselling and keeping mostly to herself. In the two weeks since her mother's death, she was, by turns, hostile, passive, aggressive, and weepy. The last few days, she had lapsed into a kind of inertia that bordered on the comatose, barely making it out of bed in the morning in time for Sam to drive her to school, unable to concentrate, to apply herself to the task in hand. Perhaps it was too early for her to be back in school, Bonnie had suggested, but Lauren had been adamant. She'd be all right, she insisted, if everybody would simply leave her alone. Only Amanda seemed able to bring a consistent smile to her face. And Rod, whom she always waited up for, no matter how late he got home.

Perhaps they should take a few days and go away somewhere as a family, Bonnie had suggested to Rod, a few days to try to really get to know one another. Bonnie was beginning to feel like an outsider in her own home. All she wanted was for Rod's children to give her a chance. Perhaps they might go into therapy together. As a family. As a unit. But Rod said he couldn't afford a few days away right now, nor could they afford extensive therapy. What they needed was time, he insisted. Sam and Lauren had already taken Amanda into their hearts; it was only a matter of time before they allowed Bonnie in as well.

I hope you're right, Bonnie thought, quickly dicing through the carrots, then on to the English cucumber and tomatoes, to the beat of the latest in teenage angst, wondering how Sam could bear to be in the same room with anything so loud. She supposed she could go upstairs and ask him to turn it down, but she didn't want to do that. She'd never been allowed the luxury of loud music as a teenager. Her mother's health had been too precarious, her migraines too frequent. Bonnie and Nick had never been permitted to play their radios above a whisper. Not that Nick ever listened to what he was told.

Besides, the loud music was curiously welcome. It had a way of taking over, of banishing everything else to the back corners of the mind, of outlawing anything even approaching serious thought. As long as drums were pounding through their kitchen ceiling, she didn't have to think about the insanity of her recent actions – her visit to Caroline Gossett yesterday afternoon, her visit to Elsa Langer today, her scheduled visit to Dr Greenspoon on Friday. What was the matter with her anyway? Did she really think her amateur sleuthing was going to accomplish anything? Did she seriously think that by assuming an active role in the investigation, it meant she was still in control of her life? Was the illusion of control so necessary to her wellbeing?

Bonnie threw all the vegetables into a wooden salad bowl and tucked the bowl into the refrigerator, checking her watch. It was almost five o'clock. Rod was going to be late again; Sam and Lauren were in their respective rooms; Amanda was at a birthday party and wouldn't be home till close to six. Bonnie could afford to take a few minutes to relax, put her feet up, read the newspaper. Or she could finish getting dinner ready and put away the laundry.

She opted for putting her feet up. She lifted the newspaper off the kitchen table, where it had been lying since this morning, and after a cursory glance at the front page, turned quickly to the Life section and Dr Walter Greenspoon. Homework, she told herself. Research.

Dear Dr Greenspoon, the first letter began. *I'm afraid my husband might be gay. He has shown no interest in me sexually for some time, and lately, he's been increasingly distant emotionally as well. Also I found some gay literature at the bottom of his drawer. I'm just sick about this, although it would go a long way toward explaining a lot of things. We haven't had sex in some time, but I'm still worried about AIDS, which I understand has a long incubation period. Am I at risk? Should I confront my husband about my suspicions or say nothing? I love this man, and it would break my heart to lose him. I don't know what to do. Can you help?* It was signed, *Adrift.*

Dear Adrift, came the immediate reply. *You need to talk to your husband at once. A marriage cannot survive with secrets, and in your case, this secret could kill you.*

'Great,' Bonnie said. 'That'll relax me.' She put the paper down, stood up, and headed for the laundry basket she'd left at the foot of the stairs this morning. 'Might as well get this over with.' She lifted the heavy plastic basket into her arms and carried it up the stairs, the music growing louder, less melodic, with each step.

She put the freshly laundered bed sheets in the linen closet by the master bathroom, her underwear in the top drawer of her dresser, and Rod's underwear two drawers down. Next came his socks – most black, a few brown, all knee high. Bonnie opened the bottom drawer, prepared to toss the socks on top of the others, then stopped. *I found some gay literature at the bottom of his drawer,* she recalled instantly. 'Don't be silly,' she said, her fingers playing with the top of the pile. 'The last thing I'm worried about is that my husband is gay.'

Then what are you worried about? a little voice asked.

'I'm not worried about anything, thank you,' Bonnie said, but her hands were already underneath the rows of socks, pretending to be straightening them, to be making more room. 'Nothing but a lot of socks,' she announced. 'No deadly secrets here.'

And then her fingers touched an unfamiliar fabric, not wool or nylon, but . . . a plastic bag, she realized. 'A plastic bag full of socks,' she said, extricating the bright pink bag, noting the bold red heart painted on its side, and the curving black letters that spelled out *Linda Loves Lace* across its side. 'Not socks,' Bonnie said, peeking inside, slowly pulling out a delicate, see-through lavender bra and panties, complete with a matching garter belt and stockings. 'Everything *but* socks,' she said, extricating two lavender chiffon scarves, as she lowered herself to the floor, a wide smile creeping across her face.

Rod hadn't bought her sexy lingerie in quite a while. He used to do it all the time, she recalled, especially when they were first married. He'd surprise her with a little package – bikini panties, black lace teddies, push-up bras, not unlike this one. She examined the underwired bra, turned it over, checking the size. 'I thought it looked a little optimistic,' she said, noting that it was a size too large. 'A bit of wishful thinking,' she said, wondering what the scarves were for.

The phone rang. Bonnie pushed herself off the floor, answered it on its second ring. 'Hello?'

'How're you doing?' Diana asked, not bothering to identify herself. 'I had a few minutes and I thought I'd check in, see if the police were still giving you a hard time.'

'They've left me alone for a few days, but I'm not sure if that's good or bad.'

'Anytime the police leave you alone is good. So, how are you feeling?'

'Okay, I guess.'

'Just okay? What can I do to make you feel better? Go ahead, ask for anything. Your wish is my command.'

Bonnie held up the lavender lace brassière, her fist pushing against the half-cup 'In that case, I wish for bigger breasts.'

Diana didn't miss a beat 'Bigger breasts coming right up. Tits 'R' Us. Actually, you can have mine. What do you need them for?'

Bonnie laughed, telling her friend about finding the sexy lingerie in the bottom of Rod's drawer

'You're sure he's not a cross-dresser?' Diana asked

'Oh, God'

'Just kidding. Anyway, I gotta go. I just wanted to touch base, see how you were coping.'

'Coping's a good word. Listen, why don't you come for dinner Friday night?'

'This Friday?'

'You have other plans?'

'No. You're sure it's not too much? I mean you have your hands full. I should be cooking for you.'

'You don't cook,' Bonnie reminded her friend

'This is true. Your place it is. Seven o'clock?'

'See you Friday at seven.' Bonnie replaced the receiver, her fingers playing with the garters on the skimpy little belt, absently snapping each one open.

'Excuse me,' a voice said from the doorway.

Bonnie quickly stuffed the intimate items back into the plastic bag, turning to see Lauren, wearing the top of her school uniform over a baggy pair of jeans, hovering at the entrance to the room. 'Hi, sweetheart. Is something wrong?' Bonnie asked.

'I can't find my purple T-shirt,' Lauren said, careful not to look directly at Bonnie.

'I washed it,' Bonnie told her, crinkling the pink plastic bag into a ball inside her fist, and returning it to Rod's bottom drawer before reaching into the laundry basket for Lauren's purple T-shirt.

'You don't have to wash my stuff,' Lauren told her. 'I can do it myself.'

'It was no trouble,' Bonnie assured her. Please let me do at least this much for you, she added silently.

Lauren walked slowly into the room, took the shirt from Bonnie's outstretched hand. 'Thanks.'

'You're welcome,' Bonnie said gratefully.

Their fingers touched briefly, and in the next instant, Lauren was gone.

'Sam?' Bonnie knocked gently on the door to his room. 'Sam, can I come in?' She knocked again. What am I doing? she wondered. Did she really expect him to hear her timid knock over all the screeching and wailing that was going on inside his room? She knocked louder, banging

132

her fists repeatedly against the door. 'Sam,' she yelled, 'Sam, can I come in?'

The door to his room suddenly opened, the music erupting into the hall like lava from a volcano, threatening to swallow everything in its path. 'I have your laundry for you,' Bonnie yelled over the sound, pointing to the basket in her arms.

'Oh, great,' Sam yelled back. 'Thanks.' He stepped aside to let her enter the room.

Bonnie hesitated briefly, then crossed the threshold, glancing around to make sure the snake was in his tank, pleasantly surprised to find the room still in one piece. She put the laundry basket down on the sofa, then brought one hand to her ear. 'You don't find that just a little loud?' she asked.

Sam moved to the stereo, turned the volume down to a more acceptable level. 'Sorry.'

'No problem,' Bonnie told him, wishing she knew how to reach him, to get him to open up, to talk about his mother. Their relationship had obviously been something less than loving. Witness his strange reaction after he'd been told of her death. Where's her car? he'd asked. *Ding dong, the witch is dead.* But surely he'd been in shock then, surely he had to be feeling something now other than the total indifference he continued to display. 'It doesn't bother L'il Abner when the music's that loud?' Reluctantly, Bonnie's eyes traveled to the snake.

'Not at all,' Sam said. 'Snakes are deaf.'

'Really?'

'He can feel the vibrations, but he can't hear anything.' Sam walked over to the tank, tapped his fingers gently against the glass.

Warily, Bonnie approached the tank. The snake stretched toward her, as if on alert. Bonnie swallowed, forced herself to look closely at the reptile. 'He's really quite beautiful,' she admitted.

'I think so.' Sam's voice filled with almost parental pride.

'How big did you say he'd grow?'

'To about twelve feet, fifteen if he were living in the wild.'

'Amazing.' Bonnie wondered if she was talking about the snake or her close proximity to it. 'What's that on the bottom of the tank?'

'Western African coral,' Sam said. 'Or you can just use gravel.'

Bonnie pointed at the other assorted paraphernalia in the tank. 'And what's all this stuff for?'

'The thermometer is so I can regulate the temperature inside the tank. It shouldn't go higher than ninety-five degrees. Are you really interested in any of this?' he asked sceptically.

'Yes.' Bonnie realized it was true. 'Please, tell me.'

Sam's face grew instantly animated. 'Well, the warmer snakes are, the faster they grow. At night, I turn the temperature down to seventy-two, but no lower than that, because snakes are cold-blooded and they wouldn't be able to metabolize their food.' He pointed at the large rock to the far left of the tank. 'That's a heating rock. See the plug?'

Bonnie nodded.

'I keep the rock at eighty-five degrees. And these lights here are also for warmth.' He indicated a floodlight on the top of the tank. 'This one here's a hundred watt, and this long one that runs the length of the tank is a vita light that mimics the sunlight and gives him vitamins. That's his drinking water,' he said, pointing to a plastic red container filled with water. 'He loves the water. Sometimes, he curls up inside it. I keep it at ninety degrees. And that log is for shade, and when he wants to play.'

'Play?'

'Boas are very playful.'

Boas will be boas, Bonnie thought, but didn't say. 'And the cardboard box?'

'He likes to crawl in it to go to sleep.'

The snake's head banged at the top of the glass. Bonnie took an involuntary step back. 'He can't get out, can he?'

'Not yet. But when he gets bigger, I'll have to put weights on the top so he won't be able to lift it up. Right now he only weighs about ten pounds, but boas are unbelievably strong, and when they're full grown, they can weigh up to two hundred pounds.'

'Jesus.'

'Do you want to hold him?'

'What?'

'He won't hurt you. He's really very friendly.' Sam was already pushing the glass top aside, lifting the snake out of the tank.

'No, Sam,' Bonnie protested. 'I don't think this is necessary.'

'There's nothing to be afraid of.' Sam stretched the snake out for her to admire. 'Isn't he magnificent? See that iridescence. He's almost purple in places. In the sun, he's almost green. See how the colors get stronger and the pattern gets more concentrated closer to the tail.'

Bonnie's eyes traveled the length of the snake's body, then watched in horror as Sam brought the snake's head to his mouth.

'See, he won't hurt you.' The snake's tongue flickered toward Sam's lips.

'What's he doing?' Bonnie forced her feet forward.

'Snakes sense heat with their tongues. Their tongues are always moving. Look how long his tongue is.' He turned the snake's head in her direction. 'See this dark strip that goes right through his eyes.'

Bonnie looked closely at the eyes on either side of the snake's head.

'Snakes don't have eyelids, so they never close their eyes,' Sam explained, clearly the teacher here. 'Why don't you touch him? He feels great. Like silk.'

'Like silk,' Bonnie repeated numbly, her arm stretching toward the snake as if it had a life of its own. Her fingers touched the snake's body, as gently and as carefully as a lover's caress. Sam was right, Bonnie thought, stroking the snake's long body with growing assurance. It did feel like silk.

'Do you want to hold him?' Sam offered.

Oh God, no, Bonnie thought. 'All right,' she heard herself say. Was she crazy? What in God's name was she doing? 'What do I do?'

'Here.' Sam guided one of her hands toward the back of the snake's head, the other toward its tail.

'What if he starts squeezing?'

'We could get him off. We're still stronger than he is. Just don't drop him,' Sam warned. 'He hates to be dropped.'

Bonnie held on tight, felt the snake strain against her grip, amazed at the power she felt undulating in her hands. I must be out of my mind, she thought. 'I've been terrified of snakes all my life,' she said.

'You're doing great,' Sam told her.

The snake twisted its head toward her, its tongue flicking into the air. He really was magnificent, Bonnie thought, temporarily mesmerized by the sight of him, by the fact she was actually holding him in her hands. Her body swayed, as if under hypnosis. If someone had told her a week ago, an *hour* ago, that she would be standing next to a boy with blue-black hair, and an earring in his nose, holding onto a four-foot-long boa constrictor, she would have said they were crazy. And yet, here she was, not only holding the damn thing, but actually enjoying the sensation, the transference of power from the snake's body to hers. Undoubtedly, *she* was the one who was crazy.

Suddenly, the snake stiffened, shifted coils, like one of Amanda's slinky toys. He strained against her fingers and palms, threatening to spill out of her grip, to topple onto the floor. She couldn't drop him, she reminded herself, struggling to maintain her grip. Hadn't Sam just told her that he hated to be dropped? 'Maybe you should take him now,' Bonnie said, wondering what she would do if Sam refused, if he were to simply laugh and walk out of the room. Oh God, of all the stupid things she had done in the last few days, this was by far and away the stupidest. Did she really think this was the way to reach Sam? To get him to open up, talk about his mother? Did she really think that the way to a boy's heart was through his pet boa constrictor?

'Sure,' Sam said, easily lifting the snake from her arms, returning him to the tank in one fluid motion, fitting the lid tightly in place.

Bonnie felt suddenly light-hearted and giddy. She heard laughter, realized it was her own. 'I did it.' She laughed. 'I did it.'

Sam laughed with her. 'You were terrific,' he said.

'Yes, I was,' she agreed.

'My mother would never go near him,' Sam mumbled, then ran a hand across his mouth, as if erasing his words.

Bonnie held her breath, desperate to bombard the boy with questions, but aware she had to tread very carefully. 'No?' was all she said.

'She said he was slimy and disgusting,' Sam continued, eyes on L'il Abner. 'But he's not slimy at all.'

'No, he isn't.'

'She wasn't interested.'

'Yet she let you keep him in the house. My mother would never have done that,' Bonnie said, knowing this was true. She hadn't been allowed any pets as a child. Her mother's allergies, she was told, remembering the puppy that Nick had brought home one afternoon, only to be told he had to take it right back to where it belonged. 'It belongs with me,' he'd begged, to no avail.

'I guess.'

'What was your mother like, Sam?' Bonnie ventured, softly.

His familiar shrug returned. 'I don't know,' he said, after a brief pause. 'We didn't spend a lot of time together.'

'Why was that?'

'You'd have to ask her.' He laughed, a strangled and truncated sound, and rubbed the side of his nose with his hand.

'That doesn't get in your way?' Bonnie pointed to the ring in his left nostril.

'You forget about it,' he answered, a shy smile briefly illuminating his face, then immediately disappearing.

'Talk to me about your mother,' Bonnie said, watching him stiffen, his body swaying, like the snake now stretching toward the top of his tank.

Sam said nothing for a very long time. 'You think I should be sad that she's dead,' he said finally.

'Aren't you?'

'No. Why should I be sad?' His eyes challenged hers. 'She was a useless old drunk. She never loved me.'

'You don't think your mother loved you?' Bonnie repeated.

'It was only Lauren she loved,' Sam continued. 'She didn't have any use for me.' Again, he scratched at the side of his nose. 'And I had no use for her. That's why I'm not sad she's dead.'

'It must have been very hard for you.'

'What?'

'Growing up with a mother who drank, who had no time for you, who never showed you any affection.'

'It wasn't hard.' Defiance laced unconvincingly through his words.

'You must be very angry with her.'

He sneered, raised his hands into the air. 'She's dead. How can I be angry with her?'

'Just because people die doesn't mean our anger dies with them.'

'Yeah? Well, it's no big deal.'

'What about your grandmother?' Bonnie asked, switching gears.

'My grandmother? What about her?'

'I saw her today.'

'Yeah? She knew who you were?'

'No.'

Sam laughed. 'Didn't think so.'

'What did you say?' a voice asked. Bonnie turned to see Lauren, ashen-faced in the doorway. 'Did you say you saw our grandmother?'

Downstairs, a door opened and closed. 'Bonnie?' Rod called. 'Bonnie, are you home?'

137

'Upstairs,' Bonnie called in return, her voice filled with surprise. 'I thought you were going to be late.'

'I told Marla enough was enough,' Rod said, his footsteps on the stairs. 'I have a home, I have a family, I have a beautiful wife I'm not spending enough time with.' He approached the door to Sam's room, stopped when he saw Bonnie with his two children. 'What's going on?' he asked.

Chapter Fifteen

They were sitting on the end of the bed. 'I have a surprise for you,' he said.

Bonnie smiled at her husband. 'You're full of surprises tonight,' she said, listing them silently in her mind. For starters, his early arrival home, followed by his seemingly unflappable good spirits, his lack of anger when he learned of her trip to see Elsa Langer, his insistence on putting the finishing touches to dinner, on serving it, on helping Bonnie with the clean-up. He'd even sat and watched while Lauren read Amanda a bedtime story and then put her to bed, then spent a half-hour more alone with his older daughter. 'I think Lauren really appreciated the time you spent with her tonight,' Bonnie told her husband.

'I enjoyed it,' Rod said. 'She's really a very lovely young lady.'

'I wish there was something more I could do for her.'

'Just be yourself. She'll come around.'

'What did you two talk about?'

'Marla, mostly.'

'Marla?'

'You know how kids are impressed with celebrity.' He shrugged dismissively. 'She wanted to know what she was really like, if she was involved with anyone, that kind of thing.'

'Is she?' Bonnie recalled vaguely that Marla was between husbands at the moment.

'I have no idea,' Rod said. 'I'm her director, not her confidant. But I guess we'll find out soon enough.'

'What do you mean?'

'Dinner on Saturday night.'

'What dinner on Saturday night?' Bonnie asked. Had she missed part of the conversation?

'Dinner at Marla's house this Saturday,' he told her. 'Did you forget?'

'Forget? This is the first I've heard about it.'

'I told you a month ago about this dinner,' Rod said, 'although I'm hardly surprised it slipped your mind in the light of all that's happened.'

'Rod, I don't think I'm up for an evening with Marla Brenzelle. Besides, we don't have a sitter.'

'We have two teenagers.'

'We can't do that,' Bonnie protested. 'You know how Joan felt about using her kids as baby-sitters.'

'They're my kids, too,' Rod reminded her. 'And I think they'd enjoy it. They love Amanda, and she's crazy about them. Besides, I think it'll make them feel more like part of the family. Isn't that what you're always talking about – becoming a real family? They're good kids,' Rod said quietly, sounding somewhat surprised, as if he'd just been introduced to these strangers who were his two older children.

And perhaps this was the case, Bonnie thought, knowing that, much as she was loath to admit it, Caroline Gossett's assessment of Rod as a father hadn't been too far off the mark. The truth was, he'd never spent much time with any of his children, including Amanda. At first, he claimed she was too little, too delicate for him to hold. He was uncomfortable around babies, he'd explained, although that scarcely accounted for his discomfort now that Amanda was three years old.

Bonnie had always rationalized Rod's aloofness from his daughter as a fear of losing her. He'd already lost one baby girl to a tragic accident and his older children to divorce. He was afraid to get too close, afraid to allow himself the luxury of loving Amanda unconditionally, afraid of being hurt again. At least that's what Bonnie had been telling herself until Caroline Gossett told her otherwise.

Perhaps all that was motivating Rod now was a desire to prove Caroline wrong. Whatever it was, if Bonnie's visit to Caroline Gossett accomplished nothing else but to get Rod back on track as a father, it had been worth it, she told herself, taking her husband's hand in hers. 'What's my surprise?' she asked, banishing Caroline Gossett from the room.

'Close your eyes,' Rod instructed.

Bonnie did as she was told, feeling like a little kid, starting to giggle. She felt him leave her side, heard a drawer open, followed by the crinkling sound of a plastic bag. A hot pink plastic bag with a big red heart on its side. *Linda Loves Lace*, she read silently, trying to arrange her features into an appropriate configuration for surprise.

'Okay,' he said. 'You can open them.'

Bonnie opened her eyes, saw her husband standing in front of her, his hands tightly gripping the pink plastic bag. 'What is it?' she asked.

He dropped the bag gently into her lap. 'It's been a while since I got you anything,' he said, sheepishly. 'I thought this might jog a few pleasant memories.'

Bonnie feigned intrigue, then mild shock, as she withdrew the sexy bra and panties from the bag, followed by the garter belt, stockings and scarves. 'My, my, what have we here?'

'You always looked great in lavender,' he told her. 'And out of it,' he added. 'Are you going to try it on?'

'Now?'

'Unless you have other plans.'

'I have no other plans,' she said, standing up, Rod blocking her way, surrounding her with his arms, drawing her into a tight embrace.'

'I don't think you have any idea how much I love you,' he said.

'I love you too.'

'I've been a jerk.'

'No, you haven't.'

'I've been burying myself in my work, trying to ignore everything that's happened, not taking your concerns seriously enough, not being here for you and the kids . . .'

'You're here now.'

'I love you.'

'I love you more,' Bonnie said.

'I can't wait to see you in this.'

'The bra looks a little ambitious.' Bonnie held it to her breasts. 'Oh, well. What is it they say? More than a handful is a waste?'

'I always thought it was a mouthful,' he told her.

Bonnie felt her heart quicken. 'I like the way you think,' she told him, and he kissed her again, this time his tongue probing the insides of her mouth. Bonnie thought immediately of the snake, its forked tongue stretching toward Sam's lips. Instantly, she recoiled.

'Something wrong?' Rod asked.

Bonnie shook away the unfortunate image with a toss of her head. 'Let me slip into something less comfortable,' she whispered, sliding out of her husband's arms, and hurrying toward the bathroom, closing the door behind her, fumbling with the buttons on her blouse.

In the next minute, her blue skirt and white blouse were on the floor, along with her white cotton bra and panties. She stared at her naked body, immediately sizing up its faults: her breasts could be bigger; her butt could be higher; her stomach could be flatter; her arms could be firmer. Her face would no longer be mistaken for that of a teenager. She lifted the flesh at either side of her eyes, thinking of Marla Brenzelle. A little nip here, a little tuck there, a few pounds of well-placed plastic here, a few acres of discarded fat there.

She stepped into the bikini panties, pulling them over her slender hips. They were sheer and fit high on the hips, dipping into a deep V above her pubic hair. She sucked in her stomach, twisted at the waist. Why couldn't she have one of those tiny little waists, like the models in the latest editions of *Vogue* and *Bazaar*? 'Could I have one of those, please?' she asked her reflection.

'Maybe,' she heard a voice respond. 'Who's asking?'

'Oh God, don't start thinking about that crazy old woman now,' Bonnie said. Not when her husband was waiting for her in the next room, feeling sexy and loving. Her hands fumbled with the garter belt and stockings, wondering what she was supposed to do with the scarves. 'Something tells me they're not for my hair,' she said, taking a last look at herself, thinking that, objectively speaking, she didn't look all that bad. So what if the bra was a little big. It wouldn't be on for very long anyway. It had been a while since she'd dressed up for her husband this way. Would he be disappointed? She took a deep breath, opened the bathroom door, and stepped into the bedroom.

Rod had turned off the overhead light, and the room was in darkness, the moon providing only a sliver of light through the curtains. 'Don't move,' Rod directed, a disembodied voice in the dark. 'I want to look at you.'

Bonnie stopped, her breathing coming in short, shallow bursts. 'What if someone comes in here?' she asked.

'No one's coming in here.'

'Sam's still awake. I can hear the stereo . . .'

'No one's coming in here,' Rod repeated. He sat up, his face now clearly visible, his eyes slicing through the darkness like a knife through butter.

'Rod . . .'

142

'Do you have any idea how beautiful you are?'

'Tell me.'

'Come here,' he directed. 'I'll show you.'

In the next instant, she was beside him on the bed and he was all over her, his hands and lips competing for inches of her flesh, his fingers delicately caressing her on top of the flimsy fabric, ultimately unhooking, unsnapping, and discarding everything until she lay naked beside him.

'I didn't know what to do with these,' she confessed, opening her fists and releasing the chiffon scarves. They expanded upon contact with the air, like a sponge in water.

'I can show you what these are for,' he whispered. 'How adventurous do you feel?'

'Adventurous?'

'You always loved adventure,' he teased.

'What . . . ?' she asked, afraid to finish the sentence.

'I'll show you. Give me your hands.'

'My hands?'

'Ssh. Don't speak.'

'What . . . ?'

'Don't speak,' he said again, kissing her gently on the lips. 'You'll like this, I promise.'

In the next second, a scarf was wrapped around each wrist, and each wrist was secured to a bedpost above and behind her head. 'Rod, what are you doing?'

'Relax,' he told her. 'Close your eyes. Enjoy.'

'I don't think I can relax.'

'There's nothing to be afraid of,' he told her. 'I'm not going to do anything you don't like.'

'But I'm not sure I like this.'

His response was to kiss her. Again, she felt his tongue deep inside her mouth. Again, she thought of the snake, tried to banish it from her brain. Why couldn't she just relax and enjoy herself, the way her husband was directing?

Because it's hard to relax when your hands are tied behind your head, a little voice said.

Not when you know nothing bad is going to happen, she admonished the voice. Not when all you have to do is lie back and let yourself go. Not when your husband is merely trying to spice up your lovemaking.

143

When had their lovemaking ever required spicing up? Hadn't this part of their relationship always been the most natural? Hadn't they always fit together like a hook and eye, two conjoining pieces of a puzzle?

A horse and carriage? the little voice added playfully. Two peas in a pod? A hand in a glove?

What was she doing? Was she trying to wreck everything?

Maybe, a distant voice cackled. Who's asking?

Bonnie closed her eyes tight, forced her mind to go blank. She wouldn't think of anything but what was happening right now. And right now her husband was tracing a series of tiny lines across her naked body with his tongue, moving down between her legs. Her body arched to accommodate him, her hands struggling to touch him, to caress him, but unable to reach him.

When had tying up become part of his fantasies? Certainly, he'd never shared such impulses with her before. Maybe it had been something he'd decided on the spur of the moment, standing in Linda Loves Lace. Perhaps Linda herself had suggested it. Perhaps he'd been too embarrassed to refuse.

Or perhaps it was Rod who'd suggested the scarves. Perhaps he'd been inspired by a movie he'd seen, or, more likely, by something someone had confided on his TV show. *Do you have a secret sexual fantasy you'd like to share with our millions of viewers? Call 1-800 . . .*

Everybody had fantasies, Bonnie told herself. Just as everyone had secrets, a little something of themselves hidden from others. You couldn't possibly know everything about everyone else. So what if Rod had never shared this fantasy with her before? He was sharing it now. She was its prime beneficiary.

Instantly, Bonnie thought of the insurance policies Rod had on her and his children, policies of which she hadn't even been aware until so recently. How well did she really know this man, who was pushing his way inside her, to whom she'd been married for five years? *'You don't know my husband very well,'* she'd said to Caroline Gossett.

'Maybe you're the one who doesn't know him,' Caroline had replied.

'You're beautiful,' Rod was saying. 'So beautiful. I love you so much.'

'I love you, too,' Bonnie said, tears running down her cheeks. What was the matter with her? Where were these ridiculous thoughts coming from? Of course she knew her husband. He was a good man, a kind and wonderful man. They had a good marriage. She had no reason to be suspicious of him. If she wasn't careful, she could end up letting other people's petty and jealous suspicions ruin everything. If she wasn't careful, she would end up like her mother.

Oh, great, she thought, her arms straining at their delicate ties, inadvertently tightening the knots at her wrists. It wasn't bad enough that she'd allowed Caroline Gossett and that crazy old woman from the Melrose Mental Health Center into the room – now her mother was in bed with them too.

'Are you ready?' Rod was asking, sitting back, lifting her legs over his shoulders.

Bonnie nodded, focusing on her husband's handsome face, as he plunged toward her, like an image in a 3-D movie, pounding into her over and over again, his lips fastening on her lips, his arms stretching toward the bedposts, his fingers intertwining with hers, locking in place.

'I love you,' he said again. 'I love you. I love you.'

Bonnie felt as if she were on a merry-go-round, traveling in ever-increasing circles, growing dizzy with delight, every fiber of her body stirring, reaching for the brass ring, as the music of the carousel built to an impossible climax. Hold on tight, she thought, arching her back, wrapping her legs around the back of her husband's neck. In just a few more seconds, the ride would be over.

'Daddy?' a thin voice called from somewhere far away. 'Daddy?' The voice slithered onto the carousel, wrapped itself around the neck of one of the wooden ponies, stretched toward Bonnie's throat.

Bonnie opened her eyes as Rod pulled abruptly out of her, throwing the bed sheet across their naked torsos, although nothing could hide the fact that Bonnie's hands were tied.

'I don't feel well, daddy,' Lauren cried, her voice a moan. 'I feel really sick.'

'Okay, sweetheart,' Rod said. 'Go to your bathroom. I'll be right there.'

Lauren quickly fled the room. Rod jumped out of bed, grabbing for his bathrobe.

'Rod, for God's sake, untie me,' Bonnie urged.

He was immediately at her side, fumbling with the chiffon scarves. But her squirming had rendered the scarves too tight around her wrists, and he was only able to untie them from around the bedposts.

'My God, what she must think,' Bonnie said, trying to work the stubborn scarves off her wrists, but unable to do so. 'Seeing me tied to the bed like that.'

'She couldn't see anything. It's pitch black in here. Her eyes didn't have time to adjust to the dark.'

'We don't know how long she was standing there.'

'Daddy!' Lauren cried from down the hall. 'Help me.'

Rod ran from the room as Bonnie struggled to her feet, her body cramping in protest at having been so rudely disturbed. Just a few more seconds and it would have been all over, she thought, going to her closet, pulling on her bathrobe, tucking the chiffon scarves inside its sleeves as she headed for the bathroom at the end of the hall. A few more seconds and they would have been finished, her body would have been satisfied, her wrists would have been freed.

Was Rod right? Had it been too dark for Lauren to make out what was going on? Or had she seen everything? My stepmother, the pervert, Bonnie thought, approaching the bathroom, the unmistakable sound of someone retching coming through the door. Bonnie took a deep breath, then entered the room.

Lauren was hunched over the toilet, her auburn hair clammy against her forehead, her face ashen, her body racked by a succession of violent heaves. Rod stood by the window, looking as if he were about to be sick himself.

'Why don't you go back to bed,' Bonnie told him, moving to the sink. 'I'll take care of things in here.'

Rod needed no further prodding. His lips twitched into something approaching a grateful smile, and then he was gone. Bonnie soaked a washcloth in cool water, and pressed it against Lauren's forehead. 'Take deep breaths,' she urged as Lauren shoved her hand aside. 'Come on, honey. Take deep breaths. It'll help.'

Lauren struggled to comply. For a few seconds, it looked like she might be all right, then the heaving started up again. Bonnie tried again to apply the cool compress to Lauren's forehead. Again, she was rebuffed.

Obviously the dinner she'd made tonight hadn't agreed with Lauren's delicate stomach. Bonnie sat down on the edge of the bathtub, feeling guilty, wondering why she'd sent Rod away. Lauren didn't want her here. It was her father she'd called for. Certainly Bonnie could think of more pleasant ways to spend the balance of the night than watching someone throwing up. Yet she didn't leave. She waited, feeling the enamel of the tub through the warmth of her velour bathrobe. 'You're a good girl,' she heard her mother say.

'I feel so sick,' Lauren moaned, tears flowing from her eyes.

'I'm sorry, sweetheart. I wish there was something I could do to make you feel better.' Bonnie wondered again whether Lauren had seen her tied to the bedposts, whether that might be adding to her misery. 'This might help,' she said, again holding out the damp washcloth. This time, Lauren offered no resistance, allowing Bonnie to press the soothing compress against her forehead. 'Is that better?'

'A little.'

'Keep taking deep breaths,' Bonnie advised.

'My stomach hurts so much. I feel like I'm going to die.'

'You're not going to die, I promise you. You're going to be fine. Just fine.'

Lauren fell back against the wall, Bonnie immediately surrounding her with her arms. She wiped the girl's forehead, then moved the cloth to the back of her neck. 'How's that?'

'A little better.'

'Good.' They sat this way for the better part of an hour. 'Do you think you're ready to go back to bed now?' Bonnie asked, no longer able to block out the unpleasant smell of the small room, beginning to feel queasy herself.

Lauren nodded, allowed Bonnie to lift her to her feet. One arm wrapped itself around Lauren's waist, the other held her trembling hands.

'Slowly,' Bonnie cautioned. 'We're not in any hurry.'

'What's that?' Lauren asked suddenly, nodding toward Bonnie's wrist. A lavender chiffon scarf peeked out from underneath the velour bathrobe.

Bonnie dropped her hand to her side, her fingers pushing the scarf back inside the sleeve. 'It's nothing,' she said. 'The lining of my bathrobe is ripped . . .' Her voice broke off. She led Lauren to her bedroom.

'I'm sorry if I disturbed you and Daddy,' Lauren said.

'You didn't disturb us,' Bonnie said quickly, wondering again how much Lauren had seen earlier, praying that Rod was right, that it had been too dark for her to make out anything. She helped Lauren into a fresh nightgown, then tucked the girl into her bed. Then she leaned over and kissed her on the forehead before heading for the door.

'Bonnie,' Lauren called after her weakly.

147

Bonnie stopped. 'Yes?'

'Could you sit with me until I fall asleep?'

Tears filled Bonnie's eyes. This has been quite a night, she thought, returning to Lauren's bed and sitting down, making sure the chiffon scarves were tucked safely out of sight. Then she took one of Lauren's hands inside her own, and waited until the child fell asleep.

Chapter Sixteen

On Friday afternoon, Bonnie went to see Dr Walter Greenspoon.

It hadn't been a good day. Rain clouds had been hovering since early morning, and the cool temperatures were more suited to October than May. Lauren still wasn't feeling well, leading Bonnie to suspect that it wasn't her cooking that had done the child in, but a case of the flu. Whatever it was, Lauren was still in bed when Bonnie left for school that morning. She hadn't bothered waking her up, deciding the girl needed her sleep more than she needed whatever was on the curriculum of Bishop's School for Girls.

Rod had disappeared early again. Another breakfast meeting at the studio in preparation for the coming Miami conference. Nothing further had been said about the possibility of her accompanying him to Florida. That option seemed to have disappeared with Joan's murder. Besides, how could she even think of going anywhere and leaving the children? Despite the fact that the police had called yesterday with the news that test results revealed the blood thrown on Amanda to be animal, and not human, the fact remained that someone had hurled a pail of blood at her innocent baby. The child was in danger, just as Joan had warned.

I'm in danger, Bonnie thought, her car climbing Mount Vernon Street in Beacon Hill, watching as a white Corvette pulled away from the curb just ahead. My child and I are in danger, and nobody seems overly concerned. The police are indifferent; my husband is in denial; nobody has a clue what to do next.

Except maybe Joan's killer, Bonnie thought, a shiver vibrating through her upper torso. Somebody walking over her grave, her mother would say.

It's up to me, Bonnie thought, pulling her car into the spot just vacated. She stared up at the elegant red-brick house that was the office of Dr Walter Greenspoon, then checked her watch. It was ten minutes to two.

Just what was she planning on saying to the good doctor? What did she think she could get him to say about Joan?

Bonnie leaned back against the tan leather seat, closing her eyes and shaking her head. She certainly hadn't had much success so far. Josh Freeman was still studiously avoiding her. He hadn't set foot in the staff room since their last meeting, and every time she passed him in the halls, he lowered his head and quickened his pace, refusing to meet her gaze. Then there was Haze – he'd missed her last two classes, and the phone calls she'd placed to his grandparents had gone unanswered. She'd left a message asking them to attend next week's open house, but she didn't hold out much hope of seeing them there. Her talk with Caroline Gossett had raised more questions than it answered, and her visit to Elsa Langer had been an exercise in futility. So, what exactly did she think she'd accomplish by coming here and lying to Boston's premier pop psychologist?

'Oh, well,' Bonnie said, pushing open her car door and stepping onto the sidewalk, 'it keeps me off the streets.'

The red-brick townhouse was typical of the homes in this most exclusive section of Boston. 'Stately' was the adjective most often applied, and it was the right one. The eighteenth-century dwellings were cared for by prim and prosperous hands, the top windows arched, the small front gardens neatly contained inside low wrought-iron railings, the brass knockers on the latticed doors shining, as if never touched. Bonnie walked slowly up the eight front steps, eyes scanning the discreet side panel of doctors' names, pressing the button for Dr Greenspoon's office.

'Name, please,' the voice said clearly through the intercom.

Bonnie jumped back, looked around, as if to make sure she was the party being addressed. 'Bonnie,' she answered, hesitating. 'Bonnie Lonergan.'

The buzzer sounded – short, low-key, to the point. Bonnie pushed open the heavy front door and stepped into the black-and-white-tiled foyer. A gold arrow on the wood-panelled wall indicated that Dr Greenspoon's office was on the second floor. Bonnie proceeded up the blue-carpeted stairs.

Dr Greenspoon's office was located to the right of the staircase, behind double mahogany doors. Bonnie knocked gently, as if not sure she wanted to be heard. Another buzzer clicked open the door, and Bonnie stepped inside the office.

Two secretaries, one black, one white, both young and impeccably groomed, sat behind a large curved desk. They looked up in unison and smiled solicitously as she approached. Brass name plates identified them as Erica McBain and Hyacinth Johnson. 'Ms Lonergan?' Erica McBain asked, her husky voice a well-practised whisper.

'Yes,' Bonnie answered, noting that the secretaries' clothes seemed to have been selected to coordinate with the décor. Soft shades of gray and rose were everywhere, from the deep rose of the matching love seats by the window to the pale rose of Hyacinth Johnson's blouse, from the muted gray of the carpet to the charcoal grey of Erica McBain's skirt. Bonnie felt out of place in her green-and-white-checkered pant suit, like a weed in an otherwise well-tended garden. Surely her outfit alone would reveal her as the impostor she was, and she would be unceremoniously yanked from the premises

'The doctor will be with you shortly.' A well-manicured hand with raspberry-colored nails pushed a clipboard across the desk. 'If you wouldn't mind filling this out. The doctor's fee is two hundred dollars an hour, payable after each session.'

Bonnie glanced at the clipboard. Name, address, phone number, social security number, age, occupation, marital status, referral, childhood illnesses, recent illnesses, medications, reason for visit. 'Oh, God,' Bonnie muttered. So many lies to be written.

'Sorry?' the secretary asked 'Were you not aware of the doctor's rates?'

'It's not that,' Bonnie said, scarcely aware of the amount. 'I don't have a pen,' she said, knowing she had at least half a dozen in her purse.

'Here you go,' Hyacinth Johnson rolled a black ballpoint pen across the top of her desk. 'Why don't you have a seat?' Dark eyes blinked toward the matching love seats

'Thank you.' Bonnie carried the clipboard to the sofas, lowered herself into one, surprised to find it firmer than she expected. What am I supposed to do now? she wondered, her hand gripping the pen, her fingers refusing to write. Come on, she urged. You've come this far. Just fill in the blanks. A half-truth here, a half-truth there. You're the teacher – do two half-truths equal one whole truth? Enough of this nonsense. Name: Bonnie Lonergan. Address: two hundred and fifty Winter Street. They aren't going to check, discover that the name doesn't match with the address. Give them your phone number, for heaven's sake. They just need it for their files, in case they need to get in touch with you. They aren't going to go to the phone company, looking for discrepancies. Excuse me, but our investigation shows no one by the name of Bonnie Lonergan living at this address and registered to this phone number . . .

Bonnie couldn't remember her social security number, although she'd always known it by heart, and had to fumble in her purse for her wallet. She found it, dropped it, watched her driver's license tumble onto the carpet, reveal her true identity for all to see. Except that nobody was looking. Erica McBain and Hyacinth Johnson were too busy answering the phones and working at their computers to worry about her misplaced identity.

'This is ridiculous,' Bonnie muttered under her breath, copying down her social security number. She had to calm down. Otherwise she'd have a nervous breakdown right in the doctor's office, and he'd have her committed. Which might not be such a bad idea, she thought.

'Ms Lonergan?' a male voice asked, and Bonnie jumped. Once again, her wallet slipped off her lap to the floor. The man knelt down to retrieve it, Bonnie recognizing his bald head from his newspaper photograph. She held her breath as Dr Walter Greenspoon picked up her wallet, his thumb across her driver's license, blotting out her name. 'Why don't you come inside?' he asked, returning the wallet to her clammy hand.

Bonnie nodded at the secretaries, although neither was looking her way, and followed Dr Greenspoon into his office, a wonderful room that was all windows and built-in bookshelves. Two burgundy leather sofas sat across from one another, a long oval glass coffee table between them. A large mahogany desk sat off to one corner, as well as another small glass table and two pink-and-gray-pinstriped chairs. Several large plants stretched toward the ceiling from corners of the room.

Walter Greenspoon himself was about fifty years of age and larger than Bonnie expected. Maybe it was because his picture in the paper revealed him only as a tidy grouping of head and shoulders that she was so surprised by his almost unruly size. He was well over six feet tall, with the massive chest and muscular arms of a running back. As if to balance this exaggerated masculine image, he wore a pale pink shirt and red paisley tie. His eyes were blue, his chin soft, his voice an interesting blend of gentle authority. 'I'll take that,' he said, indicating the clipboard.

'I haven't finished . . .'

'That's all right. We can finish it together. Have a seat.'

Bonnie sat down on one of the burgundy leather sofas, Dr Greenspoon sitting directly across from her on the other. She watched while he perused the information she'd already jotted down.

'Bonnie Lonergan?'

Bonnie cleared her throat. 'Yes.' She cleared it again.

'How old are you, Bonnie? Do you mind my asking?'

'I'll be thirty-five in June,' she told him.

'And you live in Weston, I see. Nice area.'

'Yes.'

'And you're married?'

'Yes. Five years.'

'Children?'

'A daughter. She's three. And two stepchildren,' she added, then bit down hard on her tongue. Why had she told him that?

'What's your occupation?'

'I'm a high school teacher. English,' Bonnie answered, wondering at what stage she could comfortably interrupt this needless exchange of information and get to the point of her visit. Still, it was probably a good idea to ease into things, to get the doctor to relax, as he was undoubtedly trying to do with her, before she began prodding him for information.

'Do you like teaching?'

'I love it,' Bonnie answered, truthfully.

'That's good. I don't talk to a lot of people who are satisfied with their work, and that's a shame. Are you having any medical problems?'

'No.'

'No migraines, stomach cramps, dizziness?'

'No, I'm disgustingly healthy. I never get sick.'

He smiled. 'Are you taking any medication?'

'Birth control pills.' Was that the kind of medication he meant?

'Any childhood diseases?'

'Chickenpox.' Guiltily, she touched a small scar above her right eyebrow. 'My mother warned me not to scratch.'

'That's what mothers are for. Why don't you tell me a bit about her?'

'What?'

'I just like to get a little background on my patients before we begin,' he said casually.

'I don't really think that's necessary,' Bonnie told him. 'I mean, I'm not here to talk about my mother.'

'You don't want to talk about her?'

'There's nothing to say. Besides, you know about her,' Bonnie stumbled, suddenly remembering she was supposed to be Joan's sister. Had Dr Greenspoon forgotten who she was supposed to be as well?

'I know about her,' he repeated.

'Dr Greenspoon,' Bonnie began, 'I'm Joan Wheeler's sister.'

Walter Greenspoon laid down the clipboard on the seat beside him. 'I'm sorry. I must have mixed things up. Forgive me. Were you and Joan close?'

'Not really.' Bonnie breathed a sigh of relief. At last, the truth.

'Still, you must have been stunned by her murder.'

'Yes, I was.'

'Do you want to talk to me about it?'

'Actually, I was hoping you would talk to me,' Bonnie told him.

'I'm not sure I follow.'

Bonnie looked into her lap, then up at the doctor, then back at her lap. 'I know that Joan had been seeing you.'

'She told you that?'

'Yes.'

Dr Greenspoon said nothing.

'My sister had a lot of problems, Doctor, as you know. She'd lost a child; she was divorced; she was an alcoholic.'

Still the doctor said nothing.

'And I know that she was trying to get her life back together. She told me that she was determined to stop drinking, and that she was seeing you.'

'What else did she tell you?'

'That she was worried about something. Someone, actually,' Bonnie corrected, wishing she knew what the doctor was thinking. 'Her ex-husband's wife and daughter,' Bonnie said, holding her breath until it hurt and she was forced to release it.

'She was worried about her ex-husband's wife and daughter?' Dr Greenspoon said, in that infuriating way he had of repeating everything she said.

154

'Yes.'

'Why would she be worried about her ex-husband's wife and daughter?'

'I don't know. I was hoping you could tell me.'

There was a moment of silence. 'Perhaps you could tell me a little more.'

'I don't know any more.' Bonnie heard her voice rise. She fidgeted in her seat, brought her hands into her lap, cleared her throat, started again. 'I don't know any more,' she repeated, her voice imitating the calm of the secretaries outside the door. 'I just know that she was very worried about them. She told me that she felt they were in some kind of danger.'

'She thought they were in danger?'

'Yes. She made quite a point of telling me that she was afraid for them, and she asked me whether I thought she should contact her husband's ex-wife and warn her?'

'Warn her of what?'

'That she was in danger,' Bonnie repeated in frustration. Was Dr Greenspoon stupid or was he being deliberately obtuse? Maybe his two young secretaries actually wrote his advice column and the good doctor merely lent his head, shoulders and stamp of male authority to the project.

'Why are you here exactly?' the doctor asked, after a pause.

'Well, I've been worrying a lot about what she said,' Bonnie told him, stuttering over her words. 'I mean, I didn't give it much thought initially. I just assumed Joan had been drinking and she was talking her usual nonsense. But then, after she was murdered, I started to think more about it, and I started to worry that maybe I should be doing something . . .'

'Aren't the police investigating the matter?'

'I don't think they're giving it a very high priority, no.'

'And you think they should?'

'I think that one woman has already died, and another woman and her child might be in danger.'

'You think there's a connection between the two?'

'You don't?'

'I'm not sure what to think.'

'I was hoping you could help me,' Bonnie said.

'Help you with what exactly?'

'Well, if there's anything that Joan said to you that might be beneficial . . .'

'I can't divulge anything that was said in this office between Joan and me,' the doctor explained gently.

'But if it would help save lives . . .'

'I can't break a patient's confidence.'

'Even if the patient is dead? Even if the patient has been murdered? If there's a real danger that someone else might die?'

'I'm cooperating with the police as best I can. I've already shared with them everything I think might be pertinent.'

'But the police aren't doing anything.'

Dr Greenspoon lifted his hands into the air, palms up. 'I have no control over that, I'm afraid.'

'Dr Greenspoon,' Bonnie began again, trying a different approach, 'please try to understand. My sister is dead. She's been murdered, and no one seems to have any clue who killed her. I was hoping that maybe you might be able to tell me something that might help us find her killer.'

'I wish I could,' the doctor replied.

'Was Joan afraid of something? Of someone? Did she say anything about any of the men in her life? About a Josh Freeman, for example? Or a Nick Lon—' She broke off abruptly. 'Someone named Nick,' she said.

'You know I can't divulge that information.'

'Dr Greenspoon, the police found something in Joan's home,' Bonnie began, trying yet another approach. 'They found a scrapbook.'

Walter Greenspoon's expression grew quizzical. 'A scrapbook?'

'A scrapbook about Joan's ex-husband's new family. Everything from their wedding announcement to pictures of their little girl. It was almost as if Joan was obsessed.'

The doctor said nothing, obviously waiting for her to continue.

'Was she obsessed, Doctor?'

'Why don't you tell me more about what was in the scrapbook,' Dr Greenspoon said.

Bonnie took a deep breath, sensing for the first time that he might be willing to help her. 'Mostly it was about the woman Rod married. Rod is Joan's ex-husband,' Bonnie clarified.

He nodded. 'And the woman's name?'

156

'Barbara,' Bonnie said quickly, wondering why she'd selected that name for herself. She'd never liked the name Barbara. 'There were announcements about Barbara's mother's death and her father's remarriage, about some trouble Barbara's brother had gotten himself into a few years back, stuff like that, as well as articles about Rod's progress at the network.'

'And you think this scrapbook holds the key to Joan's murder?'

'I don't know what to think. I don't know what to think about anything,' Bonnie wailed. 'That's why I'm so frustrated. Nobody will tell me anything. And I was hoping that if I came to you, you might be able to help me. You don't have to divulge any confidences. You don't have to tell me anything that Joan said to you. Just tell me whether or not you think Barbara and her daughter might be in any danger, and if you have any suspicions, whom they might be in danger from.'

'What kind of trouble had Barbara's brother gotten himself into?' Dr Greenspoon asked.

'What?'

'You mentioned that there was an article in the scrapbook about some trouble Barbara's brother had gotten himself into.'

Bonnie fought to keep her breathing under control. 'Conspiracy to commit murder,' she whispered finally.

'Conspiracy to commit murder?' the doctor repeated.

'Barbara's brother was a small-time hood with big ambitions,' Bonnie said, finding it strangely comfortable to talk about herself in the third person. 'It was funny, actually, because when he was little, he always said he was going to be a cop, that was all he ever wanted to be. At least, that's what it said in the newspapers,' Bonnie lied, wondering in what recess of her memory she'd held that little gem from the past. 'What is it they say? Cops and criminals are two sides of the same coin?' she said trying to recover her composure.

'Seems to me I've heard something like that,' the doctor agreed.

'Anyway,' Bonnie continued, 'he and his so-called "partner" got into trouble over some land development scheme, but the charges were dropped. A few years later, they were convicted of conspiracy to commit murder.'

'Tell me about it.'

'Well, I only know what I read in the papers,' Bonnie said, fingering the small scar above her right eyebrow, 'but apparently, it was some phoney investment scheme gone sour. One of the parties, who'd already given Barbara's brother a lot of money, got suspicious of how the money was really being spent, and threatened to go to the police. My . . . Barbara's brother and his partner hired a hit man to kill this guy, only the hit man turned out to be an undercover cop. Isn't that always the way?' Bonnie laughed nervously, wondering if Dr Greenspoon had caught her near slip. 'I mean, you keep reading about these people hiring hit men to kill somebody, and the hit man always turns out to be an undercover cop. I don't think there are any real hit men in America. I think they're *all* undercover cops.' Bonnie laughed again, a touch hysterically. 'Anyway, they went to jail. Nick got three years; his partner, ten, because he already had a record, and because it was rumored that he had mob connections. Nick was just small potatoes.' Bonnie's voice drifted to a halt.

'Is this the same Nick you mentioned earlier?'

'Yes. His name and phone number were in Joan's address book. So there does seem to be a connection, don't you think?'

'What do you think?' Dr Greenspoon asked. 'Do you think your brother might be involved in Joan's murder?'

Bonnie stopped breathing, the full impact of the doctor's words slowly seeping into her brain like thick syrup through a sieve. She opened her mouth to protest, thought better of it. What was the point? 'How long have you known I'm not Joan's sister?' she asked quietly.

'Since you called for an appointment,' he told her. 'Did you think I wouldn't know that Joan Wheeler was an only child?'

Bonnie closed her eyes, felt the leather cushion beneath her sinking to the floor. How stupid could she be? she wondered.

'Do you want to tell me who you really are and what you're doing here?' the doctor asked.

'I'm Bonnie Wheeler,' Bonnie told him. 'Joan was my husband's ex-wife. I'm the woman Joan thought was in danger.'

'I thought so,' Dr Greenspoon said, 'especially once you said her name was Barbara. Bonnie . . . Barbara. Two Bs.'

'To be or not to be,' Bonnie mused out loud, and the doctor chuckled. 'If you knew I wasn't Joan's sister, why didn't you just cancel the appointment?'

Walter Greenspoon shrugged. 'I figured that whoever you were, you obviously knew Joan, and just as obviously, you needed help.'

'I'm sorry,' Bonnie told him, her eyes still closed. 'I should have known I wouldn't get away with it.'

'I think you did know,' he told her simply.

Bonnie ignored the implications of his remark. 'You won't tell me anything?'

'For what it's worth, I can assure you that if Joan had said anything during our sessions that might point the finger at her killer, I would have shared that information with the police.'

'Did she ever say anything about me?' Bonnie pressed.

'More than that, I can't tell you.'

'So you won't help me,' Bonnie said, dejectedly, rising to her feet.

'On the contrary,' Dr Greenspoon said, 'I think I can help you a great deal, if you'll let me.'

'You're saying I need therapy?'

'I think you're a woman in torment,' he said gently, 'and that therapy could be very beneficial to you. I hope you'll give it some serious thought.'

Bonnie walked to the door of his office and pulled it open. 'I'm afraid one visit is all I can afford,' she said.

Chapter Seventeen

There was an unfamiliar black car in her driveway when Bonnie arrived home. 'Now what?' she asked, peeking in the car's front window, wondering whether Lauren had company. Except that Lauren didn't seem to have any friends, and she'd been feeling so sick the last few days, it was doubtful she'd have picked now to invite anyone over. Maybe she'd called the doctor, Bonnie thought, quickening her pace, key reaching for the lock.

The smell hit her as soon as she opened the door. Thick, pungent, full of exotic spices. 'Hello?' she called. Was somebody cooking something?

'We're in the kitchen,' Lauren called back.

She sounds healthy and cheerful enough, Bonnie thought, wondering what was going on. 'Lauren? Whose car is in the driveway?'

He was standing in front of the stovetop, hunched over a large pot, his back to her, his slim hips inside a pair of tight jeans, his blond hair falling forward, a large wooden spoon in his right hand. Even before he turned around, Bonnie could see his face, sense his impish grin.

'What are you doing here?' she asked, her voice so low she wasn't sure she'd spoken out loud.

He pivoted on the heels of his brown leather boots, spun slowly toward her. 'I thought you wanted to see me,' he said, 'and I decided it was high time I paid my big sister a visit.'

For an instant, Bonnie was too stunned to speak. Nicholas Lonergan, looking tanned and fit and tough as ever, brought the wooden spoon to his lips and licked at the bright red sauce clinging to it, as if it were an ice cream cone. Bonnie's glance shifted to Lauren, sitting at the kitchen table in her baby-blue housecoat, her skin color back to normal, her eyes traveling warily between Bonnie and her brother, as if she were courtside at Wimbledon. 'I don't understand,' Bonnie said to Lauren, trying to keep her voice steady. 'He came over and you just let him in?'

'He's your brother. I didn't think you'd mind.'

'How did you know he's my brother?' Bonnie demanded, her voice raised. 'He could have been anyone.'

'I recognized him from his pictures in my mother's scrapbook,' Lauren shot back defensively.

'Ladies, ladies,' Nick interjected with infuriating calm. 'No fighting over me, please. Play nice.'

Bonnie closed her eyes, felt her body sway. Let this be a bad dream, she prayed. Let me open my eyes and see no one.

'I'm sorry if I've done something wrong,' Lauren was saying, her words cutting into the edges of Bonnie's fantasy. 'He's your brother. Maybe he made a mistake, but he's paid his debt to society.'

'That I have,' Nick concurred, his voice crawling inside Bonnie's head, forcing her eyes open. 'And one of the things I learned in the slammer is how to cook. And nobody, and I mean nobody, makes a meaner spaghetti sauce than yours truly.'

'Meaner being the operative word,' Bonnie said.

Nick smiled, revealing the chipped front tooth he'd received in a fist fight when he was barely into his teens. A tough guy, even then, Bonnie remembered. 'Come on, Bonnie, loosen up. Sit down, put your feet up, enjoy a little fine cuisine . . .'

'It smells wonderful,' Lauren said.

'You're feeling better, I take it,' Bonnie remarked.

Lauren nodded. 'I woke up around ten, and I felt fine. All better.'

'Well, that's good anyway,' Bonnie said, avoiding further eye contact with her brother, trying to decide how to handle his presence in her home.

'Nick got here about an hour ago. He made me a cup of tea.' Lauren held up her empty mug as proof.

'A regular Julia Child.'

'Would you like a cup?' Nick asked.

'Just what do you think you're doing, Nick?' Bonnie asked, ignoring his offer, unable to contain herself any longer. 'What are you doing in my kitchen?'

'Making you dinner,' Nick said simply.

'I don't need you to make me dinner.'

'I wanted to do something for you.'

'I think you've done enough already.'

'What's done is done,' Nick said, after a pause. 'I can't change the past.'

'Nick was telling me what it's like to be in jail,' Lauren said.

Bonnie said nothing, focusing on her brother's face, still able to make out the young boy hiding behind the man's features. He'd always had an interesting face, even as a child. The kind of face that was constantly changing, buffeted by moods and circumstance, one minute sweet and kind, the next minute hard and cynical. A lover's eyes and a killer's smile. Full of the devil, as their mother used to say. 'You look good,' Bonnie conceded finally.

'Thank you. So do you.'

Bonnie leaned back against the kitchen counter, grateful for the support. 'I understand you have a job.'

'Yup. I'm in the travel business now. Anywhere you want to go, just give me a call. I'll get you the best deal in town.'

'I'll keep that in mind.'

'My dad's going to Florida the end of next week,' Lauren volunteered. 'With Marla Brenzelle.'

'Really.' It was more commentary than question.

'There's some sort of conference in Miami,' Lauren continued. 'He'll be gone almost a week.'

Bonnie glared at Lauren to be quiet. What was the matter with the girl? She'd barely said two words since her mother's death, and now there was no shutting her up.

'Think it's wise to let your husband trot off to Miami with the likes of Marla Brenzelle?' Nick asked, obviously enjoying Bonnie's discomfort. 'That's one hot-looking woman.'

If you like quilts, Bonnie was about to respond, thought better of it. Now was hardly the time or the place to get into an argument with her brother over some minor irrelevancy. There were too many important issues that needed to be discussed, pivotal questions that needed to be answered. *Exactly what was your relationship to Joan Wheeler? What was your name doing in her address book? Where were you on the day she was murdered? Did you kill her? What were you doing lurking in the school yard hours before someone emptied a pail of blood over the head of my innocent child? Could you be that someone? What are you doing back in my life?*

163

Yet how could she ask any questions about Joan with Lauren sitting right there? How could she demand answers about her daughter when Pam Goldenberg would be bringing Amanda home any minute? How could she get into any of this now when Diana was coming for dinner? 'Jesus Christ,' she muttered. She'd forgotten all about Diana. She hadn't gone grocery shopping; she didn't have anything prepared; she hadn't warned Rod about Diana's visit.

'Something wrong?' Nick asked.

'Just how much spaghetti sauce have you made?' Bonnie asked.

'Enough for the neighborhood,' came Nick's immediate response.

'Good,' Bonnie said, eyes drawn to the front window as Joan's red Mercedes pulled into the driveway and Sam and Haze bounded up the walk. 'Looks like we'll be needing it.'

'Do you want to tell me what's going on here?' Rod asked under his breath, pressing against his wife's side, indicating the living room filled with people. Diana, looking beautiful in a white sweater and black pants, was holding Amanda on her lap and reading her a story, Sam hovering nearby on the avocado-green sofa, watching, and maybe even listening. Lauren sat in one of two coral-and-white-striped wing chairs, Haze balancing precariously on its arm, occasionally leaning over to whisper something in her ear. Nick was temporarily back in the kitchen, putting the finishing touches to his self-proclaimed infamous pasta.

'Nick was already here when I got home,' Bonnie explained, pretending to scratch her nose, talking behind her hand. 'He'd already started dinner. And then Sam brought Haze home and asked whether he could stay, and I'd forgotten I'd invited Diana . . .'

'How are you holding up?'

'Surprisingly,' Bonnie confessed, 'I'm actually enjoying myself. It's nice to have a house full of people, and everyone seems pretty relaxed, like they're having a good time. How are you?'

Rod leaned over and kissed the tip of her nose. 'Well, it's not the quiet evening alone with my wife I'd been counting on, but I guess I can cope.'

Bonnie nodded. She was learning not to count on anything these days. Nothing, it appeared, ever proceeded the way it was supposed to. No one could be counted on to behave predictably. Her brother, for example, the golden boy, of whom great things were expected, but who instead dropped out of college to wander aimlessly around the country, disappearing into a life of crime, surfacing only when he ran out of money, ending up in prison. What was he doing now standing over the hot stove in her kitchen, happily preparing dinner for eight? And Haze, a boy whose disruptive behavior regularly interfered with her teaching, a boy whose tattooed arms angrily advertised his anti-social attitude, who'd threatened her, and skipped her last several classes, obviously saw nothing odd about inviting himself over for dinner.

And she was enjoying himself, Bonnie marveled, patting Rod's elbow as she headed for the kitchen, thinking that maybe now might be a good time to catch a few minutes alone with Nick.

He was chopping an onion as she approached, the knife in his hand moving with careless precision. 'Don't come too close,' he cautioned, not even bothering to turn around, as if he'd been expecting her. 'It'll make you cry.'

Probably true, Bonnie decided, thinking the onion an apt metaphor for the last few weeks of her life. She kept peeling back layers, only to discover more layers hidden inside. The more secrets she peeled away, the more secrets remained, guarding the skeleton buried at its core. The closer she got to the center, the sharper the onion's sting, the greater the likelihood of her tears.

'How well did you know Joan?' Bonnie asked, without further preamble.

'That's not what you want to ask me,' Nick said, sprinkling the bits of onion into the sauce, stirring it.

'It isn't?'

'You want to know whether or not I killed her,' he said, his back still to her.

'Did you?'

'No.' He swung around, smiled. 'See how easy that was?'

'What's the connection, Nick? What were your name and number doing in Joan's address book?'

'I called her a while back,' Nick admitted, after a pause. 'Asked her about looking for a house for me. I won't be staying with the old man forever, you know.'

Bonnie shook her head in disbelief. 'You're trying to tell me that you were house-hunting, and that you just happened to pick my husband's ex-wife as your realtor? Is that what you're seriously trying to tell me? That it was a coincidence?'

'Of course it wasn't a coincidence.' A hint of impatience crept into Nick's voice. 'I knew who Joan was when I called her. Maybe I thought it would be fun. Maybe I knew it would get back to you. Maybe I just wanted to find out how you were doing.'

'There were easier ways to find out how I was doing.'

'You made it quite clear you didn't want anything to do with me,' Nick reminded her.

'With good reason,' Bonnie said.

'Still angry Mom cut you out of her will?' he said, pointedly.

Tears sprung immediately to Bonnie's eyes. Don't cry now, she told herself. 'She didn't cut me out . . .'

'That wasn't my doing, Bonnie. I had nothing to do with what happened there.'

'No, you're never the guilty one, are you, Nick? You're just an innocent bystander moving from one disaster to another.' Bonnie swiped at her tears with the back of her hand. Damn it, why did she always have to cry when she got emotional?

'Told you not to get too close.' Nick pulled a tissue from the pocket of his jeans, extended it toward her.

Reluctantly, Bonnie took it, wiped her eyes, blew her nose.

'What would you have done with the house, anyway?' Nick asked. 'You couldn't wait to get away from that place. Bustin' your ass to get good grades, working part-time, putting yourself through college, putting as much distance as you could between yourself and the rest of us . . .'

'That's not true.'

'Isn't it?' He looked around the kitchen. 'And you did it. I mean, look at all you've got here. Nice home, good career, successful husband, beautiful little girl.'

'Stay away from her, Nick.'

'I think she likes me.'

'I mean it, Nick.'

'So do I. I really think she took a shine to me. Imagine, she didn't even know she had an Uncle Nick. Shame on you, Bonnie. How do you think Mom would feel about that?'

'You have no right to . . .'

'No right to what? To speak of the dead? She was my mother too.'

166

'It's your fault she's dead,' Bonnie said quietly.

The corners of Nick's mouth curled into a sad little half-smile. 'You're going to blame me for that one too?' he asked.

Diana's beautiful face suddenly popped into the doorway, her dark hair falling loosely around her shoulders. 'What can I do to help?' she asked, her eyes as blue as the waters of the Caribbean.

'You can relax and have Rod fix you another drink,' Bonnie said, still patting her eyes with the tissue. 'Onions,' she explained.

'They're deadly.' Diana stepped forward, took the tissue from Bonnie's hand, gently dabbing at some wayward mascara. 'That's better. Now you're perfect. That's a great outfit.'

Bonnie glanced down at the green-and-white-checkered pant suit she'd been wearing all day. 'I look terrible. But thanks for lying.'

'Hey, I'm a lawyer. I never lie.'

'You're a lawyer?' Nick asked. 'What's your specialty?'

'Mostly corporate and commercial.'

'Just what I've been looking for,' Nick said easily. 'I'm trying to put together a few deals. Think you might be interested?'

'Depends on the deal.'

'Why don't I call you when I get things a little more firmed up in my mind?'

'Why don't you stick to the task in hand?' Bonnie indicated the spaghetti sauce that was starting to bubble.

'Right you are,' Nick said, inhaling the rich aroma. 'Ladies,' he said, bowing deeply from the waist. 'I believe dinner is ready.'

'So, how long have you guys been friends?' Nick asked Diana, nodding toward Bonnie. They were grouped around the dining room table, Rod at one end, his children at either arm, Bonnie at the other end, Amanda on her left, Diana at her right, Nick and Haze buried in the middle. It was a small room, longer than it was wide, with peach-colored walls that matched the dozen baby roses Diana had brought and Bonnie had placed in the center of the pine table.

'Our husbands worked together for a while. And I just live around the corner,' Diana said. 'This is delicious, by the way.' She dipped her French bread into the sauce.

'There's lots more,' Nick said. 'I'll be happy to get you some.'

'Give me a minute.'

167

'You just live around the corner?' Sam asked, his interest clearly piqued. He'd barely taken his eyes off Diana all evening.

'One twenty-eight Brown Street,' Diana said. 'But I'm only here weekends now, and sometimes not even then. I have an apartment in the city, and it's easier and more convenient to just stay put, now that I'm single again.'

'You could have let Greg have the house,' Rod reminded her.

'Why should I?' Diana asked. 'It was *my* house.'

'Oh, that's right. Part of your divorce settlement from husband number one.'

'You've been married twice?' Lauren asked.

'Marriage doesn't seem to agree with me.'

'I don't know about that,' Rod argued. 'I'd say it's done pretty well for you.'

Diana pushed her now-empty plate toward Nick, brought her napkin to her full lips. 'I will have some more of this fabulous pasta, Nick, if you don't mind.'

Nick was instantly on his feet. 'Anybody else?'

'I'd like some more,' Bonnie confessed quietly, handing her plate to Nick, trying not to notice his self-satisfied grin.

'Me, too,' Lauren said, following Nick into the kitchen.

'So, you live alone?' Sam asked Diana.

'Yes, and I love it,' Diana told him. 'No one to answer to, no one to cater to, no one to pick up after. I go to bed when I want; I eat when I want; I do what I want. Not that I don't miss having a man around from time to time,' she qualified. 'There are always a few things around the house that need fixing. Stuff that requires a man's touch.' She smiled toward Sam.

'I'm pretty good at fixing things,' Sam said, eyes sparkling.

'Are you?'

'Yeah, I can pretty much take anything apart and put it together again.'

'Sam's really good with his hands,' Haze said, with a sneer.

'Well, maybe we can work something out,' Diana said. 'I have a few cupboards where the doors are just barely hanging on, and I've been taking showers in the dark for months now because I can't figure out how to replace the light bulb.'

'Taking a shower in the dark sounds kind of sexy,' Haze said.

'Not when you're alone,' Diana told him.

168

'We could fix that,' Haze said.

Bonnie squirmed in her seat, wondering if there was some way she could kick Diana under the table, stir her toward another line of discussion. Diana was a natural flirt, and a virtual magnet for men of all ages. And Haze had a way of deliberately misinterpreting even the most innocent of remarks.

'I'd be happy to have a look at the light,' Sam said. 'See what I can do.'

'That would be great,' Diana said. 'I'd pay you, of course.'

'That's not necessary.'

'I insist.'

Sam shrugged. 'Okay. When would you like me to come over?'

'How about tomorrow?'

'How about Sunday?' Sam asked, as Lauren returned to the room carrying two plates of pasta, Nick right behind her with two more. 'I was kind of planning on visiting my grandmother tomorrow.' He shifted uneasily in his seat.

'Sunday's fine,' Diana said.

'You're going to visit Grandma Langer?' Lauren asked, her voice incredulous.

'I was thinking about it.'

'Why? I mean, she probably won't even know who you are.'

'She might.' Sam stared toward his lap, clearly uncomfortable with the discussion.

'Who's Grandma Langer?' Nick asked.

'My mother's mother,' Lauren answered, her eyes clouding over with the sudden threat of tears. 'She's at the Melrose Mental Health Center in Sudbury. Isn't that where you said, Bonnie?'

Bonnie nodded, surprised both by Sam's announcement, and the fact that Lauren had asked her a direct question.

'Maybe I should go too,' Lauren whispered.

'Why don't I take you guys there?' Bonnie offered, silently preparing a list of reasons to counter the objections she knew were coming – I know the way; I've been there before; it might be easier with an adult present – surprised when no objections came.

'Grandparents are a wonderful thing,' Nick said.

'I live with my grandparents,' Haze said. 'It's a drag.'

Nick leaned across the table toward Amanda. 'Did you know you have a grandfather, Mandy?'

Amanda nodded, blond curls bouncing around her chubby cheeks, freckles of spaghetti sauce dotting her chin. 'Grandpa Peter and Grandma Sally. They live in New Jersey,' she said proudly.

'Not your daddy's parents,' Nick corrected. 'I'm talking about your mommy's daddy.'

'Nick . . .' Bonnie warned.

'You've never met him,' Nick continued, 'but he doesn't live very far from here, and his wife makes the best apple pies in the whole world. Do you like apple pie, Mandy?'

Amanda nodded enthusiastically. 'They're cool!'

'Cool?'

'That's what Sam always says.'

'Cool, Amanda,' Sam said, laughing. 'Give me five.' He stretched the palm of his hand toward Amanda. Amanda giggled and slapped at it with her own.

Bonnie laughed out loud, marveling at their easy rapport.

'Maybe you can convince your mother to take you to see your grandfather some day,' Nick continued. 'I know he'd love to see you.'

Bonnie dropped her fork, pushed her plate away from her, her second helping untouched. 'I'd better see about coffee,' she said.

Bushes of pale pink peonies stretched toward her as Bonnie made her way up the stone walkway of the Melrose Mental Health Center. Except that it wasn't the Melrose Mental Health Center, she realized, twisting in her bed, the realization that she was dreaming falling softly across her brain like mosquito netting. She tried to wake herself up, to pull herself away from the Center's front door, but the door was already opening. It was too late. She had no choice but to step over the threshold.

'Welcome home,' Nick said, waiting for her at the top of the stairs.

'What are you doing here?' Bonnie asked.

'I live here,' he told her. 'Are you here to see Mother?'

'She said she wanted to talk to me,' Bonnie said, leaning over to smell the flowers of the wallpaper.

'Come on up.'

Don't go, a little voice whispered as Bonnie turned over on her pillow.

Bonnie started up the stairs, her fingers running along the wall beside her, tripping from flower to flower, like a bee gathering pollen. She reached the top of the stairs and stopped. The door to her mother's bedroom lay open before her.

Don't go in there, a little voice warned. Wake up. Wake up.

Bonnie slowly approached the door, seeing the shrouded figure of a woman sitting up in bed, her face in shadows. Suddenly, Amanda was at Bonnie's side, tugging at her arm. 'Mommy, Mommy,' she called. 'Come on in. We're having a party.' She produced a large pointed paper hat and held it over her head. Immediately, blood poured down, soaking Amanda's hair, covering her face and shoulders.

'No,' Bonnie moaned, tossing from side to side in her bed.

'It's just spaghetti sauce,' Amanda giggled, strings of spaghetti twisting through her hair like tiny snakes.

'Have some,' Nick said, pushing a large wooden spoon toward Bonnie's mouth.

'Too many onions,' Bonnie said, swallowing, her stomach instantly cramping.

'Bonnie,' her mother called weakly from the bed. 'Bonnie, help me. I'm not feeling very well.'

'Too much apple pie,' Bonnie told her. 'We should have Dr Greenspoon take a look at you.' She reached the bed, tried to make out her mother's face in the shadows. Again, her stomach cramped. She doubled over, cried out.

'Bonnie, what's wrong?' Nick asked with Rod's voice, then again from somewhere beside her, 'Bonnie, Bonnie, what's wrong? Bonnie, wake up.'

Her mother shifted in her bed, her face slowly emerging from the shadows.

Bonnie strained to see her, stretching forward in her bed, her heart pounding wildly, pains shooting through her stomach. The pains woke her up, intensifying as her eyes opened and she realized she was no longer dreaming. In the next minute, she was on her knees in the bathroom, throwing up into the toilet, Rod beside her, smoothing her hair away from her face.

'It's okay,' he was saying later, sitting beside her on the tile floor, holding her in his arms, rocking her gently back and forth, in much the same way she had held Lauren just days ago. 'It's okay. You're okay now.'

'Jesus Christ,' Bonnie groaned. 'What was that?'

171

'You must have caught whatever bug Lauren had,' he said.

'I never get sick,' Bonnie protested.

'It happens to the best of us.'

'No,' Bonnie said, letting Rod help her to her feet, lead her back into the bedroom. 'It's just a bad dream. I'll be fine in the morning.'

'Get some sleep,' Rod said, tucking Bonnie into bed and kissing her on the forehead.

'It's just a bad dream,' Bonnie repeated, eyes closing as her head touched the pillow. 'I'll be fine in the morning.'

Chapter Eighteen

'It's just a few more blocks,' Bonnie told them. 'We'll be there in a minute.' She glanced quickly over her shoulder at Sam and Lauren in the back seat of her car, the abrupt motion sending a fresh wave of nausea spiraling through her body like a corkscrew. Don't you dare throw up, she warned herself silently. You are not sick. You never get sick.

So what was last night all about?

Last night was about a lot of things, she told herself, concentrating on the road ahead. Last night was about Dr Greenspoon saying too little, and Nick saying way too much. Bonnie jerked the car to a stop at a red light. How dare her brother come into her home, uninvited, unannounced, and proceed to take over her kitchen and disrupt her life, oozing charm and spaghetti sauce and ill-timed bon mots. *Did you know you have a grandfather, Mandy?* Where did he get off calling her daughter Mandy? Nobody ever called her that. And now the child was insisting she liked it. Last night when Bonnie was putting her to bed, she'd asked Bonnie to call her Mandy instead of Amanda. Like Uncle Nick does, she'd said. No wonder Bonnie had been sick.

She should never have let him stay. As soon as she saw Nick standing there in her kitchen, she should have ordered him from the premises, told him he was no more welcome here now that he was out of prison than he'd been before he went in. That's what she should have done. Why hadn't she?

'Is that it?' Lauren leaned forward in her seat, her elbows pressing into the front seat, her warm breath on the back of Bonnie's neck as she pointed toward the sprawling white structure ahead.

'That's it.' Bonnie turned into the long, winding driveway.

'It looks pretty nice.' Lauren bounced back in her seat, Bonnie's stomach lurching with every vibration.

What was she doing back here? Bonnie wondered, looking for a place to park. Why hadn't she stayed in bed, as Rod had advised before he left for the studio? Because it wouldn't have been right to let Sam and Lauren come here on their own, she'd told him, and besides, she wasn't sick, despite feeling flushed and faint. She took several long, deep breaths. I will not throw up, she said silently, pulling into an empty space at the far corner of the long lot, watching the scenery blur. I will not throw up again. I am not sick. I never get sick.

She shut off the car's engine, and pushed open the door, swallowing the outside air in one sustained gulp. But the air was heavy with humidity and provided no comfort. Within seconds, Bonnie was coated in sweat, her bare arms glistening with perspiration, as if she'd been freshly varnished. 'It's hot,' she said as Lauren stepped out of the car.

'Not really,' the girl said.

'Are you feeling all right?' asked Sam.

'Fine,' Bonnie insisted, bringing her hand to her forehead. Why was she feeling her forehead? She didn't have a temperature. She wasn't sick. She'd merely eaten too much last night. Something in her brother's infamous spaghetti sauce hadn't agreed with her, the same way that something in the dinner she'd prepared earlier in the week hadn't agreed with Lauren.

You must have caught whatever bug Lauren had, Rod said.

'Which way?' Lauren asked, as they stepped through the front door of the Melrose Mental Health Center into the expansive lobby, Sam lingering, falling behind as they walked to the nearby bank of elevators.

This was your idea, Bonnie wanted to remind him, still surprised he'd suggested it.

They stepped into a waiting elevator, several people already inside, the correct button already pressed. The doors closed, Bonnie's stomach sinking to the floor as the elevator lifted. She unbuttoned the top button of her striped shirt, pushed her hair away from her face, wiped some perspiration from her upper lip.

The elevator bounced to a stop. Water rose to the top of Bonnie's throat. She swallowed it down, once, then again, bolting from the elevator as soon as the doors opened, running toward the ladies' room across from the nursing station.

'Are you okay?' Sam called after her.

She got to the bathroom, closed the door, and fell to her knees in front of the toilet, her body racked by a painful succession of dry heaves. 'Jesus,' she muttered, trying to catch her breath, gasping for air. 'How long does this go on?' Another spasm shook her, pummeling through her insides like a boxer's fists. Tears stung her eyes as she collapsed against the bathroom wall, her hair sticking to her neck and forehead, her body shaking, one second hot, the next cold. 'I am not sick,' she said out loud, forcing herself back to her feet, confronting her image in the mirror above the sink. 'Do you hear me? I am not sick.'

Maybe *you* aren't, her ghostly image seemed to answer.

Bonnie splashed cold water on her face, and smoothed back her hair, pinching her ashen cheeks in hopes of restoring some color to them. She pulled a paper cup from its dispenser beside the sink and poured herself some water, trusting herself with only a tiny sip. 'You're fine now,' she admonished her reflection. 'Understand? No more nonsense.' She pushed her shoulders back, took one last deep breath, and opened the washroom door.

Sam and Lauren were nowhere around.

'Sam?' she said, attracting the attention of an elderly gentleman wandering the halls in his pyjamas.

'Did you call me?' he asked.

Bonnie shook her head, then wished she hadn't, the motion upsetting her already delicate equilibrium. They'd obviously gone ahead without her. And why shouldn't they? she asked herself, walking slowly toward Elsa Langer's room. The woman was their grandmother, for heaven's sake, even though they had little recollection of her, and she probably none of them. Still, they didn't need Bonnie to make introductions Probably she should just wait for them in the waiting area.

Too late, she thought, as the door to Elsa Langer's room swung open before her. 'Remember me?' the old woman asked from her wheelchair, allowing Bonnie just enough room to step inside.

'Hello,' Bonnie said absently, her attention focused on Elsa Langer, who was sitting up in her bed, propped up against several pillows, her lunch on a tray in front of her, Sam sitting in the chair beside her bed, Lauren standing beside her, both studying her blank face, seemingly mesmerized.

'I'm Mary,' the woman in the wheelchair said. 'I don't think we were properly introduced the last time you were here.'

'I'm Bonnie,' Bonnie told her, eyes riveted on Elsa Langer. Sitting

175

up, the old woman looked even more fragile than she had lying down, her body a mere skeletal outline of a human being, her skin all but disappearing into the whiteness of her bedclothes and sheets, her eyes blank and unseeing, like empty sockets.

'You came at lunch time,' Mary said. 'I already finished mine.' She indicated her empty tray. 'Chicken soup, macaroni and cheese, and vanilla custard. That's what I ordered. I don't know what they ordered for Elsa.' She wheeled herself over to Elsa Langer's bed and lifted off the top of her lunch tray, revealing a singularly unappetizing-looking arrangement of soft beige foods. 'Yup, same as me,' Mary said. 'But she won't eat it. She never eats unless I feed her.' She lifted a spoon from the tray, like a conductor raising his baton.

'Can I do it?' Lauren asked immediately. 'Please?' she asked the woman in the wheelchair.

'Maybe,' the woman said. 'Who's asking?'

'My name is Lauren,' Lauren told her. 'Elsa Langer is my grandmother.'

'Lauren, you said.'

'Yes, and this is my brother Sam.'

'Sam?'

Sam said nothing.

'Didn't know she had any grandchildren,' Mary stated, staring at Bonnie. 'Isn't it funny? You live with someone for years, you think you know everything about them, and then you discover you didn't know them at all. Don't you think that's funny?' she asked Bonnie.

Bonnie ignored the question. 'I'm sure she'd be happy if you fed her,' Bonnie told Lauren.

Lauren smiled, although the smile was quick, almost too brief to notice. 'Here, Grandma,' she said gently, lifting a spoonful of the chicken noodle soup to her grandmother's mouth, the spoon gingerly prodding the woman's dry lips apart. Lauren tipped the spoon toward Elsa Langer's throat, brought it back empty. Some liquid dribbled down her grandmother's chin, and Lauren quickly wiped it away with a napkin. 'Isn't that good, Grandma?' she asked, as Bonnie often asked Amanda. 'Isn't that good?' She tipped another spoon into the old woman's mouth, then another. 'She's eating,' Lauren exclaimed proudly, another smile appearing, this one lasting slightly longer than the first. 'Do you want to feed her, Sam?' she asked.

176

Sam shook his head, slumped lower in his chair, although his eyes never left his grandmother's face.

'She loves soup,' Mary proclaimed.

'Do you remember us, Grandma?' Lauren was asking.

Elsa Langer said nothing, her lips parting slightly to admit the spoon.

'You haven't seen us since we were really little. Do you remember us? Joan was our mother,' Lauren continued softly, her voice cracking at the sound of her mother's name. 'Do you remember her?'

Elsa Langer slurped at her soup.

'Joan is dead,' Mary said.

'I'm Lauren and this is my brother, Sam,' Lauren continued, her arm moving rhythmically between the soup bowl and her grandmother's mouth. 'We're Joan's children. Do you remember us at all, Grandma?'

'I'm sure she knows deep down who you are,' Bonnie told her.

'Why do you say that?' Sam asked, sitting up in his seat, leaning forward, eyes darting between Bonnie and his grandmother.

'It's just a feeling,' Bonnie admitted, the odor of the macaroni and cheese reaching up into her nostrils, curdling her stomach.

'Does my grandmother ever talk to you?' Sam asked the woman in the wheelchair.

'Maybe,' the woman replied. 'Who's asking?'

'Sam,' he told her, his eyes rolling to the top of his head. 'Sam Wheeler.'

'It's hard to keep all these names straight,' Mary announced. 'I mean, we don't have visitors for weeks on end, and suddenly, it's like a parade.'

'What do you mean?' Bonnie asked.

'Another gentleman was here this morning. A good-looking man too. Reminded me of my late husband, may he rest in peace.'

'Someone else was here?' Bonnie asked.

'Maybe. Who's asking?'

'Do you remember the man's name?'

'Maybe. Who's asking?' Mary repeated stubbornly, prodding at her dentures with her tongue.

'Bonnie. Bonnie Wheeler. Do you remember the man's name?'

'What man?'

Bonnie closed her eyes, took a deep breath. 'The man who was here earlier this morning.'

'He didn't say. But he was a good-looking man. Reminded me of my late husband, may he rest in peace.'

'Can you tell me what he looked like?' Bonnie pressed.

'He looked like my late husband,' Mary repeated.

'Do you remember what color hair he had?' Bonnie asked.

'I think it was blond,' the woman said.

Bonnie immediately pictured her brother standing over the stove in her kitchen, his blond hair falling into his face.

'Or maybe it was gray,' Mary said.

Bonnie saw Rod's face tilting toward hers as he'd tucked her in bed last night, his prematurely grey hair accentuating his boyishly handsome face.

'Maybe it was brown,' Mary mused, unaware of the havoc she was causing to Bonnie's insides. She suddenly thrust her dentures out of her mouth, balancing them on the tip of her tongue.

'Oh, gross,' Lauren said.

Bonnie's stomach reeled.

Mary popped the dentures back inside her mouth, clicked them sharply into place. 'Can I have her vanilla custard?' she asked, her hand reaching toward the tray.

'I think my grandmother might like to try her custard,' Lauren said, with surprising authority, lifting the small cup of custard away from Mary's grasp. 'Wouldn't you like to try some custard, Grandma?' Lauren scooped a tiny amount onto the edge of a small plastic spoon, and placed it delicately on her grandmother's tongue. 'Do you like that, Grandma? Is it good?'

Slowly, Elsa Langer's face turned toward her granddaughter, her eyes slipping into gradual focus, like a kaleidoscope.

'Grandma?' Lauren asked. 'Grandma, can you see me? Do you know me? Grandma, it's Lauren.'

Elsa Langer stared at her granddaughter, as everyone in the room leaned forward. No one breathed. 'Lauren?' the old woman said, the word a sigh.

Lauren's eyes grew wide with wonder. 'Did you hear that, Sam?' she whispered. 'She knows me. She knows who I am.'

'Grandma,' he said quickly, jumping out of his chair, lurching toward the bed, almost upsetting her lunch tray. 'It's me, Sam. Do you remember me?'

178

'Lauren,' Elsa Langer repeated, eyes not moving from her granddaughter.

'I'm here, Grandma,' Lauren said. 'I'm here.'

But the focus in Elsa Langer's eyes was already shifting, retreating, disappearing.

'Where does she go?' Lauren asked, several seconds later, when it became obvious she wasn't coming back.

'I'm not sure,' Bonnie said.

'Do you think she really knew who I was?'

'I'm sure she did.'

Sam pushed himself off his grandmother's bed, walked to the door. He said nothing, but it was obvious he was ready to leave.

'Do you think she's thinking about anything?' Lauren asked, watching her grandmother's face.

'I don't know.'

'I think she must be thinking about something,' Lauren said.

'I don't think she thinks about anything,' Sam said impatiently. 'And you know what else I think? I think it's better that way.' He opened the door and walked from the room.

'Testy young man,' Mary said, dentures clicking in and out of her mouth. 'Just like my late husband. May he rest in peace.'

'We should go,' Bonnie said, gently touching Lauren's shoulder, grateful when Lauren didn't automatically pull away.

Lauren leaned forward, planted a delicate kiss on her grandmother's cheek. 'Goodbye Grandma,' she said. 'We'll be back again soon. I promise.'

Elsa Langer said nothing. Bonnie led Lauren from the room.

'Bonnie was sick on the way home,' Lauren told her father as soon as they walked in the front door, Sam immediately disappearing up the stairs to his room.

'I wasn't sick,' Bonnie insisted.

'You had to pull over. Sam had to drive home.'

'I got a little dizzy,' Bonnie explained, seeing the worry in her husband's face. 'I don't think the air-conditioner is working properly in my car.'

'You look awful,' Rod said.

'Thanks,' Bonnie told him. 'Where's Amanda?'

'Mrs Gerstein took her to the park.'

'When did you get home?' she asked.

'About half an hour ago.' Rod took Bonnie's elbow, guiding her to the stairs. 'Now I want you to get into bed and get some sleep.'

'Rod, don't be silly. I'm fine.'

'Don't argue with me. You have the flu; you should be in bed. I'll call Marla and cancel tonight.'

'I'll be fine by tonight,' Bonnie protested, wondering why. The last thing she wanted to do was have dinner with Marla Brenzelle.

'All right, we'll see how you're feeling later. Meanwhile, go upstairs, get undressed, and get into bed. I'll bring you up some tea.'

'Rod . . .'

'Don't argue with me.'

'Apparently Elsa Langer had another visitor this morning . . .'

'We'll talk about Elsa later.'

'But . . .'

'Later,' he insisted.

'This is silly,' Bonnie muttered, becoming angrier with each step up the stairs. 'I'm probably just overtired. I'll sleep for half an hour, then I'll be fine.'

When Bonnie opened her eyes, Lauren was standing at the foot of her bed. She looks beautiful, Bonnie thought, pushing herself up on her pillows, thinking she must be in the middle of a dream. Lauren was wearing a bright blue little dress that started in the middle of her breasts and stopped in the middle of her thighs. It made her look very grown up, Bonnie thought, wishing she could have looked like that at fourteen, wishing she could look like that now. 'How beautiful you are,' she said, her mouth dry.

'Thank you,' Lauren smiled, self-consciously. 'How are you feeling?'

'I'm not sure,' Bonnie said honestly, wetting her lips with her tongue. 'What time is it?'

'Almost seven thirty.'

'Almost seven thirty?' Bonnie looked over at the clock on the night table for confirmation. Could she really have been asleep all afternoon? 'My God. I have to get up. I have to get ready.'

'You're not going anywhere,' Rod said, coming into the room, wearing a deep green silk shirt and black pants, looking wonderful.

'I don't understand,' Bonnie said, struggling to get out of bed.

'Lauren's volunteered to be my date tonight,' Rod told her.

'What?'

'Honey,' Rod began, 'you have the flu. Stop being so stubborn and admit it. You feel like shit. There is absolutely no way you're up to going out tonight. One look at Marla and you'd probably throw up all over her, which would not do a great deal to enhance my career. So please, do us all a favor, and stay in bed.'

'Do you mind?' Lauren asked timidly.

'Mind? Of course not,' Bonnie told her, secretly delighted with the way things were working out.

'I already fed Amanda dinner and got her settled into bed,' Lauren said.

'You did?'

'She's great with her,' Rod said proudly.

'And Sam's here, if you need anything.'

'Thank you,' Bonnie said, renewed fatigue settling over her like a heavy blanket. Have a good time, she wanted to tell them, but she was asleep before the words could come out.

She was dreaming of tomatoes, lots of fat red tomatoes in the produce section of a small grocery store. Bonnie picked up one tomato, turned it over in her hand, then squished it between her fingers, watching thin veins of tomato juice trickle down the back of her hand to her arm.

She lifted both arms to the ceiling, tomato juice cascading, as if from a waterfall, across her face, sneaking between her lips, inside her mouth. She opened her mouth wide in order to drink more.

Bonnie woke with a start, a stale taste permeating the inside of her mouth. She needed a glass of water, she thought, climbing out of bed and shuffling toward the washroom, glancing at the clock. It was almost ten thirty. Three more hours lost, and she still didn't feel any better.

She poured herself a glass of water and drank it slowly, praying it would stay down. The stale taste remained, so she squeezed some toothpaste onto her toothbrush and vigorously brushed her teeth, the normally cool mint taste curiously dull and ineffective. She swirled some water around in her mouth and spit it out, her spittle laced with traces of blood. 'Great,' she said, shuffling back out of the room. 'Just what I need.'

181

The upstairs hall was almost in total darkness, except for the small night light in the shape of a ballerina that shone outside Amanda's bedroom. Bonnie slowly approached her daughter's room, the light from the television flickering under Sam's door, muffled electronic voices squeezing toward her bare feet, licking at her toes.

Amanda was sound asleep in her bed, her covers bunched around her knees, her hands thrown back above her head, her head across her left shoulder. Bonnie pulled the covers up, tucked them under Amanda's chin, kissed her lightly on the forehead. 'I love you, sweet thing,' she whispered.

I love you more, she heard the walls echo as she left the room.

Bonnie stopped for an instant in front of Sam's room, peering at the closed door as if she could see right through it. She heard the noise of the television – a man talking, a car accelerating, a woman screaming – and turned aside, about to return to her room, when she became aware of another sound, a sound so low she almost missed it, a sound so haunting she found herself frozen to the spot.

She stood this way for several minutes, ear pressed against the door, listening to the sound. It was as if the walls were moaning, she thought, as if someone were trapped inside, begging for release. The walls are crying, she thought, pushing open Sam's door.

On the television, a scantily clad young woman was screaming as she ran from a masked knife-wielding attacker. Bonnie's eyes traveled from the TV to the top of her once majestic oak desk, on which L'il Abner lay pressed against the glass of his tank, to the sofa on which Sam sat, watching the television with tears streaming down his face, his lips slightly parted, a low hum vibrating from his throat, as if he were lost in the throes of some medieval chant.

'Sam?' Bonnie approached him gingerly. 'Sam, are you all right?'

The low moan continued even as he turned to her, as if it had a life of its own, as if it didn't depend on Sam for its existence. Bonnie's hand reached out; her hand touched Sam's shoulder. She felt him flinch, but she didn't withdraw and he didn't pull away. Slowly, she lowered herself into the seat beside him, her arm snaking around his side.

'What is it, Sam? Please, you can talk to me.'

The wailing grew louder, more intense. Bonnie fought the urge to bring her hands to her ears. Instead, she drew the boy toward her, pressing his face to her chest, feeling his wet tears through her nightshirt, the moan growing louder, as if emanating from an echo chamber.

His arms encircled her, quickly tightening their grip, as if trying to pull her into the center of his grief, as if he were hanging on for dear life. Which perhaps he was, Bonnie thought, allowing him to cling to her, smoothing back his long black hair, her eyes alternating between the woman being butchered on the TV screen and the snake now stretching toward the top of the glass tank. Suddenly, Sam's body exploded in a series of violent sobs.

Bonnie rocked Sam back and forth in her arms like a baby. 'It'll be all right, Sam,' she told him. 'It'll be all right.'

They sat this way for a long time, Bonnie's lips pressed against the top of Sam's head, the smell of his freshly washed hair filling her nose. The movie ended. The snake continued exploring the inside of his tank, his head occasionally prodding its glass top, as if trying to escape.

Eventually, Sam stopped crying. 'I'm sorry,' he said, refusing to look at her.

'Don't be sorry,' Bonnie said, temporarily forgetting her own discomfort. 'And don't be embarrassed. You have nothing to be sorry for, nothing to be embarrassed about.'

'I'm crying like a stupid little kid.'

'You don't have to play the tough guy, Sam,' Bonnie told him. 'Talk to me. Tell me what's going on inside your head.'

There was a long silence. 'She didn't know me,' Sam said finally. 'She didn't know who I was. She knew Lauren, but she didn't know me.'

'I'm so sorry, Sam,' Bonnie said. 'Maybe the next time we go . . .'

Sam shook his head. 'No, I'm not going back there.'

'She's a sick old woman, Sam,' Bonnie told him. 'Who knows what's going on inside that confused mind of hers?'

'She knew Lauren.'

Bonnie said nothing.

'I just want somebody to love me,' Sam blurted out, the words escaping his mouth in a great anguished sweep.

'Oh God, sweetheart,' Bonnie cried with him. 'I'm so sorry for the pain you're feeling. I wish I could do something to make it all go away. I wish there was something I could say . . .'

Sam shook his head roughly from side to side. 'It doesn't matter.'

'It *does* matter,' Bonnie told him. 'Because *you* matter. You're a person who deserves to be loved, Sam. Do you hear me? You deserve to feel loved.'

Sam said nothing, refusing to look at her.

Bonnie sat watching him for several minutes. It was obvious that he was deeply embarrassed by his outburst, that he would say nothing further. 'I'd better get back to bed,' she told him.

'Can I get you some tea or something?' Sam offered.

Bonnie smiled, tenderly patted Sam's cheek. 'Some tea would be nice,' she said.

Chapter Nineteen

By the following Wednesday, Bonnie was feeling better and Lauren was starting to complain about feeling nauseous again. 'Why don't you stay home today,' Bonnie told her, laying a delicate hand on the girl's forehead. Lauren didn't pull away.

'Do I have a fever?'

'No, you're nice and cool, but there's no point pushing it. Stay in bed today. If you're not any better by tomorrow, I think you should see a doctor.'

'What about you?' Lauren asked, shivering beneath the blankets of her bed.

'I'm fine,' Bonnie insisted. 'Just a little tired.' The events of the last month were finally catching up with her: Joan's murder; the police investigation; the sudden additions to her family; the re-emergence of her brother; her fears for herself and Amanda. Immediately, Bonnie thought of Dr Walter Greenspoon. '*You seem to be a woman in torment,*' he'd said. Or words to that effect.

Well, of course he'd said that, Bonnie thought, impatiently. How else would he continue making his two hundred dollars an hour if he didn't drum up new business?

'You don't look fine,' Lauren was saying.

'It's my hair,' Bonnie said quickly, catching her reflection in the mirror over the vanity table. It was true – her hair , normally shiny and luxurious, if unruly, had been looking dry and lifeless the last few days. It hung on her head like an old mop, refusing to cooperate with her brush or her blow-dryer. Maybe what she needed was a new haircut. 'Will you be all right here alone?' Bonnie asked. 'Do you want me to see if Mrs Gerstein is available?'

Lauren shook her head. 'I don't need a baby-sitter, Bonnie.'

'All right, but I'll call you later to see how you are making out. And

185

if you start feeling sick to your stomach, remember to take deep breaths.'

Lauren nodded. 'I think I'll try to sleep now.'

Bonnie tucked the covers up under the girl's chin. 'I'll have Sam bring you some tea,' she said, then left the room.

'I feel perfectly fine. I feel perfectly fine,' Bonnie repeated to her reflection in the teacher's washroom at school.

You may feel perfectly fine, her reflection admonished, but you look perfectly awful.

Her reflection was right, Bonnie conceded, noticing that her skin was beyond pale, almost transparent. Wan, Bonnie thought, understanding the full meaning of the word for the first time. *Of an unnatural or sickly pallor; showing or suggesting ill health, fatigue, unhappiness; lacking in forcefulness, competence, or effectiveness.* Yes, certainly all of the above, in one little three-letter word. The English language was an amazing thing.

She should never wear olive drab, she decided. Another word that said it all. Drab – *dull, cheerless, lacking in spirit, brightness.* That was her all right.

Did the color of her dress also explain the queasiness in her gut, the renewed waves of nausea that had been sweeping through her insides all day? Of course, her students hadn't helped. They were restless, disinterested, uncooperative. Haze had been particularly objectionable – the way he slumped down in his seat at the back of the room, his legs extended full-length into the aisle, his black boots scuffing the gray tiles at his feet, his obscenely tattooed arms raised behind his head, supporting its weight, as if he were reclining in a hammock. He knew nothing, but he had an answer for everything. He never had his homework done, never had his assignments completed, never showed the slightest interest in anything she had to say. 'Why do you even bother showing up?' she'd demanded. 'Because I want to be with you,' had come his immediate response.

The class had laughed and Bonnie's stomach had turned over. It had been turning over ever since. Staring into the mirror, she wondered whether she and Lauren were doomed to keep reinfecting one another. 'I don't have time to think about that now,' she said, brushing some fresh color onto her cheeks. But the additional color looked forced, as if it had no relationship to the rest of her face. Far from adding life, she looked embalmed, as if she'd come straight from the undertaker's table. She looked like a corpse, she thought.

No one ever looks good under this kind of lighting, she told herself, glaring at the fluorescent lights overhead, returning the blush to her purse and fishing around for her lipstick, applying it with an unsteady hand, so that she missed part of her lip on one side and went over it on the other. Now I look like a drunk, she thought.

A drunken corpse.

Like Joan.

At least Lauren was feeling a little better, Bonnie thought gratefully. She'd slept most of the day, had slept right through Bonnie's noon-hour phone call, and was still sleeping when Bonnie got home from school. But she woke up just as Bonnie was leaving for the school's spring open house with the news that she was hungry. Bonnie had left her and Rod sitting at the kitchen table, eating dinner together. Sam had already gone out.

Bonnie took a couple of deep breaths for luck, snapped her purse shut, and tucked her hair behind her ears. Maybe she didn't look as bad as she thought, she told herself, stepping into the hall and proceeding up the stairs toward her classroom. She hoped not too many parents would show up. Maybe then she could get home early, get into bed, sleep away her demons, wake up feeling better, like Lauren, her normal color and appetite restored. She reached her classroom, unlocked the door, stepped inside and flipped on the light, taking a quick look around. Everything seemed to be in order.

Bonnie glanced at her watch, then at the clock behind her. Two minutes before seven o'clock. Maybe she'd be really lucky, and nobody would show up at all.

'Mrs Wheeler?'

Bonnie turned to see the elderly couple standing in the doorway. Both looked well beyond the years one would expect for the parents of teenagers. They were dressed simply, in shades of white and blue. His hair was gray, peppered with brown, hers the reverse, brown salted with gray. Neither was smiling. 'Yes,' Bonnie answered. 'Can I help you?'

'We're Bob and Lillian Reilly,' the woman said.

Bonnie stared at them blankly. She had no one named Reilly in any of her classes.

'Harold Gleason's grandparents,' the man explained.

187

'Oh, of course,' Bonnie said quickly, amazed she could have forgotten she'd specifically requested they attend. 'Haze's grandparents. I'm sorry. I'm obviously not thinking very clearly. Come in.'

'Your message said you wanted to speak with us tonight,' Lillian Reilly stated.

'You said it was very important,' her husband stressed.

'It is,' Bonnie told them, indicating the rows of desks. 'Please, have a seat.'

'I prefer standing, thank you,' Bob Reilly told her, his wife's eyes darting skittishly around the classroom.

'I'm so glad you came,' Bonnie said. 'I don't think I've seen you at the school before.'

'We don't bother much with school,' Lillian Reilly told her.

'I doubt you'll have anything to tell us we don't already know,' her husband said.

Bonnie smiled. At least there'd be no beating around the bush. 'I was hoping maybe there were some things you could tell me,' Bonnie said.

'Such as?'

'Tell me about your grandson,' Bonnie began. 'What he's like at home, if he's happy, if he gives you a hard time, what it's like to be raising a teenager at your age. Anything you think might help me to understand him a bit better.'

'Why would you want to do that?' Bob Reilly asked.

'Your grandson is failing, Mr Reilly,' Bonnie said, matching his bluntness with her own. 'And that's a shame, because I think he has lots of potential. He's a very bright boy, and I think that maybe with a little encouragement at home . . .'

'You think we don't encourage him?'

'Do you?'

'Mrs Wheeler,' Bob Reilly said, walking slowly down one aisle and back up again, 'you want to know about my grandson? My grandson is just like his mother was, a lazy, good-for-nothing-but-smoking-dope kid, who thinks that the world owes him something. And maybe it does, who knows? But that doesn't make much difference does it? Things are the way they are, like it or not. His mother finally understood that, and sooner or later, Harold will have to understand it too.'

'And in the meantime?'

'In the meantime, we try to keep out of each other's way as much as we can. We told Harold that he can keep living with us as long as he keeps passing in school. Now you tell us he's failing . . .'

'It's not that he doesn't have the brains to pass . . .' Bonnie said quickly.

'He just doesn't do any work, he doesn't hand in his assignments, he disrupts the class,' Bob Reilly said. 'Is that what you were going to tell us?'

'I thought that maybe together we might be able to figure out some way to help him . . .'

'And just what is it that you expect us to do, Mrs Wheeler?' Lillian Reilly asked. 'We can't force him to do the work, and we certainly aren't prepared to do it for him.'

'Of course you aren't, but maybe if you took more of an interest . . .'

'Do you have teenagers, Mrs Wheeler?' Bob Reilly interrupted.

'I have two stepchildren who are teenagers,' Bonnie answered.

'And how much do they appreciate your interest?'

'Well, they might not always show it, but . . .'

'Thank you, I believe you've answered the question.' Bob Reilly put a hand on his wife's elbow. 'Come on, Lillian. I told you this was going to be a waste of time.'

'Are you afraid of your grandson, Mr Reilly?' Bonnie asked suddenly. 'Mrs Reilly?'

Bob Reilly stiffened, his wife's eyes lifting nervously to his.

'Your grandson has a lot of anger inside him. I'd like to help him before it's too late.'

'Is that why you sent the police out to question him?' Bob Reilly asked, catching Bonnie by surprise. 'Is that your idea of helping him?'

'Do you think your grandson is capable of hurting anyone, Mr Reilly?' Bonnie asked over the loud pounding of her heart.

'We're all capable of hurting someone,' Bob Reilly answered evenly, and led his wife from the room.

'How'd it go?' Maureen Templeton called after her as Bonnie headed down the corridor toward the parking lot at almost a quarter after nine.

'Okay, I guess,' Bonnie said. 'Lots of people.'

'You don't look so hot. Are you feeling okay?'

'I'm fine. Maybe a little tired,' Bonnie lied, pushing open the side door of the school, breathing in the warm night air. 'Can I give you a lift home?'

'No, thanks. I have my car.' Maureen pointed to the dark colored

Chrysler on the far side of the parking lot, then walked briskly towards it. There were only a few cars left in the lot, Bonnie noticed, eager to get home.

Bonnie unlocked her car door and climbed inside, waving goodbye to Maureen Templeton as the other woman pulled out of the lot onto the street. Bonnie put her key in the ignition and turned on the car's engine.

Nothing happened.

Bonnie twisted the key back and forth, pulled it out, shoved it back in, once, then twice, her foot pressing hard down on the gas. The car didn't even threaten to turn over. 'This is not what I need right now,' Bonnie muttered, feeling a row of perspiration break out across her forehead. 'Come on, don't do this to me.' Again, she pushed the key inside the ignition, furiously turning it to the right, then the left, pumping the pedal. 'Please, this is not what I need tonight.'

Bonnie looked out the car's windows into the growing darkness. Except for two other cars in the lot, she was alone. She tried the ignition one last time, understanding that her car was absolutely dead. 'Great,' she said, fighting back the angry tears as she climbed out of the car and returned to the school. Her footsteps echoed down the now-empty corridor as she headed for the staff room. There was something spooky about the school at night, she thought, its emptiness unnatural. She wondered whether the staff room would be locked, was grateful when the door opened easily.

Bonnie flipped on the light, thinking about the two cars still in the parking lot. Maybe they couldn't start either, she thought, sitting beside the phone in the corner of the room, dialing her home number. Maybe there was a flu for cars going around. 'I'm not a well woman,' she said into the receiver, hearing it ring. Rod would have to come to pick her up. It would only take him a few minutes to get here. They'd send someone to look at her car in the morning.

The phone was answered on its fourth ring. 'Hello?' Lauren said, as if she'd just been roused from a deep sleep.

'I'm sorry, Lauren, did I wake you up?'

'Who is this?' the girl asked.

'It's Bonnie,' Bonnie told her, and would have laughed had she felt better. 'Can I speak to Rod?'

'He's not here.'

'What?'

'He had to go out.'

'He did? When?'

'About an hour ago.'

'Where did he go?'

'He didn't say. Why? Is there a problem?'

'My car won't start. Who's there with you?'

'Amanda. She's asleep.'

'Rod left you alone with Amanda when you aren't feeling well?'

'I'm fine now,' the girl insisted. 'I told him we'd be okay. He said he wouldn't be long.'

'Where's Sam?'

'Out.'

Bonnie lowered her head. Clearly this conversation would get her nowhere. 'Okay, well, I guess I'll take a cab. I shouldn't be too long.'

'No problem.'

'See you soon.' Bonnie replaced the receiver, trying to remember the phone number of the local cab company, her eyes scanning the room for a phone book. How could Rod go out and leave his two daughters alone, especially when one hadn't been feeling well? And where had he gone?

She finally located the phone book on the floor by the water cooler next to several large blue bottles, two empty, one full. Bonnie pushed herself out of her chair toward it and bent down, hearing her knees snap like dry twigs. Suddenly the room was spinning. For one terrifying second, Bonnie couldn't differentiate between the ceiling and the floor. 'God help me,' she whispered, her fingers grabbing for something to hold onto as she closed her eyes, tried desperately to maintain her delicate balance. 'Stay calm. Don't panic. This will pass.' Bonnie counted to ten, then slowly opened her eyes.

The room had stopped dancing, although, like lovers not ready to part, it was still swaying. Bonnie waited, the fingers of her right hand digging into the thin phone book, twisting and tearing its edges. She wondered whether her eyes would be able to focus, whether she would be able to read the tiny print. She had to get out of here. She had to get home and into the comfort of her own bed. Damn Rod anyway. Where was he?

Bonnie pushed herself up, the phone book in her hand serving as an anchor, steadying her in place. Slowly she returned to the phone, reaching for it with one hand as she flipped to the yellow pages with the other. The loud buzz of the receiver vibrated against her ear like a pesky insect as she located the listing for the cab company and punched in the first few numbers.

It was then she became aware of other sounds – a door shutting in the distance, footsteps in the hall. Slow and deliberate, the footsteps were coming this way. *You're in danger*, Joan shouted through the phone wires. Bonnie dropped the phone, heard it crash at her feet. *You're in danger,* Joan cried again from the floor. *You're in danger.*

'And you're an idiot,' Bonnie said angrily, not sure if she was addressing Joan or herself, her heart pounding, her head spinning. 'You're making yourself crazy, that's what you're doing.'

The footsteps drew closer, hovering just outside the staff room door. Bonnie held her breath, unable to move. It's just the custodian, she told herself, come to lock up. Maybe he'd noticed her car was still in the parking lot and was checking up on her, making sure she was all right.

Was it just a coincidence that her car had failed to start?

Or had someone tampered with it?

'Oh God,' Bonnie said out loud. Much too loud, she realized, as the staff room pushed open. 'No!' Bonnie screamed as a man appeared in the doorway.

The man jumped three feet in the air. 'Jesus Christ,' he gasped, spinning around, head jerking warily over his shoulder, as if afraid someone was behind him. 'What's the matter? What's going on?'

'Mr Freeman?' Bonnie asked, steadying herself long enough to allow his features to sink into her conscious mind.

'Mrs Wheeler,' he acknowledged, as if he should have known. 'What's the matter? Why did you scream?'

'You scared me,' Bonnie admitted, after a pause. 'I didn't know who it was.'

'Who'd you think it was, for Pete's sake? The bogeyman?'

'Maybe.' Bonnie collapsed into the chair behind her. Josh Freeman stared at her with puzzled eyes.

'Are you all right?'

'I'm feeling a little dizzy.'

Josh moved directly to the water cooler, poured her a cup of water, brought it to her side. 'Have some of this.'

Bonnie took the paper cup from his hand, brought it to her lips, finished the contents in one gulp. 'Thank you.' He had a kind face, she thought, surprised, as she'd been at Joan's funeral, by the wondrous clarity of his eyes.

'Feel better?'

'Hopefully. Sorry if I frightened you.'

'No harm done,' he said.

'I didn't realize you were still here.'

'I guess we're the last ones.'

'My car won't start. I was just about to call a cab.'

He hesitated. 'Do you live far from here?'

'No. Just over on Winter Street. A couple of miles.'

Another hesitation. 'I could give you a lift.'

'Really?'

'Is the idea so shocking?'

'It's just that you've been avoiding me for some time now,' Bonnie said.

'I guess I have,' he admitted. 'Have the police made any arrests yet?'

Bonnie shook her head, trying not to appear too startled by his abrupt change in thought.

'Why don't we talk on the way home?' he suggested.

Bonnie nodded, rising unsteadily to her feet and following him out of the staff room into the long hallway. So, they were finally going to talk, and at his instigation, no less. She couldn't have planned it any better herself, she thought, a sudden twinge poking her in the ribs like a finger. Maybe it *had* been planned, the twinge warned her. Only not by her. Maybe Josh Freeman had deliberately tampered with her car. Was it just a coincidence that he was here waiting for her when her car wouldn't start?

Except why would he do that? Bonnie wondered impatiently, forcing herself to keep up with his pace. Why would he tamper with her car? Unless he'd had something to do with Joan's death, unless he was the danger Joan had been trying to warn her against. But what kind of danger could Josh Freeman possibly be to her? And why should she have reason to fear him?

If anything were to happen to her, she realized as they neared the end of the corridor, no one would know where she was. No one would know where she had disappeared. No one had seen her with Josh Freeman. No one had seen them leaving the school together. No one would know who was responsible should anything happen to her. She should run from his side immediately, scream for the police. At the very least, she should return to the staff room and call for a taxi. Common sense dictated that she go nowhere with this man.

'Coming?' he asked, opening the door to the outside, waiting for her to catch up.

Bonnie took a deep breath, then followed him outside.

Chapter Twenty

'So, what made you want to be a teacher?' he asked unexpectedly as he turned his car onto Wellesley Street.

Bonnie was pressed against the passenger door of the small foreign car, her right hand gripping the door handle, in case she had to make a sudden, unscheduled exit. 'It's just something I always wanted to do,' she answered, trying to be reassured by his awkward attempt at conversation. 'From the time I was a little girl, I just always knew I wanted to teach. I'd get all my dolls together and arrange them in rows, teach them to read and write.' What was she jabbering about? Was she afraid that if she stopped talking, he might pounce? 'Of course, I was a better teacher back then,' she said.

'Something tells me that you're a very good teacher right now.'

She forced a smile. 'I like to think I am. Of course you can't reach everybody.'

'You sound like you have someone particular in mind.'

Bonnie thought of Haze, her frustrating encounter with his grandparents. No wonder he was so angry all the time, she thought.

'How did it go tonight?' Josh asked, as if able to read her thoughts. 'Were you very busy?'

'Pretty much,' she answered. 'What about you?'

'Full house,' he said, an engaging smile appearing unexpectedly on his face. She'd never seen him smile before, she realized. He looked nice when he smiled. 'A far cry from the school I used to teach at,' he was saying.

'In New York,' she stated. Were they actually making small talk? Was he really confiding in her something about himself?

He nodded, the wavy half-smile vanishing into a thin straight line, like the line on a heart monitor after the patient has died.

'What made you come to Boston?' she asked.

'I needed a change,' he said. 'Boston seemed as good a place as any.'

'Do you like it here?'

'Very much.'

'And your family?' She suddenly recalled that his wife had been killed in some kind of horrible accident. At least that was the rumor, she remembered, a feeling of dread seeping into her veins, like an intravenous drip. Maybe it hadn't been an accident at all. Maybe he'd murdered his wife, just like he'd murdered Joan, just like he was about to murder her. Maybe all this small talk was simply a way of relaxing her before the kill.

'I'm alone,' was all he said.

'It must be hard to start over in a new city when you don't know anyone,' she ventured, her voice quiet, strained. It was hard to carry on two conversations at once, even if one conversation was all inside her head.

'I didn't expect it to be easy.'

'Have you made any friends?'

'Some.'

'Did you consider Joan a friend?' She'd meant the question to sound casual, but her voice stuck on Joan's name, underlining it and dislodging it from the rest of the sentence, sending it bouncing off the car windows.

'Yes, I did,' he said, eyes resolutely on the road ahead.

'Were you having an affair?' Bonnie asked, throwing caution to the proverbial wind. What the hell, she reasoned. If he'd killed Joan, if he was planning to kill her, she might as well die knowing *something*.

'No,' he said, after a pause. 'We weren't having an affair.'

'Would you tell me if you were?'

'Probably not,' he said, the wavy little half-smile temporarily reappearing.

'What exactly was your relationship?' Bonnie asked, knowing she'd asked the question before, wondering if, once again, he'd tell her it was none of her business.

'We were friends,' he said instead. 'Kindred souls, you might say.'

'In what way?'

He thought for several seconds. 'We shared an inner emptiness, if you will,' he said finally, a trifle self-consciously. 'We'd both known great tragedy. It drew us together, gave us some common ground.'

196

Bonnie phrased her next statement carefully. 'I understand that your wife died in an accident . . .'

'A car accident, yes,' Josh said quickly. 'She and my son.'

'Your son?'

'He was two years old.'

'My God. I'm so sorry.'

Josh nodded, gripping the steering wheel tighter, his knuckles growing white with the strain. 'It was winter. The roads were bad. Her car hit some black ice and skidded into oncoming traffic. It wasn't anyone's fault. It's a miracle really that more people weren't killed.'

'That's so awful.'

'Yes, it was.' There was a long pause. 'So, you see, I understood some of the grief Joan carried around inside her all the time. I knew what it was like to lose a child. I knew what she was going through.'

'When you were together, what did you talk about?' Bonnie asked.

'What do friends talk about?' he mused. 'I don't know. Whatever was uppermost in our minds at the time, I guess. The real-estate business, teaching, her kids, her mother . . .'

'Her mother?'

'That surprises you?'

'What did she tell you about her mother?'

'Not much. That she had a drinking problem, that she was in a nursing home.'

'You knew Joan's mother was in a nursing home?'

'Was it a secret?'

'Have you ever visited her?'

'No. Why would I?'

Bonnie stared out the front window, consciously trying to slow things down. The conversation was moving too rapidly, was in danger of getting away from her. She needed time to digest everything he had told her, time to organize her thoughts. He was giving her too much information too fast. Why, she wondered, when he'd been so unwilling to talk to her before?

'What about Sam?' she asked.

'Sam? What about him?'

Hadn't she just asked that? 'I understand he's in your art class.'

Josh Freeman nodded. 'He is.'

'Is he a good student?'

197

'Very good. He's quiet, works hard, keeps mostly to himself.'

'Has he talked to you at all since Joan was killed?'

'No. I tried to approach him once, but he made it pretty clear he wasn't interested.'

Bonnie's eyes traveled across the dark road, expecting to see the familiar side streets – DeBenedetto Drive, Forest Lane. Instead she saw Ash Street and Still-Meadow Road. 'Where are you going?' she said, bracing herself in her seat.

'What?'

'I said, where are you going? Where are you taking me?'

'I'm taking you home. Where do you think I'm taking you?'

'This isn't the way to my house,' she told him, her earlier panic surfacing. She debated whether to open the car door, whether to throw herself out of the moving vehicle.

'You said to turn west on South Street.'

'This isn't west,' she told him. 'It's east.'

'Then I guess I turned the wrong way,' he said easily. 'I've always had a lousy sense of direction.' He slowed the car, but instead of turning it around, he pulled it over to the side of the road.

Bonnie's hand tightened on the door handle, her eyes frantically scanning the road for other cars, other people. There was no one. If she tried to run, he'd chase after her. How long before his hands were across her mouth, muffling her screams?

'Do you want to tell me what you're so afraid of,' he said.

Bonnie's eyes continued searching the side of the road. 'Who said I'm afraid?'

'Do you always react so violently when someone turns the wrong way?'

Bonnie swiveled around in her seat to face him. 'Did you kill Joan?' she asked directly, deciding she had nothing to lose.

'What?!'

'You heard me.'

'Are you serious?'

'Of course I'm serious.'

'Of course I didn't kill her. Did you?'

'What?!'

'You heard me.'

'Are you serious?'

198

'Of course I'm serious.'

'Of course I didn't kill her.'

And suddenly they were laughing. It started as an impromptu burst of giggles and ended with great whoops of glee. Tears streamed down Bonnie's face.

'I think that was probably the most ridiculous conversation I've ever had,' he said.

'I wish I could say the same thing,' Bonnie told him, thinking that she'd had her fair share of ridiculous conversations of late.

'You honestly think I might have killed Joan?'

'I don't know what I think anymore,' Bonnie admitted. 'Your name was in her address book; I saw you at her funeral; you wouldn't talk to me; you deliberately ignored me. Why? Why wouldn't you talk to me?'

'I was scared,' he said flatly, his turn to stare out the front window. 'I move to a new city to try and put my life together, and the first real friend I make gets murdered. Not only that, but I find myself being questioned by the police. Pretty scary stuff, even for a native of New York.'

'What sort of questions did the police ask you?'

'Their questions were mostly about you, actually.'

'Me?'

'What my impressions of you were, if I thought you were mentally stable, if Joan had ever said anything to me about being afraid of you.'

'If Joan was afraid of *me*?'

'They made it clear you were their prime suspect.'

Bonnie laughed. 'No wonder you didn't want to talk to me.'

'It was a bit unnerving.'

'What changed your mind?'

'You,' he said, the soft wave of his smile growing bolder, threatening to linger. 'The more I thought about it, the more ridiculous the notion of you shooting anybody seemed. And then when I saw you in the staff room tonight, looking so scared and vulnerable, I decided I was being silly, and that Joan would have been quite angry with me.'

'Joan? What do you mean?'

'She liked you. She said once that if circumstances had been different, she thought the two of you could have been great friends.'

'I doubt that,' Bonnie said, uncomfortable with the notion.

'You're not that dissimilar, you know.'

'Joan and I were nothing alike,' Bonnie insisted, her good spirits quickly evaporating, her nausea hovering.

'Physically, no, but in other more important ways . . .'

'I've never had a problem with alcohol, Mr Freeman.'

'I wasn't alluding to Joan's drinking,' he said, as Bonnie squirmed in her seat. 'I was thinking more of her honesty, her persistence, her sense of humor.'

'Did Joan ever say anything to you about my daughter?' Bonnie asked, changing the subject.

'Just that she was a beautiful little girl.'

'Anything else?'

'Not that I can remember.'

'What about my brother?'

'Your brother?'

'Nick Lonergan.'

He looked puzzled. 'The name doesn't ring any bells.' He paused, his head tilting toward her, forcing her eyes to his, like a slow magnet. 'What are all these questions about, Bonnie? What are you afraid of?'

Bonnie took a deep breath, releasing it slowly, watching it form a thin patch of film on the car's front window. 'I'm afraid that nobody believes that whoever killed Joan might be after me and my little girl. I'm afraid that nobody believes we're in any danger, and that they won't believe it until it's too late.' She started to cry.

In the next second, his arms reached out for her, drawing her toward him, hugging her tightly to his chest while she sobbed. 'It's okay,' he was saying, soothing her as if she were a child. 'Let it out. It's okay. It's okay.'

'I'm so scared that somebody is going to hurt my baby,' she sobbed, 'and there's nothing I can do to stop them. And I'm so tired, and I feel so sick, and I never get sick, goddamn it. I never get sick.'

'Nobody's going to hurt your little girl,' Josh Freeman told her, smoothing her hair with repeated strokes of his hand.

She looked up at him. 'Do you promise?' she asked, feeling foolish, but needing to hear the words.

'I promise,' he said.

By the time he pulled into her driveway, Bonnie's tears were dry. 'I'm sorry,' she whispered. 'I had no right to lay that on you.'

200

'Don't be sorry,' he told her. 'Are you all right?'

Bonnie nodded. Rod's car was in the driveway, although Sam was still out in Joan's red Mercedes. 'I think I'll make myself a cup of tea and get right into bed.'

'Sounds like a good idea.'

Bonnie pushed open the car door. 'Thanks for being there,' she told him sincerely, climbing out of the car as the front door to her house opened and Rod appeared in the doorway.

'Anytime.'

Bonnie closed the car door and Josh backed out of the driveway. In the next second, Rod was at her side. 'Who was that?' he asked, folding her inside his arms, kissing her cheek. 'Where's your car?'

'In the school parking lot,' she told him. 'It wouldn't start. Josh gave me a lift home.'

'Josh?'

'Josh Freeman, Sam's art teacher.'

'That was nice of him.'

'He's a nice man,' she said.

'Wasn't he at Joan's funeral?'

'They were friends,' Bonnie said, about to say more when Rod interrupted.

'Bonnie, you're not sticking your nose in where it doesn't belong, are you?'

'What do you mean?'

'You know what I mean. Let the police deal with Joan's murder, Bonnie. You're an amateur. You could get hurt.' He led her inside the house.

'Josh wouldn't hurt me,' Bonnie said, more to herself than to her husband, amazed at her change of heart. Less than half an hour ago, she was afraid the man was about to kill her. Now she was convinced he'd never hurt her. 'Where were you tonight?' she asked, as they entered the kitchen. 'I called to see if you could pick me up, and Lauren said you'd gone out.'

'I left some work at the studio that I needed to do for tomorrow, and I had to drive back and get it. Made me so damn mad. It was the last thing I needed.'

'Tough day?'

'Are there any other kind?' Rod brushed some stray hairs away from

Bonnie's forehead. 'How about you? How are you feeling?'

'Not great.'

'Feel like a cup of tea?'

'You read my mind.'

'That's what I'm here for.' He moved directly to the kettle, filled it with water, put it on the stove. 'Why don't you go upstairs and get into bed. I can bring this up when it's ready.'

Bonnie smiled gratefully, walking slowly to the stairs, fatigue pulling on her legs like heavy weights. She reached the top of the stairs, automatically turning toward Amanda's room.

'My sweet angel,' she whispered over her daughter's bed, staring down at the child's sleeping face, once again struck by how much she resembled her older half-sister. She wondered if Lauren had ever gone to bed tightly clutching a Big Bird doll, if she'd refused to give up her favorite blanket to be washed in case the 'good smell' got washed out, if she'd ever fallen off her tricycle and cut her cheek. Bonnie bent over and planted a delicate kiss along Amanda's tiny scar, careful not to wake her. 'I love you,' she whispered.

I love you more, she heard Amanda call after her silently as she crossed the hall. The door to Lauren's room was closed, although the light was still on. Bonnie knocked gently.

'Who is it?' Lauren called from the other side.

'It's Bonnie,' Bonnie told her, hesitating to open the door without permission. 'Can I come in?'

'Okay,' Lauren said, and Bonnie pushed open the door. Lauren was sitting up in bed, her school books spread around her.

'How are you feeling?' Bonnie asked.

'Okay, I think. I *hope*. I'm sick of feeling sick.'

'I know what you mean. How'd the party go on Saturday night? We never got chance to talk about it.'

'It was great,' Lauren said, her face filling with animation. 'You should have seen Marla. She was wearing this black dress cut down to her toes. She looked spectacular. She said to tell you she was sorry you couldn't be there.'

'I'll bet.'

'I think she has a crush on Dad,' Lauren said.

'Really?'

'She was hanging around him all night. Every time he said anything, she'd giggle, even when it wasn't funny. It was pretty gross.'

Bonnie chuckled, although the image of a giggling Marla in a dress cut down to her toes and hanging all over her husband was not one she wished to keep in the forefront of her mind. 'But you had a good time?'

'The best.'

'I'm glad.' She turned to leave.

'Bonnie . . .'

'Yes?'

'Can I talk to you a minute?'

Bonnie steadied herself at the side of Lauren's bed. 'Sure.'

'I wanted to ask you something.'

'Okay.'

'It's personal.'

'Okay,' Bonnie repeated. Did she really want to hear this?

'It's about you and my dad.'

'What about us?'

There was a long pause. 'I saw you last week.'

'You saw us . . . ?'

'In bed.'

Oh God, Bonnie moaned silently.

'I didn't mean to. It was when . . .'

'I know when it was,' Bonnie said quickly, pushing several of Lauren's books out of the way and sitting down on the edge of the bed. 'What exactly is it you want to ask about?'

'Your hands were tied,' Lauren said after another long pause, her words suspended in the heaviness of the air between them. She shook her head, obviously unable to corral the thoughts circling in her brain.

'That confused you,' Bonnie stated.

Lauren nodded.

Me too, Bonnie thought. 'We were making love,' she said instead. 'We just thought it might be fun to try something new.' What else could she say?

'Was it?' Lauren asked.

'It was interesting,' Bonnie replied honestly, trying to imagine herself having this conversation with her own mother. It was impossible. Her mother never so much as mentioned the word sex. She'd learned most of the gory details from her younger brother.

'Thank you,' Lauren said quietly.

'For what?'

'For being honest. I could never talk about these things with my mother,' she said, as if privy to Bonnie's most secret thoughts.

'No?'

'Don't get me wrong,' Lauren said immediately, already on the defensive. 'She was great. My mother was great. It was just that there were certain things she was uncomfortable talking about.'

'I hope you know that you can talk to me about anything,' Bonnie told her. 'I may not have all the answers, but I'm willing to listen to the questions.'

Lauren lowered her eyes to the bed, as if scanning one of the texts. 'I have a geography test on Friday,' she said.

'Can't help you there, I'm afraid,' Bonnie told her with a laugh. 'I was absolutely useless in geography. Failed every test.'

Lauren laughed. 'So there's hope for me.'

'There's definitely hope for you,' Bonnie told her, patting her hand. And for us, she added silently, hearing Rod's footsteps on the stairs. Everything was going to work out fine.

'Aren't you coming to bed?' Bonnie asked as Rod lifted the now-empty cup of tea out of her hands.

'I have some more work to get finished,' he told her. 'I'll be up as soon as I can.' He kissed her forehead, left the room.

Bonnie sat in her bed, staring absently at the Salvador Dali lithograph on the wall, with its faceless bald woman sketched in blue. 'She looks good compared to me,' Bonnie said, climbing out of bed and making her way to the bathroom, where she washed her face and brushed her teeth, swiveling the water around in her mouth for several seconds, then spitting it into the sink.

The sink was full of blood.

Bonnie pulled back. 'Jesus.' She took another gulp of water, swirled it around in her mouth, spit into the sink. More blood. As soon as she felt better, she'd have to get a new toothbrush. The bristles on this one were way too hard.

And while she was out buying that toothbrush, she just might stop in and have her hair done. She definitely needed something. Her hair had never looked so dry and lifeless before. She looked positively godawful, she thought, staring at her reflection.

The woman in the mirror stared back silently, a thin trickle of blood dripping from the side of her mouth toward her chin.

Chapter Twenty-One

The next morning, Bonnie called a mechanic to look at her car. The young man, whose white name tag on his gray shirt identified him as Gerry, spent a few minutes looking underneath the car's hood, turning various knobs, and examining assorted wires and valves. 'Everything looks okay to me,' he told her, his dark brown hair pulled back into a ponytail that ran halfway down his back. 'You say it wouldn't start?'

Bonnie nodded, dropping the car keys into Gerry's open palm as he climbed into the driver's seat. She watched him stick the keys in the ignition, then twist them slightly to the right. The car started immediately.

Bonnie shook her head in amazement, careful not to shake too long or too hard. She was still feeling nauseated, had spent most of the night tossing and turning, unable to find a comfortable position. It hurt even to turn over in bed. As a result, she'd spent most of the night lying on her back, waiting for morning. Sam had given her a lift to school this morning. When she asked him where he'd been last night, he said, simply, 'Out.'

'I don't get it,' Bonnie told the mechanic. 'I tried it half a dozen times last night. It wouldn't start.'

'Maybe you flooded the engine.'

'It never even turned over. It was absolutely dead.'

'Well, it's alive and purring now,' Gerry told her, turning off the ignition, then restarting it again immediately, as proof. 'You might want to take the car in, though, get it checked out. But it seems to be working fine now.' Once again, he turned off the engine, then climbed out of the car. 'How do you want to pay for this?' he asked.

After Gerry left, Bonnie stood looking at her white Caprice, trying to remember exactly what had happened last night. She'd said goodbye to Maureen Templeton, gotten into her car, tried repeatedly to start it, and nothing had happened. She remembered frantically pressing on the gas. Could she have flooded the engine?

'Car trouble?' a familiar voice asked, coming up behind her.

Bonnie didn't have to turn around to know who it was. Even if he hadn't spoken, his scent would have given him away. Did the boy never change or wash his clothes, or had he already been smoking dope this early in the morning? Coffee and a self-rolled cigarette – a little something to start the day.

'It seems to be all right now,' Bonnie told him, turning around, squinting into the sun. The boy's handsome face was half hidden by his uncombed hair. Even so, the mottled, purplish bruise at the side of his chin was clearly visible. 'What happened to your face?' she asked, her hand reaching out reflexively.

He flinched, pulled away. 'Walked into a wall,' he said, then laughed, a hollow sound.

'It looks more like you walked into somebody's fist.'

Haze lifted one tattooed arm, brought his hand to his chin. 'Yeah, the old man still packs a wallop.'

Bonnie's mouth opened in stunned surprise. 'Your grandfather hit you?'

'Do me a favor, Mrs Wheeler,' Haze said. 'Don't bother my grandparents anymore. They don't appreciate getting calls from the school.'

'I can't believe . . .'

'It's a tough world out there, Mrs Wheeler,' Haze said, balancing on the heels of his black boots. 'You never know when someone might be waiting to punch your face in . . . or disconnect the battery of your car so it won't start . . .'

'What?'

'. . . or throw blood on a cute little kid . . .'

'My God.' Bonnie felt her legs about to give way. 'Are you saying . . . ?'

' . . . or even shoot you straight through the heart,' he concluded, nonchalantly. 'The police paid us a visit about that, you know.' He rubbed his jaw. 'My grandfather didn't appreciate that visit very much either.' He laughed. 'They asked a whole lot of questions about whether I knew anything about what happened to Sam's mom or to your little girl. What's her name? Amanda? Yeah, real cute kid. It'd be a shame if something happened to her. I'd keep a real close eye on her, if I were you. Well, I gotta go. Don't want to be late for my first class.'

Bonnie watched him walk away, too stunned to speak. She wanted to chase after him, wrestle him to the ground, pin him down, pummel his face with her fists if necessary, in order to get the answers from him that she needed. Except that his grandfather had already done that.

Was it any wonder the boy was the way he was? Was she really surprised he needed a narcotic to get him through the day? And could she really be feeling sorry for him after all he'd just implied? My God, the boy had been in her home less than a week ago; he'd sat at her dining room table with her family, and eaten her food. Was he telling her now that he'd tampered with her car, that he'd emptied a pail of blood over her daughter's head, that he was a cold-blooded killer?

Bonnie looked toward the school, watching as a steady stream of students filed through the doors, hurrying to get inside before the bell. Haze would be waiting for her at the back of her class, his feet stretched insolently out in front of him, she realized, falling back against her car door. In the next instant, she was inside the car, pulling out of the parking lot, and heading for Newton.

'What did he say to you about my daughter?' Bonnie demanded, barely giving Captain Mahoney time to get out of his chair.

'Hold on here a minute, Mrs Wheeler,' the captain said, tucking his white shirt inside his brown trousers and straightening his brown-and-gold-striped tie as he stepped out in front of his desk. 'I can see you're upset . . .'

'Tell me what Harold Gleason said to you about my daughter,' Bonnie repeated, trying to calm herself down by taking deep breaths.

'He said he didn't know what we were talking about,' Captain Mahoney told her.

'Did he have an alibi for the time my daughter was attacked?'

'He claimed he was on his way home from school.'

'Can he prove that?'

'We can't prove he wasn't,' Captain Mahoney said.

'So that's it? He says he didn't do it, and you say okay?'

'We have no proof he did anything wrong, Mrs Wheeler. Your daughter couldn't give us a description . . .'

'My daughter is three years old.'

' . . . and we just can't arrest someone for behaving provocatively,'

Captain Mahoney said. 'You should know that.'

Bonnie ignored the inference. Did he really still consider her the prime suspect in Joan's murder? 'What about Joan?' she asked. 'Did he have an alibi for the time of Joan's death? Was he on his way home from school that day too?'

'It was a PD day,' Captain Mahoney reminded her, pointedly. 'He said he was with your stepson.'

The air buzzed painfully around Bonnie's ears, like a dentist's drill.

'Your stepson also claims they were together. They say they were just hanging out, not doing anything in particular, that they don't know if anybody saw them together or not. Do you think they might be lying?'

'I think Haze might be lying, yes.'

'And your stepson?'

'I'm sure my stepson had nothing to do with his mother's death,' Bonnie said, one hand reaching toward the back of a nearby chair for support.

'Are you?'

Silence. More buzzing, the drill moving closer, digging deeper.

'Could I trouble you for a glass of water?' Bonnie asked.

Captain Mahoney left the room and returned seconds later with a paper cup filled with cold water. 'Are you feeling all right?' he asked, as Bonnie sipped slowly at the contents of the cup. 'You're looking a little green around the gills.'

'It's my hair,' Bonnie said impatiently, although she wasn't sure if her impatience was directed more at Captain Mahoney or herself. 'Maybe if you stopped concentrating on my family and started looking in other directions, you'd have more luck finding Joan's killer,' she told him. 'I should go. Sorry if I wasted your time.'

'Always interesting talking to you,' he called after her. 'We'll be in touch.'

'What can we do for you today?' the young woman was asking, scissors in hand.

Bonnie was sitting in a barber's chair, staring at her reflection in the long mirror that ran the full length of the downtown beauty salon. Behind her stood a tall young woman wearing a large green felt hat that completely hid the fact she had any hair. Not a good sign in a hairdresser, Bonnie thought, then remembered that Diana claimed Rosie was the best hairdresser in Boston. Certainly she always did a great job on Diana's hair, Bonnie thought, deciding that she couldn't look much worse. 'I need something new.' Bonnie pulled at the ends of her hair.

'It's very dry,' Rosie said, crinkling a fistful of Bonnie's hair in her palm. Bonnie thought it might break off in her hand. 'We should probably give it a treatment. Are you in a hurry?'

'I have all day,' Bonnie told her, wondering what on earth had possessed her to come here. She'd called the school, told them she wasn't feeling up to par and didn't think she should risk infecting the students, and now here she was in downtown Boston, sitting in the window of Rosie's Hair Emporium, about to have her dry hair treated and trimmed. What if somebody were to see her?

'I think it could use a treatment, and a good cut,' Rosie said. 'What do you think?'

'I'm in your hands,' Bonnie told her. 'Do whatever you think is best.'

'I love it when you talk that way,' Rosie said.

'I was wondering if I could see Dr Greenspoon,' Bonnie said, addressing the wall above the well-coiffed heads of Erica McBain and Hyacinth Johnson. 'I know I don't have an appointment, but it's really very important.'

'I'm sorry,' Hyacinth Johnson said, managing to sound as if she meant it. 'The doctor isn't in today.'

'Damn,' Bonnie muttered, louder than she had intended. 'I really need to see him.' Look at me, she wanted to shout. Look at what I've done to my hair. Can't you see that I'm a sick woman, that I need to see the doctor as soon as possible?

'We've had a cancellation for next Wednesday at ten o'clock, if you'd like that.'

'No, that's too late.'

'I'm afraid I have nothing before that at all.'

'That's all right,' Bonnie told her. 'I really don't need to see the doctor. It was just an impulse thing.'

Impulse? she wondered. She'd been sitting outside the doctor's office for almost two hours, debating whether or not to come inside. Could that be considered an impulse? And how could she say she didn't need to see the doctor? She was crazy, for God's sake. Certifiable. Look at what she'd done today, for example. She'd bolted from the school parking lot without a thought, stormed into police headquarters in Newton to further antagonize Captain Mahoney, and then driven into Boston to have her hair butchered by Rosie the Riveter. How could she have given that crazy woman in a hat permission to do whatever she wanted with her hair? She looked worse than before, for God's sake. At least when her hair was longer, she'd been able to pull it back or push it forward. How could she do anything with two inches of hair? Hadn't anyone told Rosie that the waif look was dead? Didn't she know that thirty-five was too old to be a pixie? What would Rod say when he saw her?

He'd tell her she was crazy, she decided. And he'd be right. She was crazy. That's why she'd driven directly here from the hairdresser's, why she'd parked outside and sat there for two hours trying to work up the courage to come inside. She was nuttier than a fruitcake, as Rod would say. Weren't those the exact words he'd used to describe his ex-wife to the police? Well, now he could say it about the two of them. Both his ex-wives were nuttier than fruitcakes. Something else they apparently had in common.

She was nuts, and she was making herself sick, Bonnie told herself. It was as simple as that. She couldn't cope with all the changes in her life, and this was her body's way of telling her she needed help. The psychosomatic flu. And the remedy was only two hundred dollars an hour.

'I think I will take that appointment, if that's okay,' Bonnie said.

Hyacinth Johnson calmly wrote the information down on a small card, as if she was well used to patients changing their minds, and handed the card across the desk to Bonnie. 'Ten o'clock next Wednesday morning,' she repeated. 'We'll see you then.'

'I don't see your name on the guest list, Mrs Wheeler,' the elderly security guard was saying, tired brown eyes scanning his clipboard for her name.

'My husband doesn't know I'm coming,' Bonnie said. 'I thought I'd surprise him.' Surprise was right, she thought, hands picking at whatever hair she had left, trying to fluff it up, give it more volume.

'I'll have to call down, I'm afraid.'

'That's fine.'

'I hate to have to do that to you,' the old man apologized. 'But they're very strict about regulations.'

'I understand.'

'I could lose my job if I just let you walk in.'

'I'll tell my husband what a fine job you do.'

The security guard smiled, and picked up the phone resting on the high counter just inside the entrance to studio WHDH. 'I almost didn't recognize you,' he said. 'You've done something different to your hair.'

'You like it?' Bonnie asked hopefully, not sure how long she could maintain an upright position.

'It's different.'

'I thought short hair might be a nice change.'

'It's short.'

Oh God, Bonnie thought. It must be truly awful if even the elderly security guard couldn't think of something nice to say to her. Don't be silly, she told herself in her next breath. He's hardly an arbiter of high fashion. Even if he doesn't like your hair, others might find it appealing. Besides, it's only hair. It'll grow back.

It'll take two years for this to grow back, she realized, leaning against the counter for support, watching as the security guard hung up the phone.

'They're sending someone right up for you,' he told her.

'Thank you.' Bonnie looked around the black marble foyer of the downtown highrise, just blocks from fashionable Newbury Street. Maybe after she was finished here, she'd go shopping, buy a new outfit to go with her new haircut. Maybe she'd even ask Diana to join her. Diana's office was somewhere close by. They could go shopping, have coffee, gossip, all the things that girls were traditionally supposed to do. *Sugar and spice and everything nice. That's what little girls are made of.*

What was she doing here? Why had she decided to interrupt her husband in the middle of the afternoon, when he was frantically trying to prepare for Miami? If she was smart, she'd leave now, just turn on her heels and exit the premises, tell the guard she'd made a mistake, that she was sorry she'd bothered anyone, my best to the wife and kids . . .

'Bonnie, Bonnie, is that you?' Marla's voice cut through the black marble like an electric saw through glass, splinters everywhere. She strode toward Bonnie, her svelte body encased in a bright purple dress, her corn-blond hair a series of cascading ripples falling to her shoulders.

Bonnie's hand was instantly at her own hair, self-consciously pulling at a few wisps around her ear. 'You didn't have to come out . . .' she began.

213

'I heard you were here, and we're on a break in the taping . . .'

'My God, you're taping. I'd forgotten.'

'That's all right.' Marla's hand was on her elbow, pulling Bonnie toward the corridor to the right. 'It's always a pleasure to see you. Did you do something new to your hair?'

'I felt like a change,' Bonnie said.

'You got it,' Marla told her, pulling open the door marked Studio. They continued down the narrow, dimly lit corridor.

'I'm really sorry to be bothering you . . .'

'Nonsense. You're no bother. I don't think you've been down since we changed the set.'

'No, it's been a while.'

Several attractive young women in short skirts passed them in the hall, half bowing in Marla's direction. 'The new set is such an improvement,' Marla was saying. 'Rod's idea, of course. He got rid of all those grays and greens, and replaced them with peach and blush, which, of course, is much more flattering, and much more feminine, don't you think?'

Bonnie said nothing, understanding that no response was required.

'I can't tell you what a pleasure it is working with your husband. I've had directors before, let me tell you, and there are directors and directors, let me tell you. Anyone can point a camera in the right direction and tell people where to sit, but it takes a good director to understand what makes people tick, and how to make sure everything runs smoothly. And your husband is the best. Just the best,' she said, almost wistfully, leading Bonnie past a door marked Make-up and another one labelled Green Room, although the walls were pink. 'Our guests wait in there,' Marla confided, her voice low. 'It's really cute how nervous they get. Don't you have school today?' she continued in one breath.

'We finished early,' Bonnie told her, thinking this was true. She *had* finished early. *Very* early.

'The studio's in here.' Marla guided Bonnie through yet another heavy gray door. And suddenly they were in a darkened world of cameras and monitors, where thick cable lines ran like creeping vines along the floor, and hung from the ceiling like exotic plants. The audience, some three hundred people, most of them women, sat in tiers of comfortable chairs, eyes glued to the peach-colored sofa and blush-tinted swivel chair on the lit podium at one end of the studio. There were silk potted palms

214

and vases filled with fresh-cut flowers at strategic intervals around the ersatz living room. On the back wall hung a large modern tapestry in shades of pink, mauve and beige. Marla was right – it was a vast improvement over the old set. Rod had always had a good eye. 'Why don't you sit over there?' Marla said, acknowledging with a wide smile an adoring woman fan in the front row. 'That way, if you have any questions you want to ask one of our guests, I can get to you easily.'

'I don't want to ask any questions,' Bonnie said.

'You never know,' Marla told her. 'You might relate. We have a very interesting show today.'

'I'm sure you do, but I just wanted to see Rod for a few minutes. I really don't have time to watch the whole taping.'

'There's only half an hour left. Besides, he can't see you till after the taping anyway. He's in the control room.' Marla pointed to a glass-enclosed room high above their heads at the back of the studio. 'So why don't you just sit down and make yourself at home, and sit back and enjoy the show.' She all but pushed Bonnie into the empty seat in the second row. 'I'll tell the cameraman to make sure he gets a shot of you.'

'Please don't do that.' Immediately, Bonnie's hand shot to her hair.

'Don't be silly, and don't be shy.' Marla was already moving away from her. 'And remember to speak up if you want to challenge any of our guests.'

'I don't even know what the show's about,' Bonnie protested, weakly, grateful to be sitting down.

'Oh, didn't I tell you? It's all about extramarital affairs.' She smiled, displaying all her perfectly capped teeth. 'We're calling it "Wives Who Hang On Too Long". See you later. Enjoy.'

'She's having an affair with my husband,' Bonnie was saying, pacing back and forth in front of Diana's desk like a lion in a cage.

'Bonnie, calm down.'

'Don't try to tell me I'm imagining this.'

'I'm not trying to tell you anything,' Diana said. 'I'm just trying to understand what happened.'

Bonnie walked to the floor-to-ceiling window of the modern office tower and looked down at the street some twenty floors below. It made her feel dizzy, and she immediately pulled back, bumping into the sharp corner of Diana's green marble desktop.

215

'Why don't you sit down?' Diana offered, indicating the two green-striped wing chairs across from her desk.

'I don't want to sit down,' Bonnie snapped. 'I'm tired of sitting down. I've been sitting down all day.' She pictured first her car seat, then the barber chair at Rosie's salon, then the soft wine-colored armchair in the darkened studio. ' "Wives Who Hang On Too Long", she called it,' Bonnie spat into the air. 'Can you imagine? She actually had the gall to say that to me.'

'Bonnie,' Diana reminded her 'that was the name of the show. What else could she say it was called? She didn't make it up for your benefit. She had no way of knowing you were going to drop by.'

'It was the *way* she said it,' Bonnie told her. 'The insinuation was too blatant to miss. She was implying that I'm one of those wives. You weren't there. You didn't hear her.'

Diana pushed herself out of her high-backed black leather chair and walked around, leaning against the front of her desk. 'Okay, so let me see if I have this straight,' she began in proper lawyerly fashion, tugging at the jacket of her wheat-colored suit. 'You had a run-in with one of your students so you decided to skip school and get your hair done . . .'

'I know it's awful . . .'

'It's not the most flattering cut you could have selected,' Diana agreed, 'but that's not the point.'

'I'm not sure I know what the point is,' Bonnie said.

'Which is exactly the point,' Diana said, pouncing on Bonnie's words. 'You *always* know what the point is. You never do anything without thinking it through well in advance. Suddenly, you're skipping school and cutting your hair off and dropping in unannounced to the studio. Why? What's going on?'

'My husband is having an affair,' Bonnie insisted. 'That's what's going on.'

'With Marla Brenzelle? I can't believe it. Even Rod has more sense than that.'

'I know it sounds ridiculous at first, but it all makes sense.'

'What makes sense?'

'Rod's been working very long hours lately. He leaves early in the morning, and doesn't come home till late at night. Sometimes he even goes out after he's come home.' She thought of last night.

'He's preparing for an important convention in Miami. Doesn't he leave in a few days?'

'With Marla,' Bonnie reminded her.

'She's his boss.'

'She has big tits.'

'Excuse me?'

'Remember that sexy lingerie I found in Rod's drawer, the stuff I assumed was for me, except that the bra was too big?'

'Bonnie, that hardly means . . .'

'It was for Marla, that's why. Not for me. Diana, I'm not imagining this. Remember I told you that Caroline Gossett said Rod always used to cheat on Joan.'

'You're not Joan.'

'I'm his wife. Same difference.'

'Not quite. Joan happens to be rather dead.'

There was an abrupt silence.

'Well, that was hardly the smartest thing I've ever said,' Diana said, shaking her head in disbelief. 'Are you going to confront him?'

'So you believe me?'

Diana shrugged. 'I don't know,' she said. 'The evidence is very flimsy.'

'Stop being a lawyer for a few minutes and just be my friend.'

'Would a friend tell you she thinks your husband might be having an affair?'

Bonnie sank into one of the wing chairs, felt it scratchy against her bare neck. 'I don't know. I don't know what to think anymore. I'm so tired. I feel so lousy all the time.'

'Okay, here's my advice,' Diana told her, kneeling beside Bonnie, placing her hands on top of her friend's. 'Don't do anything for now. Wait until Rod gets back from Miami. Hopefully, by then you'll be feeling better, you'll be thinking more clearly, your hair will be longer . . .'

Bonnie tried to laugh, found herself crying instead. 'I'm sorry.'

'For what?'

'For acting like such an idiot, for bursting into your office in the middle of the afternoon . . .'

'You don't have to apologize.'

'I just don't know what to do.'

217

'Go home and get into bed,' Diana told her. 'You really don't look well, and it's not just your hair. Maybe you should see a doctor.'

'I'm fine,' Bonnie insisted, getting out of the chair.

'Are you going to be all right to drive home?'

Bonnie nodded. 'I'll call you later,' she said.

Chapter Twenty-Two

On Saturday, Rod was packing to leave for Miami.

'I don't see how I can leave you when you're feeling this way,' he was saying, even as he crammed his toiletry case inside his suitcase.

'I'll be fine,' Bonnie told him, balancing precariously on the side of the bed, watching him, trying to look as healthy as she could.

'You don't look fine.'

'It's my hair.'

'What hair?' he joked. '*She's* got more hair than you do.' His gaze traveled to the Salvador Dali lithograph on the wall. The faceless bald woman outlined in blue stared blankly back at Bonnie.

'I was thinking of buying a wig,' Bonnie told him.

'Do me a favor, Bonnie. Don't do anything.' He stopped his packing, sat down beside her. 'Look, this is crazy, my going away now. You're in no shape to take care of three kids by yourself. What if Lauren gets sick again? Or Amanda?'

'They'll be fine. We'll all be fine,' Bonnie insisted.

'Why don't I call Marla and tell her I won't be there till Monday? The meetings don't start till then anyway. I won't miss anything.'

'You said you had to leave early to get things ready . . .'

'They'll manage without me.'

'They can't.' Bonnie stood up, folded the last of Rod's shirts and put it in the suitcase, as if this effectively ended the discussion. 'Come on, Rod, you'll only make me feel guilty if you don't go.'

He opened his mouth to protest, then thought better of it. 'All right, but you have the number of the hotel. If anything happens and you want me back here, you call right away.'

'Nothing's going to happen.'

'And if you don't feel any better by Monday, I want you to see a doctor.'

'I've already made an appointment,' Bonnie told him, thinking that Dr Walter Greenspoon probably wasn't the kind of doctor Rod had in mind.

'Good. Now you're starting to make some sense.' He looked around the room. 'Have I got everything?'

'Your bathing suit?'

'I won't have time to swim,' he told her, kissing the tip of her nose. 'What time is the limo getting here?'

Rod checked his watch. 'Ten minutes. You're sure you're going to be all right?'

'I'm sure.'

He closed his suitcase, zipped it up, lifted it off the bed. 'Where are the kids?'

'Lauren's reading Amanda a story in her room. Sam's at Diana's.'

Rod looked startled. 'What's he doing there?'

'Apparently, Diana found a whole slew of odd jobs for him to do. She's paying him ten dollars an hour.'

'The woman has more money than brains,' Rod said dismissively, carrying his suitcase to the doorway. 'Amanda,' he called out, 'Lauren. Where are my girls? Come say goodbye to Daddy.'

Don't go, Bonnie wanted to say, watching him as he hugged his daughters to his side. Stay here and look after us. Let someone else go to Florida. Let someone else keep Marla company. Stay here with us where you belong. Sleep beside me in our bed. Don't crawl into bed with a woman I despise. Don't forget how good we are together.

Bonnie sighed, but said nothing. How could he remember how good they were together when the last time they'd made love had been that awful evening when Lauren first got sick? Since then, he'd either come home too late from work, or she was feeling too sick. Last night, she'd hoped she could muster up the necessary energy, but in the end, nausea had proved more powerful than desire. The idea of making love had been about as appealing as running the Boston Marathon.

And now Rod was leaving for one whole week amidst the palm trees of Florida, in the company of a woman with whom he was probably having an affair, and she was not only not telling him to stay, she was urging him to go, telling him she'd feel guilty if he didn't.

You're a good girl, she heard her mother say.

No, not good, Bonnie thought, as Rod beckoned her inside his arms, beside his other two girls. Stupid. She was stupid to allow her husband to go off to Miami with Marla. And yet, realistically, what choice did she have? How could she keep him if he really wanted to go? At best, she would only be postponing the inevitable.

'Are you going to take good care of your mother?' Rod asked Amanda.

'Mommy doesn't feel well,' Amanda said, her face serious.

'No, she doesn't. So you're going to have to be a very good girl and do exactly what she tells you.'

'I will.'

'I'll help,' Lauren said. 'I can take Amanda to the park later, if she'd like.'

'The park?' Amanda started jumping up and down.

'Later,' Lauren qualified, straining to sound very grown up. 'If you're a very good girl.'

'I'm a good girl,' Amanda said, and Bonnie shuddered.

'You don't have to be a good girl,' she whispered.

'What? Did you say something, honey?' Rod asked.

The phone rang.

'I'll get it,' Lauren offered, running into Bonnie's bedroom and answering the phone in the middle of the third ring. 'Hello.' A slight pause. 'I'm afraid she can't come to the phone right now. Can I take a message?'

There was another pause, this one longer, more ominous. Bonnie could feel Lauren holding her breath.

'When?' she heard Lauren ask in her smallest little-girl voice, an audible catch in her throat. Then, 'How?' Another long pause. 'Yes, thank you for calling. I'll give her the message.'

'Who was that?' Bonnie asked as Lauren walked slowly out of the bedroom, her face drained of color, her eyes void of sparkle. 'Lauren, who was that? What did they say?'

'What is it, honey?' Rod asked.

'That was one of the nurses from the Melrose Mental Health Center,' Lauren answered, her voice seeming to emanate from somewhere across the room. 'My grandmother passed away last night.'

'What?' Bonnie couldn't believe her ears. 'How?'

'The nurse said that she slipped into a coma a few days ago, and that she died last night. I don't believe it,' Lauren continued, her voice an echo of Bonnie's thoughts. 'How can this be? We were just there last week.'

'She was an old woman,' Rod said. 'And she was suffering. It's better this way.'

'But we were just there,' Lauren repeated numbly.

'Which was very fortunate, when you think about it,' Rod told her. 'You got to see your grandmother again before she died. And she got to see you. I'm sure that made her very happy.'

'She knew who I was,' Lauren said, a tiny smile appearing on her lips before disappearing under a spray of tears.

Rod drew his older daughter into his arms. 'I'm sorry about your grandma, honey.'

'Grandma Sally died?' Amanda asked her mother, her mouth agape, her eyes giant blue circles, as if she had colored them in herself.

'No, honey,' Bonnie told her. 'Grandma Sally is fine. This was Lauren and Sam's grandma.'

'Not my grandma?' Amanda repeated.

'No, not your grandma.'

'Your mommy?' she asked.

'No, honey,' Bonnie answered, not really up for this conversation at this particular time. 'My mommy died a few years ago.'

'How old was she when she died?'

'Sixty,' Bonnie answered absently, picturing her mother sitting up in bed, her face hidden in the shadows.

'How old are you?' the child asked, nervously.

'A long way from sixty,' Rod told her, cutting in, taking charge. 'Don't worry. Your mommy's going to be around for a long, long time.'

'But you're sick. Are you going to die?' Amanda persisted, grief washing across her face, sliding her sweet features one into the next, like wax melting.

You're in danger, she heard Joan cry out suddenly. *You and Amanda.*

A shiver traveled through Bonnie's body like an electric current. 'I'm not going to die. I'm going to be fine.'

You're in danger, Joan cried again. *You and Amanda.*

'Nobody's going to die here,' Rod said forcefully. 'Have we got that? Nobody dies while Daddy's away.'

There was a loud knocking on the front door, followed by the bell.

'That'll be my limo,' Rod said, checking his watch.

'He's early.'

'I'll tell him to wait.'

'No, you're ready,' Bonnie told her husband. 'Go. There's no reason to stay.'

'I see three reasons standing right in front of me,' Rod said.

Maybe she was wrong, Bonnie thought hopefully. Maybe Rod wasn't having an affair with Marla. Maybe she'd gotten herself all upset for nothing.

'Three reasons to come back safely,' Bonnie told him.

Rod leaned forward and kissed her gently on the lips. 'I'll call every night.'

'You don't have to do that.'

'Try and stop me,' he said.

I wish I could, Bonnie thought, watching him as he disappeared down the stairs and into the waiting limousine.

Bonnie was asleep when she heard the doorbell ring. At first she thought it was part of her dream – she was wandering the halls of the Melrose Mental Health Center and fire alarms were going off – but then she realized that it was the doorbell. She opened her eyes, looked over at the clock. It was a quarter past two. The bright sun shining through the bedroom window told her it was still afternoon. At least she hadn't slept the entire day away, she thought, waiting for someone to answer the door, wondering who it could be. But no one answered the persistent ring, and Bonnie was forced to drag herself out of bed.

Lauren must have taken Amanda to the park, she remembered, slipping a robe over her nightshirt and gliding down the stairs. Sam was probably still at Diana's. Rod's plane would be just touching down in Miami. She wondered whether Marla was a white-knuckle flyer, and whether Rod's steady hand was clamped reassuringly over hers.

The doorbell rang again. 'Coming,' Bonnie called out, reaching for the door and pulling it open.

Joan was standing on the other side. 'Love your hair,' she said, pushing past Bonnie and walking toward the living room at the back of the house.

Bonnie stared at Joan's back, the woman's titian tresses cascading down her back. So, this is a dream after all, she thought, relaxing as she followed Joan into her living room and sat across from her on the avocado-green sofa. 'You look well,' Bonnie told her husband's ex-wife, checking the woman's more-than-ample bosom for signs of bullet holes. There were none. Joan looked immaculate in an all-white linen pant suit, as striking in death as she had been in life.

'More than I can say for you,' Joan shot back. 'Got anything to drink?'

'How about some tea?' Bonnie asked.

'Tea? Are you kidding? I never touch the stuff. Tea's not good for you. Didn't you know that?'

'No, I didn't know that.'

'Got any brandy?'

'I think so.'

'Get one for yourself too,' Joan called after her as Bonnie went into the dining room, located the bottle of brandy in the cabinet, and returned with two small glasses, already poured. 'Cheers,' Joan said, raising her glass to Bonnie's in a toast, downing the contents of her glass in one gulp.

Bonnie sipped gingerly at her drink. 'What are you doing here?'

'You don't have much time left,' Joan told her matter-of-factly, depositing her now empty glass on the coffee table. 'Can't you feel it? Don't you know time's almost up?'

'You have to help me,' Bonnie urged, rising from her seat, moving imploringly toward Joan.

'You have to help yourself,' Joan told her, picking her brandy glass off the coffee table and raising it to her lips. Bonnie watched Joan guide it toward her open mouth, saw that the glass was full. But just as it reached her mouth, Joan tilted the glass down toward her throat, spilling the brandy across the front of her jacket, the white linen growing deep red, burning a large hole in her chest, like acid.

'Joan!' Bonnie screamed, watching the woman fade into the air, until all that was left was a large burgundy stain in the middle of the living room rug.

And then the dream ended, and everything faded to black.

'Bonnie,' a voice was calling. 'Bonnie, are you okay? What are you doing down here?'

'Mommy!' Amanda shouted happily, jumping into Bonnie's lap just as Bonnie was struggling to open her eyes. 'Are you all better now?'

Bonnie glanced quickly around the room, trying to understand what was happening. Was this another dream? It was getting increasingly difficult to differentiate between the two.

She was sitting on the sofa in her living room, Amanda on her lap, her pudgy fingers playing with what was left of her hair. Lauren was standing in the doorway, a look of surprise on her face. There were two small brandy glasses on the coffee table in front of her, one empty, the other almost full. There was a large red stain on the carpet in front of her.

'Was someone here?' Lauren asked.

'We went to the playground,' Amanda said. 'Lauren pushed me on the swings. Sooooo high,' she said, and laughed.

Bonnie looked from Lauren to the empty glass, to the floor, then back to Lauren. 'I must have been walking in my sleep,' she said after several seconds.

'Wow,' Lauren said. 'Did you have something to drink when you were asleep?'

Bonnie summoned up some saliva, tried to determine if it tasted of brandy. 'I think I may have had a sip of something.'

'Looks like most of it ended up on the floor,' Lauren said. 'I'll clean it up.'

'You don't have to do that.'

Lauren was already on her way to the kitchen. 'It's okay. I don't mind. Would you like me to make you some tea?'

'*Tea? I never touch the stuff,*' Joan said. '*Tea's not good for you. Didn't you know that?*'

'No,' Bonnie answered, hugging Amanda tightly to her chest. 'No tea, thank you.'

'I thought you might like something to eat,' Sam was saying as Bonnie opened her eyes to see him standing at the foot of her bed.

Bonnie pushed herself up on her elbows, looking toward the clock. It was almost seven. 'Is it morning or night?' she asked, looking out the window, the indifferent gray sky no help at all.

Sam laughed. 'It's night.' He brought the tray he was holding to the bed, laid it gently across her lap.

Bonnie wasn't sure whether she was relieved or disappointed. On the one hand, she hadn't lost too much time. On the other, she had the whole night to get through. Maybe some food would help, she thought, faint stirrings of hunger mingling with her general nausea. She hadn't had much to eat in the last week. Maybe that was the reason she was so weak. She should eat something to get her strength up. 'What did you bring me?' she asked.

'Some chicken noodle soup and some toast. And some tea.'

'I think I'm all teaed-out,' Bonnie said, lifting the spoon to her mouth, slowly sipping at the hot soup. 'This is good,' she smiled. 'Thank you.'

'My pleasure.' Sam lingered by the side of the bed.

'How'd it go today?' she asked.

'Great,' Sam told her. 'I tightened some loose screws, packed up some old clothes and books into boxes for the Salvation Army, stuff like that. Diana asked me if I'd like to wallpaper her bathroom.'

'And would you?'

'Yeah, I think so. I can give it a try anyway. She has to be in New York for a couple of days next week, and she gave me her key, said to see how I make out.'

'Good for you,' Bonnie told him, swallowing another spoonful of soup, taking a small bite of toast, savoring the blackberry jam slathered across the top of it.

The phone rang.

'That's probably your father,' Bonnie told him, as Sam picked up the receiver and extended it toward her without a word. 'Hello?' Bonnie said, watching as Sam shifted self-consciously from one foot to the other. 'Hello?' she said again when no one answered. There was a strange click, then the line went dead in her hands. 'Probably a wrong number.' Bonnie handed the receiver back to Sam, who returned it to its carriage. 'What are you up to tonight?' she asked, when he made no move to leave.

'No real plans,' Sam said. 'Haze might drop over later.'

'Haze?'

'If that's all right.'

'I don't know . . .' Bonnie began, when the phone rang again. She glanced at it warily.

'I'll get it,' Sam offered, barking hello into the receiver. Don't mess with me, the growl said. 'Oh, hi, Dad,' he continued, sheepishly. 'How's Florida? Yeah, she's right here. Hold on.' He handed the phone to Bonnie. 'I'll give you some privacy,' he mouthed, backing out of the room.

Bonnie forced some levity into her voice. 'Rod? Hi. How was your flight?'

The flight was good, he told her. Some turbulence at the beginning, then clear sailing, he said, laughing at his mixed metaphor. He asked how she was feeling, and she lied and said much better, she thought the worst was over. He told her to take it easy, not to try to do too much. She told him the same. He said he loved her. She said she loved him more. They said goodbye.

Bonnie hung up the phone, finished her soup and toast, and fell asleep.

In her dream, she was carrying a tray of food up the stairs toward her bedroom. As she neared the top of the stairs, she smelled something both familiar and oppressive. The sickeningly sweet odor of too many flowers, she knew at once, reaching the landing, proceeding along the hall to her room, rock music trailing after her from a discreet distance.

Sam was in the bathroom papering the walls. She recognized the wallpaper immediately – the dark paper she'd grown up with, with its oppressive assortment of flowers threatening to tumble from the walls and bury her alive.

'What are you doing?' she demanded. 'Take that paper down right away.'

'I can't do that,' Sam said calmly. 'It's what she wanted.' He pointed toward the bed.

Slowly, Bonnie's eyes followed his finger to the bed. Elsa Langer was propped up against the pillows, staring at Bonnie as she approached. But the closer Bonnie got to the bed, the less distinct Elsa Langer's features became. They blurred, then faded into nothingness. By the time Bonnie reached the bed, she had no face at all, like the woman in the Dali lithograph come to life.

Or was it death? Bonnie wondered, awaking with a start, her heart pounding, the rock music catching up with her, filling the space around her. Sam's stereo, she realized, reassured by the sound, looking toward the window, noting the full moon. Maybe the moon was the cause of all these strange dreams she'd been having. At least she hadn't been walking in her sleep again, she thought, recalling that the last time she'd walked in her sleep, she'd been about Lauren's age. Her mother had found her asleep at the front door, a packed overnight case in her hands. That was just after her father had left, she remembered.

Bonnie heard movement, strange voices, some laughter in the hall, the music growing louder. 'Sam?' she called out. 'Sam, is that you? What's going on?'

'It's not Sam,' the voice said, as a figure stepped into the room. He was tall and slim, his muscular arms stretched out shoulder height. Haze, Bonnie realized, her breath catching in her throat as she saw the snake extended and twisting between his hands. 'How are you feeling, Mrs Wheeler?' He took several steps toward her.

'Where's Sam?' Bonnie asked.

'Outside, having a smoke.'

Bonnie heard laughter. 'What's going on?'

'Sam's just having a few kids over,' Haze said, stretching the snake as if it were a piece of rope. 'He didn't think you'd mind. We've been very good little boys and girls.'

'I'm not feeling very well,' Bonnie told him. 'I'm afraid you'll have to leave.'

Haze walked to the foot of the bed, holding the snake by its tail, swinging him lazily back and forth.

'Be careful,' Bonnie advised. 'He hates to be dropped.'

'That so?' Haze asked, waving the snake from side to side like a pendulum.

'Please go away,' Bonnie said, trying to sound strong and in control. 'I'm not feeling very well.'

'What'd you do to your hair?' Haze asked, coming closer.

Bonnie closed her eyes. Please let this be another dream, she prayed.

'Haze?' a young girl called from the hallway. 'Where are you?'

'Right here,' Haze said, wrapping the snake around his neck like a shawl, and retreating from the room. 'Catch you later, Mrs Wheeler,' he said.

Bonnie walked calmly into the bathroom and threw up.

The phone rang at just after three o'clock in the morning. Bonnie groped for the receiver, pushed it to her ear, mumbled hello, waited for an answer. There was nothing. 'Hello,' she said again, about to hang up when she heard the same strange click she'd heard earlier. Then, once again, the phone went dead in her ears.

You're in danger, Joan shouted at her through the receiver. *You and Amanda.*

Immediately, Bonnie was out of bed and running down the hall to

Amanda's room. She pushed open Amanda's door and rushed to the side of her bed, relaxing only when she saw her daughter comfortably asleep on her back between a stuffed pink teddy bear and Kermit the Frog. She kissed Amanda's forehead and slowly backed out of the room, trying to will her breathing back to normal. What was the matter with her? She was acting like a crazy person. Had she no control over her emotions at all?

The house was quiet. Everyone had left. If there'd actually been anyone here, Bonnie thought, no longer able to distinguish between what was real and what wasn't. Maybe she dreamed the whole unpleasant episode with Haze. *I'm dreaming my life away*, she thought, the words to the old Everly Brothers song filling her head.

She checked on Lauren, found the girl stretched diagonally across her bed, her blankets bunched up around her feet. Bonnie brought them gently up to Lauren's shoulders, then tiptoed from the room.

Then she looked in on Sam, saw him lying, fully clothed, on top of the sofa, the light from the full moon throwing a spotlight on his face, emphasizing a resemblance to his mother she'd never noticed before. Bonnie turned, was about to leave the room, when her bare feet brushed against something on the floor. It crinkled, scratched at her toes. A piece of paper, she thought, scooping it up. No, not paper, she realized. A photograph. The picture of Amanda taken at Toys 'R' Us the previous Christmas, its silver frame lying broken beside it on the floor.

Bonnie picked up the frame, about to put it on the desk when she froze, the light from the moon throwing interesting shadows across the top of the glass tank. Bonnie stared into the tank, then slowly started to shake. The tank was empty. The snake was gone.

Chapter Twenty-Three

'You're early,' Hyacinth Johnson said in greeting as Bonnie entered Dr Greenspoon's office the following Wednesday morning.

'Am I?' Bonnie looked at her watch, feigned surprise. In truth, she'd been waiting in her car for over an hour at the bottom of the street, having left her house immediately after Amanda had been picked up and Sam and Lauren had gone off to school. She hadn't wanted to spend one more minute at home than she had to. God only knew what might be waiting for her around the next corner.

She'd woken Sam up as soon as she saw L'il Abner's empty tank, and together they'd searched the house, to no avail. Sam had called Haze first thing Sunday morning, asking whether his friend had absconded with his prized possession. But Haze claimed to know nothing of L'il Abner's disappearance, although he allowed as to how he might not have secured the lid on the tank properly when he put the snake back. He'd been pretty loaded, he said.

Once again Bonnie and Sam searched the house from top to bottom, every corner, every closet, every cupboard, every windowsill. Nothing. 'He'd go where it's warm,' Sam told her, so they'd checked, and then rechecked at regular intervals throughout the balance of the day and night, the furnace room and the hot-water tank, but still L'il Abner failed to appear.

Bonnie now took a seat in the waiting area of Dr Greenspoon's office, noting that Hyacinth Johnson and Erica McBain were both dressed in layers of black and white. Did they consult on their wardrobe, plan it out days in advance? she wondered, grabbing a magazine from the coffee table, flipping carelessly through articles on the latest scandals involving the royal family and Michael Jackson, her thoughts unable to settle on anything other than the missing reptile. She remembered once reading about a man who'd discovered a snake in his toilet when he went to the

231

bathroom in the middle of the night. He'd opened the washroom door, flipped on the light, and there it was, rising from the toilet bowl like a periscope. 'Please don't let that happen to me,' she prayed out loud. 'It's more than I could bear.'

'I'm sorry. Did you say something?' asked Erica McBain.

'Just talking to myself,' Bonnie told her. Isn't that what crazy people do? she wondered.

'I do that all the time,' Erica said, as if to reassure her.

When repeated searches had failed to uncover the missing boa constrictor, Bonnie called the exterminators, the plumber, the humane society, even the zoo. There was nothing anyone could do. If the snake had gotten outside, she was told, probably someone would spot him sooner or later and call the police. If he'd somehow managed to get inside the pipes of the house, it could be days, weeks, months, even years before he resurfaced, if ever.

'Damn Haze anyway,' Sam muttered, visibly shaken. 'I told him to leave Abner alone.'

Damn Haze is right, Bonnie thought to herself. 'He'll turn up,' she said to Sam. 'We'll find him.'

'He'll be getting hungry soon,' Sam fretted. 'He can get mean when he's hungry.'

Since then, Bonnie hadn't slept. She was literally frightened of her own shadow. Last night, she'd lain awake, jumping at the slightest shift in the light from the moon through her bedroom curtains, repeatedly checking on Amanda and Lauren, and comforting Sam, who'd dropped two small white rats into L'il Abner's tank in hopes of enticing the snake to come home.

'Would you like a cup of coffee?' Hyacinth Johnson offered. 'I just made a fresh pot.'

'No, thank you.' Bonnie thought that the last thing she needed was a jolt of caffeine. On the other hand, she needed to keep her strength up. She couldn't let herself get dehydrated. The only nourishment she'd had all morning was a small glass of orange juice. 'On second thought, maybe I will have some coffee, if it's not too much trouble.'

'No trouble at all. How do you take it?'

'Black, thank you.'

'There you go,' Hyacinth said a few seconds later, depositing the delicate pink-flowered china cup and saucer on the coffee table in front of Bonnie.

Bonnie thanked her again, lifting the cup of hot coffee to her lips, feeling the steam filling her nostrils, being absorbed into her pores. She'd always loved the smell of fresh coffee.

She remembered accompanying her mother to the grocery store as a small child, waiting with eager anticipation while her mother emptied the coffee beans she'd selected into a grinder. Bonnie would inhale deeply as the beans were ground into aromatic dust, their scent swirling around her head like a soft rain, ultimately settling on her skin like an expensive perfume. Over the years, the visits to the grocery store had grown less frequent, then stopped altogether. Eventually, her mother did all her grocery shopping over the phone from her bed. The days of freshly ground coffee were gone.

The door to Dr Greenspoon's inner office opened and an attractive older woman stepped out, the doctor right behind her. The woman, who was around sixty, was dressed in a smart brown Armani pant suit, her blond hair pulled into a fashionable twist at the back. Seeing her, Bonnie felt dowdy, the shapeless ecru-colored dress she was wearing surrounding her like a tent. How much weight had she lost in the last few weeks? she wondered, thinking it substantial.

'Make a series of appointments for Mrs King,' Dr Greenspoon instructed his secretaries, then took the older woman's hands in his own. 'Try not to worry too much, and I'll see you next week.' He looked over at Bonnie. 'If you'd like to wait inside my office,' he told her, 'I'll be there in a moment.'

Bonnie walked silently into the inner office and took her place on one of the burgundy sofas. The same sofa and the same seat she'd sat in the last time. Was that significant? Would the good doctor notice?

Her eyes drifted into the corners of the room, circling the potted plants, peeking through the window blinds. Looking for snakes, she realized, feeling foolish, a habit she wondered if she'd ever break. Maybe Dr Greenspoon could help her.

'Sorry to keep you,' Dr Greenspoon was saying a few minutes later, closing the door behind him and taking up his position on the other sofa. He looked natty in his gray seersucker suit and open-necked blue shirt. 'How have you been?'

'Fine,' Bonnie replied automatically.

'I see you've done something different with your hair.'

'I see you've mastered the art of understatement.'

The doctor laughed.

'Do you like it?' Bonnie asked, aware she was testing, although she wasn't sure what.

'More important,' he said, 'do you?'

'I asked you first.'

'It has potential.'

'To do what?'

Again he laughed, a nice sound, easy, one that was comfortable with itself. 'To grow into something a little more flattering,' he answered.

This time it was Bonnie who laughed. 'Thank you for your honesty.'

'Was there a reason you cut your hair?' he asked.

'Does there have to be?'

'There usually is.'

Bonnie shrugged. 'It was looking a little lifeless,' she began, then stopped, the word conjuring up images of Elsa Langer. How strange that she'd died just after Bonnie had discovered she was alive. 'I haven't been feeling quite up to par,' she continued. 'It's why I decided to see you again.'

'What is it you think I can do for you?'

'I'm not sure. But somebody has to do something. I don't think I can stand feeling this way much longer.'

'How is it you feel exactly?'

'Rotten,' Bonnie told him simply. 'I'm nauseated all the time, I throw up, everything hurts . . .'

'Have you seen a doctor?'

'I'm seeing you.'

'I meant a medical doctor.'

'I know what you meant.'

'I know you did.'

She smiled. 'No, I haven't.'

'Why is that?'

'Because my symptoms are obviously psychosomatic.'

'Really? What makes you say that?'

'Dr Greenspoon,' Bonnie began, 'you said it yourself the last time I was here. I'm a woman in torment. I believe those were your exact words, and, much as I hate to admit it, you were right. A lot has happened in my life recently, not much of it pleasant. I'm dealing with a lot of shit, Dr Greenspoon, if you'll pardon the vernacular, and obviously I'm not coping very well. This flu, or whatever it is, is just my body's way of reacting to all the stress.'

'That may very well be,' Dr Greenspoon said. 'But I still think you should get it checked out. How long have you been feeling this way?'

'On and off for about ten days,' Bonnie told him.

'Ten days is too long. You need to see a doctor, rule out the possibility of infection, or more serous illness . . .'

'I'm not running a fever,' Bonnie said, impatiently. 'What will a doctor do except tell me to drink lots of fluids and stay in bed?'

'Why don't you find out?'

'Because I don't have the time or the energy to subject myself to a lot of useless tests. Especially when I know that these symptoms are all in my head.'

'How do you know that?'

'Because I never get sick.'

'So you said the last time you were here. Do you interpret getting sick as a sign of weakness?'

'What? No. Of course not. I just don't have the time to get sick.'

'And other people do?'

'That's not what I'm saying.'

'Are you saying that you think sickness is something you can control?'

'Are you saying it isn't?'

'I guess I think it all depends,' the doctor told her. 'Some things are a question of mind over matter, and I'm certainly not going to suggest that one's attitude doesn't play a role in one's physical wellbeing. But that doesn't mean a good attitude is going to prevent cancer, or that a lousy attitude is going to bring on certain death. My father-in-law is eighty-four years old. Ever since I can remember, he's been complaining about his back, his neck, his arthritis. He's been convinced for twenty years now that he's dying, that he'll never see another birthday, another new year, another summer. He has the worst attitude I've ever seen, and you want to know what? He'll live forever, long after the rest of us, with our unbounding optimism and sunny dispositions, have packed it in.

'People get sick, Bonnie. There are some things that are out of our control. As a society, we don't like to accept that. It makes us feel insecure. So, as a result, we have a lot of desperately ill people feeling guilty because they think that if only they'd had a more positive outlook, they wouldn't have gotten sick, and that's baloney. It's just another example of society blaming the victim, as far as I'm concerned. We think that as long as what happens is the victim's fault, then it won't happen to us.

'The human body is not infallible. It's prone to all sorts of infections and viruses, and our susceptibility can depend on any number of different factors, including diet, exercise, general conditioning, and stress. But mostly, good health depends on good genes. And a lot of plain dumb luck.' He smiled. 'Of course, there could be a simpler explanation for the way you're feeling.'

'And what is that?'

'Is there a chance you could be pregnant?'

'What?'

'Is there a chance you could be pregnant?' he repeated, although they both knew she'd heard him the first time.

'No,' Bonnie scoffed. 'Not a chance in the world. I'm on the pill.' Hadn't she told him that the last time she was here?

'The pill isn't one hundred per cent foolproof. Isn't it possible, what with everything that's happened in the last little while, that you might have forgotten to take it for a day or two?'

'No, it isn't possible. I take it every day without fail. I never forget.'

'You sound very sure.'

'I *am* very sure. I decided a long time ago that I only wanted one child. I'm very careful to make sure there are no accidents.'

'That's very interesting. Why is that?'

'Why is what?'

'Why did you decide you only wanted one child?'

'You don't think the world is overcrowded enough?'

'Is that why you did it?'

'You don't think that's a good enough reason?'

'It's a perfectly admirable reason. But is it *your* reason?'

'I don't understand.'

'If you're so adamant about wanting only one child, I'm curious as to why you haven't had a tubal ligation.'

The remark caught Bonnie off guard. A slight trickle of perspiration broke out along the top of her forehead. 'I'm not a fan of unnecessary surgery,' she said.

'Could there be another reason?'

'Such as?'

'You'd have to tell me. You have a brother, if I remember correctly.'

Bonnie found herself holding her breath, waiting for Dr Greenspoon to continue.

'Older or younger?' he asked.

'Younger, by six years.'

'That's a long time.'

'My mother suffered several miscarriages in between.'

'I see. So your brother must have been very special to her.'

'Yes, he was.'

'And how did that make you feel?'

'How did that make me feel?' Bonnie repeated, dully. 'I really don't remember. It's a long time ago. I was only a child.'

'A child who'd had her mother's undivided attention for six years. I imagine it was quite a shock to suddenly have to share her with someone else.'

'Are you suggesting I was jealous of my brother?' Bonnie asked. Was he really resorting to this oldest of psychiatric clichés?

'I think it would be only natural.'

'I loved having a brother, Dr Greenspoon. Nick was the sweetest baby in the world.'

'Then why are you so adamant about having only one child yourself?'

'My husband already has two children from his first marriage,' she reminded him. 'Besides, some people are only suited to have one child. They know deep down that there isn't room in their hearts for more than one. They know they couldn't love both children equally, that one would end up getting short shrift.'

'Is that how you feel?'

'Isn't that what I just said?'

'No. You said *some people*.'

Bonnie bit down on her bottom lip. 'Just an expression.'

'Tell me about your family.' Dr Greenspoon leaned back into the sofa and unbuttoned his jacket.

'I've been married for five years,' Bonnie said, relaxing a little now that they were on more comfortable terrain. 'I have a daughter, Amanda.'

237

'Your family of origin,' he corrected. 'Your parents.'

Bonnie immediately stiffened. She cleared her throat, leaned back, then forward, crossed then uncrossed her legs, tugged at her hair. 'My mother is dead,' she said, her voice so low that Dr Greenspoon had to lean forward again to hear her. 'My father lives in Easton.'

'How long ago did your mother die?' Dr Greenspoon asked.

'Almost four years ago. She died a few months before Amanda was born.'

'That must have been very hard for you, losing your mother just as you were becoming one yourself.'

Bonnie shrugged.

'Was her death sudden?'

Bonnie said nothing.'

'Is that a difficult question, Bonnie?' Dr Greenspoon asked, curiosity bringing his eyebrows together at the bridge of his nose.

'She'd been sick a long time,' Bonnie answered after another long pause. 'But it was still sudden.'

'You weren't expecting her to die?'

'She'd been sick for years,' Bonnie told him impatiently. 'She had allergies, migraines, a weak heart. She'd been born with some sort of heart defect, so there were a lot of things she couldn't do.'

'She spent a lot of time with doctors?' Dr Greenspoon asked.

'I guess,' Bonnie admitted uneasily. 'What are you getting at?'

'You don't think it's curious that your mother had all these physical problems, yet you deny yourself even the possibility of being sick? That she spent a lot of time with doctors, yet you won't even consider going for a check-up?'

Bonnie twisted in her seat, her right foot tapping furiously on the floor. She shrugged, said nothing. Why had she come here? He was only making her feel worse.

'How did she die?' Walter Greenspoon asked.

'The doctor said it was a stroke.'

'You don't agree?'

'I don't think it was quite as simple as that.'

'How so?'

'I'd really rather not get into all that right now.'

'As you wish,' the doctor said easily. 'What about your father?'

'What about him?'

'Is he healthy?'

'He seems to be.'

'Are you close?'

'No.'

'Can you tell me why?'

'My father walked out on my mother a long time ago. I didn't see a whole lot of him after that.'

'And you naturally resent him for that.'

'It was very hard on my mother.'

'Was that when she started getting sick?'

'No. She'd been sick before. I told you, she had a bad heart. But she got worse after he left, no question about that.'

'And your brother? Did he live with your father or did he stay with you and your mother?'

'He stayed with us.' Bonnie laughed. 'It's ironic when you think about it because now he's living with my father and my father's wife, wife number three, if you're counting, and they're all living in my mother's house. Happy as peas in a pod.'

'*You* don't sound very happy.'

Bonnie laughed again, louder this time. 'It's really funny how things turn out, don't you think, Dr Greenspoon?'

'Sometimes.'

'Look, why are we talking about all this? It's not relevant to anything.'

'How often do you see your father?' Dr Greenspoon asked, as if she hadn't spoken.

'I just saw him a few weeks ago,' Bonnie answered, knowing this wasn't exactly an answer to the question Dr Greenspoon had asked.

'Before you started feeling sick?'

'Yes.'

'And when was the last time you saw him before that?' he continued, refusing to let her off the hook so easily.

'The last time I saw him before that was at my mother's funeral.'

Dr Greenspoon took several seconds to consider her answer. 'Do you blame your father for your mother's death?'

Bonnie scratched at the side of her nose, pulled at her hair, rocked back and forth in her seat. 'Look, what are you trying to say? Are you trying to tell me that my long-pent-up feelings of hostility toward my – what was it you called it? – my family of origin? – that these long-

239

repressed feelings are the cause of my current symptoms?'

'Do you have long-repressed feelings of hostility?' he asked.

'I don't think it takes a genius to figure out the answer to that one, do you, Doctor?'

'Have you ever talked with your father about your feelings?'

'No. What for?'

'For you.'

'What possible good would it do? He's not going to change.'

'You wouldn't be doing it for him.'

'You think if I talked to him, that I would suddenly start to feel better? Is that what you're trying to tell me?'

'It might prove liberating. But what's important here is not what *I* think – it's what *you* think.'

Bonnie stopped rocking, sat perfectly still. 'In that case, I think I could have saved myself a lot of money if I'd gone to my family doctor for a check-up instead of coming here.'

'Probably true. Do you *have* a family doctor?'

'No,' Bonnie admitted. Amanda had a pediatrician, and Rod went for annual check-ups, but she had no one.

'Would you let me recommend someone for you?'

'Why? You obviously think my problems aren't physical.'

'I think we're dealing with two very different things here,' he told her, 'one of which we can clear up fairly easily with a visit to the doctor. The other will require more time.'

'I just want to start feeling better,' Bonnie told him, verging on tears. She hated feeling this helpless, this out-of-control.

Dr Greenspoon walked over to his desk, pressing down on his intercom. 'Hyacinth, can you get Paul Kline for me on the phone?' He looked back at Bonnie. 'His office is just around the corner, and he owes me a favor. He's a nice man. I think you'll like him.'

A moment later, the intercom on his desk buzzed. 'I have Dr Kline on line one.'

'Paul,' Dr Greenspoon said immediately. 'I have someone I'd like you to have a look at right away.'

Chapter Twenty-Four

'Take a deep breath. That's good. Now, let it out. Good. Again.'

Bonnie took another deep breath, then slowly released it. Again the doctor complimented her on her breathing. Again she felt strangely grateful.

'And one more,' Dr Kline instructed, maneuvering the stethoscope underneath the blue cotton robe the nurse had given her to put on. The metal felt cold against her bare skin. 'How long has it been since you had a check-up, Mrs Wheeler?'

'I can't remember,' Bonnie told him. 'Years.'

'And the general state of your health?'

'Good. I never get sick,' she told him with less conviction than earlier such pronouncements.

'Do you have a gynecologist?'

'I saw one when I was pregnant,' Bonnie said, although, in truth, she'd only availed herself of the woman during her last trimester, and only then at Diana's insistence. 'I'm not sick,' she'd told Diana. 'I'm pregnant.' 'I'm not pregnant, am I?' Bonnie asked now, surprising herself with the question she hadn't meant to ask. 'I mean, I couldn't be pregnant. It's not possible.'

'When was your last period?' Dr Kline asked.

'Three weeks ago. And I'm on the pill. And I never forget to take it.'

'Then the odds are you aren't pregnant,' Dr Kline assured her. 'It's a little early to be having morning sickness, particularly such severe symptoms. But we'll do some blood tests and get a sample of urine. That should help explain why you've been feeling so poorly. Turn this way,' he said, drawing down on her lower eyelid and shining a narrow beam of light into her left eye.

Dr Greenspoon was right – Dr Kline was a nice man, not too tall and a little on the plump side, but possessing a natural grace and dignity. He

241

was about forty years old, had thinning brown hair, and warm hazel eyes. His hands were small and soft, his fingers surprisingly long. When he touched her, it was always gently, as if he understood she was fragile, bur firmly, as if to reassure her of his own strength.

The office, on Chestnut, only a five-minute walk from Dr Greenspoon's office, was on the ground floor of a three-story brownstone that had been converted into a mini medical building. Stately old wooden beams mingled with the latest in technology and equipment. Built-in bookshelves filled with giant medical tomes lined the walls. A traditional eye chart was tacked to the wall opposite the window, surrounded by a coterie of impressive degrees. A graduate of Harvard medical school; a member of the college of physicians and surgeons; several other diplomas she was too tired to read. Pictures of Dr Kline's family lined the top of his large, cluttered desk. Three sons and a pretty, dark-haired wife, the snapshots charting the children's growth from babies to teens, the wife remaining remarkably the same throughout, give or take a few pounds. Dr Kline's nurse, a woman about Bonnie's age, with frosted hair and an engaging smile, stood discreetly off to one side of the room, looking eerily like a statue by Dwayne Hanson, monitoring the proceedings without moving.

'How's your vision been?' Dr Kline asked, peering into her other eye.

'Fine.'

He handed her a piece of black plastic, instructed her to place it over her right eye, then read the third line of the eye chart on the opposite wall. She did. He then asked her to put the plastic cover over her other eye and read the fourth line. She did that too. 'Good,' he said, pulling gently on her ear lobe, examining the inside of her ear with another instrument. 'Any earaches?'

'No. Why? Do you see something?'

'A little wax. We can get rid of that easily enough.' He moved to her other ear. 'Dizziness?'

'Sometimes.'

'And you said you were nauseated.'

'All the time.'

'Vomiting?'

'On a number of occasions. What does that mean?'

'Could be an inner ear infection.'

'What does that mean?' she asked again.

'Inner ear infections manifest themselves in different ways. It usually affects your balance, which can result in dizziness, nausea, general malaise.'

'And what can be done about it?'

'Not much, unfortunately. It's viral, so antibiotics are of no use. It's something you basically just have to wait out.'

'So there's nothing you can do,' Bonnie stated, as if she'd known it all along.

'I didn't say that,' he told her, his hands on her throat, pressing on her glands.

'You said we just have to wait it out.'

'I was referring to inner ear infections. I'm not sure that's what we're dealing with here. Open your mouth and say "aw".'

Bonnie opened her mouth. Dr Kline stuck a tongue depressor inside it, pressing down against the back of her tongue. 'Aw,' she said, and immediately felt herself gag.

'You all right?' Dr Kline removed the tongue depressor, discarding it in a nearby wastepaper basket.

'You're the doctor. You tell me.'

'Well,' he began, 'you don't have a fever; you don't have a cold; your eyes are fine; your lungs are clear; your throat is good; your nasal passages are clear, and you don't have swollen glands, at least in your neck. Let's see about the glands in your groin. Could you lie down, please?'

Bonnie stretched back on the examining table. Immediately the doctor's hands were pressing into her stomach and groin. The area felt tender, and she winced.

'That hurt?' he asked.

'A little.'

'A few swollen glands here,' he said, manipulating the glands at her groin. 'Okay, you can sit up now.' He handed her a small bottle. 'Why don't you give me a urine specimen in this,' he said. 'Debbie will show you where to go, and when you come back, we'll draw some blood.'

'And then what?'

'Then we'll wait a day or two for the results, and we'll go from there. In the meantime, I'm going to give you a prescription for some antibiotics that I want you to start taking right away.'

'I thought antibiotics wouldn't help.'

'They won't help if the infection is viral. If it isn't viral, you could start to feel better as early as tomorrow. At any rate, it's worth a shot. Are you allergic to penicillin?'

'Not that I know of.'

He scribbled something on a piece of paper. 'Okay. Then let's try these. Take two immediately, then one every six hours after that. You can take them with food or without, it doesn't matter. If you're not feeling any better in a couple of days, we'll know that whatever is making you feel this way is viral. But hopefully, these will do the trick. At any rate, I'll call you with the test results as soon as they come in. Call me if you don't hear from me by Friday. Now go get me that specimen.'

Bonnie did as she was told, peeing into the small bottle, then returning to the doctor's office to let him draw blood. He filled four vials. 'That's a lot of blood,' she told him, surprised by how dark her blood looked in the small bottles. 'Are you testing for AIDS?'

'Should I be?' he asked.

'Isn't it standard?'

'No, it's not.' His eyes narrowed, peered deeply into hers. 'Should I be testing for AIDS, Mrs Wheeler?'

There was a long pause. 'I don't know,' Bonnie answered finally. What was she thinking?

'Have you taken any intravenous drugs in the last decade?'

'No, of course not.'

'Have you had any blood transfusions?'

'No.'

'Have you engaged in any high-risk sexual activities?'

Bonnie pictured herself tied to her bed, her legs wrapped around her husband's shoulders. 'What do you mean exactly?' she stammered.

'Anal intercourse, multiple partners, sex with someone who's infected,' he rhymed off with disconcerting nonchalance. 'Are you in a monogamous relationship, Mrs Wheeler?'

'I've never been unfaithful to my husband,' Bonnie answered.

'And your husband?'

'I don't know,' she admitted, after a pause. Dear God, what was she saying?

'Then why don't we do the test? That way, you won't have to worry.' Dr Kline patted her hand, then squeezed her trembling fingers.

Bonnie nodded, watching as he drew one final vial of blood from her veins. How could she have told the doctor she wasn't sure whether or not she was in a monogamous relationship. Could she really believe that Rod was having an affair? Did she trust her husband so little? If so, why had she insisted he go off with Marla? Why was she anxiously waiting his return? Was she turning into one of those women she'd always felt vaguely sorry for, the kind who stood by her man, no matter what indignities he threw her way? The kind who buried her frustrations and disappointments so deep, it made her literally sick?

Like her mother.

Bonnie thanked Dr Kline for his time, got dressed, then found a nearby drugstore and filled the prescription, finding a water fountain and taking two pills right away, as directed. Ever the good girl, she thought ruefully, returning to her car, sitting behind the wheel, not moving.

Where to now? she wondered, in no hurry to return home. She could go to school, she thought, but what was the point? They'd already hired a substitute for today, and besides, the day was half over. She could go shopping, but she wasn't really in the mood. Nor was she up to walking, reading, exercising, or even a movie, simple pleasures she'd taken for granted a few short weeks ago.

Maybe the antibiotics would work. Maybe by tomorrow she'd start to feel better. Or maybe they wouldn't work. Maybe nothing would work because nothing was the matter. Not with her body anyway. Maybe she wouldn't start to feel better until – until what? *Until she dealt with her long-repressed feelings of hostility toward her family of origin?*

Give me a break, she thought, starting the car, pulling away from the curb. So much psychobabble, so much mumbo-jumbo. Two hundred dollars for a piece of advice any first-year psychology student would have given her for the sheer pleasure of hearing himself talk. What a waste. And what lousy advice. What possible good could come from confronting her father? He'd never understand. She doubted he'd even listen.

You wouldn't be doing it for him, Dr Greenspoon had said.

'I'm not doing it at all,' Bonnie said out loud, stepping on the accelerator, turning up the radio full volume, letting the Rolling Stones block out all traces of conscious thought.

It was almost an hour later when she pulled up in front of the house at four hundred and twenty-two Maple Road in Easton. 'Now what?' she asked her reflection in the rearview mirror. 'What are you doing here? You drove all the way out here against your better judgement, and just what is it you think you're going to accomplish? Is your father going to apologize? Is that what you want? Is he going to explain? As if you'd believe anything he said. Why are you here?' she asked again.

You're here to take control of your life, her reflection answered silently, as Bonnie pushed open the car door, her feet unsteady as they felt for the ground. You're here so that you can reclaim your future, and the only way you can do that is by confronting your past.

Joan's death had thrown her into a kind of limbo, reintroduced her to a family she'd tried to leave behind. Now they were standing in front of her, blocking her path, not allowing her to move forward with her life. All she had to do was confront them, say her piece and leave. She never had to see them again. It was simple, she told herself, wobbling up the front path, trying to organize all the things she wanted to say, her thoughts scattering as soon as her hand touched the doorknob.

The door opened and Steve Lonergan stood before her, wearing dark blue pants and a blue-and-red-checked shirt, his broad face void of all expression, his eyes reflecting neither surprise nor curiosity. He stepped back to let her come in. Wordlessly, Bonnie stepped over the threshold, hearing the door close behind her like a prison gate clanging shut.

'Who's here, Steve?' Adeline Lonergan stepped out of the kitchen into the front hall. She was wearing an old-fashioned apron over a bright yellow dress. 'Oh,' she said, stopping as soon as she saw Bonnie. 'My goodness, Bonnie. I almost didn't recognize you. What have you done to your hair?'

'I'm sorry, Adeline, would you mind if I had a few minutes alone with my father? Please?' Bonnie asked, temporarily blinded by the whiteness of the walls.

'There's nothing we have to say to each other that Adeline can't hear,' her father said stubbornly, hands folding across his chest, like Mr Clean, Bonnie thought, trying to reduce him to manageable size.

'That's all right, Steve. I have things to do. You talk to your daughter. I'll be in the kitchen if you need anything.'

Father and daughter said nothing.

'Why don't the two of you go into the living room?' Adeline ventured. 'I think you'll be more comfortable there. Would either of you like

246

something to drink?' she continued when no one moved.

Steve Lonergan shook his head, walked slowly into the living room.

'Nothing for me, thank you,' Bonnie concurred, following after him. Why had she come? What did she hope to accomplish? What in God's name was she planning to say?

'I understand you saw your brother,' her father said, facing her in the middle of the room.

Bonnie turned away, pretending to study the interior, but the abundance of soft greens, whites and yellows was too much for her brain to absorb, and she reluctantly brought her gaze back to her father. 'Yes, he dropped over unexpectedly.' And uninvited, she almost added, but didn't.

'He treated you to some of his famous spaghetti sauce, did he?'

'*Infamous* is the word I believe he used.'

'Whatever it is, it's damn good.'

'Yes, it was,' Bonnie agreed. Except that I've been sick ever since, she added silently.

'He says that my granddaughter is a regular little doll.'

'Yes, she is.'

'I don't suppose you have any pictures of her,' her father said, then looked to the window, as if he hadn't spoken at all.

Bonnie hesitated, reluctant to share even this much of her child with her father. 'Actually, I do have a couple of pictures in my purse,' she relented, fishing inside her beige leather handbag, and pulling out a small red leather case, holding it toward her father. He took the case immediately, pulling out a pair of reading glasses from the front pocket of his shirt and balancing them across the bridge of his nose. 'The picture on the left is when she was four months old,' Bonnie explained. 'The one on the right was taken last year. She's changed a lot since then. Her hair's longer. Her face is a bit thinner.'

'Looks like her mother,' Steve Lonergan said.

Bonnie quickly returned the photographs to her purse, dropped her hands to her sides. 'Actually, everyone says she looks more like Rod.'

'And how is your husband?'

'He's well. He's in Florida right now, at a convention.'

'Left you to look after his kids, did he?'

Bonnie looked at the floor, her brown shoes sinking into the pale green broadloom. Like quicksand, she thought, wondering how long she could keep her head above ground. 'I didn't come here to talk about Rod,' she said.

'Why did you come?'

'I'm not sure,' she admitted after a pause. 'There were some things I felt needed to be said.'

'Say them,' her father directed.

'It's not that easy.'

'You've had over three years to prepare.'

Bonnie took a deep breath, tried to speak, couldn't.

'What are you doing here, Bonnie?' her father asked simply.

'What are *you* doing here?' Bonnie snapped in return, pouncing on his question. 'What right do you have to be in this house? How dare you come back here! How dare you make a mockery of my mother's memory!' Bonnie stepped back, stunned by the ferocity of her outburst.

'You think that's what I'm doing?'

'I think you have no business being here. You hated this house. You couldn't wait to leave it.'

'I always loved this place,' he corrected her, 'although I hated that damned floral wallpaper, I'll admit that. But after your mother and I agreed to a divorce . . .'

'You walked out. You gave her no choice.'

'She never really liked this house, you know. I had to talk her into moving out here. She preferred the city. But she insisted on keeping the house as part of the terms of our divorce, probably to spite me more than anything.'

'Probably to keep from disrupting the family any more than necessary,' Bonnie said. 'Maybe she felt we'd gone through enough changes.'

'Maybe. Guess we'll never know now.' Steve Lonergan paused, swallowed, looked toward the window. 'At any rate, after she died and left the place to Nick, he asked me if I was interested in buying it from him. He needed the cash more than he needed a big house, and Adeline and I agreed to help him out.'

'Everyone's always trying to help out old Nick.' Bonnie shook her head in amazement.

'Maybe he's not as strong as you are, Bonnie.'

'And the meek shall inherit the earth,' Bonnie said, noting the presence of the Bible still on the coffee table.

'Who is it you're really angry at, Bonnie?' her father asked.

'What's that supposed to mean?'

'I'm not the one who died and left the house to your brother,' her father reminded her.

Bonnie started pacing between the sofa and the wing chair. 'If you're trying to tell me the person I'm really angry at is my mother, you're absolutely wrong. I know who I'm angry at. He's standing right in front of me.'

'Why are you angry?'

'Why?' Bonnie parroted.

'Why?' he repeated.

'Why do you think?' Bonnie yelled. 'You walked out on your family.'

'I walked out on an intolerable situation.'

'Intolerable for whom? It wasn't my mother who was out every night gallivanting around.'

'No, your mother was home in bed every night.'

'She was sick.'

'She was always sick, dammit.'

'Are you blaming her?'

'No. I'm just saying that I couldn't live that way any longer.' He brushed his hand along the top of his scalp. 'I'm not trying to make excuses for myself, Bonnie. I know I took the coward's way out. But if you could try to understand for a few minutes what it was like for me. I was still a relatively young man. There were things I wanted to do. Your mother never wanted to go anywhere. She never wanted to do anything. She had no interest in making friends, or traveling, or even making love.'

'She was sick,' Bonnie repeated.

'So was I,' her father shot back. 'Sick of living that way, of feeling like my life was already over, of sleeping every night beside someone who recoiled whenever I tried to touch her. Bonnie, you were a child then, I didn't expect you to understand. But you're an adult now. I was hoping you'd have a little compassion.'

'Where was your compassion?'

'I tried, Bonnie. I tried for years.'

'Then you walked out. She was never the same after you left.'

'She was exactly the same and you know it.'

'You walked out and you never came back.'

'It was what she wanted.'

'She didn't know what she wanted. She was sick . . .'

'I was suffocating. I couldn't breathe. Her sickness was infecting us all.'

'So you left two children alone to look after her?'

'I didn't know what else to do.'

'You could have taken us with you!' Bonnie shouted, stunned by the words coming out of her mouth. She burst into tears, then collapsed on the sofa. 'You could have taken us with you,' she sobbed.

For a long while, nobody spoke. After several minutes, Bonnie felt her father at her side, his hand on her shoulder.

'Don't,' she said, shrugging off his hand. 'It's too late.'

'Why is it too late?'

'Because I'm not a little girl anymore.'

'You'll always be *my* little girl,' he told her.

'You have no idea,' she told him, refusing to look at him. 'You have no idea how much I cried, how every night I prayed that you'd come back for us. One night, I even walked in my sleep, packed a suitcase, and waited for you in the front hall. But it wasn't you who found me. It wasn't you who woke me up.'

'I'm so sorry, Bonnie. I tried to reach out to you on numerous occasions. You know that.'

'Yes, you were always very good about introducing us to your new wives.'

'You made it very clear whose side you were on, that you didn't want anything to do with me.'

'I was a child, for God's sake. What did you expect?'

'I expected you to grow up.'

'You abandoned us. You abandoned *me*.' A fresh onslaught of tears racked through Bonnie's body.

'I'm so sorry,' her father said. 'I wish there was something I could say or do.' His voice drifted to a halt. He walked to the window, stared out onto the street.

'Are you happy?' Bonnie asked, eyes on the gradual slope of his back. 'Does Adeline make you happy?'

'She's a wonderful woman,' her father said, turning around to face Bonnie. 'I'm very happy.'

'And Nick? You think he's really getting his act together?'

'I think he is, yes. Why don't you give him a chance?'

'I don't trust him.'

'He's your brother.'

'He broke our mother's heart.'

'He's not to blame for her death, Bonnie,' her father said.

Bonnie swallowed, brushed the tears impatiently from her eyes, said nothing. 'I should get going.' She stood up, walked into the hall, feeling her father behind her.

'Is everything all right?' Adeline asked, coming out of the kitchen, one hand clutching a large wooden spoon.

'Everything's fine,' her husband told her, looking to Bonnie for confirmation. Bonnie nodded, eyes wandering to the stairs.

'I'm making apple pies,' Adeline said. 'There's already one in the oven. It should be ready any minute, if you'd like a piece.'

'I really have to get going,' Bonnie said absently, drawn toward the stairs as if by a magnet.

'Would you like to see how we've changed the bedrooms?' Adeline asked.

Bonnie's right foot was already on the first step, her left hand on the wall. Something was pulling her up the stairs, beckoning her forward. What was she doing? she wondered, slowly mounting each step, watching the white walls bleed and darken, then fill with flowers, their odor swirling through her head, making her dizzy. Don't be silly, she told herself, looking toward the bedroom at the top of the stairs. It's just the apple pies in the oven. There's no odor. There are no flowers.

Just like there's no one waiting in the upstairs bedroom, Bonnie told herself, reaching the top of the landing and crossing the hall, pushing open the door to what was once her mother's bedroom.

The woman was sitting in the middle of the bed, her face in shadows.

'We've changed everything, as you can see,' Adeline was saying from somewhere beside Bonnie. 'We thought blue was pretty for a bedroom, and I've always been partial to mirrors.'

'Could I have a few minutes alone?' Bonnie asked, eyes on the shadowy figure in the middle of the bed.

'Certainly,' Adeline said, confusion causing the word to waver in the air. 'We'll be downstairs.'

Bonnie heard the door close behind her. It was only then that the figure in the bed leaned out of the shadows and beckoned Bonnie forward.

251

Chapter Twenty-Five

'Come closer so I can see you,' the figure said, the voice surprisingly strong.

Bonnie pushed her feet toward the bed, catching her reflection in the floor-to-ceiling mirror behind the light wood headboard, seeing it rebound in the smaller mirror on top of the dresser on the opposite wall. Except that instead of a woman in a shapeless ecru-colored shift, she saw a young girl of eleven, wearing a pale white cotton dress, her shoulder-length brown hair pulled into a ponytail by a shiny pink ribbon.

'How are feeling today?' the young girl asked the woman in the bed, approaching cautiously.

Shadows danced across the woman's face, like waves. 'Not very well, I'm afraid.'

'I've brought you some breakfast.' The girl lifted a heavy plastic tray for the woman's perusal.

'I couldn't eat anything.'

'Couldn't you try? I made it myself. Two eggs over easy, just the way you like them.'

'I couldn't eat any eggs.'

'Some orange juice then.' The child held the glass toward the bed.

'You're a good girl,' the woman said, falling back against her pillows, ignoring the tall glass of juice in the girl's hand.

The child drew closer, brought the glass to the woman's lips. 'Are you having a bad day?' she asked.

'I'm afraid so.'

'Headaches?'

'Migraines,' the woman qualified, bringing her hands to the sides of her temples, closing her eyes.

The waves washed over the woman's face, then disappeared, taking with them any signs of life, leaving only a pale, vaguely bloated mask, its pain evident, even in repose. Lost somewhere in all that pain was a beautiful woman, the child liked to imagine, a woman with sparkling blue eyes and a bright, expansive smile.

The child lowered the tray to the night table beside the bed and brought her small hands to the woman's face, smoothing her thick brown hair away from her forehead, and gently massaging the area around her high cheekbones.

'Not so hard,' the woman cautioned, and the child relaxed the pressure in her fingers. 'That's better. Here,' she pointed, indicating the area around her slightly upturned nose. 'My sinuses kept me up half the night. I don't think your father got any sleep.' She opened her eyes. 'Where is he? Has he gone out already?'

'It's after eleven o'clock,' the child told her. 'He said he had work to do.'

'On a Saturday?'

The child continued rubbing, said nothing.

'He's out with one of his women,' her mother said.

'He said he had work to do.'

'Nice work if you can get it.'

The child pulled back.

'No, don't stop. It feels good. You have good fingers. You make your mother feel much better.'

'Do I? Do I make you feel better?'

A sudden loud noise reverberated throughout the house. Bonnie spun around, her adult frame colliding with the child in the mirror. 'What was that?' she heard her father call out from downstairs.

'It's nothing, Steve,' she heard Adeline call back. 'I dropped a mixing bowl. It's nothing to worry about.'

'What's that noise?' the woman in the bed asked, as Bonnie returned to the body of the eleven-year-old girl.

'Nick's playing cops and robbers again,' the young girl answered.

'Bang, bang!' Nick shouted, bursting into the room, wearing a large tin badge and brandishing a toy gun in their direction. 'Bang, bang! You're dead.'

'Nick, you have to be quiet,' the young girl urged. 'Mommy's not feeling well today.'

'Bang, bang,' Nick insisted, oblivious. 'I shot you. You're dead.'

'You shot me,' the woman in the bed agreed, a faint laugh in her voice. 'I'm dead.' She closed her eyes, her head slumping over her right shoulder.

Nick laughed loudly and ran from the room, his eleven-year-old sister chasing after him. From her position at the foot of the bed, Bonnie watched them go.

'Come closer,' the woman in the bed beckoned again.

Bonnie straightened her shoulders and approached the bed, her fingers brushing up against the sky-blue comforter. Instantly, flowers spread across its surface, like weeds. Bonnie stared into the mirror, watching another image take shape, this one taller than the previous one, the hips fuller, the breasts more developed. The image twisted in and out, grew wider, then thinner, distorting this way and that, like a reflection in a funhouse mirror.

'Your father's left us,' her mother said from the bed, her face tight with anger.

'He'll be back,' the teenage girl assured her.

'No, he won't.'

'He just needed a little time to himself. He'll be home soon.'

'No, he's not coming back. He's with her.'

'Her?'

'That woman he's been seeing.'

'He won't stay with her.'

'He won't be back.'

Bonnie watched the teen's eyes fill with tears. 'I'll take care of you, Mommy,' she heard the girl say.

'I'm supposed to see Dr Blend on Friday. How will I get there?'

'I'll take you.'

'I'm afraid,' the woman cried out, and the girl rushed to her side. 'My heart is pounding so wildly I'm afraid I'm going to have a heart attack.'

'What can I do?'

'Get me my pills. They're right here by the bed.'

The girl's hands struggled to open the small bottle of red and yellow capsules. She dropped two into the palm of her hand, held them to the woman's lips, watched her swallow them easily without water. 'Are you all right?'

The woman shook her head.

'What can I do?'

'Nothing. You're a good girl.' She wiped some perspiration off her forehead with the backs of her fingers, looked around the darkened room. 'Where's Nicholas?'

'He's hiding from the neighbors,' the girl said, afraid to upset her mother, but reluctant to lie. 'He put handcuffs on Mrs Gradowski, then flushed the keys down the toilet. Mr Gradowski had to call a locksmith to get them off. He's really mad.'

Her mother laughed, delighted, as she always was, by Nick's high jinks. He could do no wrong, it seemed. The teenage girl shook her head in wonder and dismay, then faded from sight.

'I still can't see you,' the figure in the bed said to Bonnie. 'You'll have to come closer.'

Bonnie inched her way up the side of the bed. But someone was directly in her path, blocking her way, a young woman she knew intimately, she realized, stepping into the woman's shoes, assuming her wary posture, the woman's breath tightening in her chest.

'I'm getting married,' she announced, then waited. 'Mother, did you hear what I said? I said that Rod and I are getting married.'

'I heard you. Congratulations.'

'You don't sound very pleased.'

Her mother bit down on her lower lip. 'So you're deserting me too,' she said.

'No, of course not. Nobody's deserting you.'

'You're moving out.'

'I'm getting married.'

'Who will look after me?'

'Dr Monson said that you're well enough to look after yourself.'

'I'm no longer seeing Dr Monson.'

'We can get a housekeeper.'

'I don't want strangers in my house.'

'We'll work something out. Please, Mother, I want you to be happy for me.'

The woman in the bed turned her head away and cried.

'Don't cry, Mother. Not now. Now is a time to be happy,' Bonnie said, her voice ricocheting back and forth between the two mirrors, echoing against the stillness of the room. 'Can't you ever be happy for me?'

'Sit down, Bonnie,' her mother said, as Bonnie felt her stomach swell with her expected child. She perched nervously on the side of the flowered spread. 'We have to talk.'

'You should rest, Mother. Dr Bigelow said . . .'

'Dr Bigelow doesn't know a damn thing. Haven't you learned anything in all these years?'

'He said you had a stroke, that it was worse than the last one . . .'

'I want to talk about my will.'

'Please, Mother, can't we talk about it when you're feeling better?'

'I want you to understand.'

'Understand what?'

'Why I've done what I've done.'

'What are you talking about?'

'I'm leaving the house to Nick.'

'Mother, I don't want to talk about this now.'

'He needs something to ground him.'

'You're going to be fine. We can talk about this when you're stronger.'

'He's not as strong as you are,' her mother said, using Bonnie's words. 'That's why he's always getting into trouble. You have to help him.'

'Nick's a big boy, Mother. He can take care of himself.'

'He isn't guilty of trying to kill anyone. You know that. You'll see, he'll be acquitted. Just like the last time. He won't have to go to jail. It's all been a horrible mistake.'

'Mother, you have to stop worrying about him. It's not doing you any good to worry.'

'He was always a handful,' her mother said, almost proudly. 'Not like you. I could always count on you to do the right thing. You're my good one.' A smile tugged at the corners of her lips, but the stroke had rendered much of her face immobile, and the smile refused to stick. 'But, oh, how he made me laugh with his silly games. All the time shooting his gun. Bang, bang,' her mother said, her eyes smiling even if her lips could not. 'You understand, don't you, Bonnie?' her mother repeated. 'You already have a house, and a husband, and a baby on the way. Nick has nothing. He needs something to ground him.'

'Do whatever you want, Mother,' Bonnie heard herself say. 'The house doesn't matter to me. None of it matters to me.'

'You lied, didn't you?' the figure in the bed asked now, reaching out to grab Bonnie's hand, to force her back into her own reflection. 'You were always such a bad liar.'

Bonnie tried to pull away, but the hand was too quick, too strong. She felt herself being tugged inexorably toward the figure on the bed. 'No,' she protested. 'Please leave me alone.'

'Look at me,' the woman ordered.

Bonnie immediately shielded her eyes. 'No. No.'

'Look at me,' the woman commanded again, skeletal fingers prying Bonnie's hands away from her face.

Bonnie's hands fell to her sides. She opened her eyes, stared directly at the woman in the bed as all the shadows of the past fell away.

Her mother stared back at her, thick brown hair pulled back and secured with an antique silver clasp, eyes as deep and as cold as an arctic ocean, pale skin stretched tight across proud cheekbones, delicate upturned nose over an unconvincing smile. 'You look tired,' her mother said, securing the top button of her white quilted housecoat.

'I haven't been feeling very well,' Bonnie told her.

'Have you seen a doctor?'

'Yes.' She paused, swallowed. 'I thought maybe you could help me.'

'Me? How?'

'I'm not sure.'

'Why did you come?'

'I wanted to see you.'

'What is it you think I can do for you?'

'I don't know,' Bonnie told her honestly, searching the walls for answers, finding none. 'Did you know that Nick sold the house to Daddy right after you died?'

'He needed money for lawyers.'

'You gave him money for lawyers.'

'The house was too big for him. And besides, he loved to travel. Remember how he took off after college, went across the country on his own . . .'

'Stop making excuses for him.'

'He's my son.'

'I'm your daughter!'

Her mother said nothing. Bonnie found herself gazing into the mirror, confronting the endless repetitions of mother and daughter that refracted back at her. Generations of mothers and daughters, she thought, as close as their own reflections, and as unreachable.

'I didn't realize the house meant so much to you,' her mother said.

'It isn't the house,' Bonnie cried. 'I don't care about the house.'

'Then I don't understand.'

'I care about *you*. I love *you*.'

'I love you, too,' her mother said evenly.

'No,' Bonnie argued. 'There was only room in your heart for one child, and that child was Nick.'

'That's ridiculous, Bonnie. I always loved you.'

'No. You *depended* on me. You *counted* on me. I was your good one, remember? I was the good little girl. The good egg, you used to call me. You *relied* on me. But it's Nick you loved.'

'This is nonsense, Bonnie,' her mother protested, aggravation tightening each word like an elastic band. 'I expect more from you.'

'You always expected more from me,' Bonnie told her. 'And I always provided it. Didn't I? Didn't I always come through? Didn't I always go that extra mile?'

Her mother said nothing.

'All my life, I tried to make you happy. I tried to please you. I tried to make you feel better. When I was a little girl, I used to think maybe you were sick because of something I'd done, and I thought that if I could just be the perfect little girl and not give you any trouble, then you'd get better. Even when I was older, and I understood intellectually that your problems had nothing to do with me, I still thought I could make you well again. I made bargains with God. I promised Him everything if He'd just make you well again, if He'd make you happy. And after Daddy left, I felt even more responsible. I tried even harder. I cooked, I cleaned the house, I made straight As in school. When Nick started acting out, I acted good enough for both of us. But no matter how hard I tried, no matter how much or how long I prayed, no matter how good I was, you didn't get better. You never left the house except to go to the doctor's. Do you realize that you never once came to see me in a school play? That you never met any of my teachers? That you never even came to my college graduation?'

'I was sick!'

'You were always sick!'

'And you blame me?'

'No!' Bonnie cried, then, 'Yes! Yes, I blame you.' She let out a deep, anguished cry. 'What kind of life was that for a child? We couldn't have friends over. We couldn't speak above a whisper. We couldn't play the radio loud or have pets or even fight. We had to be careful of everything we said or did in case it might upset you and you took a turn for the worse. The doctors kept urging you to get out of bed, to get out of the house. They told you you could lead a normal life, that you weren't an invalid who had to be confined to her bed . . .'

'Doctors,' her mother scoffed again. 'What good are they?'

'Well, you should know. You had enough of them. You changed every time one told you something you didn't want to hear. You always found someone new who'd listen to your litany of aches and pains, someone who'd prescribe more pills. Did you ever think it might be the combination of all the pills you were taking that contributed to your stroke?'

'That's nonsense. You know as well as I do that I had a heart condition . . .'

'A heart murmur. Millions of people have heart murmurs. They lead full, productive lives.'

'I had allergies; I had migraines.'

'You had a husband and two children who needed you.'

'I tried my best.'

'You didn't try at all!' Bonnie closed her eyes, felt the room spin. 'You abandoned us long before Daddy ever did.'

There was silence.

'It isn't the house I cared about,' Bonnie said finally, corraling her thoughts into words, trying to make sense of all she was feeling. 'I understood on a rational level why you left the house to Nick. I did. It's just that it made me feel so left out. So abandoned all over again.'

Bonnie stood up, walked to the dresser, stared back at her mother through the layers of glass. 'When I found out I was pregnant, I couldn't wait to tell you. It had been a lousy few months. Nick had been arrested. You'd had your stroke. And I thought my news would save you.' Bonnie laughed. 'After all those years, after everything that had happened, I still thought I had the power to cure you. And if I didn't, my child surely could. My baby would pull you through, give you the strength you needed, the will to live, the desire to see her smile her first smile and take her first step. I convinced myself that you'd be there for my child in a way you'd never been there for me, that you'd be the perfect grandmother, knitting sweaters and baking apple pies.' Reluctantly, she pictured Adeline downstairs in the kitchen. 'But you couldn't even do that, could you?' Bonnie pressed on. 'You had to go and die before Amanda was born. You never even allowed me the pleasure of showing you my child.'

'You think I did that on purpose?' her mother asked.

'I don't *care* if you did it on purpose,' Bonnie told her. 'I only care that you weren't there, that you've never been there. Not for Daddy, not for Nick, not for Amanda, and certainly not for me.'

Her mother folded her hands one inside the other, stared into her lap. 'What's happened to you, Bonnie?' she asked bitterly. 'You were always such a good girl.'

'I wasn't such a good girl!' Bonnie screamed, watching the mirrors shake, jarring loose past reflections – the anxious adolescent in her white dress, the worried teenager, the concerned young woman in her early twenties, the nervous bride-to-be, the agitated expectant mother – watching them cower, cover their ears. 'Do you know how many times I wished you were dead?' Bonnie cried out. 'Do you have any idea how many times I wished your heart would simply give out?' she demanded, feeling her own heart rip, then tear, with the admission. 'Do you know that as often as I prayed for you to get better, I prayed you'd go to sleep and never wake up? Oh God, I'm not a good girl. I'm not good at all.' Bonnie lowered her head into her mother's lap and sobbed.

After several minutes, she felt her mother's hand on the back of her hair, her fingers stroking her neck. 'I love you,' her mother whispered, her voice going faint.

'I love you more,' Bonnie cried softly.

'It's all right,' a voice was saying. 'It's all right, Bonnie. Everything's going to be all right.'

Bonnie slowly lifted her head, saw Adeline standing beside her, her fingers gently stroking the back of her neck. Bonnie looked at the bed, felt the sky-blue bedspread flat beneath her fingers. The bed was empty. Her mother was gone.

'Your father and I heard you crying,' Adeline said. 'We were concerned.'

'I'm sorry,' Bonnie told her, wiping her eyes. 'I didn't mean to worry you.'

'No, don't be sorry. It's all right to be sad. It's all right to cry.'

Bonnie nodded, forced herself to her feet. 'I should go.'

'Do you have to?' Adeline asked. 'Nick just called. I told him you were here. He said he'd be home in a few minutes.'

'I can't wait. I have to get back.'

'Your father and I would be delighted if you'd stay for dinner. You could call home, invite the whole family. It would be our pleasure . . .'

'Thank you, but no,' Bonnie said quickly. 'Rod is out of town, and I haven't been feeling very well.'

'Another time then, perhaps.'

'Perhaps,' Bonnie repeated, taking one last look around the room before leaving the ghosts and shadows of the past behind.

Chapter Twenty-Six

He was waiting for her when she got home.

'Josh,' Bonnie acknowledged in grateful surprise, climbing out of her car, seeing him standing in her driveway, fighting the urge to rush into his arms.

'Car's working all right now, I see,' he said.

She checked her watch, more than a little embarrassed by how pleased she was to see him, hoping it wasn't obvious in her face. 'What are you doing here?' she asked, noting it was almost five o'clock.

'They said at school that you were still sick and I thought I'd drop by and see how you were doing, bring you some chicken soup.' He held up a large bottle of clear liquid.

Bonnie smoothed her short hair self-consciously, and opened the front door, her wary eyes circling the floor before motioning for him to follow her inside the house. 'Hello?' she called, walking directly into the kitchen, taking the bottle of chicken soup from Josh's hands, placing it on the counter. 'Anybody home? Lauren? Amanda?' Bonnie marched back into the front hall, rechecking her watch. 'Sam?' Her eyes returned warily to the floor. L'il Abner? she mouthed silently. Where was everyone?

'They're at Diana's,' Josh said from somewhere behind her.

Bonnie spun around. Too fast. Her head kept spinning. 'What?'

Josh held out a piece of white paper. 'They left you a note on the kitchen table. Here.' He extended the piece of paper toward her. Bonnie reached for it, lost her balance, felt her body sway. In the next instant, she was in Josh's arms, the room dancing around her head.

'Let me get you some water,' Josh said, leading Bonnie back into the kitchen, propping her up in one of the kitchen chairs, keeping a watchful eye on her as he ran to the sink and poured her a glass of cold water.

'Haven't we done this before?' Bonnie asked.

Josh smiled, pressed the glass to her lips. 'Are you all right? Should I call a doctor?'

Bonnie took a long sip. 'I saw a doctor this morning. He gave me some pills.'

'Is it time to take one?'

Bonnie looked toward her watch, but she could no longer determine which hand was long and which hand was short. They blurred and intertwined, lost between numbers that said nothing to her at all. 'Not for another hour,' Bonnie told him, remembering that it had been almost five o'clock just minutes ago. She took another sip of water. 'I'll be okay. I think I just tried to do too much today.' She was exhausted, she realized, desperate to lie down. All that driving. All those memories. Confronting one's family of origin wasn't exactly a walk on the beach, she decided, thinking of Rod in Florida, wondering what his children were doing over at Diana's.

'What does the note say?' Bonnie asked.

'Bonnie,' Josh read. *'Went to Diana's to start papering her bathroom. Took Amanda with us. Back by six.* Signed, *Sam and Lauren.'* He returned the paper to the table. 'Can I fix you a cup of soup?'

Bonnie smiled. 'Thanks. Soup sounds good.'

In the next second, he was at the counter, emptying the contents of the bottle into a pot, stirring it gently as it heated.

'This is delicious,' Bonnie told him, moments later, savoring the soothing liquid as it snaked its way down her throat.

'My mother's secret recipe.'

'Really?'

'No. My mother was a lousy cook. And I'm a lousy liar. I bought this at a small deli in Wellesley.'

'I'm a lousy liar too,' Bonnie told him, so pleased he was here. 'Thank you for the soup. It was very kind of you to think about me.'

He smiled. 'Anytime.'

'I think maybe I should lie down for a while before everyone gets back,' she said, finishing the last spoonful.

Josh helped her into the living room, watching as she lay down on the sofa. 'What time does your husband get home?'

Bonnie drew her knees up to her chest, burrowed her head into the soft green pillow, closed her eyes. 'He's away this week. At a convention in Miami.'

'Does he know you're this sick?'

'He'll be home soon.' Bonnie raised her chin just enough so that she could peek out from beneath barely lifted lashes without actually having to open her eyes. She saw Josh fold himself into one of the chairs across from the sofa. 'You don't have to stay. I'll be okay.'

'I think I should wait until someone gets home. I don't think you should be alone,' he told her, his tone indicating further protest was useless.

Thank you, Bonnie said, although no words were spoken, and she was already drifting off to sleep.

'Mommy!' Amanda squealed, running toward her, just as Bonnie opened her eyes. 'We've been papering. It was cool.'

Bonnie propped herself up on the sofa, bringing her feet to the floor, Amanda immediately jumping into her lap. 'I can see you've been very busy.' Bonnie wiped some white paste from the child's cheek.

'It was fun. Sam said I'm a natural.' Amanda giggled.

'He did, did he?'

Amanda nodded proudly. 'What's a natural?'

Bonnie laughed as Sam and Lauren entered the room. Both wore fashionable faded and torn jeans and old T-shirts, their hair tied behind their ears and dotted with white dust. Even the ring in Sam's nose was flecked with white. 'Whose car is in the driveway?' Sam asked.

'That's mine,' Josh Freeman stated, coming into the room.

Where had he been? Bonnie wondered, then wondered why he was here at all. Had he really come just to see if she was all right?

'Hi, Mr Freeman,' Sam said. 'What are you going here?'

'Slaving over a hot stove,' came the immediate reply. 'I thought I'd make you guys some dinner,' he explained. 'I didn't think Bonnie would be up to it, and I make a mean hot dog.'

'Hot dogs?' Amanda clapped her hands with delight.

'And baked beans,' Josh added with a wink.

'You didn't have to do that,' Bonnie told him.

'Is it time for your pills yet?' he asked.

'What pills?' Lauren said.

'Bonnie was at the doctor's,' Josh explained. 'He prescribed some antibiotics. I'll get them.' He returned to the kitchen before Bonnie could protest.

'What did the doctor say?' Lauren asked.

'Not much. He says it might be an inner ear infection.' She shrugged. 'Or it might not.'

'We played dress-up at Diana's house,' Amanda announced.

'She got into Diana's closet,' Lauren said sheepishly. 'I tried to stop her.'

'Diana has pretty things,' Amanda said.

'Yes,' Bonnie agreed. 'But I don't think she'd appreciate you playing with them. I hope you put everything away exactly where you found it.'

Amanda pouted prettily, her lips arranging themselves into a large pucker that begged to be kissed.

'I helped her,' Lauren said.

The phone rang.

'Do you want me to answer that?' Josh Freeman called from the kitchen.

'Please.' Bonnie thought it was probably Rod, and wondered what he'd make of the strange male voice answering his telephone.

'Who the hell is Josh Freeman?' Rod was asking seconds later, as Bonnie took the phone from Josh's hands, sitting down on a kitchen chair Josh pulled over for her.

'Sam's art teacher,' Bonnie whispered. 'Remember? He was at Joan's funeral.'

'What's he doing there?'

'He came by to see how I was feeling. How's everything in Miami?' she asked, changing the subject, not really sure what Josh Freeman was still doing there.

'Miami is great. Everything's going even better than we hoped. The affiliates are crazy about Marla. She has them eating out of the palm of her hand.'

Josh extended his palm toward her. A single white tablet rested across his long and sturdy lifeline. Bonnie took the pill, popped it inside her mouth, and swallowed it with the glass of water that Josh held in his other hand.

'How are you feeling?' Rod asked, almost an afterthought.

'About the same. I went to a doctor. He prescribed some antibiotics.'

'What doctor?'

'Dr Kline.'

'Who's he?'

'Someone Diana recommended,' Bonnie lied, thinking it easier than having to tell him about her visit to Dr Greenspoon. Not that she planned on keeping it a secret. It was just too complicated to get into over the phone.

'Did you find the snake yet?'

Bonnie's eyes automatically shot to her feet. 'Not yet.'

'Well, try not to worry about him. I think he's history.'

Bonnie nodded, watching Sam come into the room, grab a soft drink out of the fridge.

'Bonnie, are you there?'

'Yes, I'm sorry. I'll try not to worry.'

'Okay, look, I've got to run. Marla's arranged some sort of major meeting with one of the network honchos for seven o'clock, and I've got some notes to go over. I'll call you tomorrow. I miss you,' he added before hanging up.

'Tomorrow,' Bonnie repeated, returning the phone to its carriage as Josh Freeman brought a plate full of hot dogs to the kitchen table.

'Dinner's ready,' he announced as Sam, Lauren and Amanda arranged themselves eagerly around the table. 'Hot dogs for everyone.' He looked at Bonnie. 'Chicken soup for you.'

The phone rang at precisely two twenty-three in the morning. Bonnie jumped up, arms lurching wildly in front of her, as if to protect herself from the sound. It took several seconds for her to understand what was happening, another few seconds to find the phone and bring it to her ear. 'Hello?' she said breathlessly into the receiver.

Nothing.

'Hello? Dammit, who is this?'

Still nothing, then a strange click, then nothing again.

'Hello? Who is this? Is someone there?'

A dial tone was her only response. Bonnie slammed the phone into the receiver and burst into tears. The one good sleep she'd had in days, undisturbed by nausea or nightmares or wayward twitches, and it had been shattered. Maybe the antibiotics were helping after all, she thought, wiping away her tears and getting out of bed, flipping on the light, doing a quick check of the floor, the windowsill, the curtains.

She walked into the hall. She might as well make her nightly rounds, she decided, eyes skirting the baseboards as she looked through the

267

shadows into Sam's room, the snake's tank illuminated, the two white sacrificial rats curled into little balls on its gravel-strewn bottom. Snakes, and now rats. I can't believe this is my life, Bonnie thought, continuing down the hall, stopping in front of Amanda's open door, her heart sinking.

Hadn't she cautioned Amanda to keep the door to her room closed until they found L'il Abner? 'Remember to close it again if you wake up in the middle of the night and have to go to the bathroom,' she'd warned. And here it was, wide open.

What could you do? Bonnie wondered, stepping inside her daughter's room and peering through the darkness. Amanda was a child, not even four years old. She couldn't be expected to worry about everything. That's what mothers were for.

Slowly, Bonnie's eyes adjusting to the dark, she approached Amanda's bed, hand resting on the large stuffed kangaroo as she listened to Amanda's steady breathing. Carefully, Bonnie switched on the Big Bird light beside the bed. The child stirred slightly, but didn't open her eyes. Bonnie took a quick glance around. There were bears; there were dogs; there were frogs. No snakes, Bonnie thought with relief, switching off the light and returning to the hall.

Lauren's door was closed. Bonnie pushed it slightly open and peeked inside, closing it again when she heard Lauren's delicate snore. Then she returned to her room and crawled back into bed, where she lay awake until morning.

Josh Freeman called her the following afternoon. 'I'm on a break,' he told her. 'I just phoned to see how you were doing.'

'Did you call me last night?' Bonnie asked immediately.

'Last night? When? You mean, after I left?'

'I mean last night at exactly twenty-three minutes after two.'

'Why on earth would I call you at almost two thirty in the morning?'

'I'm sorry,' Bonnie apologized. 'I'm not thinking very clearly. Of course it wasn't you.'

'Someone called you at two-thirty in the morning? What did they say?'

'They didn't say anything. They just waited a few minutes, then hung up.'

'Did you call the police?'

'What for? It's probably just some crank.'

'It might be a good idea to keep the police informed anyway,' he advised.

Bonnie nodded, but said nothing.

'How are you feeling?'

'Actually, I feel a little stronger today,' Bonnie reported from her bed. 'The antibiotics seem to be helping.'

'Need some more chicken soup?'

'I think you brought me enough to last a week.'

'How about some company?'

'Why?' she asked, surprising them both with the question.

'Why?' he repeated.

She hesitated. 'First, you wouldn't even talk to me,' she reminded him softly, thinking how much she'd like to see him. 'Now you're bringing me chicken soup, and cooking my kids dinner. What's up?'

There was a long pause. 'I like you,' he answered simply. 'And I sensed you could use a friend. I know I could.'

The doorbell rang.

'Someone's at my door,' she told him, grateful for the timely interruption. 'I better see who it is.'

'I'll call you later, if that's all right.'

'Yes,' she said. 'It's all right.'

The doorbell rang again as Bonnie reached the bottom step. She gathered her housecoat tightly around her. 'Just a second,' she called out, her legs wobbly from their sudden exertion. 'Who is it?'

'Everybody's favorite jailbird,' came the reply.

Bonnie laid her forehead against the hard wood of the front door. When had she lost control of her life? she wondered. 'What do you want, Nick?'

'I want to see you.'

'I'm not feeling very well.'

'So I understand. Let me in. I want to talk to you.'

Bonnie took a deep breath, then opened the door.

'My God, what did you do to your hair?' Nick asked, his own dark blond hair neatly trimmed and brushed away from his forehead. He had their mother's delicate nose, Bonnie realized, standing back and letting him come inside.

'Did you call me last night?'

'Last night? No. Was I supposed to?'

269

'Someone called here at two twenty-three in the morning,' she told him, walking into the kitchen, taking the bottle of chicken soup from the fridge, pouring some into a pot and turning on the element. 'Do you want some soup?'

'You think I called you in the middle of the night? No, I don't want any soup.'

'You've done it before,' she reminded him.

'Only because you told Adeline it was important that you reach me.'

'So it wasn't you who phoned last night,' she said.

'No, it wasn't me.' He pulled up a chair, sat down. 'You want to tell me about it?'

Bonnie shrugged. 'There's nothing to tell. Someone called, then they hung up. End of story.'

'I understand Rod's away in Florida,' Nick said after a pause.

'What's that supposed to mean?'

'Nothing. It's called conversation.'

'I thought you were implying that Rod might have called.'

'It never crossed my mind. Why? Do you think it might have been Rod?'

'Of course not,' Bonnie said quickly. Did she?

'Look,' Nick told her, 'I just came by to see how you were doing. Adeline told me that you dropped by yesterday. I was hoping you'd still be around when I got back from work, but Adeline said you had to leave because you weren't feeling very well.'

'What else did sweet Adeline have to say?'

'That you and Dad had a good talk.'

'Is that what Dad said?'

'You know Dad. He . . .'

' . . . doesn't say much,' Bonnie said, finishing her brother's sentence.

'But I know he felt good about your visit, Bonnie. It was all over his face. Like some long shadow had been lifted.'

The soup started boiling. Bonnie lifted the pot off the stove, poured the hot soup into a bowl. 'You're sure you don't want any?'

'I'll have a beer, if you've got any.'

Bonnie nodded toward the fridge. 'Help yourself.'

In the next minute, they were sitting across from each other at the kitchen table, Bonnie sipping her soup, Nick his beer. Who'd have thought it? Bonnie wondered, amazed by the brain's continued capacity for surprise.

'What's happening with the murder investigation?' Nick asked suddenly.

The question caught Bonnie off guard and her hand started shaking, the soup in her spoon spilling onto the table. 'What?'

'Careful,' he cautioned. 'It's hot.' He grabbed a napkin from the side counter, wiped up the spill. 'I asked if there was anything new with the police investigation.'

'Why do you ask that?'

Nick shrugged. 'Haven't read anything in the papers for a while. I was just wondering if you'd heard anything.'

'Like what?'

'Like if the police were any closer to finding Joan's killer.'

'Your guess is as good as mine,' Bonnie told him, watching his eyes, trying to read the thoughts behind them.

Nick raised the beer bottle to his lips, threw his head back across the top of his spine, sucked the rich brown liquid into his body as if he were inhaling a cigarette. 'Nothing like a good cold glass of beer,' he said.

'Have you heard anything?' Bonnie asked.

'Me?' He laughed. 'How would I hear anything?'

'I thought the police might have been back to question you.'

'Still think I might have killed Joan?'

'Did you?'

'No.' He took another sip of his beer. 'I have an alibi, remember?'

'I'm not sure our father qualifies as an unbiased witness.'

'You were wrong about him before.'

There was silence.

'Maybe you're wrong about me too,' Nick continued.

'I doubt it,' Bonnie said stubbornly, gulping down the balance of her soup, taking the bowl to the kitchen sink, the floor shifting slightly beneath her feet. 'You're not exactly a stranger to murder, are you?' she asked. 'Or are you still insisting you were framed?'

'I was in the car when Scott Dunphy was arranging the hit,' he reminded her, as old newspaper clippings danced before Bonnie's eyes. The clippings from Joan's scrapbook, she realized, her breath catching in her throat.

'They were standing two feet away from you,' she argued. 'How could you not hear what they were talking about?'

'The car window was closed.'

'So you didn't hear a thing, and you had no idea why your shady partner was handing over ten thousand dollars in cash to a total stranger. Is that what you're seriously trying to tell me?'

'It's more complicated than you realize.'

'Is it?'

There was a moment's silence. 'I didn't kill Joan,' Nick said finally.

Bonnie nodded, said nothing. What was the point? She watched the room suddenly tilt, the ceiling slope toward the floor. She leaned back against the kitchen counter, tried to focus on the large maple tree just outside the front window, watched its branches sway with the gentle outside breeze. She shifted her gaze to the Chagall lithograph on the wall, watching as Chagall's upside-down cow slid off the roof of the house, feeling her knees grow weak. She saw Amanda's painting of square-headed people, her own head starting to feel vaguely box-like. What was happening to her? Was it time to take another pill? She tried to focus on her watch, gave up when the numbers proved indistinguishable, looked instead to the digital clock over the stove, but it, too, blurred, its numbers waving in and out. 'The clock in my car is digital,' she remembered telling the police, and then laughing at the absurdity of it all. Why hadn't anybody told her it was only going to get worse?

'Bonnie,' Nick was saying, his voice lumbering toward her as if coated in heavy molasses. 'What's happening? Are you all right?'

She took a step forward, panicking when she was unable to feel the floor beneath her feet. 'Help me,' she cried out as the room faded to black and she felt herself slipping headlong into the abyss.

Chapter Twenty-Seven

When Bonnie opened her eyes, she was in bed and Nick was sitting in the chair across from her. 'What happened?' she asked, pushing her body slowly up against the headboard.

'You fainted,' he told her, approaching the bed, sitting down gently at her feet.

Bonnie looked around, saw it was still light outside. 'How long ago?'

'Not long. An hour maybe.'

'The kids . . . ?'

'Sam and Lauren came home from school and went right out again. Something about papering Diana's bathroom. Amanda hasn't come home yet.'

'No. She was invited over to a friend's house. They'll be bringing her back about five thirty. I should get up, start to get dinner ready.' She took a deep breath. Her head felt noticeably heavy, as if it were a strain for her neck to support. What was happening? Was she having a relapse? She was feeling worse than ever.

'Stay where you are. I already told the kids we'd order pizza when they get home.'

'This is ridiculous,' Bonnie groused. 'I just can't stay in bed forever.'

'Who said anything about forever?' Nick asked. 'You're not our mother, Bonnie. A few days does not a lifetime make.'

Bonnie tried to smile, but her lips quivered, then twitched, and she abandoned the attempt. 'Since when did you turn into such a nice guy?' she asked.

'Someone called while you were asleep,' Nick told her, ignoring the question. 'Said his name was Josh Freeman. Claims he's a friend of yours.'

Bonnie nodded. 'He's a teacher at Weston Secondary. He dropped by yesterday, brought me some chicken soup.'

'Well,' Nick said, patting her feet, 'there doesn't seem to be any shortage of men to take care of you.'

Except for my husband, Bonnie thought.

'Except for your husband,' Nick said.

As if on cue, the phone rang and it was Rod. 'You're still in bed?' he asked, incredulously.

'I can't seem to shake this bug.'

'What does the doctor say?'

'He should be calling by tomorrow with the results of the tests,' Bonnie said, knowing this wasn't the answer to the question Rod has asked, but thinking it served just as well. She watched as Nick began pacing restlessly between the bed and the window.

'How are the kids?' Rod asked.

'They seem fine. Lauren's okay. So far, no one else has gotten sick.' Thank God, Bonnie thought.

'When's he coming home?' Nick asked.

'What?' Rod said. 'Who was that? Is that teacher there again?'

'It's Nick,' Bonnie told him.

'Nick?! What the hell is he doing there?'

'I'm taking care of my sister,' Nick answered, scooping the phone from Bonnie's hand and snarling into it. 'Something you should be doing.'

'Nick,' Bonnie protested, but the protest was weak, and she had to admit her heart wasn't in it.

'What the hell is going on there?' Rod demanded, his voice loud enough for Bonnie to hear.

'Your wife is sick. She fainted less than an hour ago, and it's a good thing I was here to catch her when she fell.'

'She fainted?'

'When are you coming home?' Nick asked again.

'I'm scheduled to fly back Saturday morning.'

'Change your schedule,' Nick said.

It seemed as if everybody paused to catch their breath, then, 'Let me speak to Bonnie,' she heard Rod say as Nick handed her back the phone.

'Rod . . .'

'What the hell is happening there, Bonnie?'

'I don't feel well, Rod.'

'You want me to cut short my trip, come home early, is that it?' His voice pleaded for a simple 'no'.

Bonnie closed her eyes, swallowed, the stale taste of blood clinging to her gums. 'Yes,' she said.

An uncomfortable silence followed. 'All right,' Rod said. 'I'll see what I can do about getting a flight out of here sometime tomorrow.'

Bonnie started to cry. 'I'm sorry, Rod. I don't know what's the matter with me. I don't know what to do. I'm scared.'

'Don't be scared, honey.' Rod's voice strained for sympathy. 'It's just a bad case of the flu. You'll probably be feeling much better by the time I get home.'

'I hope so.'

'All right, look, I better get going if I want to rearrange my timetable. I'll see you tomorrow, honey. Stay calm. Try to get some sleep. And get rid of that brother of yours. You were doing great until he started showing up.'

Bonnie returned the phone to Nick's outstretched hand, watched him drop the receiver into the carriage, noting for the first time how defined the muscles in his arms had become. Lots of time to exercise in jail, she thought, trying not to absorb the weight of Rod's words. *You were doing great until he started showing up.*

I thought confronting my past was supposed to make me feel better, Bonnie thought, sinking back under the covers. 'He's coming home tomorrow,' she heard herself say before drifting off to sleep.

It was dark the next time she opened her eyes. She sat up with a start, a series of small heat bombs exploding inside her, bathing her skin in sweat.

'Bonnie?' the voice asked from somewhere in the dark.

Bonnie gasped, scrambling to her knees on the bed, gathering her blankets around her, trying to decide if she was awake or asleep.

'It's okay. It's me, Nick,' the voice continued, moving closer.

Bonnie saw the figure cutting through the dim light, the long dark blond hair, the muscular arms, the curiously feminine nose in the middle of such a determinedly masculine face. 'What time is it?' she asked. How many times had she asked that question lately? Did it make any difference? Had it ever?

'It's after ten,' he told her.

'After ten? Where's Amanda?'

'She's asleep.'

'Sam and Lauren . . . ?'

'In their rooms.'

'What are you still doing here?'

'Making sure you're okay.'

'I don't understand,' she told him. 'Why the sudden concern?'

'I've always been concerned,' he told her.

There was a timid knock at the bedroom door.

'Yes?' Bonnie called weakly.

Sam slunk into the room as if he were too tall for the ceiling, his head craning forward over stooped shoulders, his eyes searching out Bonnie in the dark. 'I heard voices and I thought I'd see how you were doing,' he explained. 'How are you?'

'I've been better.'

'The pills aren't working?'

Bonnie rubbed her forehead. She couldn't remember the last time she'd taken one. 'I'm probably due for one around now,' she said.

'Where are they?' Nick asked.

'In the kitchen.'

'I'll get them,' Sam offered, and was gone.

'He's a strange kid,' Nick observed.

'So were you,' Bonnie reminded her brother. 'Always playing cops and robbers. Except in those days, you were always the good guy. What happened, Nick? What made you change sides?'

'Things happen,' Nick told her. 'People change.'

'What happened? How do they change?'

Nick pushed his hair off his forehead, a curious expression settling on his face, his eyes staring at her with an intensity even the darkness couldn't hide. She realized she was frightened.

What was he doing here? Why had he come? What was he doing back in her life, and why now? What connection did he have to Joan? To her death? Had he murdered her? Was he planning on murdering his sister as well? Was that why he had insinuated himself back into her life? Was that what he was doing here tonight? She was feeling so sick, she almost didn't care. Just do it quickly, she prayed, and get it over with. Anything was better than the way she'd been feeling the last several weeks.

Just don't hurt my child, she pleaded silently, as Nick turned away. The thought forced Bonnie's spine erect. She had to stay strong, she determined. She couldn't let anything happen to her little girl.

'I brought you some soup,' Sam said, walking carefully into the room, steam rising from the mug in his hands. He came around the side of the bed, dropping the antibiotic into Bonnie's outstretched hand, then transferred the soup from his hand to hers. 'Careful, it's hot. I put it in the microwave.'

Bonnie put the pill at the back of her tongue, blew softly on the soup, then swallowed. The pill bounced uneasily down her throat, like a ball in a pinball machine. She took another sip of the soup, felt it burn the tip of her tongue, swallowed anyway. 'How's Diana's bathroom coming along?' she asked.

'Great,' Sam said proudly. 'I think she'll be happy.'

'I'm sure she will.' Bonnie took another sip of the soup.

'She'll be back on the weekend. I'll find out then.' Sam shuffled from one foot to the other. 'I'm kind of tired,' he said. 'Is it all right if I go to bed?'

'Of course,' Bonnie told him.

'I can show myself out,' Nick said.

Sam smiled, slouched toward the hall, stopped. 'Hope you're feeling better by tomorrow.'

'Me too.' Bonnie turned her attention back to Nick. 'I'm sure you have other things to do,' she began.

'Not a thing. Actually, I was thinking of spending the night.'

'What? No, don't be silly. You can't do that.'

'Why not? I'll sleep right here on the chair. That way, I'm here in case you need anything.'

'I'm not going to need anything.'

'I'm not going to leave,' Nick said.

At first she heard the whimpering as part of her dream.

She was standing in the middle of the school cafeteria, plastic lunch tray in hand, waiting her turn at the food counter. 'Move along,' a voice beckoned, and Bonnie inched forward, a high-pitched whine hissing from the vents by her feet, licking at her bare legs.

'Is something wrong with the pipes?' she asked Rod, who was dressed in the uniform of the school custodian.

'Why don't you have a look and see?' he suggested, pulling open the square air vent in the wall by his legs. The whimpering immediately grew louder, more pronounced. Someone was trapped inside, Bonnie realized, edging closer.

'Watch out for snakes,' Rod warned as Bonnie crawled inside the long tunnel.

'Is someone there?' Bonnie called, her voice ricocheting off the tunnel's walls, slapping at the sides of her face, like a bitter wind.

'Mommy?' a small voice asked. 'Mommy, help me. Help me.'

'Amanda?' Bonnie gasped, scrambling on her hands and knees toward the sound. But the closer she got, the longer the tunnel grew, the greater the distance between them. Dirt from the tunnel walls began dropping on Bonnie's head, threatening to bury her alive.

'Mommy!' Amanda called again, her voice disappearing into the now-familiar whimper.

'Amanda!' Bonnie cried, breaking into a sweat, hand reaching into the surrounding darkness, flailing about.

Bonnie's hand touched the cool air of reality, and she woke up, perspiration trickling from her forehead to her neck. Oh God, she thought, sitting up in bed, making out the sleeping form of her brother in the chair across the room. Another nightmare to add to her collection.

And then she heard the whimpering, and she understood that it was real, that her subconscious had only incorporated it into her dream, not created it. 'Amanda!' she whispered urgently, jumping out of bed, running into the hall toward her daughter's room, the whimpering growing louder with each frantic step.

Bonnie reached Amanda's room, her breath forming a tight ball in the middle of her chest when she realized the bedroom door was wide open. Uttering a silent prayer, her breath escaping her lungs in a series of short, painful spasms, she stepped inside the room and flipped on the overhead light.

Amanda was sitting up in her bed, her small body pressed tightly against her headboard, hands at her open mouth, tears streaming down her cheeks, eyes wide as saucers, her blankets on the floor, stuffed animals all around her, the pink panda by her head, several black and white dogs at her waist, the live snake at her feet.

Bonnie gasped at the almost surreal scene before her.

The snake was coiled around Amanda's bare ankle, its body swaying hypnotically toward her. 'Mommy,' Amanda cried softly, as Bonnie stood frozen in the doorway. 'He's squeezing my foot, Mommy. It hurts. Make him stop.'

Oh God, Bonnie thought, feeling her own body sway, her head grow light. She was going to faint, she realized, then, no, no, she couldn't faint. Wouldn't faint. She had to save her daughter. Nothing else mattered. This was her child, more precious to her than life itself. There was no way she was going to let anything happen to her. She would do anything to protect her.

In the next moment, she felt herself leave her body, abandoning it in much the same way a snake sheds its skin, growing weightless as she flew through the air toward Amanda's bed, no longer thinking anything at all, an animal only, operating on pure instinct and adrenalin. Bonnie lunged at the snake, grabbing at its head with one hand, at the tight coils of its tail with the other. The snake stiffened and grew heavy in her hands, as if she'd grabbed hold of an iron pole. And then it started twisting, its head straining against the palm of her hand, its long body tensing and pushing against her grip in seemingly all directions at once. Her fingers worked to loosen the snake's coils from her daughter's foot, but it was as if the snake had fingers of its own, pulsing rhythmically against hers. He's so strong, Bonnie thought, not sure if she had the strength to hold him.

She heard noises, the sounds of her own screams, she realized, as she fought to unwrap the snake from Amanda's ankle. Almost there, she thought, her fingers digging under the snake's silken skin. She almost had him.

She pulled hard, heard a pop, like a suction cup coming free, the snake now off Amanda and struggling inside her arms. He was so heavy, she thought, so damn strong. She couldn't hold him much longer, she knew, hearing voices, turning around as Nick appeared in the doorway, his eyes wild, his arms outstretched, the gun in his hands pointed directly at her head.

She gasped, and stopped struggling, her palms opening, the snake dropping to the floor.

He hit the carpet with a thud and coiled back in fury, preparing to strike.

'Don't shoot him!' Sam screamed, knocking Nick aside and racing into the room, throwing himself over the enraged boa constrictor. Bonnie's eyes remained riveted on her brother, the gun still in his hand.

Was it the same gun he'd used to shoot Joan? she wondered. Was he going to shoot her now as well?

Out of the corner of her eye, Bonnie saw Sam, wincing with pain, as he rose to his feet, the snake still putting up an impressive show of resistance. Shaken and breathing hard, giving only a fleeting glance in Nick's direction, Sam carried the reptile out of the room.

Bonnie waited until she heard the top of the tank being fitted back into place before sinking to her knees and bursting into tears.

'Mommy!' Amanda cried, jumping out of bed and into her mother's arms.

'Are you all right, baby?' Bonnie asked, kissing Amanda's cheeks, patting her hair, stroking the bruise already forming a chain around the child's ankle, like a rope burn.

'What's going on?' a voice asked from the doorway. Bonnie turned, saw Lauren hovering behind Nick, his gun nowhere in sight. Was it possible she'd imagined it?

'We found the snake,' Amanda said.

Bonnie heard laughter, realized it was her own. 'We certainly did,' she said.

'The snake is here?' Lauren drew back, looked warily at her feet.

'Sam has him.'

Lauren's eyes shot to Nick. 'What are you still doing here?' she asked, clearly confused by what was happening.

'Not much,' Nick said, and laughed, moving to Bonnie's side, helping her to her feet. 'Are you okay?'

'I think so,' she told him, pulling out of his arms. 'But I think Sam may have been bitten.'

'He's been bitten before,' Lauren told them. 'The bites sting, but they're not poisonous.'

Bonnie lifted her daughter into her arms, still feeling the weight of the snake's resistance in her hands. Did she have any strength left? she wondered.

'That was very impressive,' Nick said. 'Remind me not to mess with you.'

Bonnie stared at her brother. Explain, her eyes said.

He stared back. Later, his eyes said in return.

'Are you going to kill us?' Bonnie asked her brother after everyone else

280

was finally settled and asleep. The snake was in its tank; the rats were gone.

'Is that what you think?' Nick asked. 'That I'm here to kill you?'

'I no longer know what to think,' Bonnie said honestly, every muscle in her body crying out to lie down.

'I'm not here to hurt you, Bonnie.'

'Why then?'

'I thought I could protect you,' he said, after a pause.

'I didn't think convicted felons were allowed to carry guns.'

'They're not.'

Bonnie sank down on the foot of her bed. What was the point in trying to talk to her brother? Did she really think he'd tell her anything? 'Do you think we should have insisted that Sam go to the hospital?' she asked instead.

'He said he thought a few extra-strength Tylenol would get him through the night, that he'd see a doctor about his bites in the morning, if he felt it was necessary.'

Bonnie nodded. She'd helped Sam wash the bitten area thoroughly, watched while he applied a special antiseptic ointment. He'd said nothing about seeing the gun in Nick's hand. Perhaps she'd imagined the whole thing.

She'd put Amanda to bed in Lauren's room, Amanda quickly settling into the crook of Lauren's arm, Lauren's other arm draped around her waist, their breathing gentle echoes of one another as they drifted off to sleep.

'Is that the gun that killed Joan?' Bonnie asked, suddenly aware of the butt-end of the gun tucked into the waist of Nick's jeans.

'The gun that killed Joan was a .38,' Nick said matter-of-factly. 'This is a .357 Magnum.'

'Is that supposed to make me feel better?' Bonnie asked, realizing that it did.

'I would never hurt you, Bonnie. Don't you know that?'

'What's going on, Nick?' she asked.

He said nothing.

'Look,' she began, 'I'm sick; I'm tired; I think my husband's having an affair; I've spent half the night wrestling with a snake. I'm not sure how much more I can take. I'm starting to lose it, Nick. My life no longer makes any sense. And if you don't start giving me some answers soon, then you're just going to have to shoot me, because otherwise I'm going to get on the phone and call the police, and tell them that my brother, the jailbird, is in my bedroom with a .357 Magnum tucked into the waistband of his jeans.'

'I don't think that will be necessary.'

'If you won't talk to me, then maybe you'll talk to the police,' she repeated.

'Bonnie,' her brother said calmly, walking toward her, 'I *am* the police.'

Chapter Twenty-Eight

By the time Rod came home, Nick was gone.

'How are you, honey?' Rod asked, wrapping Bonnie in a warm embrace at the front door, then drawing back, taking a long, close look at her. 'You look like hell,' he said.

Bonnie brought her hand to her hair, her fingers trying to stretch the bangs onto her forehead. Tears sprang to her eyes. She'd spent almost an hour in the bathroom trying to make herself presentable for Rod's return. She'd showered and given her hair a special treatment that promised to add new life to damaged ends, then brushed her teeth, careful to avoid scratching her gums, although they bled anyway. She'd even applied make-up, trying to disguise her sallow cheeks with a soft pink blush, adding layers of mascara to her thinning lashes, moistening her dry lips with pink-tinted gloss. And she'd gotten dressed for the first time in several days, exchanging her perspiration-soaked housecoat for a pretty floral print dress. And still he said she looked like hell. Well, maybe after the silicone wonder that was Marla Brenzelle, her husband had forgotten what a real woman looked like, especially when she wasn't feeling well. Real women don't go to Miami to wrestle with television executives, she thought, glancing up the stairs. They stay in Boston and wrestle with snakes.

'How are the kids?' Rod walked into the kitchen, rifled through his mail.

Bonnie followed after him. 'Fine.' She checked her watch. It was either ten minutes after one or five minutes after two, she was unable to decide which. Either way, the kids were in school.

'Have you spoken to the doctor?' Rod asked.

'I called his office this morning, but the test results still weren't in. Apparently the lab's been especially busy.'

'Who is this doctor anyway?'

'Dr Kline,' Bonnie said. 'I told you. Diana recommended him.'

'I thought she saw a Dr Gizmondi.'

'Does she?'

'Don't you remember? She went on and on about him one night. I only remember because the name was so unusual.'

'Maybe she switched,' Bonnie said weakly. She wasn't up to telling Rod the truth of who'd sent her to see Dr Kline. Not yet anyway. As soon as she was feeling better, she'd tell him about her meetings with Dr Greenspoon, she rationalized, wondering when that would be. Hadn't Dr Kline told her that inner ear infections could drag on for months?

'You look like you haven't slept in days,' Rod said.

Had he always had such a penchant for stating the obvious? 'We found the snake,' she told him.

'You did? Where?'

'In Amanda's room,' Bonnie told him, declining to elaborate, something else she was holding back. You kind of had to be there, she thought, images of her brother immediately filling her head.

No wonder she hadn't slept. She sank into one of the kitchen chairs, studying her husband as he studied his mail, her mind racing through the events of the previous evening, replaying the encounter with her brother in every detail, as she'd done repeatedly since Nick left the house this morning.

'Bonnie,' she could still hear him say, 'I *am* the police.'

Panic mingled with curiosity. 'What do you mean? What are you talking about?'

'I mean, I'm still playing cops and robbers, Bonnie, still chasing the bad guys.'

'I don't understand. You *are* the bad guy. You went to prison.'

'I went to prison, yes.'

'Since when do they let convicted felons become police officers?' Anger hovered, threatened to erupt. This really was too much. If it was true, no wonder society was in such a mess.

'Since my going to jail was a necessary part of the plan,' he told her. 'The follow-through of an elaborate scheme to nail Scott Dunphy, break up his operation, put him away.'

Bonnie scoffed, shook her head, grew dizzy. 'You're trying to tell me you're an undercover cop? Is that what you're seriously trying to tell me?'

'It's called deep cover, if you want to get technical,' Nick said, 'and yes, that's what I'm seriously trying to tell you.' He paused, as if debating with himself whether or not to continue. 'I shouldn't be telling you anything. I'm taking a chance, Bonnie. I'm trusting you.'

'You're trusting me,' Bonnie repeated, numbly.

Nick nodded.

'So I'm just supposed to trust *you?*' she asked in return. 'I'm supposed to believe that all these years you've been living some sort of double life, making friends with people like Scott Dunphy, becoming part of their organization, just so you can get enough evidence to put them in jail?'

'It's what I do, Bonnie.'

'Appearances to the contrary.'

'Things aren't always what they seem.'

'So I've been told.' She took a deep breath, tried arranging her thoughts into some kind of coherent order. 'The land development scheme . . .'

' . . . was part of it.'

'But you were found not guilty; you were let go.'

'We screwed up. Someone jumped the gun. There wasn't enough evidence to convict. We had to start again.'

'And the other charge? Conspiracy to commit murder?'

'We got him good that time.'

'But you went to jail.'

'I had to protect my cover.'

'I don't believe you.'

'It's the truth.'

'You're a cop?!' Bonnie gasped, incredulously, afraid to believe him, more afraid not to. 'But how could we not know? How could you keep it from your family?'

'I had no choice. It was for your protection as much as mine.'

'You're saying that those years you were away, the years you supposedly spent bumming around across the country . . .' she began.

'I was in training with the Federal Bureau of Investigation,' he said finishing the sentence for her. She felt oddly grateful he hadn't used the letters FBI.

'And you couldn't tell anyone, not even your own mother, not even when she was dying?'

'I didn't know she was dying.'

'You let her die believing . . .'

'I didn't know she was dying,' he repeated, his voice cracking, threatening to dissolve. 'Hell, Bonnie, she'd been dying all my life.' He brought his hand to his head, pushed his hair roughly away from his forehead. 'But she didn't die because of me, Bonnie. You have to know that. You have to know she didn't die because of me.'

Bonnie lowered her head. 'I know that,' she whispered after a long pause. 'I guess I've always known that.' She looked away, then back at Nick. 'It was just easier to blame you for her death than it was to accept the fact that she was a self-absorbed hypochondriac who abused prescription drugs and whose body simply couldn't take it any more.' She took a deep breath, exhaled slowly. 'It's funny,' she said. 'I always thought I was such a lousy liar. But I've been lying to myself pretty good for years.'

And suddenly they were in each other's arms, crying on each other's shoulders.

'Don't cry,' he was saying, crying himself. 'It's okay now. Everything's going to be okay.'

'Does Dad know the truth?' she asked when their tears were dry.

'He does now,' Nick told her.

'And Captain Mahoney? Has he known all along?'

'Not in the beginning, no. I was a suspect, just like everyone else.'

'But he knows now.'

'Yes. But of course, the fewer people who know, the safer I am. It's as simple as that.'

'None of this is simple.'

He waited, fixed her with his most serious stare. 'Please don't say anything about this to Rod.'

Bonnie folded her hands in her lap, massaged her sore wrists. The last person to give her that little piece of advice was Joan, and look what happened to her. 'But he's my husband.'

'Does that mean you trust him?' came the immediate reply.

Bonnie said nothing for several seconds. 'Is there a reason I shouldn't?'

'The man's ex-wife was murdered,' Nick reminded her, unnecessarily. 'Your husband stands to profit substantially from her death, as he would from yours. We know that Joan was worried about you. We know she knew something she wasn't supposed to.'

'What do you mean?' Bonnie asked. 'What do you know? What are you saying? How are you involved in this? What's your connection with Joan?'

'She called me a few weeks before her death,' Nick explained. 'Or rather, she called Dad. She didn't know I was back at home. She told Dad she was worried about you, but she wouldn't say why, just that we should keep a close watch on you. Dad didn't know what to make of it. He said it sounded like she'd been drinking, but still a phone call like that, out of the blue . . . So I called her, went to see her, tried to find out what was going on. But I couldn't get her to say any more. One thing was certain, she was genuinely worried. I went to see Rod at the station, tried to feel him out, pretended I had some nutty idea for a series. For a few scary minutes there, I actually thought he liked the idea. Anyway, he was his usual affable self. Nothing seemed out of line. I started to think maybe Joan was talking out of the bottom of the bottle, but then the next thing I knew, she was dead. And you were the prime suspect in her murder.'

'I didn't kill her.'

'I know that.'

'But you've been keeping an eye on me.'

'For your protection.'

'So it *was* you I saw in the school yard that morning.' Bonnie pictured her brother emerging from the shadows of the nearby trees.

'You've got good eyes. I had to get out of there pretty damn fast.'

'Was it also you who paid Elsa Langer a visit?'

He nodded. 'After you said you'd been to see her, I thought it might be worth checking her out. Unfortunately, she was pretty much checked out already.'

'So where does that leave us?'

There was a long pause. 'There's only one person who had both motive and opportunity, no alibi and a missing .38.'

'You're saying you think it's Rod?'

Nick looked toward the floor. 'I'm saying it's a real possibility.'

Bonnie shook her head vigorously, despite the dizziness it induced. 'I can't believe it. I've lived with the man for over five years. I can't believe he could kill anyone.'

'You don't want to believe it,' her brother said.

'You actually think Rod murdered his ex-wife, that he might be planning to kill me and our daughter?' The words sank into the pit of Bonnie's stomach, like stones into water.

'Who else stands to profit by your deaths?'

No one, Bonnie had to admit, although she refused to do so out loud. 'But how can I stay here if I believe that? How can I keep living with him?'

'You don't have to,' Nick told her. 'You can take Amanda, move out.'

'Where would we go?'

'You could move in temporarily with Dad.'

Bonnie shook her head. 'I can't do that. Rod is my husband. He's Amanda's father. I refuse to believe he had anything to do with Joan's death. I refuse to believe he'd do anything to hurt Amanda or me.'

'I hope you're right. But I'd get Rod to cancel the insurance policies he has on you and Amanda, just in case. And if he refuses, I'd get the hell out.'

I'd get Rod to cancel the insurance policies he has on you and Amanda, Bonnie repeated in her mind, the words gaining momentum with each breath she released, until they were careening out of control, slamming painfully against the base of her brain.

'What's the matter?' Rod was asking now, rushing to Bonnie's side, kneeling on the floor in front of her chair. 'You went white as a sheet.'

'I want you to cancel the life insurance policies you have on Amanda and me,' Bonnie told him, staring straight ahead, afraid to look at him.

'What?'

'I want you to cancel . . .'

'I heard you,' he interrupted, pushing himself back to his feet, taking several steps into the center of the room. 'I just don't understand where this is coming from all of a sudden.'

'It's not all of a sudden,' Bonnie said. 'I've been thinking about it for weeks. I'm not comfortable with the whole idea, and I want you to cancel the policies.' And if he refused? she wondered. What would she do? Could she really pack up her daughter and her belongings and move out?

'Consider it done,' Rod said.

'What?'

'I said consider it done.'

'You'll do it?'

Rod shrugged. 'Actually, I've been thinking about cancelling them myself. I'm paying a hell of a premium on the damn things, and it doesn't really make sense when we could be using that money elsewhere.' He paused, smiled weakly. 'You *are* planning on getting better, aren't you?'

Bonnie smiled, then laughed, then cried. How could she have doubted him? she wondered. It was this damn inner ear infection. It was fogging her brain, not allowing her to see things clearly.

Immediately, Rod returned to her side. 'Bonnie, what is it? What's happening? Talk to me, honey. Tell me what's going on.'

Bonnie collapsed into Rod's arms, sobbing against his shoulder. 'I'm so tired,' she cried. 'I'm just so damn tired.'

Rod put his arm around her, lifted her gently to her feet, led her toward the stairs. 'Let's get you into bed.'

'I don't want to go to bed,' Bonnie said, hating the whine in her voice. 'You just got home; I want to hear about your trip.'

'You'll hear about it later. I want to check in at the studio anyway for a few minutes.'

'You're going out?'

'Just for a little while. I'll be back before you wake up, I promise. And then we can have the whole weekend together, and I'll bore you to tears with tales of my Florida exploits.' They reached the top of the stairs. 'And I want to speak to this Dr Kline when he calls, because enough is enough. If he can't do something to make you feel better, we'll find somebody who can.' Rod guided Bonnie into their bedroom, started unbuttoning the front of her dress.

'Kiss me, Rod,' Bonnie begged softly, her cheeks slippery with tears.

He kissed the side of her mouth, then each eyelid in turn before moving to her lips. She felt his lips on hers, as soft as a cotton ball, she thought, as he slid her dress off her shoulders. She heard it fall to the floor, his hands already unhooking her bra. Did she have the strength to make love? she mused, wondering if this was his intention, as he sat her down on the bed. He brought her feet up, laid her back against her pillows, brought the bedspread up over her shoulders. Clearly, making love was not his intention. 'Get some sleep, honey,' he whispered, moving to the curtains, pulling them closed, returning the room to the darkness Bonnie had lately grown so accustomed to. She watched his shadow slip from the room, then closed her eyes.

When she woke up, it was almost four o'clock. She looked around the empty room. Where was everyone? Then she remembered – Sam and Lauren would be finishing up at Diana's; Amanda was at day care; Rod was at the studio. Still? she wondered. Hadn't he promised he'd be back before she woke up? 'Rod?' she called, pushing back the bedspread and swinging her feet off the bed. 'Rod, are you home?'

No one answered.

The phone rang. She picked it up before it could ring again.

'Is this Mrs Wheeler?' the voice asked.

'Yes,' Bonnie answered.

'Will you hold for Dr Kline?'

'Yes,' Bonnie said, wiping the sleep from her eyes, smoothing her hair, as if she wanted to look presentable for when he came on the line.

'Mrs Wheeler,' he began. 'I have the results of your tests.'

'Yes?'

There was a slight pause. 'It appears that there's a high level of arsenic in your bloodstream, Mrs Wheeler. I'm not sure how . . .'

'What?' Bonnie demanded, sure she must have heard him incorrectly. 'What did you say?'

'Your blood samples reveal a significantly high level of arsenic in your system,' he repeated, his tone deceptively businesslike. 'I don't understand it, frankly. An amount this high can't be accidental.'

'What are you talking about?' Bonnie yelled. 'How could there be arsenic in my bloodstream?'

There was silence. 'Try to stay calm, Mrs Wheeler.'

'Are you suggesting that someone is trying to poison me? Is that what you're trying to tell me?'

'I'm not trying to tell you anything, Mrs Wheeler. I was hoping you'd be able to tell *me* something.'

'I don't understand,' she said, then faltered, her mind racing too fast for her words to follow. 'How . . . where . . . ?'

'Arsenic can be found in any number of household products,' Dr Kline told her. 'Insecticide, rat poison, weedkiller.'

'But wouldn't I know if someone were adding poison to my food?' she demanded. 'Wouldn't I taste it?'

'Arsenic itself is tasteless. It's entirely possible you wouldn't know you were taking it. At any rate, we can discuss all this later. Right now, I'd like you to check into the hospital.'

'What?'

'I'm affiliated with Boston Memorial. I can arrange for you to be admitted . . .'

'I can't,' Bonnie said adamantly. 'I can't go to the hospital now. I can't leave my daughter.'

'Mrs Wheeler, I don't think you understand the seriousness of your situation. We need to treat this quite aggressively, get the poison out of your system.'

'I can't go into the hospital. Not yet,' Bonnie told him, trying to make sense of everything he'd said. Was it possible? Had someone really been trying to poison her? 'I can't leave my daughter. I won't leave her.'

'Try and make some arrangements for her. In the meantime, have your pharmacist call me. I'll give you a prescription for a stronger medication. The antibiotics you've been taking aren't strong enough, although they're probably the reason you're still alive.' He paused. 'And don't eat anything that you don't see prepared in front of your eyes.'

'But I haven't eaten anything in ages,' Bonnie told him. 'Just tea, and chicken soup.'

'Home-made?'

'No, a friend brought some over.' She pictured Josh Freeman's handsomely disheveled features. *I thought you could use a friend*, he told her. *I know I could.*

'Is there any of that soup left?' he was asking.

'What?'

'Is there any soup left?'

'I don't know.'

'If there is, you should have the police analyze it.'

Bonnie was having difficulty keeping up with the conversation. Was he hinting that the soup Josh brought over had been poisoned? 'This is ridiculous,' she said. 'I was sick long before my friend brought over the soup.'

'Do you remember the first time you got sick?' Dr Kline asked.

Bonnie frantically searched her memory for the first such occasion. 'It was in the middle of the night. My brother had been over earlier. He'd made a spaghetti dinner,' she said, the words tumbling out, her tongue tripping over them. 'But nobody else got sick,' she added quickly. 'And my stepdaughter had been sick with the same sort of thing all week.'

After Rod had helped make her dinner, Bonnie remembered, a chill twisting through her body like an electric shock. And Rod had been home the night Nick cooked his infamous spaghetti special. Was it possible he'd added some extra spice of his own?

She held her breath, trying desperately not to allow the thought circling her brain to land. Could it be that Rod and Nick were in it together? she asked herself when she could delay the question no longer. That together they'd conspired to kill Joan, just as they were conspiring to kill her now? That Lauren was at risk as well? Was it possible that everything her brother had said to her yesterday was a lie? That he had deceived her again, as he had been deceiving people all his life? 'I have to go now, Dr Kline.'

'Mrs Wheeler, you should be in a hospital. At the very least, you should contact the police immediately . . .'

Bonnie hung up the phone.

It couldn't be, she thought, rocking back and forth on the bed, trying to clear her head. She had to focus, get her thoughts in order, make some sense of what she had learned. She was being slowly poisoned, that much was clear. Arsenic – found in any number of common household products. At first, the poison had been given to Lauren either by accident or by design, as a way of averting suspicion, to make Bonnie think she was dealing with a simple case of the flu. And then she'd gotten sick. And stayed sick. Rod was always there, making sure she had enough liquids, making sure she drank her tea. He knew about her long-standing aversion to doctors.

But Rod had been away all week, and she hadn't gotten any better, even with the antibiotics, which meant she was probably still being poisoned. What did it mean? Was Josh somehow involved? And if he was, was he acting alone or was he working with Nick? Or with Rod? Possibly it was all three of them together.

'This is crazy,' Bonnie moaned. 'I'm thinking crazy.'

What about Sam? Bonnie questioned with mounting horror, realizing that Sam was the one constant, the one person who was always around. He'd been so solicitous, making her tea, carrying bowls of soup to her bedside. It would have been relatively easy for him to add a little something unexpected to her food. Just as it would have been oh-so-easy for him to hide the snake, set it loose on her little girl.

'Oh God,' Bonnie thought. 'It can't be. It just can't be.' Bonnie grabbed the phone, quickly dialed the Newton police. 'Captain Mahoney, please,' she said.

'I'm afraid the captain isn't in the station at the moment,' came the response.

'Then let me speak to Detective Kritzic.'

'I'm afraid she isn't here either. Perhaps someone else could help you.'

'No, I'll have to call back.' Bonnie dropped the phone into the receiver, stood up, sat back down, stood up again. She was running out of time. She had to get dressed and get out of here, she realized, running into her closet, pulling a blue jersey over her head and a pair of jeans over her hips, running out of the room. She didn't know where she was going. She didn't know what she was planning to do, but she had to get out of the house before anyone came back.

She'd stop by the day-care center and pick up Amanda, take her . . . where? She couldn't go to her father's house – Nick would be there. She couldn't go to Diana's house – Sam would be there. She couldn't go to Weston Secondary – Josh would be there. And she certainly couldn't stay here with Rod. She didn't know where to go. She didn't know whom she could trust.

She thought of Diana's apartment in the city, and called Diana's office. Of course she'd let her use it. 'Diana Perrin,' Bonnie said clearly into the receiver.

'Ms Perrin will be back in the office on Monday,' Diana's secretary informed her. 'If you'd care to leave your name . . .'

Bonnie slammed down the receiver. She didn't have time for this. She had to get out, go to the police station, hope Captain Mahoney and Detective Kritzic would be back. She grabbed her purse, feeling dizzy and weak, raced down the stairs, was almost at her front door when she realized she'd forgotten the bottle of soup.

It was hidden near the back of the fridge, and at first she didn't see it. It was only as she was closing the refrigerator door that she saw the tall bottle, with only a few inches left of the clear liquid inside it. She grabbed it, feeling it cold and slippery in the palm of her hand, and ran with it out the front door, almost losing her grip on it as she fished through her purse for her car keys. She found them, only to watch them tumble out of her fingers and fall to the driveway. 'Oh no, please no,' she wailed, grabbing for them and watching everything else fly from her hands, her purse, her house keys, her wallet, the glass bottle. 'No!' she yelled, watching the bottle crash to the driveway and shatter, the clear liquid spilling onto the pavement and disappearing, like rain. 'No, damn it, no,' she cried, bursting into tears as she knelt amidst the large slivers of glass to retrieve her wallet and keys.

It was then that she heard the sound of a car approaching, slowing down, turning into the driveway. Rod was home, she understood. She'd waited too long. She wasn't going anywhere.

She closed her eyes, pushed herself slowly to her feet, heard the car stop and a door open then slam shut. Footsteps walked toward her, stopped just inches from her face. The stale scent of marijuana encircled her. Only then did she open her eyes.

Haze stood before her.

Was he there to put a bullet through her heart?

'Sam home?' he asked without further preamble.

Bonnie found herself laughing out loud. Haze regarded her strangely, took a step back.

'He's at Diana's,' Bonnie said, still laughing. 'He wanted to finish papering her bathroom before the weekend.'

'I'll find him,' Haze said, climbing back into the ancient dark blue automobile and backing out of Bonnie's driveway.

For an instant, Bonnie stood paralyzed, unable to move, barely able to breathe. In the next second, she was in her car and on the road, her hands tightly gripping the steering wheel, heading toward School Street and her daughter, still not sure what she was going to do when she got there.

Chapter Twenty-Nine

'Where are we going now, Mommy?' Amanda asked, fidgeting in her car seat. They'd stopped at a drugstore, where Bonnie bought Amanda a bag of potato chips and had the pharmacist call Dr Kline. Fifteen minutes later, she had her prescription, and two pills were already traveling through her veins, trying to rout the poison in her blood.

'I thought we'd go for a drive, sweetie,' Bonnie told Amanda, swiveling toward the back seat, smiling at her daughter, wondering if the smile looked as false as it felt. How long could she keep driving? she wondered. Sooner or later, they had to go somewhere.

'I don't want to go for a drive,' Amanda protested. 'I want to go home. I want to see *Sesame Street*.'

'We can't go home yet, sweetheart. There are some things I have to do first.'

'What things?'

Bonnie decided to go to the police. Less than ten minutes later, they were in Newton. 'We have to stop here for a few minutes,' Bonnie told Amanda, pulling her car into the parking lot at the back of the station.

'I don't want to go here.' Amanda folded her arms across her chest, threatened tears.

'Please don't cry, sweetie. This won't take long.'

'I want to go home. I want to watch *Sesame Street*.'

Bonnie unbuckled Amanda's seatbelt, lifted her from her seat, Amanda's body stiffening with indignation.

'Come on, honey. Please cooperate. I'm not feeling very well.'

'I want to go home.' Amanda started kicking her feet.

Bonnie carried her daughter, kicking and squirming, toward the front entrance.

'You're not nice,' Amanda told her. 'You're not cool.'

'I need to talk to Captain Mahoney,' Bonnie announced to the officer at the front desk, as Amanda fell mercifully silent.

The young male police officer stared at her with no trace of recognition. 'He's not here right now. Can I help you?'

'Is Detective Kritzic here?'

'Not at the moment. What seems to be the problem?'

Bonnie lowered Amanda to the floor, then leaned forward toward the officer. 'I'm being poisoned,' she said.

Well, that was a colossal waste of time, Bonnie thought, angrily pulling out of the police parking lot, checking the digital clock. Over forty minutes gone, and for what? So some cynical pimply-faced youth barely out of high school could ask her a bunch of inane questions, only to tell her that since the alleged poisoning took place in Weston, it was really out of his jurisdiction. 'But I'm sure Captain Mahoney would be interested . . .' she began, then stopped, her energy drained. What was the point? She'd check into a motel somewhere for the night, and call Captain Mahoney in the morning. She certainly wasn't about to drive back to Weston now.

'I'm hungry,' Amanda whined after several more minutes. 'Where are we going now?'

Bonnie looked around, startled to find they were on Lombard Street. She slowed down, inched her way up the street.

'Where are we Mommy?'

The house at four hundred and thirty Lombard Street looked exactly the same as it had little more than a month ago. Even the For Sale sign hadn't been touched. The police had removed the yellow tape from around the premises. People could now cross without impunity. No doubt the house had been thoroughly cleaned. Joan's blood had been carefully wiped away. Only her ghost remained.

Bonnie stopped in front of the house, her eyes following the path to the front door. If only she hadn't taken that path, she thought now, wondering how different things might have been. If only she hadn't listened to Joan. If only she hadn't answered the phone that morning. So many if onlys. Would they have made any difference?

'Whose house is this, Mommy?' Amanda asked.

In response, Bonnie pulled away from the curb. 'No one's,' she told her daughter, wondering how long it would take to sell the house now that it was the site of a homicide, if the Palmays had been forced to lower the asking price. She returned to Commonwealth Avenue, following it to Chestnut and then heading up into West Newton Hill.

The house at thirteen Exeter Street also looked the same, with its greenish-beige exterior and enigmatic stained-glass windows. There were no outward signs that the house was empty. Even the grass had been kept well trimmed, as if someone still lived here.

Bonnie stopped the car, turned off the engine. 'Where are we?' Amanda demanded again.

Bonnie opened her car door, climbed out, and unhooked Amanda from her special seat, carrying her to the front lawn of Joan's house.

'Is this a church?' Amanda asked, eyes on the windows.

'No, honey. This is where Sam and Lauren used to live.'

'Are they here now?'

'No.' Bonnie led Amanda up the front walk to the large wooden double door.

'Are we going inside?'

Were they? Bonnie reached inside her purse, pulled out her keys, found the right one, pushed it into the lock. She'd all but forgotten she had a key to Joan's house. Until she'd dropped the keys in her driveway, seen Joan's house key winking at her from underneath a piece of broken glass.

Had she known from that moment that she was headed here?

The door opened easily, and Bonnie stepped inside, Amanda darting into the front foyer. Bonnie remembered her first visit to this house, heard the echo of Lauren's voice calling down the stairs for her mother, recalled the look of confusion on Lauren's face as she peered over the top railing and saw her father, felt her angry fists on her face, tasted the blood at her lip.

What was she doing back here now?

Amanda skipped into the living room. 'This is a funny house, Mommy,' she said, jumping from one Indian rug to another, as if they were chalk squares on pavement, stopping in front of the large brick fireplace.

'Be careful, honey,' Bonnie cautioned. 'Try not to disturb anything.'

'What's disturb?' Amanda asked.

'Don't touch anything,' Bonnie explained, continuing through the medieval-looking dining area into the kitchen at the back of the house. She quickly located the pantry, and opened its doors.

It was almost empty. A few boxes of dry cereal, some instant coffee, a box of raisins, a five-pound bag of sugar sat on the shelves, but little else. An iron, still in its box, lay on the bottom shelf, next to a stack of unopened white paper napkins.

Bonnie simultaneously closed the doors to the pantry and opened the one to the broom closet beside it. Two brooms fell forward to greet her, one electric, one regular. Bonnie propped them back into position, then closed the closet door, continuing on to the sink, moving like an automaton, as if every move had been carefully programmed for her in advance.

'Can I have some milk?' Amanda asked.

'They don't have any milk.' Bonnie knelt down, opened the cabinet under the sink.

'Don't they like milk?'

'No one lives here now, sweetie, remember? The milk would go bad.' Bonnie's eyes scanned the contents of the cabinet – a dark green garbage pail, a plastic container full of assorted sponges and scrubbing pads, two kinds of dishwashing detergent, a small bottle of Mr Clean.

'Can I have some water?'

'No, honey.' Bonnie pushed the bottle of Mr Clean aside.

'Is the water bad too?'

'It's not our house,' Bonnie reminded her.

'Then why are we here?' Amanda asked logically.

Because I'm looking for something, Bonnie thought, but didn't say, watching as two imaginary white rats scurried in front of her conscious mind. Insecticide, rat poison, weedkiller, Dr Kline had said. Bonnie didn't keep any insecticide or weedkiller at home. She'd never had the need for rat poison. She'd never had rats until Sam came to live with her. Bonnie reached into the back of the cabinet toward a cylindrical tin can cramped in the far corner.

'I want to go home,' Amanda pouted, leaning her full weight against her mother's back, upsetting Bonnie's precarious balance. Bonnie fell to the floor, her hand knocking over the boxes of dishwashing detergent and the bottle of Mr Clean, scattering the sponges in all directions.

Amanda giggled. 'Mommy made a mess.'

Bonnie regained her equilibrium, quickly gathering up the sponges and returning them to their container, then righting the boxes of dishwashing detergent and the bottle of Mr Clean, before extricating

298

the cylindrical tin from the back of the cupboard.

She saw the skull and crossbones before she saw anything else. DANGER, POISON, it said above it in bold black capital letters. SUREKILL, the orange letters announced over black and white stripes, then in somewhat smaller letters beneath it, RAT POISON. A drawing of a dead rat occupied the center of the label.

Bonnie swallowed, feeling dizzy and cold and numb and hot as she turned the tin around. *Precaution*, she read. *Harmful if swallowed. Keep out of the reach of children. Do not use in any areas where food may be exposed. Do not use in bulk food storage areas. Do not use in cupboards where food or cooking utensils are stored. If swallowed, do not induce vomiting. Principal ingredient: arsenic.*

Bonnie dropped the tin to the floor, watched it roll just out of reach. Amanda ran after it, grabbing for it.

'Don't touch that,' Bonnie yelled, frightening the child, who jumped back, tears filling her eyes. 'It's okay, sweetheart,' Bonnie said quickly. 'It's just very dangerous. You mustn't touch it.'

'Why did you touch it?' Amanda asked.

'I shouldn't have,' Bonnie agreed, stretching toward it, grabbing hold of it, her fingers covering the warning.

'Put it away, Mommy,' Amanda cried. 'Put it away.'

Bonnie returned it to the rear of the cabinet, made sure everything else was where she had found it.

'I want to go home, Mommy. I don't like this house. I want to go home.' Amanda was already out of the kitchen and into the front hall.

'Amanda, wait,' Bonnie called after. 'Wait for me.'

'I want to go home,' Amanda wailed, as Bonnie scooped her into her arms.

'How about we go get some ice cream?'

'I want to go home,' Amanda insisted stubbornly.

'We can't go home yet, sweetheart,' Bonnie told her.

'Is L'il Abner missing again?' Amanda asked. 'Because I'm not afraid of him, you know. Sam told me that he was just mean because he was hungry, and that he'll make sure he doesn't get hungry again.'

'That's good, pumpkin.'

'I like Sam.'

'So do I,' Bonnie told her, and realized it was true. Could he really be a cold-blooded killer? She opened the front door and stepped outside, locking it after her.

'And I like L'il Abner too. He's cool.'

'Yes, he is.'

She carried Amanda down the stairs, trying to decide her next move before she got to the car. She'd buy Amanda an ice cream cone, call the police station again, insist on being put through to Captain Mahoney, wherever he was, tell him about her discovery. Maybe he'd have some ideas. There had to be something she could do.

'Bonnie?' the woman said, waiting for her by the side of her car.

Bonnie's eyes shot to the tall blond woman in the paint-stained green smock. How long had she been standing there? 'Hello, Caroline,' Bonnie said, lowering Amanda to the ground.

'I saw the car pull up, and I thought it might be you,' Caroline began. 'But you looked so different, and I didn't recognize the little girl . . .'

'This is my daughter, Amanda,' Bonnie told her, not sure what else to say.

'It's nice to meet you, Amanda.' Caroline Gossett knelt down, extended her hand toward Amanda, who grabbed it and shook it vigorously. 'Does anyone ever call you Mandy?'

'My Uncle Nick does.'

'Well, Mandy, you're a very beautiful little girl.'

'Thank you.'

Caroline Gossett rose to her feet, looked at Bonnie. 'Are you all right?'

'I've been better,' Bonnie admitted.

'Can I do anything to help?' Caroline asked.

'I could use a glass of water.'

'Me too,' said Amanda. 'Mommy said we couldn't have any water in that house because it wasn't ours.' She pointed at Joan's house.

'Well, not only do I have nice cold water at my house,' Caroline said, 'I also have ice cream and cookies.'

'Ice cream!' Amanda parroted. 'Cookies.'

'Come on,' Caroline directed, taking Bonnie's elbow. 'You look like you could use a place to sit down.'

'Do you want to tell me what's been going on?' Caroline asked once Amanda was comfortably ensconced in the family room in front of the

TV with her bowl of Häagen-Dazs cookie-dough ice cream.

'I'm not sure I know where to start.'

'Start with that haircut.'

Bonnie smiled. 'I haven't been feeling very well lately,' she began. 'My hair was a mess. I thought cutting it might help.'

'Did it?'

'Did you know that lifeless hair, bleeding gums and acute nausea are all symptoms of arsenic poisoning?' Bonnie asked, reciting what the druggist had told her.

'What?' Caroline Gossett leaned forward on the living room sofa. 'Are you saying that you've been poisoned?'

'Apparently there's a high level of arsenic in my bloodstream.'

'I don't understand.'

Bonnie sank back into her chair, took another long sip of water, her eyes filling with tears. 'Someone's been trying to poison me.'

'My God. Do you know who?'

Bonnie shook her head. 'Obviously someone close to me,' she admitted reluctantly. 'Probably the same person who killed Joan.'

'What do the police say?'

'That I'm in the wrong jurisdiction.'

'What?'

'It's a long story. Captain Mahoney wasn't there. I'll have to try him again later.'

Caroline stood up, walked to her kitchen, returned with her portable phone. 'Try him now,' she said.

Bonnie punched in the number for the Newton police station, told the operator she wanted to speak to either Captain Mahoney or Detective Kritzic, was told they were still out, did she want to leave a message?

'Give them this number,' Caroline said, and Bonnie did as she was told.

'Thank you. I hate imposing on you this way.'

'Christ, you're amazing.' Caroline shook her head. 'Someone's trying to kill you and you're worried about being an imposition. Do me a favor – don't worry. I'm delighted for the company. Besides, you obviously can't go home until you sort this out. You and your daughter will sleep here tonight.'

'I can't do that.'

'You can, and you will.'

'But your husband . . .'

'I didn't say you could sleep with him.'

Bonnie smiled, almost managed a laugh. 'I can't stay here forever.'

'I didn't say forever either.' Caroline squeezed in beside Bonnie on the chair. 'But if someone close to you is trying to kill you, then you can't go home until the police figure out who it is. Besides, you obviously need a few days to rest and recuperate. Should you be in a hospital?'

'No,' Bonnie lied. 'I have some pills.' She indicated her purse on the floor beside her feet.

'Okay, then, it's settled. You'll stay here, at least until tomorrow.'

Bonnie checked her watch. 'There's a friend of mine I'd like to call,' she said. 'Would you mind?'

'Call anyone you like.'

Bonnie punched in Diana's number at home. It was answered on the first ring.

'Diana?' Bonnie said, grateful to hear her voice.

'Bonnie, is that you?' Diana shouted into the receiver. 'Where are you?'

'I'm with a friend,' Bonnie told her, alarmed by her friend's voice.

'Rod's been calling here every five minutes,' Diana told her. 'He's absolutely frantic. I've never seen him like this. He's beside himself. He says you just disappeared.'

'I haven't disappeared.' She pictured her husband, imagined him barking questions into the phone, her brother and her stepson hovering nearby, listening. 'How's your bathroom?' she asked suddenly.

'I beg your pardon?'

'Your bathroom. I know that Sam was working hard to finish it before you got back.'

'It's fine,' Diana said, clearly distracted by the sudden twist in the conversation. 'He still has a little left to do, but it looks great.'

'And how was New York?'

'It was okay,' Diana said dismissively. 'Bonnie, what's going on? Rod says he went out for a few hours, and that when he left, you were so sick you could hardly stand up. When he came home, you weren't there. No note as to where you went, nothing. He's going crazy with worry.'

'Diana,' Bonnie interrupted. 'Listen to me. I'm all right. I'm safe now.'

'*Now?* What are you talking about?'

'Someone's been poisoning me.'

'Poisoning you? Bonnie, you're talking crazy.'

'I'm not crazy. I had blood tests taken. They show a high level of arsenic in my system.'

'Arsenic?'

'Someone's been adding arsenic to my food.'

Diana's voice dropped to a whisper. 'Rod?'

'I don't know,' Bonnie said after a pause. She could feel Diana shaking her head in astonishment.

'I don't believe it. I *can't* believe it,' Diana said. Then, 'Where are you?'

Bonnie glanced at Caroline. 'At a friend's.'

Caroline smiled.

'What friend?' Diana asked.

'I think it's safer if I don't tell you,' Bonnie said, suddenly understanding the things her brother had told her. If her brother was who he claimed to be, that is.

'Safer?'

'If you don't know where I am, then you don't have to lie to anyone. You can't be persuaded or tricked . . .'

'I'm not easily tricked, Bonnie,' Diana said.

Unlike me, Bonnie thought.

'Have you talked to the police?'

'Not yet.'

'But you're sure about this? I mean, it couldn't have been an accident?'

'How does one accidentally swallow arsenic?' Bonnie asked.

There was a slight pause. 'All right, look, what do you want me to say to Rod?'

'I don't want you to say anything.'

'Bonnie, are you kidding? He'll be calling here in two minutes. You just want me to pretend I haven't heard from you?'

'I'll speak to Rod.'

'You will? When?'

'I'll call him now.'

'What will you say?'

'I don't know. I'll think of something.'

'This is crazy, Bonnie,' Diana said. 'I feel so helpless. There must be something I can do.'

Bonnie thought of Diana's apartment in the city. She couldn't impose on Caroline's generosity indefinitely. 'There might be,' Bonnie told her. 'After I've spoken to the police, I'll have a better idea of my options. I hope,' she said, and almost laughed. 'Look, I'll call you first thing in the morning.'

'You promise?'

'I promise.'

'Because I won't move from the phone until I hear from you.'

'I'll call you first thing.'

'You sure you're all right?'

'I'm not sure of anything,' Bonnie admitted. If you couldn't trust chicken soup, what could you trust? she thought. 'I'll call you,' she said, pressing the button to disconnect, then immediately punching in her home phone number.

Rod answered before the first ring was completed.

'Rod . . .'

'Bonnie, where the hell are you? Are you all right? Where did you go?' he said, the words running together like colors bleeding into one another in the wash.

'I'm all right.'

'Where are you?'

'I'm with Amanda,' she said, sidestepping his question. 'And I won't be home tonight.'

'What?!'

'I'm sorry I made you come home early from Florida, Rod.'

'You're sorry you made me come home early? What are you talking about?'

'I'll talk to you tomorrow, Rod.'

'Bonnie, wait, don't hang up.'

'I'll explain everything tomorrow.'

'Bonnie . . .'

Bonnie turned off the phone, handed it back to Caroline, wondering if tomorrow she'd be any further ahead.

Chapter Thirty

It was almost ten o'clock the next morning when Bonnie woke up in bed alone. Amanda, who'd been curled into a warm little ball beside her all night, was gone. Bonnie looked around the large white room – white carpet, white lace curtains, white bedspread. She checked the white en suite bathroom – white tile, white tub, white towels. Amanda wasn't there.

'Amanda?' she called out, slipping on the white terrycloth robe Caroline had left at the foot of the bed, padding out of the room in her bare feet. 'Amanda?'

She continued down the wide hallway, past several closed doors, listening for any sounds, hearing muffled voices coming from the room at the end of the hall. She approached quietly, leaning against the door, feeling it open.

'Mommy!' Amanda sat, fully dressed, her hair freshly brushed, in front of a large-screen television set. 'Caroline let me watch cartoons.' She pointed at the screen where one animated figure was clubbing another animated figure over the head with a large piece of spiked wood. 'And she gave me two bowls of Corn Pops for breakfast. And chocolate milk.'

'Two bowls of Corn Pops? Aren't you lucky?'

'She said to be very quiet so you could sleep in.'

'I hope you don't mind,' Caroline said, coming up the hallway, looking wonderfully healthy in a pale lavender sweatsuit. 'You were sleeping so soundly, I didn't want to disturb you.'

'I can't believe I slept so late,' Bonnie said.

'You look much better for it,' Caroline said. 'Can I get you something to eat?'

'I'm not sure I'm ready for solid foods.'

'Not even a piece of toast? I make a mean piece of toast.'

'Okay. Toast sounds good.'

'And tea?'

'I don't think I'll ever drink tea again,' Bonnie said truthfully.

'How about some orange juice?'

'Orange juice would be great.'

'Good. It'll be ready in two minutes.' Caroline peeked in at Amanda. 'How are you doing in here, kiddo? Can I get you some more Corn Pops?'

Amanda giggled. 'I had two bowls,' she announced proudly.

'You did? How did that happen? Lyle usually doesn't let anybody share his Corn Pops?'

'How does Lyle feel about our being here?' Bonnie asked as Amanda returned her attention to the cartoons. 'I mean, *really*.'

'You heard what he said last night. You're welcome to stay as long as you like.'

'That's very generous, but why should he put up with strangers in his house? He doesn't even know me.'

'He knew Joan. He wants to see her killer brought to justice as much as I do.'

Bonnie looked to the floor, saw her bare toes wiggle back. 'I should call the police,' she said.

'I'll get your breakfast ready.'

Bonnie called Captain Mahoney. He wouldn't be in until noon, she was told. Again, Bonnie left a message, stressed its urgency. Wasn't there some way of reaching the captain before then?

Doubtful, she was told, this being a Saturday. Perhaps someone else could be of assistance.

'What did he say?' Caroline asked, as Bonnie walked into the kitchen, took a seat at the table.

'He won't be in till noon.'

Caroline deposited two pieces of toast on a plate in front of Bonnie, along with some butter, raspberry jam, and marmalade. Then she poured a tall glass of juice and handed it to Bonnie, watching while she took a sip. 'Drink up,' she instructed. 'You don't want to get dehydrated.'

'Thanks.'

'Did you take your pills?'

'A few minutes ago.'

Caroline laughed. 'I'm starting to sound like my mother.'

'She must be a lovely woman,' Bonnie said sincerely.

306

'Thank you. She was.' Caroline paused. 'So, what do you think? Is that, or is that not, the best piece of toast you ever tasted?'

Bonnie obligingly took a bite. 'Most definitely the finest piece of toast in creation.'

'Try the raspberry jam. I made it myself.'

Bonnie scooped a small bit of jam onto her toast. *And don't eat anything you don't see prepared in front of your eyes*, she heard Dr Kline intone solemnly. Immediately, she lowered the piece of toast to the plate. What was she thinking? Did she seriously think that Caroline Gossett was trying to poison her too?

'Something wrong?'

Bonnie took a deep breath. 'No, nothing.' She bit determinedly into the piece of toast, savoring the rich raspberry flavor on the insides of her mouth, then swallowing. Ultimately, she decided, she had to trust somebody. 'I should call my friend,' she said, picturing Diana waiting nervously for her call.

Caroline handed her the phone. 'I'll be in the other room.'

'You don't have to leave,' Bonnie told her, grateful for the company, listening as the phone rang once, then twice, then three times. 'I'm probably dragging her out of the bathroom,' she said nervously, letting it ring another six times before finally giving up, then trying again. 'Maybe I dialed the wrong number,' she said, knowing instinctively she hadn't, but trying it again anyway. 'I guess she must have gone out for a few minutes.' After telling Bonnie she wouldn't budge from the phone until she'd heard from her? Without putting on her answering machine?

'Maybe she's in the shower,' Caroline offered.

'That's probably it,' Bonnie agreed readily, patting her own unwashed hair. 'And actually, that's not such a bad idea. If you wouldn't mind . . .'

'Please, be my guest.'

Bonnie rose unsteadily to her feet.

'But finish your toast and juice first,' Caroline advised. 'Something tells me you're going to need all the strength you can get.'

Bonnie stood under the shower's hot blast and watched herself disappear in a cloud of steam. Not that there was much of her left to disappear. She'd lost at least ten pounds, possibly more, and her ribs protruded awkwardly from underneath her small breasts. Her legs looked like sticks, not much fleshier above the knees than below. Prepubescent, almost. Twiggy returns, Bonnie thought, with her haunted eyes and painted-on lower lashes, her close-cropped hair, and her sunken chest. Maybe Twiggy hadn't been naturally skinny after all. Maybe she'd painted on those exaggerated lashes because her own had fallen out. Maybe she'd adopted the boyish waif hairdo when her once lustrous locks had turned to straw. Maybe she'd been suffering from arsenic poisoning.

Bonnie laughed, shampoo snaking its way from her hairline into her open mouth. She spat it out, laughed again, massaged her head with forceful fingers. *I'm gonna wash that man right out of my hair*, she sang softly, then wondered why on earth she was singing. Her whole life was falling apart, someone was trying to kill her, she didn't know whom she could trust, and here she was singing in the shower. The arsenic must have already seeped into her brain.

She thought she heard something, waited until she heard it again, shut off the water when she realized it was a tapping at the bathroom door. 'Yes?' she called out, wondering if she'd heard anything at all.

'Bonnie,' Caroline called back, opening the bathroom door a crack, letting a gust of cool air inside. Bonnie felt it wrap around her torso, like a towel. 'I'm sorry to bother you, but I thought I should call you right away. It's Captain Mahoney – he's on the phone.'

Bonnie barely had time to dry off and get dressed before Captain Mahoney was at the front door. She told him everything, the words pouring from her mouth like boiling water from a kettle – the way she'd been feeling the last few weeks, her visit to the doctor, the results of her blood tests, the certainty that someone had been poisoning her, the uncertainty of who it was. 'I found some rat poison under Joan's sink,' she told him.

'You were there?'

'Yesterday.' She caught a glimmer of surprise, then impatience in his dark eyes. He fidgeted on the seat beside her, pretended to be studying the tall nude sculpture in front of the piano in Caroline Gossett's living room. Caroline was teaching Amanda how to make papier-mâché in the basement. Lyle had disappeared first thing in the morning to play golf.

'You touched it?' he asked, resignation clinging to his words, like a stubborn tickle in the throat.

'Yes.' Bonnie understood without needing to be told that her careless hands had probably destroyed whatever chance the police might have had of discovering fresh prints somewhere on its surface.

'I'm sorry. I wasn't thinking.'

He scratched the side of his head. 'Everyone's a detective,' he muttered.

'Like my brother?' Bonnie asked, waiting for his response, receiving none. 'Is he who he says he is, Captain Mahoney?'

'Your brother is not a suspect in Joan's murder,' Captain Mahoney replied cryptically.

'Is he a police officer?' she pressed.

'I couldn't say.'

'Couldn't? Or won't?'

'Your brother is not a suspect in this case,' he repeated.

Bonnie nodded. 'Then it's safe for me to contact him?'

'It's safe,' he told her, as grateful tears filled her eyes.

'Thank you,' she said. 'I didn't know which way to turn.'

'Looks like you turned in the right direction,' he said, eyes scanning Caroline's living room.

'I was lucky. Caroline's a wonderful woman.'

'Good friends are hard to come by.'

'Oh my God, Diana,' Bonnie said. 'She must be half crazy by now.' She stood up, ran into the kitchen, grabbed the phone, punched in Diana's number.

Again the phone rang once, twice, three times. She was about to hang up, dial again, when it was suddenly picked up.

'Oh good, you're there,' Bonnie said, not waiting for Diana's hello. 'I called before, but you must have been in the shower.'

'Who is this?' The male voice on the other end of the line was flat, expressionless, although vaguely familiar.

A cold sweat broke out across Bonnie's upper lip. Her breath caught in her throat, refused to budge. 'Who's this?' she asked in return.

'Detective Haver of the Weston police,' he answered. 'Who am I speaking to, please?'

'Detective Haver?' Bonnie repeated, picturing the dark-skinned police officer she'd talked to at Amanda's day-care center after the incident with the blood.

Captain Mahoney appeared at her side. 'I'll take it,' he said, and Bonnie handed him the phone without further prompting.

She watched as Captain Mahoney's eyebrows furrowed, shaping his face into a frown. She listened as his voice lowered almost to a rasp, heard him whisper, 'Yes, I see. What time was that?' She saw him shake his head, balancing the phone between his ear and neck as he reached into the back pocket of his pants and pulled out his notepad, jotted something down. 'Do you mind if I come out there, have a look around?' she heard him ask before putting down the phone.

'There's been a homicide,' he told her directly, as she grabbed for the kitchen counter.

Bonnie could barely bring herself to speak. 'No,' was all she could ultimately manage.

'A neighbor just made a positive identification a few minutes ago.'

'Please no,' Bonnie said.

'I'm afraid your friend is dead,' Captain Mahoney said solemnly. 'She's been shot.'

'Diana was shot,' Bonnie repeated, refusing to believe the words she was hearing, the words she was speaking.

'A single gunshot through the heart.'

'Oh God. Oh God, no. My poor Diana.' Bonnie's eyes traveled restlessly around the kitchen, stopped on the charcoal drawing of the mother and newborn child. She wanted to grab her own child and run, run as fast and as far away as she could. 'Is there any chance it could have been prowlers? Or maybe Diana's ex-husband? She was married twice, you know. Married and divorced. Maybe it was one of them or someone else she knew. There was never a shortage of men around. I mean, this doesn't have to have anything to do with Joan, or with me, does it? It could just be one of those awful coincidences, one of those perverse twists of fate. Couldn't it?' Bonnie asked, desperately wanting this to be the case, although she knew it wasn't so.

'A neighbor saw a car screeching out of her driveway at around ten o'clock this morning,' Captain Mahoney said. 'He got concerned, walked across the street, saw her front door was open, went inside, found her sprawled out on the floor of her living room.'

Bonnie tried very hard not to picture her closest friend lying dead on her living room floor. It couldn't be, she thought. There had to be some mistake. Diana was such a complex human being, so intense and complicated, so full of energy and contradictions. It was impossible that someone could rob her of that intensity with anything as simplistic

310

as a bullet to the heart. 'Did the neighbor get a good look at the person in the car?' Bonnie asked.

'No. But he did get a good look at the vehicle.'

'What kind of car was it?' Bonnie asked, hearing the answer almost before Captain Mahoney spoke it.

'A red Mercedes,' he said.

'We've assigned several police officers to guard the house,' Captain Mahoney was saying later, although he had to say it several times before it finally sunk in what he meant. 'They'll be in an unmarked car a few houses down the road. As well, we'll have someone out the back, just in case. And we've put a tap on your phone should he try to contact you.'

'Contact us?' Bonnie asked.

'You never know.'

'I know my brother didn't do this,' Lauren insisted from her seat at the dining room table, her arms sprawled haphazardly across the table top, her head dangling loosely from her neck, like a marionette whose strings had been severed.

They'd been sitting this way for what seemed like hours – Bonnie, Rod, Lauren, Nick, Captain Mahoney, Detective Haver, their bodies defeated, their arms and legs akimbo. Bonnie thought of another occasion several weeks ago, when another small group had been gathered around this table, only then it had been Haze instead of Detective Haver, Sam in place of Captain Mahoney. And Diana, Bonnie thought, picturing her friend, her eyes as blue as a tropical sea.

'You know Sam didn't do this,' Lauren said again, less forcefully.

'Of course we have police watching the Gleason house as well,' Detective Haver continued. 'In case they show up there.'

It turned out Diana's neighbor thought he'd seen two men in the car. Young men with long hair, he said, although he couldn't say for certain the young men in question had been Sam and Haze. It didn't matter. Neither Sam nor Haze had been seen since this morning. There was an all-points bulletin out for their arrest.

'Why would Sam want to hurt Diana?' Lauren asked, although her eyes were blank and her voice was directed at no one in particular. 'He had this huge crush on her. He wouldn't hurt her.'

Bonnie tried to block out the sound of Lauren's voice by closing her eyes. If police suspicions proved correct and Diana had been sexually assaulted before she died, then Lauren was doing nothing to help her brother's case. The medical examiner's report would take at least several days to come in, but Captain Mahoney felt certain it would show that Diana had been killed by the same gun that killed Joan, and that she had been raped either before or after death. 'Oh God,' Bonnie moaned, covering her mouth with her hand. It was all her fault. If it hadn't been for her, Diana would be alive today. Hadn't she dragged her friend into this mess? Hadn't she called her from the police station the day she'd discovered Joan's body, dragged her into Newton, even though she knew little about criminal law? Hadn't she invited her to dinner, introduced her to Rod's son? *Sam, this is Diana. Diana, this is Death.* 'Oh God,' she moaned again, burying her head in her hands.

Strong hands came to rest on her shoulders, their fingers massaging the muscles at the base of her neck. 'I'll be staying here tonight,' Nick said, his fingers applying just the right amount of pressure. 'On the couch in the living room.'

Bonnie nodded, looked toward Rod, wondering how he would react. But Rod said nothing. He sat at the far end of the table, staring blankly into space, seeming not to realize that Nick was even there, that his house was full of police officers, that there were more police outside. He was probably in shock, Bonnie thought, realizing he'd said almost nothing since she'd arrived home in the company of Captain Mahoney. Anger and outrage had vanished into horror and dismay. Diana was dead, the captain had told him, and his son was the prime suspect. He was also the prime suspect in both his mother's death and the attempt to poison his stepmother. Rod had listened to all this in stunned silence, then retreated into the dining room to sit down. He'd been there ever since, not speaking, not moving, barely breathing.

Bonnie wanted to go to him, to put her arms around him and tell him that everything would be all right, but something stopped her. How could she tell him everything would be all right when it might never be all right again? How could she comfort him when only hours ago, she'd thought he might be guilty of the crimes himself?

'I should check on Amanda,' Bonnie said, rising to her feet, swaying, sitting back down.

'I just did,' Nick reminded her. 'She's sound asleep. Which is something you should consider doing. I doubt anything will happen tonight, and those pills you're taking are pretty strong stuff. You should be in bed. You too, Rod,' he said, shifting his focus.

Rod said nothing. He continued staring at the far wall as if no one had spoken.

'Daddy?' Lauren called. She got out of her seat, walked to her father, put her arms around him, hugged him tightly, as if trying to squeeze life into him, her lips grazing the side of his cheek. 'Come on, Daddy,' she whispered. 'I'll help you up the stairs.'

Rod allowed his daughter to lead him from the room. Bonnie watched them mount the stairs slowly, planting both feet firmly on each step before continuing on to the next.

'You should really be in a hospital,' Nick said, turning back to his sister.

'Not till this is settled. Not till I know it's safe to leave Amanda.'

'They won't get far,' Captain Mahoney stated. 'Two long-haired teenagers in a red Mercedes. Shouldn't be too difficult to spot.'

Bonnie shook her head, trying to imagine where they might be, where they were headed, why they would have killed Diana.

Why? she asked herself again, the word making her head spin. Why any of it? Nothing made any sense. Sam might not have been the son of most people's dreams – he had a ring in his nose and a snake in his bedroom – and he was withdrawn and angry, moody and shy. But he was also sweet and sensitive and caring and desperate to be loved.

Was that what had happened? Had his need to be loved resulted in his misinterpreting Diana's kindness? Had his pent-up rage surfaced when she'd turned down his awkward teenage advances? Had he raped her, then killed her to keep her quiet? Had her death been an isolated act of fury or part of a larger plan?

Or was Haze the prime culprit? Was it his sperm they'd discover in Diana's body? That was the simple part, Captain Mahoney said. If Diana had been sexually assaulted, DNA testing would easily ferret out the guilty party.

'It's almost over,' Nick told her.

Bonnie nodded, praying he was right. She stood up, walked to the stairs, Nick right behind her. Captain Mahoney and Detective Haver remained at the dining room table. They would show themselves out when they were ready.

'Dad would like it if you'd call him,' Nick said in the hall. 'He's been worried about you since your visit. He knows there's all sorts of stuff going on, and I think he'd rest a whole lot easier if you'd give him a call.'

'I don't know if I can do that, Nick. I don't know if I have the strength.'

'Oh, I wouldn't waste a minute worrying about your strength,' Nick told her. 'You're one strong woman, Bonnie. If a shitload of arsenic couldn't finish you off, I don't think you have anything to worry about from a harmless old man who loves you.' He paused, and when he spoke again, his voice was strong. 'We can't do anything about the dead, Bonnie. It's the living we have to learn to pay more attention to.'

His arms reached out toward her. Slowly, Bonnie collapsed into them, folding like a soft tissue. After several seconds, she raised her head, kissed the tip of his delicate nose. Then she turned and followed her husband's path up the stairs.

He was lying on top of the bed, Lauren removing his shoes, when Bonnie entered the room.

'I couldn't get him to get undressed,' Lauren told her.

Bonnie stared over at Rod, curled into a semi-fetal position on top of the covers, his eyes open, though seemingly unfocused. Bonnie tried to imagine what he must be going through. How would she feel, after all, if a police captain were to announce some years down the road that her child was a psychotic killer responsible for the deaths of two people and the poisoning of two others? 'Are you all right?' Bonnie asked her stepdaughter.

Lauren shrugged. 'Do you think they'll find Sam?'

'I'm sure they will.'

'I'm so afraid,' Lauren cried softly. 'I'm so afraid they'll shoot him.'

Bonnie went to the child, took her in her arms. 'Nobody's going to shoot anybody,' she said. There's been enough shooting, she thought. 'I think we could all use some sleep. It's been a long day.'

'Are you going to be all right?'

'I'll be fine.'

Lauren returned to the bed, planted a gentle kiss on her father's forehead. 'I'll see you in the morning, Daddy. You'll see, everything's going to be all right now.' She tiptoed to the doorway, stopped. 'I love you, Daddy,' she said, then was gone.

Bonnie crossed to the phone by the side of the bed, her fingers moving automatically across the dial. Several seconds later, she heard her father's careful hello.

'It's Bonnie,' she told him. 'Nick said you were worried about me.'

'Are you all right?'

'I've been better,' Bonnie replied honestly. 'What about you?'

'Me? I'm fine.' He sounded surprised she would ask. 'I just wanted to make sure you were okay.'

'I'm fine. Don't worry.'

'A parent always worries.'

Bonnie smiled sadly, realized this was true. 'Can I call you back in a day or two?' she asked. 'Hopefully, by then, things will have settled down a bit . . . we could talk.'

'Call whenever you like.'

Bonnie felt tears falling the length of her cheek. 'You too,' she said.

'I love you, sweetheart.'

'Good night, Daddy,' Bonnie whispered, hanging up the phone. Then she climbed onto the bed beside her husband, and waited for sleep.

Chapter Thirty-One

It was six o'clock in the morning when Bonnie felt someone moving across the carpet toward her. A sudden shadow fell over her still-closed lids, slicing a thick diagonal line through the early-morning sun. She felt fingers, as soft and light as a feather, brush against her arm, heard a gentle voice floating toward her ear. 'Bonnie,' the voice said, 'Bonnie, wake up.'

Bonnie opened her eyes, saw her brother's face only inches from her own, bolted upright on the bed.

'It's okay,' he reassured her quickly, taking several quick steps back. 'Sorry, I didn't mean to frighten you.'

'What's happening?' Bonnie looked beside her. Rod was still asleep. She hadn't felt him move all night.

'We just got a call from the New York State police. They stopped two kids in a red Mercedes for speeding on the thruway. Looks like it's Sam and Haze.'

'What happens now?' Bonnie asked, glancing over at Rod, his eyes still closed, though she noticed a slight stiffening in his limbs, as if he were holding his breath.

'They're bringing them into Newton. We'll talk to them when they get to the station.'

'How long will that be?'

'A couple of hours.' Nick sat down on the bed, took Bonnie's hands in his own. 'You okay?'

'I just want it to be over.'

'And then you'll check into a hospital?'

'As soon as I know Amanda's safe.'

Nick's hand reached out, caressed Bonnie's cheek. 'You're one tough cookie.'

She smiled. 'I guess it runs in the family.'

'I better go,' he said. 'I want to talk to Captain Mahoney before they bring Sam in.'

Bonnie nodded. 'You'll call me as soon as you know anything?'

'I'll call you as soon as I can.'

Bonnie listened to Nick's footsteps padding down the stairs, heard the front door open and close. Then she lowered her head to the pillow, her neck and shoulders unable to support its weight any longer, and glanced over at Rod.

His eyes were open.

'You heard?' Her voice was detached, as if it were coming from someone else, as if it had no connection to her body.

'They picked up Sam and Haze on the New York thruway,' he repeated, his tone flat and unemotional, as if he were talking about strangers.

Bonnie observed the interaction between her husband and herself as if she were watching a television program, one of those true-life docudramas that had become all the rage since fact had outpaced fiction in matters of the entertainingly absurd. She saw a man and a woman, both in yesterday's rumpled clothing, their faces pale and bewildered, their postures equal measures of defiance and defeat. She wondered who these two people were, so estranged from their own lives and each other, reciting their lines as if they were actors, ill-matched and badly cast, reading from a script they couldn't quite understand. 'Are you all right?' she asked.

'Are you?' he asked in return.

'I'm feeling a little stronger. Not great, but better.'

Rod said nothing. He shifted onto his back, stared up at the ceiling.

'Do you want to talk about it?' Bonnie asked.

'No,' he said. 'What's the point?'

'The point is, he's your son,' Bonnie said.

The sound that escaped Rod's mouth was halfway between a laugh and a cry. It chipped at the air, like a shovel through ice.

'Maybe it wasn't Sam,' Bonnie offered weakly, sitting up and drawing her knees toward her chest. 'Maybe it was Haze. Maybe he dragged Sam into all this . . .' She stopped. Was she trying to convince her husband or herself? 'I just can't believe that Sam is a killer,' she continued after several seconds. 'I've spent a lot of time with him these last weeks, and I just can't believe he'd do something like this. He's a gentle boy, Rod. He's unhappy and he's lonely, but he's not a psychopath. He couldn't murder his mother. He couldn't rape and shoot Diana.'

Rod flipped over onto his other side, burying his face into his pillow, not quite muffling the sobs that twisted through his throat. Bonnie watched the trembling of his back, the spasmodic jerkings of his shoulders. She wanted to throw her body over his, to warm and protect him, like a child's security blanket. 'Everything will be all right,' she wanted to tell him, as Lauren had told him the night before. And yet, something stopped her. An invisible hand kept her an arm's length away, pushing her back into her own little corner, not letting her connect with her husband. What was stopping her? she wondered. What was keeping her from comforting the man she loved?

'It'll be all right, Rod,' she said, but the words sounded hollow, even to her own ears.

Rod continued crying softly.

Was he crying for his son or himself? Bonnie wondered. Maybe for both of them. For the relationship they'd never had; for the relationship they would probably never have now. It was too late, too late to play the doting parent, too late to make up for all the lost years, too late to cement the parent-child bonds that had never been properly set in the first place.

Or maybe not, Bonnie realized, thoughts drifting closer to home, understanding that the need for a father was something a child never really outgrew. Maybe there was no such thing as too late for a father to reach out to his child.

Bonnie watched her husband's shoulders shudder to a halt. Was the enormity of all that had happened just now sinking in? That his child could have murdered his mother? That he could have raped and killed a woman who'd tried to befriend him? Certainly, Rod would waste no tears over Joan, a woman he'd despised, or Diana, a woman he'd barely tolerated. So why such bitter tears?

'Rod . . .'

He sat up, wiped the tears from his face with the back of his hand. When he turned to her, his brown eyes seemed more opaque than ever before, like the very bottom of a mud-filled river.

319

'What is it?' she asked.

He shook his head, as if to shake loose whatever unwanted thoughts had settled there.

'Rod, please tell me.'

'The police will be conducting tests,' he said, as if he were taking part in a different conversation altogether.

'What do you mean?'

'Blood samples, sperm samples,' he continued in the now-familiar monotone. 'For their DNA tests.'

'Yes,' Bonnie said, not sure where Rod was going with this.

'It's over,' he said. 'Everything's over.'

'Rod, what are you talking about?'

There was a long pause.

'Sam didn't rape Diana,' Rod said finally. 'Neither did Haze.'

'What?'

'The sperm they'll find in Diana's body, it's not Sam's,' he repeated.

Bonnie found herself inching off the bed, backing toward the wall, though she could scarcely feel her feet on the carpet. 'What are you saying?'

'I think you know,' he told her.

Bonnie tried for several seconds to find her voice, was finally able to croak out a hoarse whisper. 'You're saying the sperm is yours?'

Rod said nothing.

'You're saying that you killed her?' Bonnie looked toward the doorway, silently measuring how many steps she'd need to the door.

'No!' Rod said adamantly, snapping out of his lethargy. 'Although that's what the police will think, that's for damn sure. They can't wait to get their hands on me.' He laughed, a strangled sound that punctured the air like a nail going into a balloon.

'I don't understand.'

'I didn't kill Diana, for God's sake. I could never do anything to hurt her.' Rod's face contorted with undisguised pain. 'I loved her,' he whispered, burying his face in his hands, so that his words were muffled. 'I loved her,' he repeated, the words now as clear, and as cold, as a mountain stream.

'You loved Diana,' Bonnie said, and waited for Rod to continue, but he said nothing further, just stared at her with those opaque, bottomless eyes. 'How long . . . ?'

'About a year.'

'All those nights you were working late, all those early-morning meetings . . .'

Rod nodded, recognizing there was no need to say the words.

'But you never liked Diana,' Bonnie protested weakly, feeling as if the floor beneath her feet had vanished, as if she were standing in the middle of a vast void, and it was only a question of time before she was sucked into its center, before whatever was left of her disappeared altogether.

'It just happened, Bonnie.' Rod lifted one hand in the air, let it float aimlessly about for several seconds, then drop to his side.

What could he say after all? That they never meant for it to go this far? That they never meant to hurt her?

'She didn't go to New York,' Bonnie said. 'She was with you in Florida.'

Rod nodded.

'She was standing right beside you when I told you I'd been to see Dr Kline, and I said Diana had recommended him.'

'She said she never heard of him.'

'That's how you knew that her doctor's name was Gizmondi, because she told you.'

'It was so unlike you to lie. We thought you might have gotten suspicious and were trying to trap us.'

Bonnie lowered her head, thinking of her misguided suspicions. 'I thought it was Marla you were having the affair with.'

'Marla?!'

Rod actually managed to look offended by the suggestion. Bonnie almost laughed. It was all starting to make sense, she thought, gathering all the pieces of the puzzle together, pushing them into their designated slots.

'The lingerie I found in your bottom drawer, that wasn't for me,' she stated, slipping into Caroline Gossett's habit of stating all her questions. 'It was for Diana.' She pictured her former friend, luxuriant dark hair resting atop high ample breasts. 'No wonder the bra size was too big.' She remembered the conversation she'd had with Diana right after finding the sexy undergarments in the bottom of Rod's dresser drawer. Obviously Diana had called Rod immediately afterward, informed him of his wife's untimely discovery, sent Rod home with instructions to be extra loving and attentive.

'So, you've been sleeping with Diana for almost a year,' Bonnie began. 'The times the three of us were together, the times you supposedly put up with her for my sake, you were actually putting up with me. That time in the police station when you were so angry about finding her there, you weren't angry at her at all. You were angry at me. Because I dragged you away from your little tryst. Isn't that so? Isn't that the reason I couldn't locate either one of you? Isn't that the reason you didn't have an alibi for the time of Joan's death? Because you were out fucking my best friend!'

'Bonnie . . .'

'The whole time I was sick, you were with her,' Bonnie said, amazed. Could she really have been so stupid? Was she such a pitiful cliché? The wife who's the last to know? 'Even after you came back from Florida, you were with her.'

'We flew back together, I dropped her off, then came straight home,' he volunteered, the words spilling from his mouth, almost as if he were eager to finally be able to talk to her about it.

Perhaps he *was* eager, she thought, listening helplessly, wanting to tell him to shut up, but unable to do so. He was making her an accomplice, she thought uneasily. 'So, you came home, checked in on me for a few minutes, then put me to bed like a good little girl and went back out to play.'

'You make it sound so callous. It wasn't like that.'

'Wasn't it?'

'It wasn't meant to be.'

'So you were there when Sam and Lauren showed up to finish wallpapering the bathroom,' she stated, picturing the scene, wondering whether she would have found it amusing had it happened to somebody else.

'I told them I'd flown back early and stopped in at Diana's to find out how you really were, if there was something you weren't telling me. They seemed to buy it . . .' His voice drifted off, as if suddenly cognizant of the fact that he should at least have the decency to be embarrassed by these revelations.

'And then you came home and found out your wife had flown the proverbial coop.'

'I was frantic. I didn't know where the hell you'd disappeared.'

'How thoughtless of me,' Bonnie said.

'I didn't mean . . .'

'So, you went back to Diana's. You must have been very relieved when I phoned.'

'We didn't know what was going on.'

'So, of course, you had to comfort each other.'

'I didn't stay the night,' Rod said.

'But you did make love.'

A minute's silence before stating the obvious. 'Yes.'

'And then you left.'

'I came home.'

'What time was that?'

'Around midnight.'

'And the next thing you knew, Diana was dead, shot through the heart just like Joan, in all probability by the same gun, undoubtedly by the very same hand. But, of course, you had nothing to do with either killing. Is that what you're trying to tell me?'

'I didn't kill them, Bonnie. I swear I didn't. You have to believe me. I'm devastated by Diana's death.'

'The reason you're so damn devastated has nothing to do with the fact that Diana is dead,' Bonnie snapped, 'and everything to do with the fact that you were stupid enough to leave your sperm in her body. Isn't that true? Your tears have nothing to do with Diana, or even your son. They're all about you. Tell me, Rod, have you ever cared about anyone other than yourself?'

He regarded her plaintively. 'I care about you,' he said, holding out his arms.

Bonnie approached him slowly, drawn by the power of his need into a tight embrace. She felt the warmth of his arms as they snaked around her body, the softness of his cheeks as they pressed against her own. How she'd always loved the feeling of being in his arms.

She pulled back slowly, stared into his unfathomably deep brown eyes. Except that they weren't so deep after all, she realized, gently extricating herself from his grip. They were surprisingly, disappointingly, dangerously shallow.

'What are you doing?' he asked as Bonnie walked to the phone beside the bed and pressed the appropriate numbers into the receiver.

'This is Bonnie Wheeler,' she said. 'I need to get in touch with Captain

323

Mahoney immediately. Yes,' she told the police operator, watching as her husband collapsed back on the bed, burying his head in his hands, 'I can wait.'

'Where did my father go?' Lauren asked, coming into the kitchen, Amanda at her side.

Bonnie was sitting at the kitchen table staring at Amanda's painting of people with box-like heads. She turned around slowly, smiling at Rod's two daughters, all red and blond curls, one face echoing the other. *Sugar and spice and everything nice. That's what little girls are made of*, she thought. 'He had to go down to the police station.'

'That was hours ago,' Lauren said. 'Shouldn't he be back by now?'

Bonnie checked her watch. It was almost eleven a.m. 'I guess the police had a lot of questions to ask him.'

'What about Sam?'

'He and Haze are at the station.' Bonnie checked her watch again, although only a few seconds had passed. She hadn't heard from either Nick or the police in several hours. No doubt there was simply nothing new to tell her at this point. Her husband, his son, and his son's friend were all being questioned. Everyone had been informed of his rights. *Mirandized*, she remembered Diana saying. Lawyers had been summoned. Hopefully, she would hear something soon.

'I want to go to the park,' Amanda said, bouncing up and down without moving her feet.

'I can't go to the park now, sweetie,' Bonnie told her.

'Why?'

'I can take her,' Lauren volunteered. 'I wouldn't mind getting some fresh air.'

'I don't know,' Bonnie said, not sure if it was a good idea for them to go anywhere until after the police called.

'Please,' Amanda pleaded.

Bonnie wondered why she was hesitating. The police had all the major suspects in the murders down at the station. Was she waiting for a call to tell her that the killer had confessed? Did she really consider that a possibility? She wasn't even sure the police would lay any charges. Could she really keep her daughter cooped up indefinitely? 'I guess you can go,' she said finally, understanding Lauren's need for air.

'Hooray.' This time when Amanda jumped up and down, her feet moved with her.

'Let me get my purse,' Lauren, said, chasing Amanda out of the kitchen and up the stairs.

The phone rang.

'Hello,' Bonnie said, picking it up almost instantly.

'Bonnie, it's Josh. How are you?'

'Josh?'

'Josh Freeman?' he asked, as if he weren't sure.

'Yes, of course, Josh, I'm sorry. I was expecting it to be someone else, that's all.'

'Is this a bad time?'

'No.' In fact, she was glad to hear from him.

'I was just wondering how you were doing.'

'A little better,' she told him. My husband and stepson are down at police headquarters, suspects in not only Joan's slaying, but that of my best friend, Diana, who, it turns out, was sleeping with my husband for most of last year. Oh, and did I mention that I have high levels of arsenic in my bloodstream? Bonnie thought, but didn't say. Some things were better discussed in person.

'I thought I might drop by a little later, if that's all right with you,' Josh said, as if reading her thoughts.

'Sure,' Bonnie said. 'That would be nice.'

'How about in an hour?'

'Sounds good.'

'See you then.'

Bonnie hung up the phone, looking forward to Josh's visit. Of course, only yesterday she'd suspected him of bringing her poisoned chicken soup, she realized, glancing back at the phone, wondering whether to call him back, tell him not to come. 'This is silly,' she said out loud. It wasn't Josh who'd tried to poison her. It certainly couldn't have been Josh who killed Diana. What possible motive could he have? Still, she thought, reaching for the phone, it wouldn't hurt to play it safe until she knew for sure. She'd call her brother, apprise him of the situation, ask him to drop by at about the same time that Josh was due over.

The phone rang just as she was about to lift it from its carriage.

'We're ready,' Lauren said, bounding down the last few stairs, her large tote bag slung over her shoulder, Amanda with a Barbie bag slung over hers.

Bonnie picked up the phone. 'Hello,' she said.

There was no response.

'Hello?' she said again.

Still nothing.

'Do you want me to pick up anything at the store while we're out?' Lauren asked.

'Check if we need milk,' Bonnie said, temporarily distracted.

Lauren went to the fridge, opened it, peeked inside. 'No, there's plenty of milk.'

'Hello?' Bonnie repeated into the receiver a third time, wondering why she didn't hang up, about to do just that when she heard the familiar click on the other end of the line. What *was* that? she wondered, recognizing the sound from somewhere, unable to place exactly where.

'Who is it?' Lauren asked, worry etching delicate creases around her huge hazel eyes.

'Who's calling, please?' Bonnie said.

Silence, then another click. Then again.

Click. Click.

The breath stilled in Bonnie's chest. She felt herself adrift in a windless sea, waiting anxiously for the next gust to propel her to shore. She was so close. All that was necessary was a gentle puff.

Click.

And suddenly she saw herself turning her car up a long driveway, parking in a busy lot, then hurrying through the front door of a beautiful sprawling white building. Something out of the old South, she remembered thinking the first time she saw it, watching herself proceed through the front lobby to the front desk, waiting impatiently by the elevators, hesitating outside the door to room three hundred and twelve.

Click.

She saw the door open, saw the old woman sitting in the wheelchair, legs like tree stumps, her face pebbled with age, her eyes hooded with boredom, wide delinquent mouth open, balancing her dentures on her rude tongue, then clicking them back into place.

Click. Click.

'Mary?' Bonnie asked warily. 'Mary, is that you?'

'Maybe,' the voice replied. 'Who's asking?'

Chapter Thirty-Two

Fifteen minutes later, Bonnie pulled her car into the crowded parking lot of the Melrose Mental Health Center in Sudbury, and raced up the front steps, through the lobby and toward the bank of elevators on the right. There was a crowd already waiting, and Bonnie leaned against the wall, trying to catch her breath and gather her thoughts.

What was she doing back here? What had prompted her to race out of the house as soon as Lauren and Amanda left for the park? To jump into her car and press the accelerator to the floor? She still wasn't feeling well. She certainly shouldn't be risking her life to talk to some crazy old woman who, in all probability, had nothing of any value to say to her.

She certainly hadn't said anything on the phone. It was Bonnie who'd done all the talking. Why was she calling? Did she have something to tell her? Did she want to talk to her about Elsa Langer?

Maybe, had come the immediate response to all her questions. Who's asking?

And so here she was, operating purely on instincts and adrenalin, standing with a bunch of strangers, all of whose faces reflected the intense desire to be somewhere else. And if any of them asked, she wouldn't be able to come up with one good reason for her being here. What exactly was she hoping to find out?

A bell sounded; a green light lit up above one of the elevator doors; the door slowly opened. There was a hurried exchange – people pushing out, people pushing in – and soon the elevator was full, the doors closing, leaving Bonnie behind, along with half a dozen others. Together, they stepped back and shuffled over to the next elevator, almost as one. *Acting as a unit*, she thought. Dr Greenspoon would be proud.

Another bell sounded; another green light indicated the imminent arrival of a second elevator. This time, Bonnie broke from the ranks, wormed her way to the front of the line, began moving inside as soon as the elevator doors opened.

'Excuse me,' snarled a middle-aged woman, whose limp hair accentuated the slackness of her features. 'I'd like to get off, if you don't mind.'

Bonnie squeezed her body into a corner of the elevator, staring resolutely at the numbers on the panel beside the door, as the elevator filled up. 'Could someone press three?' she asked, pretending to look around, as if the voice had come from someone else. She felt hot, dizzy, in danger of fainting, grateful that there were so many others in the small compartment to keep her upright. She wondered if she could survive standing on her own.

The thought struck her as appropriately symbolic, and she laughed. Immediately, and despite the lack of room, she felt those around her take a step back. When the doors opened on the second floor, those who remained behind inched even farther away.

Bonnie hesitated when the elevator reached the third floor. 'What the hell,' she whispered under her breath, stepping into the corridor. She was here now. She might as well find out why.

She inched her way slowly down the long corridor toward Mary's room, pausing for several seconds outside the door.

'Come in,' Mary called from inside. 'What are you waiting for?'

Bonnie pushed open the door.

Mary was sitting in her wheelchair by the window, looking out at the grounds below. 'They keep it very nice, don't they?' she asked, still not turning around.

'Yes, they do,' Bonnie agreed, looking around the room, surprised to see a bright pair of eyes staring at her from Elsa Langer's bed. 'Hello,' she said to the woman, who was slim and dark and almost regal in appearance. Bonnie wondered what she was doing at the Melrose Mental Health Center.

'How do you do?' the woman said, extending her hand. 'I'm Jacqueline Kennedy Onassis.'

'Don't pay any attention to her,' Mary bellowed from the window. 'She's nuttier than a fruitcake.'

Bonnie gasped. Wasn't that the phrase Rod always used when describing his ex-wife?

'First they gave me a vegetable, now they send me a fruitcake.' Mary turned from the window, angled her chair to face Bonnie. 'What's the matter? Gas?'

Bonnie cautiously approached Mary's wheelchair, noting that Mary was dressed in a clean navy-and-white-striped terrycloth robe, and that her brown hair appeared to have been freshly colored and was held in check by a variety of different-sized bobby pins. 'What did you want to see me about?' she asked.

'Who said I wanted to see you?'

'You did. When you called me. You intimated you had something to tell me.'

'I did?'

Bonnie felt her heart sink. Had she really raced out here for this? A pointless conversation with a sick old woman? Of course, if she hadn't, she wouldn't have gotten to meet Jacqueline Kennedy Onassis, she thought, smiling at the bright-eyed woman in Elsa Langer's bed.

'I thought you might have had something to tell me about Elsa Langer,' Bonnie ventured.

'Who?'

'Elsa Langer,' Bonnie repeated.

'Teddy wasn't to blame,' the woman in the bed proclaimed suddenly. 'He tried to save that girl. But he was never much of a swimmer.'

'You say I called you?' Mary asked, her hands tapping her knees with growing agitation.

'Not more than twenty minutes ago.'

'Didn't take you very long to get here.'

'I thought it might be important. You obviously went to some trouble to get my number.'

'Nah,' Mary said dismissively. 'I just asked the nurse. I remembered you told Elsa you'd leave her your number.'

'What else do you remember?'

'About what?'

'About Elsa,' Bonnie said.

'She wasn't any fun,' Mary said, pushing her lips into an unpleasant pout, then twisting them from side to side. 'She just lay in that bed all the time, never saying anything. Not that Jackie O here is any improvement.'

'Christina was a very unpleasant girl,' the woman in the bed confided.

331

'I tried to get close to her, but she wasn't having any of it. She wanted her father all to herself.'

'Tell me more about Elsa,' Bonnie prodded.

Mary began pushing at her dentures with her tongue. 'Nothing to tell. She just lay in that bed day in and day out, and then one day she died.'

'That must have been very upsetting for you,' Bonnie commented, thinking she should probably leave, but feeling tired, needing a few minutes to rest, regroup.

'Frankly, I didn't even notice,' Mary said and laughed, temporarily abandoning her fight with her dentures. 'It was the nurse who realized she was in a coma.'

'At least she didn't suffer,' Bonnie said. 'I guess that's good.'

'I guess.' Mary swiveled her chair back to the window. 'You should tell that to the little girl. It'll make her feel better.'

'Little girl?' Bonnie walked to the window, stared down at the woman in the wheelchair.

'Her granddaughter. What was her name?'

'You mean Lauren?'

'Yes, I think that was it. Well, you should know. You brought her here the first time.'

'What?'

'I kept telling her to go on a diet,' Mrs Onassis announced from her bed. 'But she wouldn't listen. She hated me. Did right from the word go.'

'What do you mean, the first time?' Bonnie asked.

'You brought both those kids here, the boy and the girl.' Once again, Mary's mouth started twisting, as if she were gargling.

'Yes, I know,' Bonnie said. 'But I only brought them once.'

'The girl came back,' Mary said matter-of-factly.

'What?' Every hair on Bonnie's body stood on end.

'She came back. Brought Elsa some custard she said she made herself. Sat on the bed feeding it to her. Wouldn't let me have any. Not very nice, if you ask me,' Mary pouted. 'I just wanted a taste.'

Bonnie grabbed hold of both arms of the wheelchair, forced Mary's eyes to hers. 'Think very carefully, Mary,' Bonnie instructed, trying hard not to panic. 'How soon after Lauren was here did Elsa slip into her coma?'

Mary flipped her dentures in and out of her mouth. 'That night,' she said.

Bonnie felt her body sway, her fingers digging into the soft rubber of the chair's arms to keep from falling. 'Oh God.' What did it mean? Bonnie looked helplessly about. Could Lauren have poisoned Elsa Langer? And if she'd poisoned Elsa Langer . . .

'It can't be,' Bonnie said. 'It can't be.'

'I thought the least she could do was give me a little taste of her custard,' Mary said. 'But no, she insisted that her grandmother eat it all.'

'I left Amanda with her. She's alone with my little girl.' Bonnie bolted for the door.

'I tried to be her friend,' Bonnie heard the woman who would be Jacqueline Kennedy Onassis cry out as she ran down the hall. 'I could have helped that girl, if only she'd let me.'

Bonnie drove like a maniac along Route Twenty, watching as Boston Post Road became State Road West, then State Road East back into Weston, where once again it became Boston Post Road. She was shivering, sweating, crying, shouting. 'No, it can't be,' she kept repeating. 'It can't be.'

Bonnie recalled how eager Lauren had been to visit her grandmother, how touched she'd been when the old woman spoke her name, how loving she'd acted toward her, sitting beside her on the bed, feeding her lunch. Could she have returned at a later date to feed her poison? When? The girl had school all day. When would she have had the opportunity?

'She stayed home from school one day,' Bonnie said out loud, remembering the day that Lauren had felt queasy, thought she might be suffering a relapse of the flu. Except that it wasn't the flu. It was arsenic.

Unless she hadn't been sick at all. Unless she was merely pretending.

'No, that's impossible,' Bonnie said. 'I saw how sick she was. I held her head for hours while she threw up. That was no act. She was really sick.'

But she got better, Bonnie thought. While I got sicker and sicker. And she was always there. She was always there.

But why? Bonnie wondered, screeching to a halt at the red light at the corner of Boston Post Road and Buckskin Drive, looking around impatiently, tapping her foot against the gas pedal. 'Why would she want to kill me?'

Bonnie thought back to the afternoon she and Rod first went to Joan's house to tell Lauren and Sam about their mother's death. She remembered Lauren's violent outburst, felt the sharp jab of Lauren's shoes against her shins, the hard smack of her fist against her mouth. She hates me, Bonnie recalled thinking.

But surely that had changed. Surely over the ensuing weeks they had moved closer, forming a bond of respect and friendship. Unless that too had been an act.

But even if she hates me, Bonnie thought, does she hate me enough to want me dead? And why would she want to kill her grandmother, a helpless old woman who barely remembered who she was?

And who else? Bonnie wondered, her foot flooring the gas pedal as the light turned green, the car streaking across the intersection as if someone had inadvertently pressed the fast forward button on a VCR.

Bonnie tried desperately not to think at all, to concentrate on the road ahead. Her thoughts were too bizarre, too crazy, more like drug-induced fantasies than anything connected to reality. Was she actually thinking that Lauren might have had something to do with her mother's murder, with Diana's death?

'No, this is ridiculous. You're being absolutely ridiculous.'

Lauren was at school the day her mother was murdered. She was at home the night Diana was killed. Wasn't she?

She could easily have skipped a class or two, Bonnie realized. The police wouldn't have bothered to check. Who would suspect a fourteen-year-old girl of killing her mother? And she could have easily slipped out of the house to kill Diana while Rod was asleep. She knew where Diana lived. She'd been there earlier that same afternoon.

But why? Why would she want to hurt Diana? And what motive could she have had for wanting her mother dead?

You're in danger, Joan had warned her. *You and Amanda.*

Was Lauren the danger Joan had been trying to warn her against?

'Oh my God.' Bonnie pictured her daughter's innocent hand inside that of her half-sister's. 'Don't you hurt my baby. Don't you dare hurt my baby.' She turned right onto Highland Street, the scenery blurring into a green fog as she accelerated along the clear road. 'Please don't hurt my little girl,' she prayed out loud.

How could she have left her daughter alone with Lauren? Hadn't Joan cautioned her enough times never to use her children as baby-sitters? Maybe those pronouncements hadn't been the drunken ramblings of a jealous ex-wife at all. Maybe Joan had been trying to warn her even then.

But why?

Always why.

It didn't make sense. It wasn't possible. Lauren couldn't have had anything to do with her mother's death, or Diana's, or Elsa Langer's, or with her own poisoning. Yes, she had access to her mother's gun; yes, she must have known where her mother kept the rat poison. But that didn't mean anything necessarily. So did Sam. So did Rod.

Except that both Sam and Rod were at the police station, and Lauren was with her little girl.

Lauren had taken Amanda to the park, but which park? There were several in the area, and they could have gone to any one of them. 'Where are you, dammit?' Bonnie demanded. 'Where did you go?'

She drove past Brown Street, inadvertently glancing toward Diana's house, saw the now-familiar yellow tape cordoning off the house. *Crime scene – do not cross.* 'Don't panic,' she told herself, turning right on South Avenue, seeing the little park at the corner of South and Wellesley, slowing to a crawl.

Some children were playing on the swings and slides, watched over by several bored-looking women, but Lauren wasn't among them, and neither was Amanda. Bonnie thought of stopping, of asking the women if they'd seen her child, but she didn't recognize anyone, and didn't want to waste any time. She doubted she would be able to speak with any coherence anyway.

Where else might they have gone? There was a little park back on Blueberry Hill Road, but it was tiny and had only a few swings, and Amanda didn't like it much. And there was the playground behind her school, the playground beside the small alleyway that was Alphabet Lane, where someone had emptied a pail of blood over Amanda's head. 'Oh God,' Bonnie moaned. Surely Lauren wouldn't try to hurt her now, not so soon after Diana's murder.

Bonnie sped up Wellesley Street to School Street, turned left. She tore up the long driveway of the day-care center, jumping out of the car in the same second she pulled the key from the ignition, running along the small walkway to the back of the school, the fully equipped playground popping into view.

There was no one there. Bonnie spun around. 'Where are you?' she cried. 'Goddam it, Lauren, where did you take my baby?' And then she saw it, discarded in the sand at the foot of one of the swings. She raced toward it, bent down, scooped the bright pink Barbie bag into her hands. So they'd been here. Been and gone. Was it possible they'd returned home?

Bonnie raced to her car, almost skidding into a tree at the side of the road as she backed it onto the street. 'Slow down,' she told herself, easing her foot off the gas pedal as she made a sharp right turn onto Winter Street. 'You're almost there.'

The house appeared at the second bend in the road and Bonnie pulled into the driveway and jumped from the car. 'Amanda!' she called even before she reached the front door. 'Amanda! Lauren!' She fumbled with her key and pushed open the door, tripping over her feet into the front hall, taking the stairs two at a time.

She saw the blood as soon as she reached the upstairs hall. Just a few red drops on the white tile of the bathroom floor, but they were unmistakable nonetheless. 'Oh my God.' Bonnie threw her hand across her mouth to keep from screaming. 'No, please, no.' Slowly, as if her feet were encased in cement, she approached the bathroom.

And then she heard a tiny squeal from behind the closed door to Amanda's bedroom and she spun toward the sound. 'Amanda?' she cried, her voice as shaky as a single tear. Her hand reached toward the door, gently pushed it open, her breath stilled in her lungs, her eyes afraid to focus.

Amanda was sitting cross-legged on the floor in the middle of the room, one hand on her knee, the other extended toward Lauren, who sat beside her, her tote bag in her lap, holding Amanda's wrist in one hand, a razor blade in the other.

'Oh my God.'

'Please don't come any closer,' Lauren said simply.

'I fell, Mommy,' Amanda told her, lifting her hand from her freshly scraped knee. 'Lauren was pushing me on the swing, and I fell off and hurt my knee. I was crying, but Lauren told me not to cry, and she cleaned it up for me.'

'I'm sorry the bathroom's such a mess,' Lauren said, as if this were the most normal conversation in the world, as if she weren't holding a razor blade to Amanda's wrist.

'Amanda,' Bonnie began, her eyes glued to her daughter's delicate veins, 'why don't you go downstairs and get some milk and cookies . . .'

'Not now, Amanda,' Lauren said with authority. Amanda didn't move.

'Lauren says we're going to become real sisters. Blood sisters,' Amanda emphasized. 'She said it wouldn't hurt.'

Bonnie felt the air around her suddenly turn to ice. Her breath had to fight its way through. 'What?'

'What did Mary have to say?' Lauren asked. 'I know you went to see her. She told you I was there, didn't she?' Her voice assumed a faraway cadence, as if she were speaking from another room.

'Yes.' Bonnie took a step forward.

'I wouldn't come any closer,' Lauren said. 'I might get nervous. My hand could slip.'

Bonnie stopped dead. 'Don't hurt her,' she begged. 'Please don't hurt her.'

'Lauren said it wouldn't hurt, Mommy. Not like when I scraped my knee.'

'That's right, Amanda.' Lauren gave her hand a little squeeze. 'I wouldn't do anything to hurt you. You're my little sister.'

'Please,' Bonnie begged. 'Let go of Amanda's hand. Let's talk. I'm sure that we can work everything out.'

'What if I don't want to talk?'

'Then we don't have to talk,' Bonnie agreed immediately. 'We don't have to say anything.'

'Just wait for the police to get here so you can talk to them?' Lauren asked.

'I have nothing to say to the police.'

'No? That's strange. I thought you'd have a lot to tell them.'

'No,' Bonnie said. 'Nothing.'

'I killed them, you know,' Lauren said evenly. 'I killed all of them.'

Bonnie felt her heart grow heavy and sink into the pit of her stomach. 'You killed your mother?' she asked, though the question had already been answered.

Lauren's voice turned petulant. 'It was her own fault. If she hadn't gone snooping in my room, she never would have found my scrapbook. That's what started it all.'

'The scrapbook was yours?'

Lauren nodded. 'Pretty neat, huh? I started keeping it the day you married my father.'

'But why?'

A cloud passed across Lauren's eyes, threatened rain. 'My father loves me, you know. He's always loved me. Even when he went away. Even when you tried to take him away from me.'

'Lauren, honey, I never tried to keep your father away from you.'

'You tried,' Lauren insisted. 'Everybody tried. But I wouldn't let them.'

Bonnie struggled desperately to make sense of what she was hearing, her eyes never leaving her daughter's delicate wrist. Perhaps if she could keep Lauren talking long enough, she'd loosen her grip. 'That's why you shot Diana?'

'She was really something, wasn't she? Pretending to be your friend. Sneaking around behind your back. Screwing my father. You know when I found out?'

'When your father showed up at Diana's?'

'No.' Lauren shook her head. 'I had it figured out way before then. I knew the first time Sam and I went over there, the time Amanda was with us. You know what Amanda found when she was looking through Diana's dresser? You found all sorts of sexy undies, didn't you, Amanda?'

The child nodded, mesmerized, though clearly confused by the direction the conversation had taken.

'You know what else she found?' Lauren continued. 'Those silly little scarves, like the kind you had tied around your wrist that night I was so sick. The same kind of scarves my father tied you to the bed with when you were having sex.'

'Mommy, why did Daddy tie you to the bed?' Amanda asked, eyes like saucers.

Bonnie lowered her head to the floor, the memory of that night filling her head like the smell of rotting fruit.

'God, that made me sick,' Lauren said. 'Almost as sick as the arsenic.'

'You gave yourself arsenic?'

'Smart, huh? I saw it in a movie once. That way you never suspected it was me, even after you found out you were being poisoned. Of course, I had to do it gradually. I could only give you a little bit at a time, so everyone would think it was the flu.'

338

'And you put the snake in Amanda's bed,' Bonnie stated rather than asked.

'He was supposed to wrap himself around her neck and give a little squeeze, but it didn't work out that way. It was no big deal. I knew I'd get another chance. Accidents happen to little kids all the time. Like falling off a tricycle. Or a swing.' She laughed. 'Besides, it was fun watching you worry.'

'Is that why you threw the blood on her? So I'd worry?'

Lauren smiled at Amanda. 'You should have seen her before they cleaned her up. She was quite a sight.'

'You threw blood on me,' Amanda repeated indignantly, trying to pull away. 'I don't like you anymore.'

'Come on, Mandy,' Lauren cajoled, tightening her grip on Amanda's wrist. 'You're not afraid of a little blood, are you? I thought you were a big girl.'

'I don't like you anymore. You're not nice. I don't want to be your sister.' Again she tried to pull away.

Lauren quickly lifted her onto her lap, held the razor to her throat.

'Please, no!' Bonnie cried. 'Please don't hurt her. Don't move, baby,' she cautioned her squirming child.

'It's all your fault, you know,' Lauren told Bonnie.

'My fault?'

'You were supposed to get arrested for killing my mother. Then I could have moved in with my father and taken my time about getting rid of Amanda. It would have been much simpler. I wouldn't have had to hitchhike and take all those damn cabs back and forth everywhere. I wouldn't have had to ask Haze to get me the blood.' She giggled. 'He's such a jerk. He thought we were just playing games. He even fixed your car so it wouldn't start.'

Tears began falling down Amanda's face, one veering off, diverted by the tiny scar along her cheek. 'Don't cry now, baby,' Bonnie told her, wondering if there was some way to distract Lauren, to get Amanda to safety.

'What about Sam?' she asked, playing for time. 'Was he involved?'

'Are you kidding? Sam thinks you're the greatest thing since Lego.' She made a sound halfway between a laugh and a cry. 'It must have been some shock when he went to collect his money and found Diana dead on the floor.'

Amanda fidgeted in Lauren's tight embrace. The razor pressed deeper into her throat. A tiny dot of blood appeared.

'Please,' Bonnie begged, 'you don't want to hurt Amanda. You don't really want to hurt her. She's your baby sister.'

There was silence.

'I don't want a baby sister,' Lauren said, her voice cold and hard, like the granite of a tombstone. 'I never wanted a baby sister.'

Bonnie felt her entire body go numb as the realization of exactly what Lauren was saying began seeping its way into her bones. 'What are you saying?' she asked slowly.

'I think you know.'

Bonnie shook her head back and forth. 'Are you telling me that you killed Kelly? That her death wasn't an accident?'

Lauren stared at her with ghostly eyes.

'But you were almost a baby yourself. You were only six years old when Kelly drowned.'

'It doesn't take much strength to hold a baby's head underwater,' Lauren said matter-of-factly. 'She was only a little bit of a thing. That's what Daddy always used to say, that she was just a little bit of a thing.' Lauren's eyes flashed in sudden anger. 'Everything was all right until she was born.'

Bonnie thought of Joan, of her long, sad decline after the death of her youngest child. 'Your mother knew it wasn't an accident,' she said.

Lauren nodded. 'She lied to protect me. She did everything to protect me.'

'But you killed her.'

'I didn't want to kill her,' Lauren protested. 'But she didn't leave me any choice. After she found my scrapbook, she got so suspicious. She started watching me all the time. I tried to reason with her. But when she discovered her gun was missing, she panicked, called you. She was going to tell you everything. Just like she told my grandmother everything one night when they were drinking.' She stared accusingly at Bonnie. 'It's your fault my grandmother's dead,' she said. 'You had to go and find her. You couldn't just mind your own business.'

'Lauren . . .'

'And now my father's going to be angry at me. He's going to think I'm a bad girl. He's going to go away again.'

'Your father's not going anywhere, Lauren. He loves you. He loves you very much.'

'Do you think so?' Lauren asked, wide oval eyes filling with tears. 'That's all I ever wanted, you know. For him to love me. Can you understand that?'

Another silence, then, 'Yes,' Bonnie told her honestly. 'I can understand that.'

Lauren swatted at her tears with the back of her hand, rubbing them into her cheeks.

Like a little girl, Bonnie thought, looking back at Amanda.

'Bonnie,' a voice called suddenly. 'Bonnie, are you there?'

Lauren's head snapped toward the sound, temporarily loosening her grip around Amanda's throat, as footsteps bounded up the stairs. In the next instant, Amanda propelled herself out of Lauren's arms and across the room.

'Mommy!'

Bonnie caught sight of Lauren fumbling furiously inside her tote bag. The gun, Bonnie realized, lunging toward the bag, grabbing hold of Lauren's arm just as her hand grasped the gun's handle.

Lauren's arm stiffened, resisted, refused to surrender. Like a goddamn snake, Bonnie thought, slamming Lauren's wrist against the floor, hearing it snap, watching the gun fall from her limp hand.

And suddenly, Josh Freeman was at her side, kicking the gun out of reach, pulling Bonnie away. 'Where the hell did you come from?' Bonnie asked, eyes still on Lauren, watching as she curled into a fetal ball.

'The front door was wide open. I just walked in. Are you all right?'

'I will be,' Bonnie said, eyes closing with relief.

Amanda ran into her mother's arms, buried her face in her neck. 'Mommy, Mommy!'

'My sweet angel, are you all right?' Bonnie's shaking fingers touched the drop of blood beneath Amanda's chin.

'What's the matter with Lauren, Mommy?'

'She's not well, sweetie.'

'Will she get better?'

Bonnie kissed her daughter's cheek. 'I don't know.' She smoothed some hairs away from Amanda's forehead. 'What about you? How are you feeling?'

'I'm okay.' She gently extricated herself from Bonnie's grasp, cautiously approached the young girl lying motionless on the bedroom floor. Bonnie watched, holding her breath. 'Don't cry now, Lauren,' Amanda told her. 'Everything's going to be all right. You'll see. Don't cry. Don't cry.' Then she sat down beside her, stroking her long auburn hair until the police arrived.

Rod was waiting for her in Captain Mahoney's office. He jumped immediately to his feet when he saw her, the chair in which he'd been sitting tumbling backward to the floor. 'Bonnie, are you all right?'

Bonnie closed the door behind her. 'I'm fine.'

He took a step toward her, stopped when he saw her body tense. 'Amanda?'

'She's frightened, confused. But I think she'll be okay. I'm going to take her to see Dr Greenspoon next week.'

'Dr Greenspoon?'

'We're old friends,' Bonnie replied, not bothering to elaborate. 'You look exhausted.'

'It's been a hell of a day,' he said, and tried to smile.

'They've taken Lauren to the hospital for observation,' Bonnie told him. 'You should probably get over there as soon as possible.'

Rod looked stricken. 'God, Bonnie, I don't know if I can do that. I don't think I can face her.'

'You have to,' Bonnie said forcefully. 'She's your daughter, and she needs you.'

Rod said nothing for several seconds. 'Will you come with me?' he asked finally.

Bonnie stared into her husband's deep brown eyes, looking for some trace of the man she once thought she knew. But all she saw was the face of a stranger, a handsome man whose gray hair made him seem curiously younger than he was, even now, in spite of everything that had happened. 'No,' she said simply.

He looked toward the floor. 'So what happens now?' he asked.

'I'd appreciate it if you could have your things moved out of the house by the end of the week,' she told him.

He nodded acceptance. 'If that's what you want.'

'I have to check into Boston Memorial for a day or two,' she continued. 'I've arranged for Amanda to stay with my father. Nick is going to drive her over there in a few minutes. I'll join them as soon as Dr Kline gives me the okay.'

'Bonnie . . .'

'Sam is going to stay with Josh Freeman overnight. You can talk to him in the morning, decide together what you think he should do.'

'Christ, Bonnie, you know I can't look after him . . .'

'I've already told him that Amanda and I would like him to stay on with us,' Bonnie said.

'I think that would probably be best,' Rod quickly agreed.

Bonnie smiled sadly. 'Yes, I thought you might.' She turned to go. 'Bonnie . . .'

She stopped, waited, held her breath.

'Can I give you a lift to the hospital?'

Out of the corner of her eye, Bonnie saw Josh waiting by the station door. *I sensed you could use a friend*, he once told her. *I know I could.* 'No thank you,' she told Rod. 'I'm getting a ride with a friend.'